PRAISE FOR

MADAM OF MY HEART

"A debut historical novel that chronicles the struggles, loves, and joys of an exceptional madam in 19th-century America. Grossenbacher's book, the first in a planned series, dramatizes the early life and busy career of a woman named Brianna Baird. Raised in Baltimore in the decades before the Civil War, Brianna dreams of one day growing up to own a seamstress shop and marry a sweet man of virtue. But her plans unravel after she meets young Spenser Brown, a sweet-talking violinist who leaves her pregnant and betrays the promises he made.... Alone and knowing little of the world, she travels to New Orleans and finds work at the notorious parlor house of Madam DeSalle. There, she earns her keep first as a seamstress and later as the exclusive courtesan of gambler Edward Spina....

"Grossenbacher's prose is both graceful and inventive. She absorbingly limns the various cities Brianna inhabits, from New Orleans and its 'web of Creole cottages, chaotic marketplaces, and secretive balconies, simmering outside her window,' to the rowdy atmosphere of frontier-era San Francisco. The occasional marvelous metaphor will surprise readers, as when 'the truth hit Brianna like a badly aimed bowling pin.'

"This isn't just a novel for lovers of history's more prurient corners; it's for everyone who likes well-deployed language and intense stories. A seamier side of American history, engagingly told through one woman's unexpected adventures."

—*Kirkus Reviews*

MADAM OF MY HEART

GINI GROSSENBACHER

JGKS Press
the past comes to life

JGKS Press
the past comes to life

WWW.JKGS PRESS.COM

This is a work of historical fiction. Descriptions and portrayals of real people, events, organizations, or establishments are intended to provide backgrounds for the story and are used fictitiously. Other characters and situations are drawn from the author's imagination and are not intended to be real.

Cover design by Clarissa Yeo at Yocla Designs
Book design by Maureen Cutajar at Go Published

Publisher's Cataloging-in-Publication Data
provided by Five Rainbows Cataloging Services

Names: Grossenbacher, Gini.
Title: Madam of my heart : a novel of love, loss and redemption / Gini Grossenbacher.
Description: Elk Grove, CA : JGKS Press, 2017. | Series: American madams, bk. 1.
Identifiers: LCCN 2016920440 | ISBN 978-0-9983806-0-5 (pbk.) | ISBN 978-0-9983806-1-2 (PDF) | ISBN 978-0-9983806-2-9 (EPUB ebook) | ISBN 978-0-9983806-3-6 (Kindle ebook) | ISBN 978-0-9983806-4-3 (MOBI ebook)
Subjects: LCSH: Brothels--Fiction. | Vodou--Fiction. | Slavery--Fiction. | New Orleans (La.)--History--19th century--Fiction. | San Francisco (Calif.)--History--19th century--Fiction. | Historical fiction, American. | BISAC: FICTION / Historical. | FICTION / Romance / Historical / General. | FICTION / Coming of Age. | GSAFD: Historical fiction. | Love stories. | Bildungsromans.
Classification: LCC PS3607.R66 M33 2017 (print) | LCC PS3607.R66 (ebook) | DDC 813/.6--dc23.

To Karl, Steven, Jon, Andrea, and my cairn terrier, Murphy,
whose patience and love made this book possible.

Part One

Vows Made in Wine

I pray you, do not fall in love with me,
For I am falser than vows made in wine . . .

William Shakespeare, *As You Like It*, 3.5.74–75

One

AS THOUGH DREAMING

New Orleans, Louisiana
May 1850

An orange twilight faded into night on the wharf, casting deep shadows into the room. Brianna sipped warm water from a flask and nibbled on stale crackers from her landlady, Madame Goulet. Night shouts floated into the boardinghouse through the open window as stevedores unloaded cargo from the last ships to arrive. A gangplank smacked on the pier, followed by the calls of sailors as they tied giant ropes and chains to the dock. Drunken laughter rose from the boardwalk, and faint strains of banjo music plunked in the distance. What was going on out there?

She peeked over the windowsill at the wharf. As the harbor quieted and stars brightened, fear tugged, and then twisted her throat. A lone stevedore coiled a rope, and then grabbed his jacket from a post and strode away toward town. The path was clear—it had to be—no time to waste. The window latch scraped shut between her thumb and forefinger.

She lifted the carpetbag and found it heavier than she had expected, its precious contents nestled inside. A small key on a string glinted on the dark-red-stained bedsheets. She looped it around her neck; its weight lodged between her milk-laden breasts.

Her pulse throbbed in her ears as she crept downstairs, out of the building, and across the street to the pier. No one must see her. Mud splashed her shoes. On the quay, she explored piles of cast-off rigging. A weight—any weight—would keep the bag from floating back up to the surface. A block and tackle rested next to a gangplank from a merchant ship. If only it weren't so heavy in her arms.

Brianna cast her legs over the side of the pier. Careful not to tear this skirt, her one and only. Was that a bump down at the end of the pier? She hunched down, her palms sweaty. It must be a boat at its moorings. Luckily, no one else lingered about. The bag unlatched easily, and she lifted the package, then settled the wood pieces underneath it. They'd weigh it down.

Time to let it go. She dropped the satchel into the water. A small splash sent ripples across the black river. The bag submerged, but my God, it was floating right back up to the surface, its maroon flowers dripping.

"No, for God's sake!" The carpetbag was bobbing out on the seaward tide—not what she'd planned at all. She grabbed a stevedore's pole lying nearby. Kneeling down on the planks, she fished the bag out of the water. What if a drunken sailor were to see her? Or worse, the night watch? She set her teeth. No turning back now. She had to do this now, this way—no other choice.

Brianna made her way farther down the long pier, dragging the damp bag, rummaging in the darkness for a lead weight. She stumbled over a heavy link of iron chain left by a dockhand inside the shelter of a giant shipping crate. A bit of luck. Would she have the strength to hoist it? Luckily, the chain yielded. Courage. Stooping, she placed the chain under the package in the carpetbag. The links clanked as she moved the bag and pulled together the leather straps.

Brianna's temples pounded in the humid air. She dangled the key from the string between her teeth and sat on the edge of the dock. Her throat constricted like a winding sheet. This time, her plan had to work.

The bag lingered for a moment on the surface, but then the Father of Waters swallowed up her secret. Bubbles surfaced at the point where the cargo descended. Finally, the tension started to melt. Her carpetbag pursued a silent pathway downward to the bottom, its final resting place the illustrious Port of New Orleans.

Meanwhile, Nancy De Salle tiptoed from Skipper Seymour's cot to the ceramic washbowl. His snoring rocked the vessel. Her eyes shifted to the porthole facing the wharf. What was that movement? She squinted. None other than a young woman on the pier, alone. Whatever was she doing? Nancy wet her fingers and rubbed them against the glass, then peered into the darkness. Backlit by the stars, the girl was outlined in silver. Sure enough. The waif placed a red pouch on the water and watched it disappear into the deep. So fascinating. Next, the poor girl sat cross-legged on the dock, her eyes closed. Nancy breathed a sigh, wiping her dirty fingers against the soiled towel on the rack. How well she knew that story.

Two

HONEYSUCKLE BREEZES

Baltimore, Maryland
May 1849

Brianna struggled under the bolts of fabric she carried from the tailor shop to the Admiral Fell Inn, her regular duty. Miss Osborne's order of bedroom curtains lay heavy in her arms today, and her boots slipped on the brick walk. Her foot turned in a muddy hole, and her ankle twisted. A sharp pain shot up her lower leg, but she clamped her teeth shut against it. She held the curtains overhead—if any moment deserved an answered prayer, this was such a moment. She yanked the hem of her petticoat out of the gushy muck, and nearly lost her balance another time. Footsteps sounded behind her, and she stepped aside to make way for women with young children who hefted food baskets home from the Broadway marketplace.

Around her, a fragrant array of spring roses bloomed red along the walkways. She stopped for a moment to catch her breath. The very sight of their vibrant scarlet blossoms lifted her spirits, and she grinned despite her heavy load and dirty hem. The sign above read THE ADMIRAL FELL INN. Along with the roses, she'd never really looked at that sign. What was on that round emblem? A fish wrapped around an anchor. Were the sailors like fish who sheltered at this temporary anchorage, missing the feminine comforts of their faraway homes? Brianna cast her eyes over the Inner Harbor, which lay across the road. In the channel, clusters of ships drifted back and forth, their sails unfurled. At the pier, the seamen in gray caps lingered, smoking and laughing.

Brianna and Annie loved to recite the names of well-known Baltimoreans who attended fancy dances at the Inn. Miss Rose, their supervisor, had warned them, *don't be so curious—you're not old enough yet to go into that ballroom*. Brianna grinned at the memory of the mistress's wrinkly lips as she spoke. *And by no means are you to go around the corner onto Thames Street. You'll see the hussies during the daytime—they come and go with men of all kinds. Married men, sailors. You're only sixteen—too young to think of such things.* Little did Miss Rose know that the more she curled her lip in disdain, the more Brianna was determined to venture there someday.

When no one answered the service door, she kicked it open with the toe of her shoe, still steadying the heavy load across her arms. Such a bother. Miss Osborne would surely make a fuss if the material fell to the ground. To her relief, she heard a friendly voice from across the lobby.

"What—oh, it's you, Brianna." Mrs. Whipple sat upright at her desk, scratching figures in her ledger with her silver dip pen. "I thought Cook would open the door." She peered over her *pince-nez* glasses. "Lovely surprise. I always enjoy our chats." Her broad smile spoke of sisterly affection.

"Where should I put them, Mrs. Whipple?" Brianna swayed under the bolts of fabric, half-blinded by the locks of hair that had fallen across her face.

The innkeeper rested her pen across her inkwell, slipped out of her chair, and pushed the load onto the counter. "I'll need a bit of time to make sure Mr. Whipple approves of the design and the colors. We'll need to match it against the rug and our chairs in the second-floor suite." She tugged on a red velvet rope and a bell chimed in the distance. She leaned over and Brianna's eyes closed as the woman's soft fingers swept the usual annoying strands of hair away from her eyes.

A tall slave approached from the hallway. "Mrs. Whipple?" He lowered his head, awaiting her orders.

Brianna settled the bolts into his outstretched arms.

Mrs. Whipple said, "These go upstairs for now, Joshua." A piece of paper fluttered in the innkeeper's hand.

"Yes, Ma'am." He shifted the fabric to his shoulders and carried it away down the hall.

Ceramic plates and cast-iron pots clattered in the distant kitchen. Colored slaves in head rags scurried around Whipple in the foyer, running feather dusters over velvet couches and mopping tile floors. Brianna pinched back a sneeze and rubbed her eyelids as she followed the mistress. Dash, that infernal dust forever brought tears to her eyes.

Whipple motioned her into the kitchen and patted the seat next to her at the servants' table. "Do sit down, my dear. Next to me." The faint beginnings of lines around her mouth framed an affectionate grin.

"Thank you—most kind." Awestruck around Mrs. Whipple, Brianna sat silent for a moment, absorbing the thrill of this special conversation. When she grew up and ran her own seamstress shop, she'd be just like Whipple. Why couldn't her family treat her this way—as an adult, an equal?

The kitchen fire's warmth blended the aromas of cinnamon, clove, and allspice. Brianna breathed in deeply, resting her feet against the wooden floor. A red-cheeked dishwasher banged pots and pans in the bubbly water of the sink. The sous-chef in a large, white apron chopped celery with a heavy knife. A young girl kneaded bread, her bare arms white with flour.

Cook set a porcelain plate of spiced nutmeats before them. A lump of butter melted away on top, like the sugar coating over apple fritters, her personal favorite.

Whipple popped a walnut into her mouth. "This will do." She placed some of them in the palm of her hand and held them out. "Care to try one or two? Maple candied walnuts for the guests this afternoon."

Brianna reached for a piece, brushing back the disobedient strands of hair with the back of her hand.

As she did so, a shadow crossed Whipple's face.

Brianna's body stiffened. Was that a sign she'd overstayed her welcome?

Instead, Whipple's eyes wrinkled with concern. "How can your parents neglect the grooming of such a beautiful young girl? The simplest of hairstyles would improve your bearing."

So it was only about her hair? Brianna relaxed into a numbing comfort.

Whipple said, "Let's take a look." Holding up her pince-nez glasses, she inspected Brianna's facial contours, nose, lips, cheeks, and eyes. She then lifted Brianna's chin in her hand and twirled a strand of her hair around her finger, angling it in front of Brianna's forehead, then tapping the top of her head. "Do you ever wear it up?"

"What? In your style? In truth I'd never considered it much. My hair's thick and bothersome. So heavy in the heat."

Whipple's eyes narrowed. "Let me see." She gathered the remainder of Brianna's curls and placed them on the crown of her head. Whipple tilted her head as she studied the style. "This is the most sophisticated look today. *Godey's Lady's Book* has many fashions, but I like to put mine into a chignon. Try it. Have your mother get you some hairpins."

Brianna held her head very still as she spoke. "I can't see the back of my head, Mrs. Whipple. We don't have a decent mirror, only an old cloudy one. Father says a looking glass is against God's law. 'I have seen all the works that have been done under the sun, and lo, the whole is vanity and vexation of spirit!' That's in Ecclesiastes."

Whipple shrugged and dropped the locks of hair. "Ah, I see. What a shame. In that case, bring some hairpins to me. I'll do the style for you here. Once you observe, you can pin the curls on your own, even without a mirror." After checking her pocket watch, Whipple arose from the chair. "Cook and I are planning the evening menu."

Brianna swiveled and observed her movements. Whipple's trim figure was silhouetted against the afternoon light of the hallway. The innkeeper walked with erect posture, chin lifted, eyes straight ahead. Commanding. There was a grace about her, a certain elegance.

Could she remember those gestures to practice later at home? She'd try. Maybe if she paid attention to every move, at least one or two would sink in. Annie could help her practice walking upright with a book on her head. Then she'd have Annie pin her hair up.

Cook's agreeable grunts punctuated Whipple's low murmurs as the two bent their heads, whispering about the number of servings needed for tonight's grand ball.

Meanwhile, Brianna contemplated the state of her own skirt. A crease had etched itself in the gray cotton beside her apron. She'd have to be more careful with the iron next time. Whipple never had a wrinkle on her skirts. Neither would she.

Over in the hall, the innkeeper pointed at the list. "*Poulet à la russe* will do for today, since you haven't been able to find decent lamb at the market."

"Yes, mum." Cook nodded.

"Prepared the cherry Tarte Tatin for the evening?"

Cook frowned, her wrinkles deepening. "Couldn't find the cherries, so I substituted pears. Some left from last week's party for the mayor's son."

"Very well, that is all."

Cook shuffled back into the kitchen, her eyes examining the paper as she walked.

Whipple paused to rearrange the bouquet of wild roses and coralbells in a cut crystal vase on the hall table.

Brianna sat mesmerized by Whipple's movements, watching the woman's fine fingers weave the stems together and fan the leaves around the flowers.

Someone touched Brianna's arm and she tensed. Cook's ruddy cheeks beamed down at her. The woman held out a plate and a napkin. "Want a Berger cookie?" Wisps of gray hair escaped from her white cap.

Brianna's nerves relaxed. "Why, thank you." She selected a warm, chocolate-covered shortbread. Without hesitation, she bit into the buttery layers mixed with cocoa and considered the kindly Cook. Despite her gruff manner, the woman showed genuine affection toward her. Why wasn't her mother this jovial sort, instead of the worn, gray shade who never spoke?

Then, Cook turned away and sank her hands deep into pie dough, her attention taken by the crust for which the Inn was famous.

No one was looking. Here was a chance to venture beyond the scullery, to explore uncharted territory.

Three

A Floorboard Squeaks

After a brief tiptoe across the hallway, Brianna paused at the door of the grand ballroom. A click echoed across the room. A blond man perched on the edge of a chair, unlocking his violin case. She brushed away the crumbs on her chin. From this distance, he looked more grown-up than other lads she'd known. Could she explore the room quietly and make it back to the kitchen before he saw her?

She stepped across the threshold, dwarfed by the high ceilings. Glittering candelabras sprayed light across the crimson wallpaper. Traces of French perfume and furniture wax lingered in the air. Silver trays of Swiss chocolates and fruit tarts graced mahogany side tables.

Brianna's mind spun in this new atmosphere. Colorful curtains featuring country scenes bedecked arched windows. Giant bunches of May roses burst from various vases. She moved sideways to a large hearth that glowed with smoky embers. Brass spittoons occupied each corner, under the shelter of potted palms. Then a floorboard squeaked under her feet—she winced. Her eyes traveled down to her scuffed boots. Such footwear did not belong in a sophisticated room like this one.

The violinist set down his bow and stood up. "Oh, hello." His voice conveyed a deep sensuality that pulled her toward him.

"I'm sorry to stop you from practicing. It's just that I . . ." Words froze in Brianna's throat. Why in blessings couldn't she think of something to say? The room grew warm all of a sudden. What would Mrs. Whipple do at a time like this?

"You didn't stop me." He raked his fingers through thick, blond hair. "I saw you eating your sweets. Cook spoils me, too."

Brianna curtsied, turned, and got a full view. A well-carved dimple sat in the middle of his chin, resting under a broad smile.

"Come," he swept his hand in a circular motion, "over here to see the dance floor."

Her first instinct was to flee back to the safety of Cook and the kitchen, yet his grin drew her closer. Should she dare? Just a little dance, maybe. She wouldn't want to get in trouble.

He met her at the edge of the polished parquet, and pointed. "Step on it here."

His hand was warm to the touch. Brianna slid her boot onto the smooth surface. "It's a wonder dancers don't slip and fall."

His voice broke into a chuckle. "The more they drink, the faster they dance, and the more they slip."

Who else did she know with such easy humor? She racked her brain. No boy she knew had such grace and charm.

He bent toward her, the smile still lighting up his face. "Miss—?"

"Baird. Brianna Baird." A tingle traveled down her back. He repeated her name in such a grown-up way. Not like at home, where the family grated out her name like wood shavings.

"A pleasure, Miss Baird. May I?"

His inviting hand reached for hers again, this time closing around her palm. Amusement flickered in his eyes. His rich voice was gentle, almost soothing. "Be brave and try the dance floor. By the way, I go by Spenser Brown. My father says we're related to a famous British poet. I wouldn't know since I've always cared most about my music." His hands tightened over hers, then loosened as though concerned about her comfort.

Brianna's breath quickened. Such unusual violet eyes. Annie would be jealous.

She let him guide her out to middle of the dance floor. Spenser took command, his posture straight, his hand outstretched, fingers pressing the middle of her back.

"Know some steps?" He tilted his head.

She hesitated, baffled at the question. But this time she found some words. "No, Father won't allow dance in the house. A man of the cloth."

He grinned in mock sympathy. "Pity. Sounds dreadful. Try some little steps for fun?"

Maybe this was going too far. After a glance back toward the kitchen, Brianna moved back a foot. "I don't know. What about your practicing? The tea dance?"

Spenser inched toward her, his voice softening. "I came in early this morning to tune the strings, and I know the pieces well enough. The rest of the quartet should be here in a few minutes. Cook always feeds us before we play."

What was the worst that could happen if she went along with him? Was she willing to endure a tongue-lashing from Cook?

The eagerness in his voice was hard to resist. "Come on. I insist." His outstretched hands drew her toward him.

At the touch of Spenser's hand resting on her waist, Brianna was drawn into a rapture. He raised her arm, placing his palm against hers. His fingertips were ridged from violin strings, and he smelled of tree sap mixed with molasses. Must be the rosin on the violin. He led her backward and forward, counting the steps: "One-two-three, one-two-three."

Crunch! Her heel landed on Spenser's ankle boot. "Sorry." She'd have to be so clumsy—here—now—after she'd just met him.

He hopped in mock pain. "Have no fear. You're not the first lady who has done that."

His feet resumed the gentle gliding, back and forth. Their rhythm fell into a kind of lullaby. After a minute or two, she relaxed in the comfort of his arms, the steps, and the lights flickering by.

"There you are, my girl!" In the middle of their third turn, Cook's shrill cry reverberated from the hallway.

Brianna halted mid-step. Spenser's arms lingered around her waist, holding her body close. Breathless, his half-open lips bent toward hers. Why couldn't this moment last forever? They'd be enjoying the kiss she'd watched many a sailor and his sweetheart do on the wharf before a ship went out to sea. Spenser was no schoolboy. He'd know how to kiss a girl.

Cook's heavy steps pounded in their direction, and Spenser's arms tightened around her. She wanted to nestle her breasts against his chest and tuck her head under his chin.

"Yes, Ma'am?" He replied sharply and drew his face away. Then he dropped Brianna's arms. A sudden emptiness filled the space between them. Was this warmth imaginary? His smile faded into the potted palms, his ardor growing cold along with the fireplace cinders.

Brianna nodded like a wooden doll in the direction of Cook's voice. She glanced at the doorway where the hearty woman had planted her feet, and cleared her throat. Cook's cheeks puckered, wrinkled as a baked apple. A stained white apron stretched over her large girth. Pieces of pie dough clung to her abdomen and littered the checkered towel wrapped over her arm.

The force of Cook's voice could snuff out a candle across the room. "You, young man, you'd better do some practicing. I heard plenty of squeaky notes at last week's dance. The ladies complained."

Spenser radiated ease and familiarity with all things stylish. Of course, that was part of being a violinist at an important inn. He strode toward Cook, an arm outstretched. "Dance with us. Teach Brianna the quadrille."

Cook paused, open-mouthed. Brianna wondered. Had he won the woman over? Would she dance with him?

The domestic's rough cheeks flamed and she strode over to Spenser's side. She halted abruptly, cast her eyes back toward the kitchen, and slung the towel over her shoulder. "Nonsense, boy. You put notions in these girls' heads."

Sensing something damp, Brianna felt Cook's hand encircle hers and yank her in the direction of the kitchen.

Cook said, "Come, Miss, before he fills you with silliness." She flapped the towel, then wiped sweat from her brow.

Brianna suppressed a giggle. "Yes, Cook, of course." She glanced over her shoulder at Spenser, who bowed low. She'd love to spend all day feeling his arms around her waist—but that was not to be, so she strode across the ballroom to the door.

At the threshold, Brianna paused, looking back at Spenser. He'd regained the platform and was now lifting his violin out of the case. Had she heard his whisper—*Come back to me*? His words contained a secret intensity, meant for her alone.

The red and feverish Cook rushed her out, murmuring. "Girls—who—aren't—careful—get—themselves—into—trouble. Courtesans—and such like."

Brianna swallowed a laugh. The woman resembled a sheepdog herding an errant lamb through the kitchen and out the door. Then she knew the force of Cook's hands moving on her back, the rush of air, the latch clicking shut. And there it was again: the roses, the harbor, the crowds milling about at the pier.

Outside on the threshold for a moment, Brianna gathered her thoughts. In truth, she'd heard Cook's voice. What had she said? Something about courtesans? She brushed off Cook's floured handprint on her sleeve. Why was everyone always so worried she'd get into trouble? After all, it was just a dance, wasn't it? So friendly, so innocent.

Brianna looked back up at the creaking sign overhead. Fish wrapped around an anchor. Cook loved to yammer at her, but she'd now proven able to handle herself around a man. Was she a fish to Spenser's anchor? With that question, she stepped out onto the sidewalk in waltz time: *one-two-three, one-two-three, back-to-me, back-to-me.* Miss Osborne's shop lay ahead on the walk, its window panes a dark blue in the late afternoon sun. As she followed the path, a ship's horn sounded, slop water flowed in the gutters, and carriage bells jingled. *Count your blessings*, Father had said. Blessings, indeed—she'd spied on The Admiral Fell Inn and she'd danced a waltz.

Four

⁂ THE GRAY WALLS ⁂

Back at her sewing table, Brianna pressed up the window and leaned out over the sidewalk. After a month of solid rain, the lowering sunlight beamed golden over the harbor. She stretched her arms overhead and turned to survey the long sewing room. Where was Miss Rose? No sign of her. Thank the Lord for a break.

More than a dozen girls were bent over with scissors as they cut out designs on slippery cloth. Others sat in chairs, stitching gowns, sleeves, and hems. Straw mannequins stood at attention, some wearing muslin patches tacked with straight pins. Dirt, mildew, and sweat clung to the gray walls. Brianna had never told anyone about her dream to own the finest seamstress shop in Baltimore. It was her secret for now. Her own shop wouldn't be closed up like this; she'd have plenty of open windows to let in the sea air. Outside, a passing hackney clattered toward the Inn. Nearly time for the tea dance.

More horses clopped on the cobblestones outside. One more peek out the window. The driver's top hat teetered as he reined in the span of spirited bay horses. A footman jumped down and swung open the doors of the cab. This time, a man sprang out; his black boots gleamed. A blue-feathered headdress emerged next. A hatpin sparkled in the dappled light. The woman took the man's hand; he guided her around mud puddles. Such finery. Soon they vanished behind the swinging doors of the hotel. The coach stirred up a dust cloud as it pulled away, veiling the entrance.

Brianna had visions of the day when she'd own her own shop, her own bearing as fine as that blue-hatted woman. A little thrill coursed through her. Her hand would rest on Spenser's arm as he twirled her around the dance floor again. She'd wear a sparkling pin, glowing in the candlelight. Brianna let out a sigh—there'd be time for that. She turned to survey her table. So many piles of material, waiting for her. For now, she was a seamstress in someone else's shop—that and nothing more.

A tinkling bell broke into her fantasy. Rows of girls clutched lunches in folded newsprint and filed downstairs to the long tables. Brianna trailed the line down the stairs. Little time to swallow her piece of dry bread and moldy cheese. *Little time to waste*, according to Miss Rose. The girls were quiet today, unusually so. Tired of the humdrum as much as she.

No sooner had she taken the last bite than the bell called them back upstairs to the monotony of pattern books and thread-on-cloth. Miss Rose shut the window and the air grew suffocating. The *one-two-three* rhythm of the waltz faded into the mechanical stamp of *cut-and-stitch, cut-and-stitch*.

Five

NO RESPECTABLE GIRL

Baltimore, Maryland
May 1849

Days passed, but despite many moments of stealing looks out the window, Brianna hadn't glimpsed Spenser. Miss Rose always had her do the finishing work on Saturdays. After taking the latest piece to the Admiral Fell, she'd come back and cleaned up the shop before her long walk home. Tomorrow would be spent in church—another day filled with dry smiles and mindless chatter. She looked forward to more daydreams about Spenser and sparkling pins.

A hand touched Brianna's forearm. She glanced over at her worktable.

"This dress is for Mrs. Whipple." Miss Rose laid out the bright-blue poplin gown as though it were a delicate child. "Mind your lace stitches around the sleeves and the hem. Those parts get the most wear."

The hatpin shimmered in Brianna's mind. "I've been meaning to ask you, Miss Rose. How does one become a courtesan?" On a typical day, Miss Rose's face was the color of milk quartz. At that moment, dark cherry blossomed on her cheeks.

Brianna could have kicked herself. Why on earth had she ever said those words? If only she could suck them back into her foolish mouth. Was it too late to crawl under the table? She bowed her head, not in shame, but resignation. Time now for one of Miss Rose's classic lectures on proper etiquette. After a moment of silence, she looked up.

Miss Rose's thin eyebrows arched. "Whatever has influenced you, my child? Well, if you must know." She lowered her voice and bent her head closer. "They've fallen from grace—who knows what has possessed them. It's a rowdy business indeed. Their gowns are sinful and their behavior even more. Ship captains and sailors. One after another. They do not live long. How they become wanton women is none of your business. Understood?"

"Yes." She nodded. Miss Rose wasn't usually this frank. Was she speaking this way because Brianna was growing up?

Rose continued. "Keep your eyes away from their windows on your walk, do you hear? And don't you tarry." Her wrinkle-worn eyes angled toward the Inner Harbor. "They live in parlor houses along Thames Street. That's where they linger, some the legal age of sixteen, down around the corner past the Admiral Fell." *Thames Street.* Rose's voice grew agitated, and her eyes widened in warning. "Make no mistake. No respectable girl goes down there."

Later on in the lobby at the Admiral Fell, Whipple was nowhere in sight, so Brianna spread out the new dress on the hardwood desk. She bit her lip, studying the stitching she'd done on the lace collar and the satin hem. What would such a smart frock look like on her? She ran her fingertips along the bodice, feeling the flat plane of the cotton and the embroidery at the edges. Although splendid, this garment was too big for her, its neckline meant for an older, well-endowed matron.

She looked down at her breasts. The curves on her small chest looked small as anthills. She'd never have the hourglass shape of the models in the broadsheets. She pushed away from the desk and stepped to the door. In the carriageway, the breeze caressed her face. The parade of her wonderings continued its march. When would she have the breasts to fill out such a dress? Maybe when she turned eighteen. Annie said she'd have plenty of time ahead of her to wear fancy things. But Annie had nothing to worry about. She'd been blessed with curvy breasts and hips. A chemise and petticoats embraced her body like a lover.

On the following Saturday, Brianna left the Admiral Fell after dropping off a new order of tablecloths, and she noticed a news sheet nailed to the side of a wall of the Inn. Its headline announced the arrival of Baltimore's own *Seaman,* a clipper ship from New York, a cause for the celebration. The last time a Baltimore clipper returned to its home port, Fells Point went wild.

Drawn toward the wharf by curiosity, she ignored Miss Rose's advice, and rounded the corner onto Thames Street, where sounds of loud snickering and sharp laughter poured from downstairs windows onto the cobblestones. In the humid sunlight, she was jostled by passersby dressed in fine cottons, straw hats, and silk parasols.

A quarter of the way down the street, Brianna stopped. How curious—a lace curtain was flapping in and out with the breeze. Distant strains of a fiddle kept time with the tinkling of a melodeon. What fine adventures could those men and women be having? She may as well stop and take a look. Surely no one among the indoor revelers would notice her out here, watching them. Dry grass crackled beneath her shoe. On the ground floor, visible through panes of wavy glass, plates of cheese, fruits, and champagne flutes glimmered on low tables. Women in low-cut corsets and slit skirts mingled with men in short sailor's jackets and bell-bottom pants. Both men and women smoked pipes, and now and then, a cloud of smoke wafted out the window, followed by a high-pitched laugh. And so what if they did notice Brianna? Would they even care? Around her, pairs of sailors heading to the pubs paid her no mind.

She anchored her hands on the decorative molding below the window frame. What a perfect listening post.

"Come here, Miss Laurel," a male voice said.

Oh, drat! Brianna hadn't expected to hear a voice. She ducked under the window frame and stayed low.

"Captain Lunsford, you're all about telling me lies." Sarcasm rang in a girl's words.

Brianna blinked up at Miss Laurel's naked derriere posed on the windowsill, surrounded by red flounce and white petticoats. Transfixed by a rebellious instinct, she wanted more, much more. She cupped her ear to catch the conversation.

"Miss Laurel, I've been lusting for you in my heart." Lunsford's voice throbbed like a steam engine.

"You'll lust a bit more after you have another glass of our famous French champagne." Using a velvety voice, Miss Laurel tantalized her companion.

"Is that what you tell all your gentlemen callers?" Lunsford's voice mingled with the rustling weeds as Brianna crouched there.

Miss Laurel's response was smooth as spun silk. "You know, there isn't but one gentleman comes to me but you—and that one's special. Here, open up and let me feed you the special raspberry *petit fours* you always crave at our tea dances."

"Luscious," Lunsford said. The sound of slurping and pouring ensued.

The girl cooed. "And you're my special frosting." Miss Laurel's bottom jounced off the windowsill, and a blue-jacketed arm encircled her waist.

After a quick intake of breath, Brianna held her hand against her mouth. She looked around in case someone saw her spying. No place to hide. More sailors passed, snaking along the street in jagged, drunken lines. Caught up in their own inebriated thoughts, they didn't appear to notice her.

The word-slurring captain spoke again. "Let's go upstairs so I can taste some more of your raspberries."

"But you promised me a waltz-in-five."

"I'd rather waltz-in-five inside you," he said.

"So, what if I say no?" Hers was an alluring voice.

"Mmm, I have something special for you today, my *petit four*."

"You do?"

Laurel's eyes were likely glistening. If only Brianna could see the whole scene.

"Yes," he said. Then she heard the sound of hands rustling—they must be underneath the girl's starched petticoats.

Brianna's hand flew to her throat. She gloried in the forbidden moment. Annie's lectures on love had nothing on this.

Then the girl's breath came fast as she spoke. "I can't wait to see your surprise."

The stairs squeaked; the man must be carrying his prize up to a room on the second story. Brianna chewed her fingers. It was then that the dance music stopped, and a rocking cadence filled the silence.

Brianna couldn't climb up the trellis to see, or she'd be caught. Maybe they wouldn't care that she was spying, but on the other hand, she might be ridiculed. Following that, other voices downstairs provided a chorus for the upstairs moaning. A window in the lower salon was open a crack. Several couples clinked glasses there while the bed squeaks above harmonized in crescendos, then diminuendos.

What did the captain and Miss Laurel look like in that bed? Their bodies were likely entwined, reposing against the soft sheets. A movement flickered at the top window. Captain Lunsford stared down at Brianna, clad only in his captain's hat. A soft gasp escaped her. Dash!

He winked, then abruptly pulled the drape. Soon, the bedsprings resumed their rhythmic notes. The melodeon accompanied a soft voice singing a ballad. Had he known Brianna was there all along? Strangely, she didn't care if he did.

Six

A POLKA

Brianna sat back on her haunches, her skirt spread across the ground. At least now she knew a little of what courtesans did. She could tell Miss Rose a thing or two. What was that? Her hand reached back to scratch her neck where something had itched. Darned mosquitoes. She glanced up into Spenser's face. It would have to be *him*—how embarrassing.

A dry tickling weed hung suspended from his fingers. "Snooping, eh?" A humorous light flickered in his eyes.

Heat rose from her neck into her cheeks. "I'm so—"

Without warning, his hands closed over her shoulders, then traveled down her arms and lifted her up.

Brianna looked up at him, smoothed her skirts, and dusted off some of the weeds. Her cheeks continued a slow burn.

"Feeling well, Miss Brianna?" Spenser gave her a conspiratorial wink, then took a quick puff from his cigar.

"Well, yes, actually I am." She set her summer bonnet squarely on her head, fighting her mortification. He must reckon she was from the mudsills, hanging about, spying into windows.

Spenser pointed with his cigar down Thames Street in the direction of South Broadway. "In that case, may I walk you back to the dressmaker's?" A stream of smoke floated out with his words.

"Yes," Brianna heard herself say. She worked to sound coherent.

Spenser's gentle hand guided her elbow, and she let him lead her. "Shouldn't you be inside the Admiral Fell?" She struggled to contain a smile.

A buoyant humor sparkled in his eyes. "I'm through for the day. Horace was playing the viola when I left." They paused in front of the Admiral Fell. The downstairs ballroom windows were flung open, and inside Brianna could see couples swirling in dance.

Of a sudden, the musical ensemble broke into a lively polka. Spenser's sparkle turned to a smolder, and his eyes held hers. "Let's practice again right here."

She stared, astonished. "But won't everyone see?" Her cheeks heated up. Was that lust in his gaze?

His former grin of amusement returned. "Come. You didn't seem to care who saw you snooping at the parlor house window. Why would you care now?" Rather than wait for her answer, Spenser grabbed her right hand and led her out to a dry patch of earth beside the Admiral Fell. He flung his cigar away, put his arm around her waist, held her arm out, and whirled her in a circle. When she faltered, he paused to show her a step or two.

Brianna glanced at an elderly couple who had stopped their walk to regard them. They held onto their cane and parasol, and shook their heads. Were they remembering their own romances?

The music poured out from the Inn, and Brianna struggled to stay in time. These dizzying polka steps were even more fun than the slower waltz. Why didn't Father allow dancing? The notes and turns sent her heart racing. Surely anything this joyful couldn't be a sin.

Spenser's violet eyes twinkled. She softened in his now-familiar arms, and his cheers encouraged her steps. As the melodeon finished a last refrain, he skipped her over to some roses lining the pathway.

Breathless, Brianna paused next to Spenser on the walk, her eyes following his broad back as he leaned over a bush. His index finger and thumb worked around some prominent thorns. Then he bent the stem of a red cabbage rose, its petals tinted with white.

"One for you," Spenser said. He plucked the young flower, then stuffed it into her bosom, piercing the lacework of her chemise. A thorn grazed her breast. It hurt, but she didn't care. He drew her to his chest, the scent of the crushed blossom between them heady, sweet, and rich. He pulled away, caressed the bare skin of her neck with the tips of his fingers, and then brushed a lock of hair back behind her shoulder. A trickle of sweat eased down the back of her chemise and a gentle warmth meandered up and down her legs. As he lifted her chin, Brianna closed her eyes, waiting for the taste of his lips.

Instead of a kiss, he jerked away and sniffed. "Fire? Gol dern, no!" White smoke curled up from the wood shavings where he'd tossed his cigar.

Brianna had to get these skirts out of the sawdust before they caught on fire, so she lifted them high and made for the street. Father said a Baltimore blaze was no laughing matter; the fire department was no match against flames in colonial rowhouses. Besides, the Admiral Fell could not afford rumors of fire—bad for business.

Spenser jumped on the smoldering weeds and stomped out the flames. He bent over, coughing. Brianna went back and stood by his side while he caught his breath. Her eyes seemed to be on fire, and tears seeped from under her closed lids. Yet, even in discomfort, she gloried in their moment together. He'd held her near, so close that she'd seen his desire burn like firelight.

A girl's voice from the end of the roadway shattered their enchantment. "Brianna, what's taking you so long? Mother's worried. You're an hour late, and she and I are waiting supper on you." Annie's parasol shielded her face and cast her blue taffeta dress in partial shade. She strode toward them, her red hair catching bits of sunlight.

A hard knot rose in Brianna's throat. "Thank you, Mr. Spenser. It was delightful." Her skirts swished as she curtsied. His violet eyes stayed focused on hers.

Disapproval layered Annie's black look. "You hadn't closed the shop, so I had to do it." Her words landed like a sharp axe on metal.

Brianna cringed, silent. If only Annie had picked another day to come and get her.

Spenser half-bowed, his eyelids lowering. He uttered quick words of detachment. "Glad you enjoyed it, Miss Brianna. Maybe next time we can go somewhere where we'll not be interrupted." He tapped the brick walk with one toe in hesitation for a moment, and afterward took long steps back toward the Admiral Fell. His broad shoulders disappeared around the corner onto Thames Street.

Brianna's eyes brimmed with wistful tears. Why did he have to go so soon? When would she see him again? Not soon enough. How long could she wait?

Annie stared after him and hissed, "Mama's so upset she's gone into one of her trances. We need to get home and eat before Father is back from the saloon. Otherwise . . . well, you know what happened last time he came home full of drink."

Brianna knew. His massive hands had twisted her arms into a painful knot. His reeking whiskey breath had concealed the remnants of her old Father, the one who'd bounced her on his knee and carved her hobby-horse just a few years back. That tender man had vanished through the doors of The Horse You Came In On Saloon. In recent months, she'd witnessed his rapid slide into disgrace.

How well Brianna remembered the day not long ago when Father tore his riding crop from the wall, took her by the arm, hauled up her petticoats, and slammed the whip against the back of her legs. Ten lashes. All for asking for money to buy a penny candy. The flush rising in her cheeks was hot, the remembered pain still raw in her memory. She followed after Annie, but she couldn't resist a long look behind her at the Admiral Fell.

That spot—*their* place. A polka she would long remember. Wisps of smoke hovered overhead.

Seven

THE OPEN DOOR

Brianna's disappointment centered in her chest as she followed Annie home on the windy walk down South Broadway through Fells Point. Her sister's red curls bounced around on her back, her sunbonnet tied in neat red ribbons. Brianna imagined the list on her own diary page labeled *Reasons Why I Hate Annie*.

Brianna trudged along, composing her complaints: when she sensed herself young and inferior, her sister acted older and superior; when she struggled in school, Annie brought home top honors; when she wrestled with her own thick, wavy hair, her sister's curls lay tidy on her collar.

Dark revenge ebbed and flowed inside of Brianna, depending on Annie's latest treatment. While Annie snored next to her that night, she might take the scissors to those way-too-perfect curls. On the other hand, maybe not. She wouldn't dare risk another whipping from Father.

Brianna felt Annie's guiding hand on hers as they crossed Aliceanna Street, bobbing between carriages and peddler's carts toward their brick rowhouse on Wolfe. Did her sister think she was still a little girl? Brianna slapped her away, and in return, Annie flashed her the usual look of disdain.

A rider and stallion barreled toward Brianna, but she misjudged his distance and wobbled into the street. The traveler's horse reared back and the rider cursed, gripping the reins. Sliding on the cobblestones, Brianna twisted her right ankle. Fierce pain shot through her foot. The pungent odor of dung pervaded her nostrils. A sharp snap rang out; a whip bit horseflesh, and horse's hooves pounded away from her down the road.

Annie bent toward her, blocking the sun.

Briana flinched at her sister's grasp, the fingers an iron grip on her wrist. She yanked her hand away. "Leave me alone." Her voice resembled the snarl of an injured dog.

When Brianna tried to rise and fell back down, Annie's hands wrapped around her waist and pulled her to her feet. Peering after the horseman, Annie said, "I've seen that man before. It all happened so fast, but I think—"

"I don't care what you think." Brianna limped the rest of the way home, all the while aiming her mutterings at Annie's back. "Your fault. Always treating me like a child."

After a purgatory of a march, Brianna and Annie reached Wolfe Street. Among the colonial brick rowhouses, theirs was the only one with a red door, and tonight that door was open. That could only mean one thing: Father was home from church early, and he was full of drink. Her stomach clenched. The family had to whisper when he was home; he complained that the sounds of their voices gave him a headache.

Brianna hobbled up the steps. Each movement taught her a painful lesson. She stepped with Annie around the walking stick Father dropped in the front entry. His tattered Bible lay open on the marble top table. She let out a long, lingering sigh. Their family's ruin seemed to deepen every day. Chaos ruled Father's mind, and Mama had resigned herself to sweeping up the daily wreckage of their lives. Mama's vibrant personality was fading away, like velvet left too long in the sun.

Eight

FAMILIAR PATHWAYS

Father had been known for his youthful boxing skills. His mates called him Spiker Baird. The former prizefighter continued to reenact his glory days every night in the kitchen. There he was again, raving along with the noise of plates breaking against the brick wall. Who was he mad at now? The vicar? A fellow reverend? A parishioner?

Hearing their shouts, Annie stopped in the entry and turned in a circle. There was a bitter edge to her voice. "Mama must have forgotten about dinner. Follow me. We can wait on the steps until it's over."

Brianna shadowed Annie up the stairs and stopped at the first landing. Her sore ankle had become a lead weight. Although all she wanted to do was lie down upstairs, she took a seat with her sister. She didn't have the strength to charge down and intervene on Mama's behalf. At least their reserve of used porcelain was stacked high in the kitchen cabinet. Father's mania for throwing and smashing was satisfied, as long as cups, plates, and teapots were handy.

At the sound of Father's voice, Annie touched her arm. Father's voice echoed from the kitchen. "Gets worse every week." She pictured him hurling another one of Auntie's old Aynsley plates against the wall. A splintering crash resounded.

"Father, stop." Mama's voice cracked like ice crunching under carriage wheels. Brianna envisioned their weak mother, ill-equipped to live with a man whose mood was soft one day, harsh the next.

Every time a plate hit the wall, Brianna's old fears and uncertainties crowded in as nosy neighbors. Did she even belong here anymore? She was almost old enough to leave home, to live in the boardinghouse with Miss Rose's seamstresses. But it was Annie who'd kept her here, coupled with her own fears for Mama's safety.

Brianna imagined the scene in the kitchen. By now, Mama would be holding up her apron to catch the flying shards as they bounced off the sideboard.

"Done *nothhing* wrong, yet the elders have *d-deemed* I've a lesser role now." Father had been drinking for a while now. He often started at noon and continued all day and into the evening. Used to be he'd not show the effects of his drinking, like all the other men at the pubs in Fells Point. Now he didn't seem to care who knew he was drunk. The despair in his voice stabbed at her heart.

"At church, they said that last month, you'd shown improvement." Mama's low voice trembled.

Another clattering of dishes signaled Father's fresh ammunition.

His voice grew brash. "Deacon Thomas Wilkins and his bloody *b-band* decreed they've had enough of my *drrrinkin'*. They're tired of seeing me *intoxicate-d-durin'* the giving of communion. I *slurrrred* my words during the *b-baptism* of Jonathan Wilks last Saturday."

Yet another dish smashed against the wall. Annie's leg pressed against Brianna's on the step. Mama named items as he threw them. "A dinner plate." Brianna gave a silent prayer: *Please, Mama, duck down—don't get hit.*

The sound of his guttural hiccup reverberated. "Cut my *zzalary* from fifteen-hundred *dollarzz* to eight-hundred *dollarzz* a year. How're we all to survive?"

"The girls are working." Mama always tried to be pleasant.

An eerie silence ensued. Father was rearming, clutching up more dishes to his chest.

Mama announced, "The cups."

He grunted.

Brianna clutched Annie's hand. Another blast of china splitting apart.

"Our girls shall not only have to work at Betsy Osborne's, but they shall also have to move *elsewhhhere*, for we will not be able to *furnishh* food and lodging for them *anymohre*."

Brianna trembled—how many fearful possibilities could crowd into her mind? He might throw them both out, or at least have them live elsewhere. Why stop at china? He may as well toss his children out, too.

"The soup tureen," Mama said.

By now, Father's face would be sneering with vengeance. He cast the dish away like a bad dream.

Then, with his usual abruptness, Father said, "Mama, I'm goin' to *ressht*."

"Stew?" Mama's muffled voice rang like a coffin bell.

"None for me."

Brianna knew that he'd already drunk his dinner, wasting what few coins he'd scraped together.

"Must you drink so often?" Mama croaked, her voice full of disillusionment.

Father's voice took on a mocking tone. "Oh, Reverend, must you have more drink? Oh, Reverend, *pleazz* buy me this, *pleazz* buy me that!"

Was Mama so used to his jeering that she didn't even respond anymore?

Then Mama said, "Here, dear, don't forget your slippers."

The priest's heavy footsteps thudded on the floorboards, and he lurched out of the kitchen, the shuffling noise of his moving bulk fading away toward the parlor.

"Mama needs help with the dustpan," Brianna whispered.

Down at the kitchen door, she peeked around the corner, and faced the battleground. Annie's warm breath fanned across the back of her neck. In the middle of the kitchen, Mama hunched over her knees, tears strolling down familiar pathways to her chin. She squatted, picking through the broken porcelain.

Mama had to be imagining the grand teas in County Down where Aunt Kathleen had served cold meats on those fine platters. Around her, shards of white, green, and yellow plates littered the floor and stuck into the walls, as though shot from a cannon. A fine white dust coated every surface. Brianna looked back at her sister. "Best we leave her alone right now so she won't know we heard Father's rampage tonight."

Annie's voice spoke of trampled dreams. "She knows."

Nine

A Boy and the Devil

Up in their bedroom a few minutes later, Annie wound a white cloth around Brianna's sore ankle while she fought back tears. "Are you trying to make me cry? Any tighter and my leg will be cold as a wagon tire." She ran her hand over her numb calf.

Brianna's ankle rose into a purple mound under the bandages. She spoke through clenched teeth. "It's getting bigger." She clung to her rag doll. Belly hunger and ankle pains were doing battle inside of her.

Annie's cool tone revealed her disapproval. "You're lucky you didn't break a bone. If you broke your ankle, you could lose your whole leg to gangrene. It happened to old Mr. Perkins, the one-legged butcher. That's why he hops around on a crutch in the Broadway market."

"Poor Mr. Perkins," Brianna said. She gazed at Mercy, the upstairs cat, who rubbed her sable back against the door frame, then leaped onto the bed and kneaded Brianna's pillow. Small clusters of duck feathers escaped where the cat's claws pierced the cotton.

Annie drew the bandage tighter. "Wouldn't have happened if you'd walked properly across the street. That young man trampled you. Wasn't he the same one you talked to in the carriageway?" She slid off the bed onto a stool in front of a cloudy looking-glass, the only one Father allowed in the house. After she untied the perfect red ribbons of her bonnet, she perched the hat on a wall hook.

Brianna nuzzled the cat and picked a feather off her nose. "I never saw the rider."

Mercy's purr filled the space between them.

"Brazen." Annie wiped the day's grime off her own face with a checked handkerchief. "And to think he's your new beau and all." She ran her tortoiseshell comb through some stray curls, then picked up her brush.

"What?" Brianna seethed, her sister's condescending tone grating on her.

"That violin player at the Admiral Fell. What's his name? Simpson? Spentley? The one who nearly ran over you on Aliceanna?"

"What makes you think he's my beau?" Her eyes watered—was the cause indignation or her ankle this time?

Annie turned and put her hands on her hips. "From your scene in the carriageway."

"He was fixing my bonnet." Maybe if she changed the subject, her sister would stop insisting he was her beau. "What makes you think it's his horse that ran me down? If he'd been the rider, he'd have jumped off to help me." Brianna chewed her lower lip.

Annie plopped down on the sagging mattress next to her. The motion bumped the cushion where Mercy lay, and the cat emitted a low growl.

Her sister reached out, her fingertips raising Brianna's chin. Annie's touch was cold and she shivered. "Slip or no slip, be careful. If Father finds out you're dallying with boys, that's the end of you."

"Stop, sister. I was toting the ballgown over on an errand for Miss Osborne. What's the harm in that?" Brianna blinked away angry tears.

Mercy glided from the pillow onto Annie's lap, and her sister ran a hand over the cat's back. "Were you going over there to see a certain someone?" Annie's wide eyes could not conceal her disapproval.

"Course not. I had the tablecloths to deliver." Brianna held her tongue. Her sister had no right to ask that. Especially not before dinner when they were both weak and hungry.

Annie's tone grew tight. "You've no business to linger over there. They ever tell you about Cousin Maggie from County Down?"

"Never heard of her." It was worth burying her dignity to hear this. Tales of their scandalous Irish relatives were better than a traveling show.

Mercy slid off Annie's lap and curled up in a ball at their feet. Annie continued. "Cousin Maggie was Aunt Kathleen's daughter, the one who gave Mama the chinaware." Annie stepped over Mercy and closed the bedroom door, something Father would never allow. "I heard it from Ralph when he came to visit from Ireland last year. He's old, you know. Twenty-one. Mama's side of the family has all the excitement. Ralph knows the family secrets."

"Go on." Brianna's pulse quickened.

Annie lowered her voice, and she bent her head toward her. "Well, Cousin Maggie died frozen in a Belfast gutter at age eighteen. Ralph said she couldn't hold her liquor."

"Sin to Moses." Brianna ached to hear more.

"And that's not all," Annie said.

"What?" Maybe there'd be even more juice.

"She went with men." Her words sounded harsh as a gavel on Judgment Day.

Brianna bit her bottom lip in fake dismay. "Don't say."

Annie folded her arms. "In the family way at the time they found her. Ralph said she was cast off by her parents, and so she drank herself to death. Her liver crusted and shrank like a rotten peach. The child didn't survive."

"The child's father?"

"Rumor has it he was a wealthy banker, already married."

"Oh." Brianna sighed. She envisioned the young girl's gray, pregnant body lying next to a roadway, the corpse frozen in the muddy gutter, sprayed by rain-drenched carts and wagons traveling past. She could see the crusty liver lying next to the girl, dark like those in the butcher shops. She remembered her terror when she had once stumbled over a corpse outside a tavern in Baltimore. Nightmares about it had filled her dreams for months. She tapped her sister's arm. "Annie, you ever, um, slipped?"

"What do you mean, 'slipped'?" Annie peered at her with narrowed eyes.

"You know, kissed a boy and such?" The oval image of Spenser's face flickered against the wall.

"Course not." Annie sat upright as the cross. "'Tis a sin."

Brianna nicked her sister's arm with the back of her knuckles. "Come now, there had to be sometime when you flounced your curls, or fluttered your eyelashes. Fess up, Annie."

"All right, once. Remember Sam Gosling, the church serving boy? During Holy Communion. The part of the service when we're at the communion rail and the boys help the minister?"

"Yes. What did Sam do?" she asked.

"Well, Father was kneeling next to me and Minister Brown was putting the host in Mrs. O'Brien's mouth when Sam turned to me and winked. Hard to ignore his big, green eyes," Annie said.

"I know. What'd you do next?" Brianna moved closer.

"What any girl in her right mind would do. I winked back." Annie sat up straighter, the image of innocence.

"Father see you?" Surely he would have noticed his daughter's flirting.

"I didn't know it at the time. He waited 'til we got home and then he let me have it. Grabbed the hairbrush and paddled me hard." Annie slapped her brush on the palm of her hand.

"Go on." Brianna fought a sense of disbelief. Had Annie ever suffered the beatings Father had lavished on her?

Annie clenched the hairbrush. "He chased me with the brush around the dinner table, calling me a hussy while Mama screamed. Then he pinned me down to the horsehair sofa in the parlor and gave it to me good. I couldn't sit down for days."

"Hmmm. Where was I? I don't remember you ever getting in trouble."

"Oh, you were too young to know about it." Annie brushed a curl back over her shoulder. "That's why I don't trifle with Father. He's dashed mean and getting meaner."

"Don't fret about me or Father. I'm not even friends with Spenser." Another jab shot from her ankle up toward her knee.

"Listen, the boy always gets his way. Older girls at school say boys like toying with us girls a lot. And that can ruin us." Annie wound an auburn curl around her finger.

"How?" Brianna asked. Annie's frankness nibbled away at her confidence.

Her sister settled back on the bed. "Boys can take away our virtue. Once it's gone, Satan's in charge."

"How can he be in control?" A breath caught in her chest.

Annie crossed her arms. "A boy and the devil can make us have a baby when we don't want one."

"I thought a lady always wanted a baby." She'd never let Annie know how much she knew about relations between men and women.

"If she's not married, a baby's a curse."

"How very sad. I've always wondered, sister. When'll you get married?"

Annie drew her close. "When I'm older and ready. It'll be a coon's age before you marry. You're but a child. Can't even walk straight in the highroad." She grinned.

Brianna stared at her swollen ankle, then laughed with her sister. The aroma of Mama's stew drifted through the house and her stomach growled. Maybe there'd be more meat this time, instead of the usual thin broth. Tonight she'd have to spoon off the white film left by the porcelain dust.

The diary page marked *Reasons Why I Hate Annie* crossed her mind. Might as well see what her sister had to say about her own moral perfection. "How do you do it, Annie?"

"What, sister?" Mercy's deep purr grew louder as Annie massaged the cat's neck.

"The right thing?"

Annie crossed her legs at the ankles. "I don't know. I just try to follow what Mama and Father taught us. Ten Commandments and Sunday school."

"I don't believe the lessons at Sunday school, and I can never remember all the commandments. I do try. In school, I've felt the switch and worn the dunce cap more than I care to recall." Brianna fingered a strip of peeling wallpaper that curled next to the bed.

"You've always been the contrary one, Brianna." Annie patted her hand. "Oh, by the way, let's keep your injury a secret. Don't want Father to know, do we? And we'd upset poor Mama. Let's go down to dinner." Annie's face took on a gentler aspect as she glanced over Brianna's ankle.

Did Annie sound kinder than usual? Maybe she wouldn't cut off her sister's curls after all. Brianna rose from the bed, and Mercy claimed the warm spot where she'd been sitting. Brianna hopped on one foot over to her carpet slippers, smoothed her petticoats down over the bandages, and inched down the stairs to dinner. Annie's speech about boys had lacked something. Where was her passion? Where was mention of the heat of a boy's touch on a girl's fingertips? Where was the shiver that accompanied a brush on the lips?

A few moments later, Annie led grace while the stew steamed in the middle of the table. She and Mama bowed their heads, whispering along with the prayer. *We thank Thee, Lord, for happy hearts, for rain and sunny weather. We thank Thee, Lord, for this our food, and that we are together.* Brianna examined her own dry hands and wondered how her sister could get her long fingers to fold so neatly during prayer. Her ankle bent and she gasped.

"Brianna?" Her mother ladled stew out of the kettle.

She forced a grin, taking a bowl from her mother. "I'm fine, Mama."

Annie shot a knowing look across the table as she passed the biscuits.

The watery mush slopped in the bowl Mama had passed over to her. Brianna pondered the potatoes nestled in gray froth, then supported her sore ankle on Louie the Labrador's back as he lay under the table, awaiting his usual scraps. She stirred the broth with her spoon. Even Louie would turn his nose up at this concoction. "Mama, is there some reason I don't see any meat in this tonight?"

Her mother sat in silent contemplation.

"Where's Father?" Annie asked.

"At The Horse You Came In On," Mama said. "He closes the place down all by himself these days. This morning, I found him asleep on our front stoop. I'm fixing to find him passed out in a gutter, the way they find Mr. Poe every now and then." Mama's face went from dull ashen to waxy white. She sank her teeth into a biscuit.

Brianna took the saltcellar from Annie's hand.

Would this silence ever end? Annie slurped her soup against the music of Louie's snores from under the table. The wooden clock performed a steady tick-tock on the mantle. Her mother studied the gray contents of her bowl as though it held the secret to life. A lone tear clung to the wrinkles under her chin.

Ten

SILVER STENCILS

Baltimore, Maryland
June 1849

A few mornings and evenings passed, casting light and shadows over Fells Point. One afternoon after an early dinner, Brianna edged around the usual dusty mosaic of porcelain on the kitchen floor. Father had been at it again. The shards of Mama's china lay in jagged circles and triangles on the wood. Brianna wrapped one of Father's large handkerchiefs across her nose and mouth to avoid inhaling the dust. White clay powder covered everything: the table lamp, the windowpanes, Mama's knitting basket, her souvenir map of Paris, and even Louie's bone.

Annie stepped to the window and raised it up as far as she could, propping it with the usual stick. She grabbed a broom and held it out to Brianna.

Taking the handle from Annie, a powerful relief filled Brianna—even an uneasy peace—as she and Annie swept Father's mess away. When would he be cured of his drinking? She'd have to pray harder.

Brianna angled her broom, trying to catch the smaller shards. What a mess. She'd helped Annie gather many of these dinnerware pieces from church rummage sales and Baltimore flea markets. She picked up a broken cup, one of her old favorites. A yellow daisy chain brightened the handle. This piece had no doubt saved Mama's life, and possibly their own.

Still holding the broom handle, Brianna peered into the dining room. Her mother's usual place at the table was empty. "Where's Mama?" Her ankle throbbed, so she rested her hip against the kitchen cupboard.

Annie picked up a broken saucer as she spoke. "Went up to bed."

"This early?" Late afternoon sunbeams played across the floor.

Annie shrugged.

"Father go out?" Brianna asked.

Her sister shifted her eyes toward the drawing room.

Brianna glided over to the fainting couch. Father lay there, stretched out. His left arm cradled Louie the Labrador, who gazed up at her with mournful, brown eyes. The man's chest rose up and down in the rhythm of sleep. She paused, wondering. How could her cruel father look so innocent?

Back in the kitchen, Annie fingered the remnants of a teapot. "Father made a bigger mess tonight." She pointed at the jumble with the broken spout. "Let's clear a path to the sink so we can do the dishes first, then sweep up the rest."

"I'll get the tray." Brianna piled the dinner dishes from the table onto a platter, brought them into the kitchen, and then settled the glassware into the sink.

Annie plunged her hands deep into the soapy water. "So, tell me more about Spenser. I'm curious." Bubbles rose up as she swished the rag back and forth over the plates.

Brianna stiffened. She wouldn't say too much. "He invited me to dance when I took some things over there from Miss Betsy." She held out a towel to her sister.

Her sister passed her a dinner plate. "He did?"

"Yep, and he said nice things to me."

Her sister's forehead wrinkled. "What'd he say?"

"Oh, I don't know. I think he appreciates me."

Annie nudged her with her elbow. "So, what would a violinist have to appreciate in a seamstress?" A bitterness tinged her voice.

"Well, he taught me the waltz."

"So he did, eh? Go on."

"And . . . he wants to kiss me."

Annie flapped the dishtowel hard against her leg, stirring dust. "The girls were saying something about him today at Miss Betsy's."

"Tell me." Brianna swallowed hard, but planted her feet.

Annie's face hardened into a clay mask. "They say he has a wife. A violinist, too. She's soon to join him, moving here from New York."

"Not true." Brianna's stomach cramped.

"Why would they lie at Miss Osborne's?" Annie rolled the dishtowel between her hands.

"Just a bunch of gossipers. I'm surprised you listen to them."

Her sister's mask grew softer. "I've told you before. You need to watch out for these scoundrels. You never know their background—where they came from."

"Well, I believe in Spenser. He's sweet." Brianna loved to say his name.

Annie moved toward her. "Come now, you hardly know him."

"You've no business intruding into my life." Feeling the water drip from her wet hands, she set her hands on her hips.

Annie's breath was warm against her face. "Oh, yes I do. I'm all you have."

Brianna listened with a heavy heart. Annie was right, yet there had to be more to life than stitching darts and piecing garments. A man like Spenser would promise her love. He'd believe in her vision of owning a dressmaker's shop.

There had to be more than—*this*. She gazed around the kitchen. The waning summer light pierced the dusty sunbeams that played over the broken porcelain. A pair of blue flies mated on the windowsill.

That night, Brianna awakened to moonlight filtering through the sycamore leaves outside the garret window. Love images had layered her dreams. Her fingers toyed with the little scabs where Spenser's rose had pricked her breast. In the air over her head, a scene unfolded—their lips met; Spenser fondled her breasts; both touched, searched, and held each other. She heard loving words whispered into deep embraces.

Perspiring, she flung off the covers to let the summer night flow over her the way Spenser's love engulfed her, carrying her far away from Father's madness. Maybe then her gloom would leave, too. The soft light gave comfort. She rested her arms behind her head on the pillow.

Another scene stretched above her. Life with a violinist. They'd keep a neat little cottage and surround it with flowers, puppies, and babies. The first child would be a boy. Ambrose, her grandfather's name. Spenser would help decorate her shop. They'd call it *Brianna's Needleworks*. Gentry from far away as New York would order gowns from her.

Brianna followed the lacy pattern of leaves outside the window. Now she'd have to practice writing her married name in her penmanship book. Every girl has to know how to write her intended's name in cursive. *Brown*. Then she'd work on *Mrs. Spenser Brown*, slanted, with loops inside loops. Fancy that. *Brown* would appear on all the account books at their new shop.

Turning on her side, she plumped her pillow and faced her snoring sister. The branches of the sycamore fluttered dark green in the night breezes. Moonglow etched silver stencils on the bedroom walls.

Diffused light spread across Annie's slumbering form. An endless supply of auburn curls poured from the back of her sleeping cap. Brianna reached over and lifted a pair of sewing scissors from the bedside table. Clip off a curl or two for good measure. Payback for Annie saying she knew all about Spenser and for calling her "contrary." Betrothed already? Humph. She'd see as much.

Her sister sprawled on the mattress, oblivious to the world and its evils. Brianna's fingers arranged Annie's red ringlets against the pillow in a zigzag pattern. With a tailor's hand, she extended the scissors and held up a curl.

The front door slammed. Father was home.

She trembled. What was she about to do? Annie had held her, hugged her, and advised her. How would she survive without her? Ashamed, she snuck open the drawer and hid the scissors far back behind her Bible and diary.

Annie slept deeply, her hands thrust under her pillows. Brianna snuggled up to her back and floated in visions of Spenser's embrace.

The following Wednesday morning, Betsy Osborne's shop hummed with busy voices. Next door, a wheelwright's clanging kept time with the flow as women measured and basted hems and sleeves.

Brianna raised the window across from her sewing table and opened the curtain extra wide. Time to see the goings-on at the Admiral Fell.

That morning, Betsy Osborne announced that their shop had received a large order. The mayor always hosted Baltimore's July Fourth ball. At this glittering extravaganza, many of Osborne's clientele danced the cotillion in their spectacular dresses to the admiration of Baltimore's mayor and high society. Osborne's girls would spend the day after such an event poring over the society columns in Baltimore newspapers, pointing out the dresses they had made.

Brianna chuckled at Annie, curls intact, who bent over the table ahead of her. Orderly ringlets peeked out from her cap. Little did her sister know how close she'd come to losing them.

How annoying that Annie continued to bait her about Spenser. He wasn't married. Brianna tied a satin sash to the hip of a voluminous red, white, and blue ballgown. Ridiculous. In her mind, his memory would remain as pure as his violet eyes, and as rich as his deep voice she could hear even now when she closed her eyes.

At the sound of carriage wheels rolling on the cobblestones, Brianna's pulse quickened, and she leaned out her window. Cook and Mrs. Whipple got into a barouche and the pair of black horses travelled up South Broadway in her direction.

Quick! She ducked back in so as not to be recognized, and turned back to pin sleeves onto the dress and measure the length. Those women from the Inn must never think she was so curious. It might get back to Spenser.

"Brianna!" A shrill voice cut into her thoughts.

She looked up at Meg from the alterations room. The girl was always untidy, her hair askew, her dress tattered, and her stockings wrinkled. Yet Meg's heart was usually in the right place.

"What is it?" Brianna controlled the needles of irritation at work in her voice.

"Have something for you." The girl teased, her brown eyes merry.

"What now, Meg?" Brianna suspected the girl wanted to borrow her new scissors. How many phrases could she invent to say *no* to her?

"Here." Something crackled in her hand. Meg looked around for Miss Betsy or any of the other supervisors. Sliding a thin envelope into Brianna's hand, she whispered, "Don't open it here."

"Thank you . . . I think." A small voice in her head wondered if it was from Spenser. She didn't dare get excited yet—did she?

Outside, a driver called and a whip cracked. Who was it this time? Brianna peered around her creation to see another carriage leave the Inn, its passengers wearing satin, lace, and feathered hats. Was Spenser among them? No. Could that mean—?

Brianna's palms grew clammy and she wiped them against her apron so as not to damage the dress. Folding the gown and its sleeve inside-out, she began stitching long, temporary tucks as she removed the pins. A short while later, another noise jolted her. This time, a landau departed from the Inn. Those hatted women must be headed to the market to buy food, or to shop for accessories for their fanciful gowns.

The Inn drew her like a nail to a magnet. She couldn't resist another peek. A curtain had opened upstairs. Was Spenser waiting for her inside? Not everyone was gone after all. Her heart settled back down. Was Spenser in one of the coaches? It's possible she'd missed seeing him depart.

On the other hand, maybe he hadn't come to the Inn at all that day. Yet, he'd usually come to practice on Wednesdays, the day the Inn was closed. The chamber trio would practice when no one else was at the hotel. And today was Wednesday. The envelope rustled with each movement of her apron pocket.

The sound of the bell lent Brianna a surge of nervous energy. Neglecting to fold her work neatly on her table as Miss Rose required, she slid off her stool and hunted under the table for her lunch pail.

Eleven

NEEDLE JABS

Baltimore, Maryland
June 1849

On summer days, Brianna and the girls took lunch in the garden behind the shop. A noon breeze and warm light greeted them in the garden. Her quivering hand patted her pocket as she strolled. She needed to find a quiet space alone, so she settled her plaid blanket on a patch of dry ground under the apple tree, and stretched her legs out under her skirts, the ground bumpy beneath her. Thank goodness Annie and the other girls were deep in gossip over on the porch. They'd hardly notice her absence.

Brianna raised a corner of her skirt, reached into her pocket, and tore open the envelope.

I will be waiting at the kitchen door at 5:00 this afternoon.
Please come,
Spenser

A current of excitement gripped her. Her brain galloped at a pace no thoroughbred could match. Conscious of little else than Spenser, she counted fifteen needle jabs on her fingers by the end of the day.

At five o'clock, Brianna drew the ribbons of her straw bonnet tighter and wove her way out of the sewing room toward the stairs. The girls' heads were bent over their piecework in the stuffy late afternoon. She latched the door behind her at Miss Osborne's and stared down the street. The sun rode low above the horizon, casting glimmers on the tides of the Inner Harbor. Clipper ships bobbed at their moorings, growing larger as she paced toward the Inn. Joy replaced her worry—Spenser waited by the half-open entry.

He closed the kitchen door behind them and dropped the key in his vest pocket. He flashed a grin. "How were you able to get away from your sister?" He turned and faced her, running a hand through his tumble of blond curls.

Brianna flushed, her heart thudding in her chest. "I told her I had to sweep the floor at Father's church before going home for dinner."

"I see." He wound his arm around her shoulders, and then gently pulled her forward down the street, stopping under the Admiral Fell sign.

"Where are we going?" Her hands shook a little. If only she didn't appear so nervous.

Spenser's low voice teased and charmed. "Around the corner on Thames, of course. For a bit of refreshment, and . . . you know . . ."

Brianna lifted her chin as though she understood completely. Yet, she did not know, so she turned and followed his broad back as he made for the corner and turned right on Thames.

At the corner, she paused. "Here?" *Here* was the territory of hussies, the brazen ones she'd spied upon the day she'd danced with Spenser in the street. Whatever would Annie say about this? One foray into forbidden land was enough alone, but to go again with a man?

He stopped and gazed at her. "Whatever is the matter?" An impatient edge lingered in his words.

"Why aren't we going back into the Inn? After all, it is empty. I thought . . ." She floundered.

Spenser shook his head, seeming disappointed. "No, I would get into trouble were I—that is, were we—to be discovered there."

Brianna stopped. "I'm not supposed to go down Thames. Miss Rose says—"

The mocking, playful grin she remembered flashed across Spenser's face. "You didn't mind Miss Rose the last time you were down here when I caught you snooping. Besides, I've a friend with a room down here where we can be alone."

Brianna swallowed, then relaxed. She may as well follow him. If she didn't go with him now, what might happen? She couldn't bear to lose him. All right, she would go down Thames if that's what it would take for them to be together. After all, it was only to the room of his friend—where was the harm in that?

"Very well," she said.

Spenser's eyes conveyed eagerness and tenderness. "Everything will be fine, you'll see. I've arranged a nice surprise for you." He stopped midway down Thames at a rowhouse across from Harborside Rope Makers. He keyed open the door, and passing the drawing room to the right, led her up a steep flight of stairs. Red brocade wallpaper and cherrywood wainscoting blurred in her vision. They stopped, breathless, at the top of the landing. Drawing a second larger key from his vest, he inserted it into the lock on the door on their left.

"But, won't someone hear us?" Brianna tensed.

He opened the door and led her inside. "Not at all. My friend says the girls in this house work at night and sleep during the day. We have a couple of hours until dark. No one will notice us."

High ceilings, cherub wallpaper, and a canopy bed. The door shut behind them.

Brianna let Spenser take her jacket off. She watched him hang it up on an empty peg next to the door. What would be the next thing he would remove?

"Hungry?" His voice was low and beckoning.

The blood beating in her ears and her desire for him made her crazy. What had Spenser asked? Oh yes, *hungry.* She summed up an answer. "I must admit, Mama usually has dinner ready this hour." A heart-shaped ring glimmered on his finger as he lifted his hand to touch her hair.

"I'll bet your Mama doesn't serve *this.*" He pointed to a silver tea tray full of finger sandwiches, some caviar, and a bottle of French champagne.

Spenser stepped closer. There it was again—the scent of rosin from his violin. "Do you think your sister believed your excuse about being late?" He lifted her chin and his eyes explored her face.

His violet eyes contained flecks of gold. If only she could lose herself inside them. She exhaled slowly. "Yes, I often do that, so she won't suspect anything, unless I get home way after dark."

Spenser's broad smile enlivened her spirits. "Oh, I could keep you late." He pulled Brianna close, and nuzzled her curls. "Your hair smells fine." His arms wrapped her into him, and she melted into the potent smells of sweet tobacco, hair pomade, and cotton starch. Tilting her chin, he pressed his mouth against her lips, and his tongue worked to open them slowly, easily, as she allowed him to explore the soft, tender reaches of passionate arousal. Her breath came fast, and his manhood surged and pressed against her.

Spenser's gentle fingers unlaced her corset. The many layers of petticoats fell away and she stood bare-breasted against his open shirt. His lips were warm. He kissed her neck, her shoulders, then worked his way down between her breasts, cupping them in each hand as she moaned. He turned and licked each nipple, running his tongue around and over them until she shuddered with pleasure. Brianna reached down and put her arms around his neck, and he raised his head, devouring her mouth. Then he lifted her up and carried her to the bed.

He lay on top of her, his pulsing manhood pressing between her thighs. She returned his deep, ardent kisses with the desire stored up during those nights of fervent dreams. Each wave of pleasure mixed with pain as she opened to Spenser. Inch by inch, he probed the secret, dark places she'd never shared with any man. They rocked together, the harmony of bedsprings loud, then soft, then loud again, until he cried out to her, his eyes wide in happy surprise. Brianna held his face as he bent over her, then cradled her, encompassing her, a last tremor moving through his body.

Spenser rested in an exhausted slumber next to her, one arm encircling her shoulders, the other resting on her belly. That ring again. Where would he get such a fine jewel? A thousand explanations were possible. A family heirloom, perhaps. Spenser was a worldly man from a worldly family. What good taste he had.

Brianna took in her surroundings. A linen canopy stretched over them. Ivory linen. Ideal fabric for a wedding dress. The room held a faint perfume, a womanly scent. Her hunger intensified. She eased off the bed, taking care not to disturb her sleeping lover. In the silence, she poured some champagne into a flute and took a finger sandwich.

Could she ever love anyone as much as she loved Spenser? She sipped her champagne and felt its fizz on her tongue. No one else could compare. He was special, meant for her. Her gaze shifted to his face where he lay napping. His long eyelashes rested on his cheeks. Brianna took bites of the sandwich, wondering. What might he be dreaming about? Was he dreaming about marriage? They must be together forever. Not a soul must come between them. The room darkened in the twilight.

Brianna paused to listen as Fells Point moved from daylight to nightfall. Outside the clip-clop of horse traffic and carriages grew more sporadic, and shop owners called good night to one another as they locked their doors. A ship's horn groaned from the Inner Harbor. Were those children chanting rhymes as they skipped home?

The clock downstairs chimed seven, so she climbed into her drawers and dressed in her chemise and corset, followed by her many layers of petticoats. Doors opening and shutting and sounds of women's voices penetrated the walls. She must hurry before the house filled with sailors and the courtesans began their business. What if someone occupied this room tonight? She went about on tiptoe. Better not to disturb Spenser—he needed his sleep.

Drops of champagne lingered in Brianna's glass. After she took the last sip, she hesitated. Was that a tinge of blood there on the sheet? Her blood? No time to clean that up. She'd leave that to Spenser. She assumed that such sheets were a common sight in the laundry at a parlor house. How many virgins had been deflowered there? More men than women, probably. She snatched her jacket from the hook, then she stole down the stairs before easing out the door into the darkness.

That night, at home in bed next to her sister, Brianna gazed up at a ceiling spider inching across the shimmering silhouette of the tree. Crossing her arms to hold her shoulders, she sensed a dull ache between her thighs. Her eyes followed the spider's path, and she contemplated it, the only sound her sister's soft breathing next to her. She'd given herself to the right man. Spenser was hers forever, and she was now a woman who would be wed in ivory linen. Shifting to her side, she patted her feather pillow. A lone, blue fly lay in silver darkness on the windowsill, its legs curled up in death.

Twelve

LIGHTNING BEFORE THE STORM

Baltimore, Maryland
September 1849

Brianna's summer swirled by in a collage of dressmaking and lovemaking. On Wednesday afternoons, the Admiral Fell was closed to visitors, the Whipples were away on shopping expeditions, and the staff enjoyed a free day. Spenser would meet her at the kitchen door and they would continue on to their brothel room on Thames Street. Their customary habit of drinking champagne and eating finger sandwiches was abandoned as the weeks went by, and instead, they did not wait to eat. The room was usually littered with her skirts and his pants cast onto a chair in hasty lovemaking.

In the secret chambers of her mind, she wondered why Spenser seemed distracted the last few times they made love. Instead of muttering his earlier words, *I love you*, and *you're beautiful*, he became increasingly silent during their love rituals, his eyes closed, his motions seemingly mechanical. Could he be hiding something—an illness, perhaps? Brianna struggled to find a reason for this, since his reserve put a layer of separation between them. Yet, she must be grateful. In time, she'd learn all about him.

When Brianna listened to the girls at Miss Osborne's talk about their crushes and prospective beaus, she sniffed. They didn't know what real love was. Spenser's loving words were more passionate and loyal than the simple caresses the shop girls discussed. He'd taught her many ways to give him pleasure. A relationship was about making a man so happy he would ask for her hand in marriage. After creating many a bride's gown, embroidering designs onto lace collars and cuffs, she yearned to prepare her own bridal trousseau.

As Brianna stitched the present set of flowers, she considered the larger set of recent events. Each brothel encounter made her more certain that her dreams of marriage, living in a house with Spenser, having children, and owning her own shop were going to come true. As she pulled a strand of thread through a French knot, she brimmed with a joy shared only with him. He'd changed the subject when she talked about betrothal or marriage yesterday, but after all, there was no doubt he wanted her. Hadn't he possessed her body in hot, throbbing embraces each week?

The next evening at home, Brianna leaned over the zinc tub, soaping the dinner dishes. Father was out drinking at The Horse You Came In On, and the house rested in blessed tranquility. Annie kept up the usual chatter in her ear. It was so easy to ignore her and to wander into a forest of romantic thoughts. She saw Spenser's heart-shaped diamond ring appear, then disappear among the bubbles. Distracted, she slopped tepid water from the basin onto Louie instead of the dishes in the basin, and he yelped.

A hand pushed her arm. "Watch out, Brianna!"

"I know it, Annie." She toweled up the mess.

She kneeled down to offer Louie a hug. Turning to the cupboard, Brianna rummaged in a box marked DOG. Then, she sat cross-legged on the floor. "Here, Louie, here's a soup bone." His eyes bright, Louie crawled across her lap, then grasped and tore the shreds of meat off the bone.

Annie's voice pierced the air. "You can't avoid the subject. You certainly are a love-struck child, if I've ever seen one." She stood stiff as a general, hand on one hip, the other hand forming the dishtowel into a noose against her leg.

Brianna pushed Louie off her lap, reeling from the burn of her sister's remark. She got to her feet and picked up Mama's baking tin. "It's not any of your business, that's all." She scrubbed a stubborn piece of Johnnycake stuck to the side.

Annie's tone bristled. "You act plumb crazy about a boy who's making you the talk of Betsy Osborne's." She worked her towel inside a cup, drying it.

Brianna fired back. "A bunch of nosy gossips. Nobody's business but my own." Wouldn't Annie leave her alone? The weight of Annie's big hands rested on her back shoulders and she flinched. It was all she could do not to kick back her heel and give her a bruised shin.

"It is everyone's business, especially where your standing is concerned. Do you know what they say about you?" Annie's voice had strange echoes of their father's disdain.

"I don't care." Brianna thrust her sister's hands off her shoulders, spraying water into the air.

"They say you're in training to be a courtesan! They say you're becoming a harlot!" Annie slid next to her, peering into her face, one eyebrow raised higher than the other.

Brianna dropped the dishwashing brush. "Who says that? They can't be my friends if they do." She swallowed, struggling to hold in her temper. Spinning around, she crossed the hallway from the kitchen to the dining room. She turned to see Louie, the bone hanging from his mouth, following her, his tail waving like a banner. At least *he* approved of her.

Her eyes took in the room. Mama hunched over in deep sleep at the dining table. Even a cannon discharging wouldn't stir her. Chubby Jezebel, the downstairs cat, napped on the rocking chair, one eye open, observing the action.

Oh no, Annie had followed her in. Brianna seethed with indignation. Why couldn't everyone leave her be?

Annie let fly an unexpected volley. "Father says there is always grain of truth in gossip. So, are you?"

"Am I what?" she shot back.

"In training to be a fallen woman?"

Brianna stepped around to glower at her sister. "Of course not! How dare they say that about me! Besides, gossip is not fair fighting."

Annie's face mingled determination with tenderness. "There's nothing fair about what could happen to you. Miss Osborne could good and well fire you. Julia Gromney said she's seen you slinking out of a Thames Street brothel on more than one Wednesday." Annie shifted the towel from one hand to the other, her knuckles whitening.

"That's absurd."

"No it's not! Obviously you have done something more than once to merit that kind of talk. The girls aren't jealous. They're concerned you might lose your—"

"My what?" Brianna challenged.

"Your reputation as a proper girl. A girl with—prospects." Annie frowned.

"I don't set store by their opinions," she said.

"Can't you see? You might lose your entire future. You probably already have." A warming flush colored Annie's cheeks.

Brianna picked up a dirty napkin from the table and rubbed it between her hands. "My future's with Spenser, and I'll settle for no less." She folded it back on the table and a new anguish began to gnaw at her.

"Recognize the truth about him." Annie's tone softened. "He's already married. Amy Jenkins knows his family."

Brianna put her hands up to her cheeks; they glowed hot with an inner fever. "You're envious. You'll both make up any kind of lie so I'll lose Spenser."

Annie shook her head. "That's a ridiculous notion. I want you to be happy, but Spenser's not the beau for you."

"He's the man I love." Brianna dropped into a chair at the dining table, and rubbed Louie's ears.

Annie tugged the chair next to her sister and sat down.

Brianna felt her sister's knees touching hers and she pulled away.

Annie said, "You give me no choice. I thought you'd listen to reason when I first questioned your relations with Spenser. I was wrong.

"But—"

"Now you must hear me out. Spenser's married to Miss Ellen Scott of the Scotts of North Baltimore. They studied together at the music conservatory."

Brianna lost her bearings for a moment. A wave of shock sideswiped her like the end-tail of a hurricane.

"Lies, all lies. Who made up all this nonsense?" Brianna's stomach churned. The paint was starting to chip on the imaginary house she'd planned to share with him.

Her sister set her mouth in an obstinate line. "She plays the pianoforte and the violin, quite well I'm told. They perform with the Baltimore Chamber Society in the Methodist Church on Friday evenings. The family owns shipping companies in New York, and her father will support them as they follow their musical careers. How Spenser ended up at the Inn is a mystery to me, but my guess is that the family isn't aware of his sideshow."

Brianna stretched out her arms to the dog. Louie's ears were soft and velvety under her fingers. "If I want to know the truth, I'll ask him. All I know is that he loves me and only me."

Ouch! Louie had nipped her hand, tired of all that ear-stretching. He extended his legs, then wobbled off to his corner mat.

Thirteen

WITH ALL LIVING THINGS

Late afternoon on the following Friday, Brianna lay on the wooden examination table. Her eyes followed midwife Louetta Morgan as she rinsed her hands in the bowl on the dresser, then dried them on a dingy towel. Bottles of herbs and potions ranged along the counter. Evil-looking forceps rested alongside an ivory-handled scalpel. The grimy sheet across Brianna's belly smelled of old, dried blood. She ran her cold fingers over the goose bumps emerging on her bare thighs.

Mrs. Morgan said, "You may sit up now, Miss Baird. I need to ask you some questions."

Brianna rose up on her elbows and looked up. "Thank you. I've been feeling awful poor lately." She patted her midsection. "Can't keep my breakfast down."

The midwife perched on the edge of the table. "There, there." Her smile lingered for a moment, then faded like a leaf in winter.

Brianna gazed into Mrs. Morgan's gaunt cheeks and wrinkly lips. In many ways, the trust she had in Mrs. Morgan and her husband, the doctor, were the strongest bonds she had with anyone. She remembered lying on the same table, feverish with ague, or nursing a cough. Those round, brown eyes had continued to look down at her in protective sympathy.

In turn, she'd told Mrs. Morgan things she'd never dream of telling her parents. Mrs. Morgan never quoted Bible verses or the Ten Commandments when she asked Brianna about her body and the new feelings she had as a growing girl—the feelings of wanting, desiring, touching herself or a boy. Instead, she had told her she was growing, that her feelings were natural, and were in tune with all living things.

Mrs. Morgan rested by her side, her observant gaze lingering on Brianna's stomach. She resumed her doctor-like questioning. "Have you been vomiting?"

"Yes, especially in the morning when I get up." She swung her legs over the table edge, and sat parallel to Mrs. Morgan.

"Head spins around like a wheel?"

"Yes, pretty often. I bumped into that mannequin yesterday at work."

"Crave certain foods?"

"I've had a great fondness for Mama's pickled beets, more than usual."

"Missed finding blood in your drawers this month?" Creases gathered around the midwife's eyes.

"How'd you know?"

She patted Brianna's hand. "You've got all the signs."

"Of what, Mrs. Morgan? Bilious attack?" *Oh, please, let it be a bilious attack*, Brianna prayed. At least that would pass in a few days.

With a sigh the woman pushed her spectacles up on her nose. "No, Miss, you're with child."

Brianna met the midwife's frank brown eyes with the same numbness as when Father cursed at her. Her elbows dug into her thighs; her head sought shelter in her hands. "That's not possible." She jerked up, rebelling against any such notion.

Mrs. Morgan reached for her husband's wooden stethoscope. "What do you mean, not possible?"

"I'm still a virgin!" In desperation, a lie would get her out of trouble. She had to try it here.

Mrs. Morgan shook her head. "Lie back down." The midwife pulled the sheet aside and placed the cold, fluted end of the stethoscope down on Brianna's belly, the other end against her ear. Brianna saw the woman squint, listening for the beating heart. "It is indeed a miracle, then, my child, if you say you have never had relations with a man. You carry a fetus. Judging from your missed courses, I'd estimate it to be of some eight weeks or more." The midwife lifted the stethoscope away and tucked the sheet back over Brianna.

Brianna's throat tightened. "But my beau promised this wouldn't happen, Mrs. Morgan. He said he was making plans for us to be married."

"I must ask you a question. Please don't fret, I ask it of all the girls in my care. So, Miss Brianna, did he use French letters?"

Bitter bile rose into her throat. "I don't know. What are you talking about?"

Mrs. Morgan helped her sit up, then put a hand on her shoulder. "French letters are a sheath a man puts over his manhood. Surely you would have seen him put it on."

As their eyes met, a tremor flowed through Brianna. "I don't remember." In truth, she'd never seen him put anything over his manhood, except her own hand. She coughed into her closed fist, irritated that she had not been more observant.

"Well, did he withdraw himself before he came? Did you feel his discharge on your belly?" The midwife wiped her hands on a dingy towel.

The words *withdraw*, *discharge*, *belly*—these were not words her family bandied about. Brianna stumbled around, finding the right words to say. "No, always the wetness was inside me. It used to run down my drawers when I walked home after—well, you know—our meetings. I thought it was water." More frightened than surprised now, she searched Mrs. Morgan's face.

Mrs. Morgan raised her gray eyebrows. "Dear girl. He did not come outside of you, but inside of you. That's how husbands and wives make babies. Have you never watched the wild critters?"

A slow anger rose inside her. Did Mrs. Morgan take her for an ignoramus? She ground out her words through clenched teeth. "I never paid animals much attention. I always thought a baby came when the girl and her beau wanted it, not before, as long as it was God's will."

Morgan put a calming hand on her arm. "No, a young, healthy girl like you can get pregnant anytime, Miss."

Brianna watched the minute hand move forward on the clock facing her. "I never reckoned." This was unfair. A child out of wedlock was not in her plan.

Morgan pulled a handkerchief from her apron pocket and wiped some beads of sweat from her own forehead. "You're a healthy girl in a delicate condition."

Brianna hopped off the table and stepped into her drawers, petticoats, and day dress. Her lower lip quivered. This was not delicate for her at all.

The midwife helped her with the many buttons and loop fasteners on the back of her gown. With each button, Brianna's anger grew in severity.

Then, like a dam, her pent-up anger broke. She whirled around and stood facing Mrs. Morgan. "I feel like you're describing a poisoned mare or cow. Not me, surely, not me." Sudden tears blurred her vision and then trickled in streams down her face. They gathered at her chin, and she swiped them away with the back of her hand to keep from wetting her embroidered apron, a gift from Mrs. Whipple.

In response, Mrs. Morgan plucked the handkerchief out of her apron pocket. "Here, take this, my dear. No need to return it. It's always hard to hear this kind of news when a girl's not married. Please come back if you decide . . . to give up the baby or to end it. I know midwives who can help you. No one need know." The midwife's kind eyes spoke of many such encounters with girls in situations like Brianna's.

Brianna looked down at the white embroidery on the handkerchief. She glanced at the array of shiny forceps and pointy scissors that had terrorized her during her visits since she was a little girl. "Father would never let me give up the child."

A frown played across the woman's face. "You plan to tell him?" She folded a towel and set it on a side counter.

"Yes, of course. I must. What choice do I have?" Brianna shriveled like a wilted cabbage from the Broadway market. The idea of confronting Father crippled her joy and deadened her will to live.

"I—I don't think that is a good idea, my dear." Mrs. Morgan fanned her fingers across her mouth.

Brianna's studied her knees and watched her hair drop in an auburn veil in front of her face. "I must have his help to raise my child." She squeezed her eyes shut, misery seeping in where joy had been.

Mrs. Morgan brushed back a lock of Brianna's hair, her look cautious, protective. "Your father hasn't treated you kindly in the past. I remember setting your broken arm when he twisted it behind your back some years ago. And what about that Christmas when he nearly choked you? Your neck bruises looked like a hanging." The midwife frowned in disgust.

Brianna's gaze lingered on Mrs. Morgan, then down at her stomach, swollen as though she'd eaten too much pudding. She fell into a strange silence. A being was growing inside her. A little person.

The midwife continued, furrows gathering around her mouth. "I think your father's humor is worsening. Rumors circulate about his troubles in the taverns. If he finds out about the child, you may be in grave danger. Do be careful. It's best if he never knows."

Mrs. Morgan left Brianna alone to dress, the examination room door banging shut behind her. A headache hammered her temple. She needed to make an effort to put her thoughts together, even though it was painful. Could she be loyal to a man who'd put her in this position? Why did Spenser make her have a baby? She didn't want to hear the answer. That couldn't be true. He did love her—he'd want this child.

But then, what about Spenser's recent distance when they made love? He'd been abrupt the last few times they'd met. Less feverish. Annie's words rang in her ears. *They say he has a wife.* That would mean he didn't care what happened to her. Or did he? Why would he be so careless if he knew he could make her expecting just like that? She bit her thumbnail.

Only one way to find out the truth. Brianna stashed Mrs. Morgan's handkerchief inside her pocket. She peeped out the window; the late afternoon sun descended behind the post office across from the doctor's. She arranged her skirts, patted her straw bonnet on her head, and marched out into the direction of Spenser and the Methodist Church.

Fourteen

STOP TO SAY A PRAYER

The thick-timbered door of the church clanged shut behind Brianna as she hastened from the vestibule into the nave. The deafening sound contrasted with the still small voice inside her head. Spenser loved her. She now had to believe that was the truth. There was no alternative. And if his wife were there—if she actually was his wife—so much the better. He'd see that *she* loved him best. Brianna paused for a moment, and let her eyes adjust to the dim interior. Her fists tightened into knots. She'd keep the child—and he'd leave his wife for her and the baby.

The church vault swept upward as its columns stretched to heaven. Candles flickered in sconces. Smoke trailed up to the rafters. The pulpit soared above the altar. The smooth stone floor softened under her shoes as Brianna strode into the nave. Instinctively, she stopped and said, "Our Father who art in heaven, Hallowed be Thy name." She folded her sweaty fingers in prayer. "Thy kingdom come. Thy will be done, on earth as it is in heaven. Please God, help me and this new life I carry inside me."

A chamber group of violin, cello, and viola emitted pure sound that floated through the church. Bach's *Jesu, Joy of Man's Desiring* captivated the listeners. As Brianna passed, she saw women and children, dressed in brown and gray, lining the first few square, prim pews. A lone lady sat in the far shadows against a column, face down as if in silent prayer. For a moment, she paused. Could it be? Sometimes she stepped in after the afternoon shift. No, Brianna decided. Annie would still be working at the shop.

From the front pew, a feathered hat turned to observe her, then turned back to hear to the strains of the music. Brianna recognized Mrs. Cecilia Rogers, a frequent customer of Miss Osborne's. She drew closer to the altar. Flickering sconces and candelabras cast an amber glow over the musicians.

The chamber trio in black performed on rickety chairs amid modest bouquets of field flowers arranged by the Ladies' Altar Society. Brianna paced along with the notes down the long, central aisle toward the altar where she belonged with Spenser, the altar where they'd say their vows. The trio grew larger, the music louder, as a mysterious force propelled her toward the sweet notes, the ethereal beauty, the sublime Spenser.

Brianna took in Spenser's powerful presence in the center of the musical group. His eyes closed in concentration; his chin rested on the violin. Drifts of blond hair framed his high cheekbones. He bit his lower lip while struggling to reach high octaves; his delicate bow plied the strings as if he was caressing her body all those many afternoons. She'd held that face and kissed that body. His manhood had pulsed inside her. She desired him now—right here. He wanted her, too. No more waiting.

Everyone there would see them united. Spenser craved to hear the news about the child—she knew he did. With each step, the altar grew larger, the musicians' faces more defined, the music louder. Each forward movement lent her a confidence only a mother has—the confidence that her baby will find its father. Not too much farther now—just a few more feet.

At the open gate leading up the altar's marble steps, Brianna smacked into the ample stomach of her former headmaster, Elder Jack McCall. He stood there, fortified as usual by the Mrs. McCall's legendary luncheon of shepherd's pie, blackberry cream tarts, and two pints of ale.

On impact, Brianna landed back on her own soft skirts, but McCall reached out both hands and pulled her up to a standing position. The sight of his wrinkled face and muscular bulk brought back a flood of childhood memories. McCall never hesitated to dole out discipline to her nor any other hysterical girl in school. This gentle giant had broken up many girl-fights on the schoolyard.

Brianna had to get to Spenser; no matter that McCall stood in her way. She pushed against his hands and she cried out, "Spenser, I must talk to you! I must!"

"No you won't, young lady!" McCall's boom echoed up to the church rafters. He lifted her up and over his shoulder much as one would heft a sack of grain.

Oh, curses! Why hadn't she thought of Elder McCall? He was sure to be at the service. He always was. Brianna knew he'd never let her nor any other ruffian ruin the Baltimore Chamber Society concert. It brought in extra revenue to his church.

Her fists pounded his back. "Spenser! Stop! Spenser! It's me, Brianna!"

She raised her head from McCall's back to view the scene. The orchestra silenced mid-note, and all eyes in the audience shifted to McCall, then her, then back to the players on the altar.

Why hadn't Spenser answered her? Surely he'd heard her voice, the intimate voice they'd shared.

Instead, his expression showed passive indifference. Rather than look at her, run to her, rescue her from the arms of the giant McCall, he acted as though Brianna were an errant fly buzzing around the communicants. Worth a flick of the eyelid but nothing more. With his bow raised, Spenser extended his legs for a moment, his attention absorbed by the young violist in the black brocade gown next to him. The young woman's sandy hair glistened in the candlelight, and she tilted her ear up to Spenser. He whispered something, and then brushed his lips on her cheek. A fashionable heart-shaped ring twinkled on the woman's left hand. It matched Spenser's.

The truth hit Brianna like a badly aimed bowling pin. Those same lips that had given her so much pleasure, those lips that had told her he loved her more than anything else on earth—those lips had lied. The boy and the devil had transformed her life and now that of her unborn child. Her dreams sputtered away, drops of wax from a spent candle.

She had been a momentary toy for Spenser, a diversion. Annie had been right after all.

Exhausted, Brianna let McCall carry her out over his shoulder, her eyes shut tight against the scene. The violist struck her bow, leading the next movement of the piece.

Once outside, Reverend McCall parked Brianna on the church steps without a word. The door clanked shut behind him and he was gone. She shuddered, not so much from the sudden chill of the evening breeze, but because she realized how inevitable Spenser's rejection had been.

Brianna bit her lower lip. A very ugly fact had made itself plain: she hadn't listened when Annie had told her the gossip about Spenser's wife. Unexpected and disquieting truths began to line up in squares, like the cobblestones on Wolfe Street. She'd ignored all of the tales at Miss Osborne's, and now she realized that sometimes gossip contains at least one grain of certainty.

She struck her knee with a balled fist. Why hadn't she steeled herself and spoken to some of the girls at the shop? Her isolation had placed her in the pickle barrel where she brined right now. She should have known better.

From Brianna's perch up on the church steps, the hitching posts looked so much smaller than down at street level. Brianna glanced at one of the several horses tied up there. It was the white stallion that had almost trampled her the day she was walking home from the Inn. Next to it, a black mare flicked its tail. The same silver design was emblazoned on both saddles. Did she need any more insulting reminders of her predicament? The white stallion chewed his bit and his dark eyes blinked. The black mare nosed him, and he snorted and shook his mane. They both stood waiting for their riders, Spenser and his wife. Brianna pictured them riding home together, their musical instruments encased in their arms.

Now she had to face Father and Mama, and watch their faces redden with rage. Brianna was trapped, suffocated. Her Christian upbringing and all its moral values hadn't done a thing for her. Father wouldn't stand for her to remain in his house. His reputation with his fellow clerics lay in ruins. He'd become the joke of The Horse You Came In On. Furthermore, Brianna's stupidity would make her the laughingstock of Fells Point.

A little girl in braids, her checked skirt bouncing around her, passed on the sidewalk below. A couple of pigs, escaped from the slaughterhouse herds, were rooting through mounds of piled refuse. A tall, long-bearded man held her hand, guiding her around the animals. Brianna stared long and hard at the father and child, her eyes staying on them until they disappeared into Kinnear's sweet shop on the other side of the street. The sun on her cheeks enlivened her memories.

Brianna had been that girl once, and Father had been as loving to her as that man was to his child. There was always hope. Maybe he'd find it in his heart to forgive her. After all, she was his youngest daughter. She remembered him reading to her, playing dolls with her, and even singing hymns to her. Where had all that gone? Her childhood had vanished, and she wasn't sure she liked this new adulthood.

She shifted her hips on the hard step. At the hitching post, the horses batted flies away with their tails. The pigs grunted among the scrap piles, their pink tails coiled like corkscrews.

A pigeon pecked at a crumb on the step below Brianna. Annie had told her tales of unwed girls in the family way. Now she was one of those girls. Shunned no matter where she went in Baltimore. And it would be worse for her child. Poor dear. An outcast even before birth, and afterward, a scapegoat at school, not allowed into church, forever labeled bastard. Brianna would have no visible means to support the girl or boy.

Annie had been right. She and the child would be abandoned by their family, then sent to live in a workhouse. Her child would suffer more than she—that is, if they survived the cold Baltimore winters in the snow and freezing rains pelting in from the Atlantic. All of this because Brianna refused to listen and believe. Why had she thought nothing like this would ever happen to her? She fished out Mrs. Morgan's handkerchief from her reticule, and held it against her face.

Shadows lengthened and evening twilight cast long shapes around her. Despair gripped her throat. Mrs. Morgan had mentioned midwives who could help her get rid of the baby if she wished. The midwife would keep it a secret. Apart from her senseless appearance at the church, no one would know about it.

No, Brianna couldn't end its life. She'd suffer even more if she were to give up this helpless child, the fruit of her vanity. Her future may lie in tatters, but her child would survive. She had made the mistake, but no one else should have to pay for it—now she would bear the burden. The pigeon cocked his head, examining her first with one eye, then the other. Brianna moaned and shook her head at the bird. After a moment, she got up, dried her tears, folded the handkerchief, and dusted herself off. The pigeon bounced down to another step.

Fifteen

INDIGESTION

Baltimore, Maryland
September 1849

Brianna mounted the stairway to the entrance of her Wolfe Street home; the door stood ajar. Father's bulk darkened the threshold. Her throat went dry. He was shrugging into his jacket, a dark scowl etched on his face. She had to summon the strength to tell him now. Surely Father would understand. Never mind his past; he'd offer her shelter, forgiveness, acceptance. He stepped back out of the way as she stumbled through the door. Brianna closed the door behind her; the doorknob clicked into the frame.

As she turned to him, her news burst out like a gunshot. "Father, there's something I've been thinking about."

Father emitted a low, canine growl. "Brianna, I've told you never to interrupt me on my way out." His fingers squeezed a brown wool cap in his hand.

"I know," she said. He'd listen now. He must. Her heartbeat rapid, she stayed planted at the door.

Father's bloodshot eyes fixed on her. "Find me sometime tomorrow, my girl. Not now. My hack is soon to arrive." He knocked her aside and swung open the door, then stepped out onto the stoop where he peered up and down the street.

Brianna regained her balance and spoke to his turned back. "Been drinking this afternoon?" Her insides quivered after she'd asked the question. Her legs were bent and she was ready to duck if he threw a fist at her.

He swiveled and faced Brianna across the threshold, his mouth curling into a hollow. "Course not."

She moved toward him, her right hand outstretched in part to protect herself. "Well, this news can't wait. It's urgent."

Father wiped his runny nose with his cap. A silence passed between them. Out at the curb, horsebells jangled. Whiffs of smoke from the driver's pipe floated up the steps. No matter. Father had to listen to her. The same father who read to her *The Talisman, Tales of the Crusaders* by Sir Walter Scott. He even acted out the parts with different voices to make it come alive for her. So long ago—Brianna knew that same dear man lived somewhere behind those wrathful eyes.

He squared his cap on his head. "If it's about more allowance, I don't have any for you this month. The Bishop's reduced all the ministers' salaries, so as you can see, I'm hardly able to put food on the table." Drops of sweat popped out on his forehead where blue veins bulged. His hands were shaking. She could see his rage boiling inside, a blister about to pop.

Brianna took another step, one foot on the threshold. "Father—" Words stuck in her throat. Why didn't she have the courage to blurt them out?

Father exhaled sharply. "Leave me alone, child."

"I can't."

"Very well. Say your peace and get on with it." He glanced out at the rig, then back inside, then crossed his arms across his upper belly.

"I wasn't feeling well yesterday."

"How's that?" He raised an eyebrow, then cast a nervous glance at the driver.

Brianna didn't have long before he would leave her in mid-sentence. She rubbed her midriff. "Indigestion."

Father's eyes flickered over her, then down the hallway. "I think we have bismuth in that brown bottle in the kitchen. Ask your mother."

"I didn't want to trouble you or Mama, so I went to see Mrs. Morgan."

Red patches darkened his sallow cheeks. "The midwife? Why are you telling me this, child? This is your mother's business, a woman's affair." He shifted from one foot to another, working his jaw. Then he took one step down the stair.

Brianna advanced to the threshold. "Please, Father, hear me out. Mrs. Morgan said I wasn't bilious or suffering colic. She says I'm with child of eight weeks or more." Her voice faltered, her bravado once again losing its battle with fear.

Father turned and regarded her with an icy stare, his greatcoat whirling in slow motion. "What did you say? Repeat yourself, Brianna. I must have a bit of wax in my ear, for I mistook you to say you're with child. Say again."

On instinct, her hands went up to ward off a blow. "I'm expecting a baby, Father."

He took a step up. His eyes glistened, lizard-like. "And who, may I ask, is the father, so I can kill the sonuvabitch with my bare hands? Who was it who took advantage of my poor little girl?"

"No one, Father. I was in love." Spenser's face appeared in Brianna's mind, his hair rumpled after making love.

Her father's voice thundered as he pressed her back across the threshold. "In love? No such thing. Only the deadly sin of lust as you lie with a man out of wedlock."

"It wasn't lust." Brianna straightened to her full height, her fists clenched against her hips.

Father's eyes bulged and he spat his words. "As surely as I stand here it was. You've sowed the great sin of the flesh, and now you'll reap the harvest of your own rotten plants. Get your things and get out. I don't know you as my daughter." He strode back outside onto the top step and waved the carriage to go along without him.

Oh no. She'd not counted on his staying here. Hadn't he wanted a drink?

Father stepped again across the threshold and poked her chest down the hallway, and with each finger jab, his purple nose and bulging red cheeks magnified his disgust under the mangy beard. "It's a whore—no daughter of mine. And no whorish daughter of mine deserves to live. You're not long for the fires of hell, saith the Lord."

Brianna put up her fists as she stumbled backward, but she was defenseless against his size. *No more*, said a little voice in her head, at which point she wheeled around and fled up the stairs to pack her bag. There again, she was guilty of misjudging someone. If she'd expected Father to accept her and the child, she'd sorely missed the mark. He'd spoken with such sullen viciousness; had he ever been kind to her? Maybe in her childlike confusion, she'd thought he was kind growing up since she had no one to compare him to. Maybe she'd thought all fathers were stern, irritable, and rigid. All the while, the man paced back and forth, his boots pounding the wooden hallway, his steps like dirt clods hitting a coffin lid.

Nauseated and disillusioned, Brianna rummaged through the dark bedroom closet. Her fingers grasped the maroon flowered carpetbag that belonged to Annie. This would have to do. She crammed her nightgown and a dress into Annie's satchel, then lugged it down the stairs. Surely Mama would protect her.

At the bottom step she cried out, "Please, Mama! Listen to me." She dropped the bag, ducked Father's outstretched arm as he grabbed for her, and scuttled over to her mother's side. Mother rested in her customary fog at the dinner table, but this time, at the sound of Brianna's voice, she raised her head and sat up.

To her surprise, Mama stood and took her in her arms, the same arms that had cradled her and protected her during times of Father's unbridled temper.

Father's boots scraped the floorboards as he followed her in to the room at a half-run.

Brianna sobbed into her mother's shoulder. "Mama, I'm so sorry. I've failed you and Annie." She smelled Mama's scent of lavender soap, a vivid memory carried from childhood. She breathed it in and clutched her mother as one may hold a precious package about to be mailed to a distant country, never to be seen again.

Father exhaled chuffs of loathing, and she pictured him standing over the two of them, a specter in his cap and greatcoat, waiting to pounce on them both.

Mama stroked her hair and held her close. "Shh . . . it's going to be all right."

Brianna whispered in the secret voice known only to daughters and mothers. "Please explain to Father that I didn't mean any harm."

For the first time in days, Mama spoke, continuing to hold Brianna close to her. "Reverend Baird, your daughter's with child. Your grandchild. She needs your help, not your condemnation. She's made a mistake, but she acknowledges that, and seeks our forgiveness."

Surely Father would listen to Mama, now that she'd mentioned the word *grandchild*. Brianna relaxed for a second and glanced up at his face. Come on, Father. Show a flicker of compassion.

Instead, his eyes flashed with haughty indignation. "For the sake of your soul, you get away from her."

Their faint spark of hope was extinguished, and her mother's face transformed. A glaze of despair suffocated any hope that once glimmered there.

Brianna and Mama stepped away from each other. He lifted Mama under her armpits and held her dangling like a lifeless doll. He spat his words. "You're no wife. Just another daughter of Satan. Now I see where the evil seed came from. And to think we prayed together all these years." He dropped her, and raised his fist, landing a mighty *thwack* across her face. Blood spurted from her nose, and she landed face down, unmoving, on the floor.

Brianna ran to the hallway and grabbed her carpetbag. Too late to save Mama, but she could still save herself and the child. She raced to the doorway, but the sound of his boots pummeled the floorboards behind her.

As Brianna reached the threshold and swayed, gaining balance to descend the steps, something kicked her so hard she flew down the front steps of her family's house onto the cobbles lining Wolfe Street. A rush of red brick and gray mortar from the sidewalk flooded her senses, and she lay dazed, head down, shaking from the impact of the blow.

"Soiled trash!" Father's bellows rang an anthem in her ears.

The world went black around her.

When Brianna came to, dusk had descended on Fells Point. Smells of onion and meat cooking wafted in the air. Dinnertime. Brianna lay there, listening to her own breathing. The force had knocked her out—only God knew for how long. She figured she'd landed hard on her left elbow, and intense pain radiated from it. Her body bruised and broken, she sprawled in the dusty lane. What was that pressure on top of her leg? Sure enough, it was Annie's carpetbag. She thrust it off and rolled over onto her back. A sudden thought entered her brain like a spike: What about the child? Was it still alive inside her? She rubbed her swollen belly to comfort the unborn and herself.

Random thoughts flashed across Brianna's mind like the stereoscope cards she and Annie had viewed at the fair. Father shouldn't have hit Mama, too. She'd expected confrontation, but not to this degree. When she sat up to recover her things, she flinched at the squeal of her front door's rusty hinges. What was he planning now? She glanced over and up the steps rising above her. He'd already injured her. Was murder next?

Father reappeared on the stoop holding a stack of dinner dishes. He then hurled them willy-nilly at her in the street, along with Bible verses she didn't recognize. Was he making new ones up as he threw?

When Brianna ducked, a butter dish caught her full in the back of her head, a dinner plate glanced off her twisted elbow, and a platter landed on her hip. She envisioned the neighbors at their windows, their hands covering their mouths. Why wouldn't any of them run to get the patrol? It was useless to ask. They were afraid of him and what he might do to them.

"*Slore*! *Slore*!" He bellowed in Gaelic. "Out of my house! You're none of mine." Father's voice echoed in her ears and reverberated down the tree-lined block. He slammed the front door so hard a crack sounded in the parlor. Either he had cracked a window or part of the door frame. She couldn't tell. The front door latched, followed by the rumble of the heavy iron bolt.

In her daze, Brianna returned to imagining their block, where house by house, candles would illuminate windows in the gathering shadows; next door, Mr. and Mrs. Douglas would peer out their dining-room curtains, gathering details to tell their friends. She heard scraping as a lamplighter moved his ladder up and down both sides of the street, stepping around her and her satchel. No one came to her rescue. In truth, no one dared. Drunken Spiker Baird was a man to fear.

Brianna pushed herself up on one elbow. Pain coursed up her arm. Poor Mama. The family house sat dark and silent. A tomb marked *Mrs. Frances Baird*. If only she could take Mama away. Well, Mama was already dead anyway. Father had beaten the life out of her. Smacked her senseless. Mrs. Morgan was right. What made her think she could confront Father? With that, Brianna let loose the sobs that had been gathering in her chest.

Sixteen

A Gray Hooded Cape

A little while later, Brianna blew out the dirt from her nose, wiping it off with her sleeve. No man could be trusted. If her own father could do this, what would a stranger do to her? She sat up and picked out the bits of dung clinging to her hair. She held her temples—such pain—and looked about. She winced, probing her swollen nose, then squinted down the next block. A curious woman in a familiar gray hooded cape leaned against a lamppost on the next block, under the light. Wasn't she the same person from the lone pew in the church? The woman untied her hood, releasing those perfect curls. Brianna rose, holding her carpetbag to her chest, and then limped toward the half-lit figure.

The young woman at the lamppost extended her arms. Brianna stood speechless and stumbled toward her. Annie reached out and held her at arm's length—no wonder, since she looked and smelled like the inside of a barn. Her sister's big hands covered them both with the cape, Annie's arms entwining hers in the semi-darkness.

Brianna drew away and regarded her sister's face. "Annie, I'm . . ." Brianna couldn't bring herself to say it. She didn't want to hear her own voice mouth the word *pregnant* out loud.

Her sister flicked a piece of dirt from her sleeve. "I know." Her voice rang with a gentle softness, so much like Mama's. "I was at church."

How irritating. Couldn't there be one place on earth where her sister wouldn't be snooping after her? She studied Annie's eyes. "So, detective, how did you know I'd be there?"

"Because I went to find you at Dr. Morgan's."

"Why?"

Annie's arms wrapped loosely around her. "You're my precious little sister. I knew you were in trouble. When you weren't at Miss Osborne's this afternoon, I went over to visit Cook at the Inn to see if you'd been there." Her fingers tugged at Brianna's head as they untangled a knot in her hair.

"What did she tell you?"

"She said she hadn't seen you, but she gave me an enticing tidbit."

A hot flare rose inside Brianna. Had Spenser told Cook something about their meetings? Had Cook betrayed her to Annie? She asked, "What kind of tidbit? I'm surprised you trust idle gossip."

"Cook told me he wasn't going to see you anymore—that his wife was Catholic, and the church would never grant her a divorce." Annie's forehead wrinkled.

The lamppost was sturdy and firm against the small of Brianna's back. Was life worth living without Spenser?

Annie's face hovered, half-shadowed in the gaslight above her. "Cook feared you might be pregnant. She had a hunch you might be at the doctor's office, so I left work to go and find you. I was so worried." Annie put her arm through Brianna's and pulled her close, but not too tight. Her sister's soft lips planted a kiss on her cheek.

Annie would have to do the thinking for them both now. "Where should we go? I must look a fright." Brianna stood quietly as Annie continued to make futile attempts to comb her fingers through her matted hair.

After a moment, Annie spoke. "Let Dr. Morgan take a look at you. To clean you up at least. You should see your face. You've all manner of scrapes and scratches on your cheeks, and your eyes are swollen." She picked up the carpetbag. "I'll carry this for you." Annie's arm sagged and she nearly dropped the bag. A scowl crossed her face. "You must have put all your earthly belongings in it."

"I was in such a rush, and then Father came at me, then he went for Mama and—"

"There, there, no time for that now." Annie's arm slid arm around Brianna, then she guided her down the cobbled street.

Mrs. Morgan opened wide the door of the colonial townhouse. Her gentle eyes grew large. She ushered the girls into the sitting room. "Victor's taking a nap, but I'll fetch him right away,"

Dr. Morgan entered, rubbing his eyes. "I heard the noise." He considered the girls, giving a sidelong look first at one, then the other. He focused his gaze on the younger sister. "So what have we here? You this time, rather than your mother?"

"I'm dirty, freezing, and I think I have a broken nose." Brianna dropped into a chair.

"What provoked him this time?" He cast a perceptive glance.

"Well, when I got home, Father wasn't too happy to hear the news about the new child, so . . ." She patted her stomach, thinking about the new life growing inside her. Was this being a little peanut swimming in a sea of liquid dreams?

"Let me guess . . . er, he gave you a lecture." The candlelight reflected off the doctor's spectacles.

Annie said, "Doctor, he gave my sister a lecture with his fists. The whole neighborhood hears Father's sermons, especially when the wind blows in off the wharf."

Brianna slumped. To top off her injuries, her right canine tooth hung by a thread and she played with it, tasting the blood that oozed across her tongue.

"Here, take this," Mrs. Morgan passed her a cotton cloth, and reached for a medical pan.

Mrs. Morgan inserted a forceps and pulled the tooth out with a yank. After a brief stab of pain, Brianna heard the ping as Mrs. Morgan dropped it in the pan.

Brianna stretched out on the same examination table as she had on her earlier visit, illuminated under Dr. Morgan's lanterns. Her right eye burned and the lid was closing up.

She followed the doctor's movements with her one good eye. He scrutinized her with tender eyes as though she were a wounded bird. He turned to his wife. "Please mix me a plaster and bring in some wet towels and a washrag."

Annie's skirts rustled as she stood next to the examination table, her hand a comforting weight on Brianna's shoulder.

Dr. Morgan made low murmurs. He must be talking to Annie. "The force from repeated blows has all but closed her eye; as you see, the red mass has turned to purple now." Brianna closed her good eye, and the darkness welcomed her.

At her side, Annie breathed concern. "The bruise looks so dark. Please tell me the marks won't be permanent."

"No, it is just in the process of healing. Nature takes its course." The doctor's words radiated kindness "She'll be an ugly duckling before she turns back into a swan again."

Was that Mrs. Morgan moving around in the background, clinking bottles and pouring water? Brianna startled when Dr. Morgan placed cold compresses against her eye and she twitched, the pressure of the cloth firing a jolt of pain through her.

Dr. Morgan and Annie cut away Brianna's chemise and the bodice of her day dress in order to free the twisted arm. Brianna bit on a rolled towel to bear the hurt, then heard a click as Dr. Morgan set the dislocated elbow.

He bandaged the arm and tied it in a sling around her neck. He spoke to Annie. "A simple dislocation. A bit of laudanum and she'll start to heal. Did you by chance bring her a change of clothing—a robe, perhaps?"

Annie said, "I only saw a dress and nightgown in her carpetbag."

"We must check the well-being of the baby," Dr. Morgan said. Brianna opened her eye. A trio of faces was peering down at her.

"But we need something to wrap around Brianna," Mrs. Morgan said. "Victor, I have an extra robe upstairs. It belonged to Mrs. Webber who expired here last week. Poor soul. I'll fetch it for the girl."

"Splendid. I'll check the baby while you do that." His tone relayed gentle concern.

The thought of wearing a dead woman's robe added to Brianna's misery. Would it still contain the stench of death? Not only was she beaten and bruised, she was also being prepared for the grave. Her eye and her arm throbbed each time her heart sent out a beat, as if they were the only active parts of her body.

The cold stethoscope against her belly gave her goosebumps. Her baby must be safe after all of this. Poor child—it wasn't the infant's fault her father rejected them both.

"The heartbeat is strong. It appears the baby is fine for now, but it may develop more slowly. A blow to the mother's stomach could have consequences for the fetus."

Brianna's muscles relaxed. Her child would survive and grow up to be healthy and happy. "Thank you, Doctor."

The mantle clock chimed the hour. Mrs. Morgan returned and Brianna let the midwife bring her to her feet, enfolding her in a robe whose scent imparted a strange mixture of peaches and medicinal herbs. The midwife's gentle hands led her to the adjacent sitting room. Brianna stretched out against the firm cushions on the horsehair sofa, and Mrs. Morgan's fingers tucked a blanket around her. A flowered needlepoint pillow cradled her head.

Out of the corner of her one good eye, she could see Annie and the Morgans as they stood over an adjacent table. What were they saying about her? If only she were a speck on the table in order to hear their conversation. It hurt too much to try and watch them, so she rolled over to one side, her ear out of the blanket. If Brianna really tried, she could pick up most of what they said.

"I'll get us some tea," Mrs. Morgan said, her footsteps tapping away in the direction of the kitchen.

"What can we do for her now, Doctor?" Annie asked.

Brianna absorbed the sounds. Chairs scraped against the wood floor, followed by rustling garments and creaking wood as Annie and the doctor relaxed into their chairs at the table.

The doctor said, "I don't really know. Miss Baird, are you talking about her state in life? Her pregnancy?"

Brianna knew he'd spoken the truth, as ugly as it was. But wait—there was more.

Annie said, "I just don't know what she can do. Where can she go? She has no future here in Baltimore. Spenser is well-connected and he would deny the child is his."

Brianna pulled the comforter over her chest, setting her arm over the top, her elbow speaking in throbs. What sort of pickle had she created for herself? She'd love to blame it all on Spenser, call him a scoundrel, tell him off over and over until she'd lost her voice, but a tiny voice spoke in her head. *You enjoyed it, young lady; indeed, you did.*

Mrs. Morgan's footsteps broke into Brianna's thoughts. China teacups rattled against the tray in the midwife's hands. Brianna heard a third chair scrape against the wood floor, followed by sounds of spoons clinking in the cup, stirring in helpings of sugar and milk.

Mrs. Morgan said, "I've heard other midwives speak of boardinghouses in New Orleans for unwed mothers. If there is room, perhaps she could stay there until the baby is born." Her tone resounded with hope.

"What would she do afterward?" Annie asked.

Brianna gave her sister a silent applause. What *was* she to do?

Mrs. Morgan spoke. "She could find an orphanage for the baby or care for it herself, depending, of course, on whether or not she can get work."

Brianna cringed. An orphanage? She'd never put her newborn in a children's home. Visions of her own red-cheeked orphan floated around her on the couch. She longed to cry out to the baby, *I'm coming to rescue you*, but she had no energy; every breath took effort.

Dr. Morgan's tenor voice filled the room. "We'll find a boardinghouse address and send her with enough money to tide her over until the child's born."

Annie said, "I'm grateful for your generosity." A tremor sounded in her voice like a distant rumble of thunder.

A tear burned in Brianna's good eye. She brushed it away.

"In New Orleans, Brianna will be able to get a midwife when her lying-in-time comes," Mrs. Morgan said.

"That would be more than we could hope for. I wouldn't dare go with her . . . Father would disown me . . . and I need to stay at home to protect Mama, but to have Brianna well and healed with her child . . . that is the best I could wish for my sister," Annie said.

"There's always the risk that the boardinghouses are filled." Dr. Morgan's voice sounded cautious.

"True," Mrs. Morgan said.

Annie said, "At least it will be a start. She has to go away, and chances are that someone at a boardinghouse could at least help her find some other lodging. Is that our only way?"

Brianna imagined a frown creeping across the doctor's lips. He said, "We don't know of anyone else who can help."

Brianna gave a silent nod, settling deeper into her pillow. This seemed like the only plan she had. She must be grateful for the Morgans' help. If she stayed in Baltimore, Father would kill her in a rage, or worse, kill Mama out of spite. She sank into the velvet womb of sleep and heard no more.

Seventeen

PELICAN FEATHER

Baltimore, Maryland
September 1849

After two weeks of recovery at the Morgans', a Thursday morning's sun lit up Brianna's lime-green parasol, a gift from the midwife. The sails unfurled, and the lines snapped and tugged against the dock. Reaching the top steps of the gangway, Brianna turned to gaze down at the small farewell party standing on Henderson's Wharf.

Dr. Morgan, Mrs. Morgan, and Annie waved up at her, when suddenly the steam whistles blew. Brianna patted the pocket in her skirt; the address of the New Orleans boardinghouse on the crackling paper was safe. Now the chilly salt air cleared her nose as she gained the upper deck, the crowds cheering and children yelling back and forth over the distance between dock and ship. They all looked so small down there, in their early-autumn jackets and coats. A man on the pier in his top hat and high boots resembled a toy from childhood. The cloaked, round-bellied matron beside him bore similarity to the playhouse doll from their tea parties.

A swell of gratitude mixed with sadness washed over Brianna. Thank God for the Morgans and for Annie. She fished out Mrs. Morgan's handkerchief and waved it at them. Annie was wiping tears from her cheeks.

The wind whirled around Brianna as the ship began to creak, its sails white against the red bricks and cobalt blue waters of the Inner Harbor. The railing was sturdy under her hands and she rocked with the vessel as it cleared its moorings. Barges, brigs, and schooners cast their lines, their crews carrying cargo up and down the gangways. Sailors cast away the giant rope holding the ship to the Port of Baltimore.

Someone tapped her shoulder. A kind face looked down at her, gray mutton chops bordering a man's cheeks. He inclined his head. "Dr. Perry at your service, Miss."

Brianna gave a quick curtsy in response, then when the deck tilted, she reached out to grab the railing again. The horizon was slanting in relation to the ship, and nausea was troubling her stomach.

"I noted you have some recent bruises on your face, Mademoiselle." His mouth crinkled with concern. "You could use a poultice to ease the swelling."

That was all she needed. Another false friend. She pulled a lock of hair over her cheek. "'Tis nothing but a fall, Doctor." She tightened her brown cape around herself as it flapped against the breeze.

Brianna was in no mood to respond. She continued to stare back at the crowds on the wharf. He persisted in hovering at her side. Why wouldn't he disappear? To be alone now, to heal—that's what she really wanted. Instead, he hung about, a wasp over honey-glazed cornbread. She wanted to move away, but the roll of the ship brought on a queasiness that immobilized her.

"Leaving is always the hardest, my dear. The return is always sweet."

Brianna turned and faced him. "But I don't know if I'll ever be coming back." Shifting the sling on her arm, she gazed down at her swelling bodice.

Maybe if she ignored him, he'd leave. She looked away and out over to water at the harbor. The majestic colonial buildings of Fells Point soon transformed into trifling red dots as the ship maneuvered out through bobbing boats on its way to the Atlantic.

Yet, Brianna continued to sense the buzz of the doctor's presence next to her as the calls of the boatswain directed the crew's activities.

He leaned over her and she blinked at the bright metal buttons on his vest. "Now, Miss, you will go back to Baltimore, you know. Maybe not soon, but sometime surely." His hand patted her shoulder. "Please call on me should you feel ill during the voyage. And let us talk about your poultice."

She grimaced, staring out at the widening channel between their ship and land. He clicked his heels, then headed off on his rounds. Not a moment too soon.

As the ship cast off from the safety of Baltimore and the fading shoreline, Brianna surveyed the only home she'd ever known. What was in store for her in New Orleans? The place was a mystery. Would it be like Fells Point? Annie had read about it and told her it was a river city with a port rivaling the Inner Harbor. Ships went back and forth from Baltimore to New Orleans all the time. All the same, Brianna couldn't imagine it, since Baltimore had been all she'd known since birth. Maybe ignorance was a good thing. If she thought about it too hard, she might get scared.

A pelican feather drifted down from overhead, and Brianna caught it and pressed its soft velvet against her cheek. "A good luck charm for us," she whispered through a sob that came out of nowhere. "It's pretty, isn't it, Ambrose or Ambrosia? I'll put it in Annie's carpetbag. Your first toy."

How many hours had it been since Mrs. Morgan's oatmeal breakfast? Hunger pangs rumbled in her stomach, so Brianna made her way down the ladder to the lower decks and her new cramped quarters. Although her ticket guaranteed a certain ration including bread, rice, water, tea, molasses, and pork, she'd have to share cooking utensils with a group of passengers. She patted the crust of bread carried in her pocket. How long would that last her?

Later, in the stifling heat of the lower deck, Brianna lay nibbling her crust of bread in her upper berth, one of dozens of bunks planted side by side. Sleepers snored, belched, and passed gas, some murmuring in languages she did not understand. The splash of waves against the ship kept time with the grunts and snores of an old woman in the berth below.

The pelican feather came in handy to bat at a fly that pestered her without mercy, buzzing and landing on her face, arms, and hands—anything exposed from the thin blanket she wrapped around her. Somewhere in the distance, a child cried softly, and Brianna thought about her baby. What will he look like? Will he like music as much as Spenser? What if it's a girl? She focused on a spot of oil on the side of the berth. Ambrosia. A perfect girl's name. Her eyes grew heavy. She tumbled into dreams, the feather clutched in her hand, resting on her chest.

During the lantern-lit darkness of the night, Brianna awoke to footsteps coming down the ladder, then stepping onto her deck. She turned in her wooden berth. If she could only see through the berths that blocked her view. She listened, and recognized one of the voices. Doctor Perry and the first mate must be on their candlelight rounds to assist passengers in their quarters.

Brianna lay on her back and pretended to slumber, her fingers entwined in her locks of hair slung across the pillow, the feather against her breast, her handkerchief clasped in her right hand. She squeezed her eyelids shut. What were these strangers doing so close to her? How dreadful—was there no privacy?

She heard the men's breathing, *in-out-in*, as they gazed into her bunk. The doctor whispered, "This woman is with child." His voice sounded gentle, a bit like Doctor Morgan's.

"How do you know, Doctor?" The first mate's whisper spanned the candle's shadows.

The doctor continued, his voice nearing her head. He held the light over her; the red veins on the insides of her eyelids grew purple. He said, "See how she round she is? She has a look in sleep only mothers have. Such peace." Something pressed on her, and Brianna felt a blanket being draped over her shoulders, then tucked into the sides of her wooden berth.

"I see now," the first mate said. "It is a rare contentment on her face."

As he moved down the hallway, the doctor's voice grew softer, but Brianna leaned toward the center deck, cupping her ear.

She heard him say, "She reminds of my wife Jenny back in Baltimore. Do you have any children?"

The first mate's voice was faint. "We're expecting one next month."

The voices sustained a low hum as they disappeared into the shadows.

Brianna wondered, did both their wives share her loneliness, pregnant and abandoned? Wait a moment. She wasn't alone. She hit her forehead with the heel of her right hand. "I'm sorry, Ambrose, for I forgot you are with me. I love you, dear." She folded her arms over her stomach and drifted into the sleep that only mothers know.

Part Two

THOUGH I AM SOLD

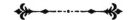

O, I have bought the mansion of a love,
But not possess'd it, and, though I am sold,
Not yet enjoy'd: so tedious is this day
As is the night before some festival
To an impatient child that hath new robes
And may not wear them.

WILLIAM SHAKESPEARE, *Romeo and Juliet,* 3.2.26–31

Eighteen

THE FRENCH MARKET

New Orleans, Louisiana
May 1850

A week after burying her package in the river, Brianna searched the bottom of her reticule for that extra gold dollar piece Dr. Morgan had given her before she had left Baltimore. Her throat squeezed: this was the last coin in her possession. Although she was broke, she walked the streets and mingled with the people of New Orleans. What could she do next? Maybe she'd find the answer here in the jumble of humanity. She smelled rotting fish on her hands—well, at least she'd be right at home here on the wharf.

How lively the French Market appeared on this early morning. Vendors chatted, unpacking wares from yellow crates. So many strange languages swirled around her. Free colored men and women, some in bright Caribbean dress, set out their wares, carvings, and fruits on tables. Bananas and plantains lay side by side on tables. Red apples, green breadfruit, and purple berries punctuated displays.

Brianna wandered past a large Haitian woman in a bright-orange headdress, its bow sweeping the air. The smooth caramel skin of the woman's face misted with sweat while she stirred a pot of gumbo and cried out, "Bowl cup dee-lish-e-oos." Brianna stopped to watch the woman's artful movements: not only did the Haitian dip and ladle out her soup for the customers, but with the other hand, she batted the flies savoring her concoction. In the distance, she heard a musical fusion—drums, fiddles, and banjos—in rhythms and combinations of notes she'd never imagined before. Whistles of steamboats filtered down the Canal Street Wharf over from the Mississippi. Her right hand closed around her last coin. She'd have to make it last.

Brianna continued meandering down the lanes under the slate-covered roof; shouts of dockworkers accompanied the beat of a headache jabbing her forehead. More vendors called out as she passed: *Alligator pie, jambalaya, fried okra, over here.* She gazed at long strings of red peppers hanging next to rows of fresh pineapples and barrels of nuts. Stray dogs lifted their legs, peeing against table legs. Ragged cats squabbled over the odd piece of meat, and mice scuffled over refuse. Again, voices rose, languages she did not comprehend. Some French, some Spanish, African dialects, sing-song voices, rhythmic voices rising and falling with swarms of mosquitoes. The flavors and aromas roiled her empty stomach. When had she eaten her last cracker?

Wending her way around tables, Brianna thought about the Goulets. Theirs had been the last place she'd found on an empty search for a boardinghouse for unwed mothers. Yesterday, she'd used her next-to-last gold piece to pay for the previous week's lodging. She remembered the moment when her landlady had bitten the coin to make sure it was good. Her pock-marked husband had leered from behind his wife, running his tongue along his lips. During her stay, he'd taken to knocking at her door in the middle of the night, and she could still hear his whispers: *Got some titty to gimme, Missy?* She shuddered. Thank God she was out of their clutches.

Last night, Brianna had slept in a shipping crate on the wharf to escape the couple's questions about where she planned to go next. She wrinkled her nose at the memory of fish rotting beside her in the crate. She'd had no choice but to leave the boardinghouse; otherwise, Mrs. Goulet would have had her work off any unpaid rent by doing chores for her dreaded husband. If she'd stayed, would she have been forced to be alone with him? Another shudder rose within her. She shook her head. No, this solution proved so much the better. She'd seek her fortunes away from the wharf in the *Vieux Carré*. By now, her package would be lying safe at the bottom of the river, nestled in the mud. She'd lost Spenser. Mistakes had yanked a curtain across the light, but now that was all in the past.

She crossed into the Poet and Love Café within the long market building. "*Bonjour*, Monsieur Ginn," she said. She'd learned to say it correctly at the Goulet's, who were forever correcting her French.

The proprietor looked up and flashed a grin. She inhaled the aroma of strong *café noir* and chicory. Fresh *beignets* steamed behind the counter. They looked like fluffy square pillows wearing white jackets of powdered sugar. Staring at them made her hungrier. Her empty stomach cramped. She'd add extra cream and watch it swirl in her *café au lait*. Maybe the coffee would distract her from hunger. Make her think about what to do.

Arthur Ginn handed her the usual large cup of chicory across the counter. He broke into her thoughts. "Would you like extra *crème*, Mademoiselle? You're getting very thin these days."

Brianna looked down at her empty pleats, wondering if he could tell. "*Merci.* That will be all." She passed a gold coin into the palm of his hand. Her last one. His fingers gathered around it like an octopus's tentacles surrounding a prize fish. She drew her hand away, tolerating his touch. He may have a slimy bearing, but he meant well.

Steam curled the tips of his gray hair, and his blue eyes creased. "*Très bien.*" He dropped her gold dollar in the till, then handed her the change.

She carried her drink to the table. As she returned to pick up the bowl of sugar and creamer, Brianna spied a tall Creole woman decorating a table across the café. The lady twisted her face away like people do when they're caught spying. Had the woman been watching her? Brianna eased into the chair, then stared out the tent flaps into the street. A warning prayer rose in her mind. *Please God, have her not be trouble.* She'd had strife with men, but she never expected to have a such a lady bothering her.

Brianna dangled the spoon in the hot coffee. The oval shape of the woman's face stayed in her mind. When and where had she seen her before? Baltimore? The ship? Here in New Orleans? She knew those features from somewhere, not too long ago. *Be still,* Brianna told herself. She was probably just one of a thousand in the crowd of black, brown, yellow, and white faces in the Crescent City.

Her stomach churned with hunger. This drink would have to satisfy her for now. She had to make that money last. The long shades of the open market suspended motionless in the still heat of late May. Brianna took off her jacket and placed it beside her on the table. No brocade Baltimore jackets here. The air lay humid, thick, and close.

Footsteps padded behind her and a pair of hands in black lace gloves anchored onto the table's edge next to her coffee cup.

"Bonjour, Mademoiselle." The woman's voice boomed, a cannon testing the depths of the Mississippi.

Brown eyes framed by sweeping eyelashes gazed into Brianna's. The hat with parrot feathers waved over her like so many palm leaves. The woman's red-painted lips cast a garish pink glow over her face. What an irritating sort to interrupt her like this.

"May I?" The woman pointed to the seat next to her, and Brianna said, "Of course." Who in God's universe was she? What did she want?

Probably another type of Goulet like the one she'd left behind. She was tempted to get up and run, but hunger and recent childbirth weakened her will.

The woman settled her many layers of petticoats on the chair; she balanced one arm against the rosewood handle of her green parasol. "My name is Nancy DeSalle," said the Creole. She shifted her crimson and yellow beads; they clicked and smacked into each other as they sailed the caramel waves of her cleavage.

Brianna said, "*Enchantée, Madame.*" By jiggety, how many folds were in the woman's bosom? She found herself gawking, so she pulled back and sat up straight. She would have to be dignified in the woman's presence. Brianna's kin in Baltimore never dressed this way—the church would excommunicate them. Now that she'd thought about it, neither she nor Annie would exhibit this kind of bare flesh. Of course, she already knew she wouldn't have enough to show anyway. What would Father say about this woman? She could only imagine his purple face, contorted with rage.

"*Comment vous appelez-vous*?" Nancy's voice was deep and rich, a broad smile lighting her face. A sickening sweet blend of perfume laced with sweat emanated from the woman's pores, causing Brianna's eyes to water.

Despite some unpleasantness, this face looked friendlier than the Goulets', so Brianna took a risk. She was past her last coin after all. "Baird . . . Brianna Baird."

"German?"

"No, Irish. Northern Ireland." The inside of her corset itched.

"Eh, *bien*. You looked lonely, my dear Irish. I thought you might like some company." Nancy turned and snapped her fingers to Mr. Ginn, who in turn carried what must have been her regular order: blueberry pastries, topped with powdered sugar and clotted cream, clustered on the silver tray.

What a wonder: the woman devoured her breakfast, flurries of sugar snowing on her bosom. The hat feathers bobbed and swayed while DeSalle talked, and Brianna's gaze followed a large diamond on her pinkie, which glistened whenever she lifted her coffee cup. What was she saying? In truth, Brianna hadn't heard a word. She was too busy wondering why this fleshy woman out of nowhere would take an interest in her. Such bright colors and exotic movements. Not at all like the prim Baltimorean matrons she knew. Yet, with so little change in her pocket, she summed up a beggar's courage. She had nothing to lose by speaking to her.

Brianna broke into DeSalle's chattering mid-sentence. "—I'm lonely." She clutched her growling stomach, hoping to silence it, then she continued. "I've no family here."

A pause ensued. DeSalle picked up her coffee and took her time with the next sip. "Do you have work here in New Orleans?" Nancy tilted her head, the feathers swishing.

"No, I've come from Baltimore. To find gainful employment." Brianna swept away a dribble of sweat from her hairline. She must look a sight—not much of an impression.

"Are you trained? In any line?" Nancy dabbed a starched linen handkerchief at the corners of her sugared lips.

Brianna's eyes followed the movements of the handkerchief, so like the one Mrs. Morgan had given her. She blinked. "Needlework. Three years at Miss Osborne's in Baltimore." She pictured the measuring tape draped over the mannequin near Miss Osborne's window. She gazed down into the deep refuge of her cup. A gnat flailed its wings, then drowned in the coffee. She fished it out with the edge of her spoon, and dropped it on the tablecloth.

Nancy sipped, her eyes looking faraway. "Well, my house could use a seamstress, I suppose. We order from Paris, but shipping takes time, and we wait months for the latest apparel. In our profession, we must look our best on every occasion."

Brianna listened and felt faint. The flaps of the tent café began a slow spin. She held onto the table edge with both hands. She must try to focus.

"Our local seamstress, Madame Garnier, has assisted us in the past, but her prices have gone up since her husband died and left her with all those brats." Wrinkles gathered around Nancy's mouth and pointed down toward her chin.

A red parrot feather floated to the ground. "What profession would that be, Madame?"

Nancy wiped sugar from her lips. "We provide essential services to the men of New Orleans."

"And what might those services be?" Why had she asked such a stupid question?

Nancy heaved a sigh. "You northern girls are so backward compared to our free children in the south." A smile lifted the corners of her mouth. "We entertain them in our beds, Mademoiselle Baird."

Brianna hesitated, then spoke. "So, you are . . ."

She sipped from her coffee cup. "A parlor house, Mademoiselle."

"Oh," Brianna said. The man and the woman in the window at the house on Thames Street flickered in her mind. She tightened her grip on her spoon. Was her life going in a circle?

The woman resumed. "Yes, Mademoiselle, but not just any parlor house." She lifted her chin as she spoke. "*Le Maison DeSalle.*" Her finely plucked eyebrows rose.

Brianna tried to arch her own brows in imitation. "*Le Maison DeSalle.*"

"Yes. The mayor's very own." Nancy's eyes gleamed. "Here, my dear, let me buy you a brioche. Poet and Love makes the most divine almond filling, and it gushes out into your mouth as you eat it."

Brianna's eyes lost their focus. Would she faint before it came to the table? She picked up a spoon and pretended to examine its every crevice.

After what seemed an eternity, the white-aproned Mr. Ginn came and lingered over them, his eyes shining. "I'm happy to see our Mademoiselle in the company of a successful community woman such as yourself, Madame DeSalle."

He turned toward Brianna. "Now, Miss, allow me." He placed the hot pastries, dripping with melted sugar, before her. Despite her instinct to grab one, she waited until he set it on her plate. She closed her eyes as almond essence filled her mouth.

Someone pressed her hand. Madame DeSalle said, "Let me arrange you a room in our house. Then we will discuss the garments you'll work on."

"Very kind." Brianna savored the almond cream, and sugar and flour. She cared little that flaky crumbs lay on her chin. All that mattered was that she had eaten. That pastry eased the top layer of stomach cramps, yet deep starvation churned below.

"My dear Monsieur Ginn, another brioche for the Mademoiselle Baird," Nancy said. "One to carry away."

Mr. Ginn smiled. "But of course. Right away. *Chocolat* and brandied orange peel for the young lady?" He plucked it from the tray and wrapped it in a lace doily. He stepped back, rubbing his hands on his apron.

"Why not?" Nancy winked, edging the envelope of pastry into the girl's rough hands.

Mr. Ginn said, "I am so pleased you have made Madame's acquaintance. I've told her all about you, Mademoiselle. I knew you would be a good acquaintance for her."

Brianna tensed. So that was how the woman knew so much about her past. Should she be mad about Mr. Ginn's intervention? Puzzled, she pictured her cat Mercy squashed between two pillows on her bed at home.

Nineteen

CHOCOLATE CREAM FILLING

Brianna devoured the chocolate cream filling while Nancy hooked her elbow, guiding her from the French Market out onto the street. If the woman threatened her, she could always run back to Poet and Love. On the other hand, DeSalle might be a showier version of her idol, Mrs. Whipple. She'd followed Mrs. Whipple's every move about the Inn, learning from someone in charge, someone to imitate as she'd planned her own seamstress shop. So, she paid attention while Nancy peppered her with the regulations posted in the upstairs rooms at the parlor house.

As they stepped out onto the street, DeSalle said, "Of course, any men visitors will need my approval. My girls drink no alcohol on the premises at any time. You will not have any money in your possession, since your earnings, room, and board are managed by the house."

Brianna stopped, struggling with uncertainty. "Does that mean I would have to ask you for any spending money?" Would she like that agreement? Her thoughts returned to Baltimore. A few seamstresses at Miss Osborne's had told her about such arrangements, when they had worked in-house at a hotel or on a private estate.

Nancy faced her. "Of course, of course, although you'll have very little use for spending money since the house provides for all your needs."

Brianna chewed her bottom lip. She and Nancy resumed their walk, stepping around a pile of steamy horse droppings. A milk truck rumbled past, followed by a boy driving a flock of sheep down to the loading docks.

She noticed Nancy's sideways glance as she spoke. "Above all, *chérie*, do your best to get along with all the girls at the house. Any fighting or discord and I'll put you back onto the street to fend for yourself." The woman's eyes took on a threatening cast. "You wouldn't want that again, now would you?"

"No, of course not," Brianna said. She digested the details along with her *chocolat*, and her nervousness lessened. She remembered Father throwing the plates. These were hardly rules. Not compared to Father's. She felt a bit of hope and reassurance. She'd do her best to get along. As long as she worked hard and did her part to be agreeable, DeSalle would meet all her needs. What more did she deserve? She'd fallen to the bottom of a well and she'd have to claw her way back out.

Brianna and Nancy DeSalle fell into an easy rhythm on their walk together on Chartres Street. Their footsteps kept time with a Congolese drummer's beat. White clouds streaked with gray sailed overhead. They passed the tall, creamy façades of the Presbytère Courthouse and St. Louis Cathedral. The Latin call-and-response of the priest and the congregation floated out through the open doors. *Morning mass*, Brianna thought. She peered into the vestibule and down the nave. Outside DeSalle guided her onward through a cluster of artists painting the scene. They dipped their brushes on easels, then dabbed paints on canvases.

A hefty Negro crossed their path as they neared the Cabildo, another tall-columned court building on her right. The man whistled a song; he pushed a large box on a wheelbarrow toward the wharf. Across from the Place D'Armes, sailing and steam ships anchored at an angle, and around them, the brown Mississippi glistened like *café au lait.* Steamboats and flatboats frothed the waters as they churned upriver.

A hunchback drove a rickety conveyance between them, the horses kicking up dust and mud on St. Peter Street. Brianna coughed into her sleeve. This wagon, crammed with colored men, women, and children, creaked by on its way from the slave market. Sweat-lined faces stared at her, blank, unseeing. Chains jangled against the wood floor. She drew back, picturing the scene a few months ago when Mr. Ginn had told her about the human trade in New Orleans. He'd told her that white and colored men of means examined naked men, women, and children, then dickered on their worth.

Plantation owners retained all rights to these human lives and their generations. Brianna had not seen such a cruel display since the time she had witnessed a slave whipping on a dock back in Fells Point. All the same, she closed her eyes. *Please God, help those unfortunates and me.* She followed DeSalle's abrupt right turn at the red brick Pontalba building onto St. Peter Street, where shoppers were strolling. Out of the corner of her eye, she spotted two men in straw hats. They paused to stare at her and DeSalle from across the narrow street.

Accustomed to flaunting her wares, DeSalle bent down to pick up a leaf, gravity tugging her breasts from her chemise. The taller man elbowed the shorter at the sight of the madam, but the other's steady gaze found Brianna's. She worked to maintain what delicate control she had over herself when all she wanted to do was get to DeSalle's house. She brushed brioche flakes from her chin.

The same man removed his hat, bowing in her direction. A man had never hailed her in such a way before, and Brianna blushed. She felt the encouraging press of Nancy's arm, so she bent her knee and the men tipped their hats. A laugh ricocheted across the street. What kind of snicker was it? At first she found it mocking, but the next moment, she thought the men were being playful, entertaining.

Brianna squinted in order to get a better view of them. The shorter man had slim, dark features. Spanish or Italian? So many cultures mixed here in New Orleans. She looked at his olive skin and black moustache. His straw hat glowed white against the dingy building behind him. He wore a pressed linen jacket, red cravat, and fine black leather boots. He looked to be a bit older. A troubling thought took hold. Could he be one of the many gamblers in town?

Twenty

THE DOUBLE EAGLE

Across the street, Edward Spina stepped back to avoid the splattering mud thrown up by a passing cart. His tall companion spoke. "I wouldn't tip my hat to those harlots if I were you, Edward."

Spina studied the young one, then the older woman whom he knew well. "Why not? Two of the finest looking ladies in the Quarter."

"Hah!" Sam said. "You've been throwing in too often with the gentry at the Bourbon Orleans. You're powerful fixed on your winnings these days, Spina. At the sight of a fallen woman, you're carrying on like a man possessed."

Edward endured Sam's clap on his back. "Ah, you trump me there, Sam. Who's the young lady with DeSalle, since you know all the sweetmeats in the French Quarter?" The lithe young girl looked so sad. So many girls like her, but she had an exceptional figure. What was her story?

Sam said, "I'll fold on that one. Never seen her before in my life, and I've spent all my years in this town. He breathed a sigh. She's sure a beauty worth having."

Spina watched him shrug. "I trust your judgment, my friend. You've always proved to be an expert on New Orleans' most comely women. Many's the time we've toasted to them."

A trace of laughter rang in his friend's voice. "For a wayward sister, she sure is a beauty. Skin like porcelain. Just look at those rags she wears. Must have been some mischief."

Spina's voice was calm and steady. "She doesn't look wayward to me, Sam. Her eyes are clear green, her face as pure as an angel's wing. See how her gold-red hair forms a halo about her head? I don't think she's a street urchin; you know, she appears newly fallen to me."

Edward remembered the small copy of a famous painting his father had brought over from Genoa. It had been hanging on the family's dining-room wall during his years growing up. Now he knew—this girl looked like Botticelli's *Madonna of the Pomegranate*. The shock of discovery excited his senses. Her flowing hair, her upturned nose, the forlorn expression: all this created an uncanny portrait of the Madonna.

Sam touched his friend's sleeve with his walking stick. "Always a poet, Spina. Were you not a clever gambler, I daresay you'd be a wandering minstrel or a priest."

The gambler pulled a double-eagle twenty-dollar gold piece from his breast pocket. He held it up, then flashed it in Sam's face. "Date on it?"

"1849, my friend." He grinned.

Spina bit the coin. "Right. A double eagle. Fresh from the Old Mint. Now, heads, you win the girl; tails, you win the old lady."

"Sure enough, let her rip," Sam said. He focused his eyes on the money.

The gold piece spun in the air as the gambler tossed it high, caught it in his palm, and slapped it onto his left hand. "Tails." Spina danced up and down.

The grin vanished from Sam's face. "Aww, all bets are off." He shook his head, then strode off in the direction of the wharf.

"Sore loser," Spina's voice echoed down the street.

Brianna watched the coin catch the sunlight. "Whatever are they doing?"

"Some bet or another, I suppose." Nancy's hat plumage rippled. "Edward Spina's a clever card player. I've seen the other gent in the Quarter before, but I've forgotten his name."

She adjusted her hat and pulled down her bodice, revealing substantial flesh. "Wait a moment. I think he wants a word with us."

Edward waved to them, then stepped across the street and up on their side of the walk. Brianna's eyes watered as DeSalle sidled closer, her perfume stench worsening in the heat of the day.

"Good morning, Madame." Spina flashed a row of white teeth. He held his hat to his chest, and planted his silver-tipped walking stick on the ground before Brianna. Shoppers milled around them on the busy walkway.

DeSalle curtsied. "*Enchantée*, Mr. Spina. Our paths have not crossed in a few days."

He bowed his head. "Indeed. I'm overdue for a visit at the Maison. You're looking well today, Nancy. Those feathers flatter your eyes."

Nancy lowered her eyelashes.

Edward turned to Brianna. "May I make the acquaintance of your beautiful companion?"

Why was his look so intense? Once again, she wanted to run away. She broke eye contact, but she could feel his eyes on her. He sure was pleased with himself.

Nancy's crayoned eyebrows lifted and she stepped between them. "Miss Brianna Baird, may I introduce Mr. Edward Spina."

He removed his straw hat and bowed low. "*Plaisir*, Mademoiselle."

Brianna bobbed a curtsy in return. All right, now that this was over, she and Nancy would be on their way—wouldn't they? Dizzy once more, she leaned against a hitching post and closed her eyes.

She opened them in time to see Madame's feathers ripple. "I've just retained Miss Baird as my house seamstress. She has considerable experience with ladies' gowns *a la mode Française*, the French style."

Brianna saw the man's eyes wandering over her body, and she tensed as a slow smile eased across his face. On its own, his face was handsome, but under the circumstances, she was far from drawn to him. Seldom had a man gazed at her with such concentration. She gritted her teeth. Was she to be examined like a racehorse? This was becoming unbearable.

"May I have permission to walk with the lady?" he asked.

Blast the man. Couldn't he see how exhausted she was? Her throat tightened. "I don't feel very well. This heat you have down here does make me peaked."

Madame DeSalle's brows pulled inward. "Mr. Spina, I want her at the house *pour le déjeuner*, for the midday meal. One can see she's tired as a young mouse." She shook her finger at him. "And not too much walking in this heat."

Brianna swallowed hard. Was she trusting herself to a gambler? Annie wouldn't approve. Father would rage. Here she was, waltzing with danger again.

Spina tapped DeSalle's arm. "*Oui*, Madame, do not worry. I will see she takes her *dejeuner*," he said. "I will have her back to you in due time." He extended his arm to Brianna.

"My dear, let us stroll, so I may make your acquaintance."

Brianna floundered in the uncertainty. Why had Madame DeSalle pawned her off to him?

The madam nudged her toward the gambler. Reluctantly, Brianna latched her arm under his. His linen jacket was crisp and pressed. Why would he be interested in her? Hadn't he noticed the stains on her gown?

Brianna grimaced at the tattered condition of her skirt. She'd fled from Father and Baltimore, but now, New Orleans was turning out to be a tempter's paradise.

Twenty-One

THE PLACE D'ARMES

After a brief stroll, they approached a bench under the live oaks surrounding the Place D'Armes. The touch of Edward's strong arm and guiding hand at Brianna's back sent a wary chill through her. She shrank away on the bench and eyed him with all the coldness she could muster.

It was her turn to examine him. Fine wrinkles blended into his face. Early thirties, she judged. He had a Roman nose, and his olive skin was deeply tanned. He crossed one leg over the other, his face directed toward the cannon in the middle of the square.

They sat for a while in silence. The buzz of dragonflies and songs of mockingbirds harmonized in the sycamore branches overhead. The *clip-clop* of horse-drawn carriages and the steam whistles from the many boats on the wharf pulsated around them in the May air. From time to time, a stale breeze rustled the fallen brown leaves around their feet. It was hard to stay quiet this long. She thought of the past few months shut up at Madame Goulet's. She hungered for conversation. Brianna had talked plenty to Ambrose, but now he was gone.

She turned with a start at his touch on her arm. Edward leaned back, and reclined against the bench seat. A wrinkle appeared between his eyes. "You're wasting away to nothing," he said, observing the rips in her skirt. "Is that all you have to wear?"

He had struck a nerve. Brianna fought against a sob. "At the moment, yes."

"Open your mouth so I may look at your teeth."

"No . . . I feel like a horse . . . whatever do you want?"

"Do as I ask, child. Ah . . . just as I thought when I first saw you."

"What?" Her hand flew to her mouth and she covered it with her palm.

"You have a tooth missing. A canine. Your upper right. How did that happen?"

"I was in a scrap. Not something I wish to share with a stranger." He wasn't a policeman, was he? Why all these questions? Her uneasiness grew as the seconds passed.

Edward's face relaxed and his tone softened. "Where are you from?"

Brianna leaned away, silent. Despite the heat, she pulled her skirts tighter around her legs. Even if she tried, she could only manage a whisper.

Undaunted, he leaned toward her. "Madame DeSalle says she has offered you a seamstress position in her parlor house." His brown eyes reflected the sunlight on the Place D'Armes.

"Yes, sir, I am most grateful to her." Brianna wiped sweat from her cheek with the back of her hand, mindful of her own filthy condition. A bath would not come too soon.

Edward frowned. "Do you know what a parlor house signifies, Miss Baird?"

She gathered her composure as she looked into his dark eyes. "Well, yes. I'll work making dresses for her . . . um . . . courtesans. That's what one calls them here in the South, is it not?"

He fingered his mustache. "You know, DeSalle will probably ask more of you than mere sewing."

Brianna leaned back against the wrought-iron bench and looked up into the branches. His words shattered her vision of her future. Though she had nothing to lose, she possessed one important thing: a last shred of pride when she'd kissed Ambrose, lying tranquil in her arms. Ambrose's sacred river burial had sent him off to eternity in the manner of the ancients.

She'd vowed to make him proud of her, never again to surrender to a silly man who trivialized her very existence. Instead she'd guard her heart against this man and all men.

"I think you're wrong, Mr. Spina. DeSalle can only ask of me what I am willing to give." Brianna punctuated her words with a sidelong glance.

Edward scowled, then batted a fly. "Yes, but she can also demand. And that's when life becomes dangerous for such a fragile beauty as yourself."

"What is your meaning, sir?" Her neck muscles tensed. She folded her arms into a tight knot.

He tapped his chin. "The word *demand* means DeSalle can take your freedom against your will."

Through the leafy canopy, Brianna saw herself in Baltimore, waving to Spenser from the end of the carriageway. What a fool she'd been to fall for his flattering words.

The gambler touched her arm and she stiffened. Yet, his voice sounded sympathetic. "This kind of demand can be cruel and cause you much pain. New Orleans is wild and hostile to young girls. Men abuse them, drug them, and throw them into the river every week, according to *The Picayune*." He fumbled in his jacket pocket and pulled out a cigar.

"Why do you bother telling me this?" Bile burned in her throat.

Edward closed his eyes for a moment, fingering a match. "I am native to New Orleans and it is part of my soul, so I know its dark underbelly. This hellhole is my territory." He puffed the tobacco to life.

Brianna peered at his profile through the smoke. "What do you mean by an underbelly?" The sun crept to midday position over the tree-lined canopy. She coughed.

Leaning back, he extended his arms against the back of the bench. "The part of our society that destroys, that cheats and lies." He blew a stream of smoke into the air. "You need to be alert, Miss Baird. Don't trust anyone in the Quarter. See that dying pelican over there under that bush?" Edward pointed his cigar to a bloody, fly-covered mess, shrouded by a red azalea.

"How horrible." Brianna drew a sharp breath.

"Indeed, Miss Baird. And that could be you if you do not watch everyone and everything around you in town."

"What must I do to protect myself?" She slapped at a mosquito nestling on her forearm.

"You have already gotten yourself into an arrangement with Madame DeSalle. Chances are if you fold your hand now, she may have a mind to hurt your reputation. Spread lies about you and such. You can't afford that. News travels fast in the Vieux Carré." Edward waved away a droning mosquito.

Brianna crossed her arms, holding onto her shoulders. There stood the cannon in the center of the great square. If only the famous General Jackson, the hero of New Orleans, would rescue her. This man might speak the truth, in which case she was in more danger than she'd imagined. White steamboats tapped against their moorings in the brown river water beyond.

A thread of fear weakened Brianna's voice. "I think myself so unfortunate."

Edward's knowing tone brought her eyes back to his. "No, Miss Baird, you don't want to think that. Life is an adventure. You have to figure out where the decks are stacked against you, and place your bet with caution."

An unchecked drop of sweat rolled down her cheek.

He continued. "My dear Miss Baird, I like you. You're a huckleberry above most persimmons. I'll watch out for you. To be honest, I find it hard to pass up an enchanting young woman like you."

Brianna's heart thumped; his dark, searching eyes could light a fire in the snow. "Nonsense." She bit her lower lip. "Away with you. You're like all the rest. How will you look out for me? Spenser said he would, and then he turned out to be a fraud." The misery of that evening at the church continued to haunt her.

"Spenser? Never heard of the scoundrel." His voice was steady. "Where is the fellow? I'd like to challenge him to a duel."

Her heartbeat quickened. "He doesn't live here. My father was supposed to protect me, and he got drunk every night. Why should I trust you when every other man in my life has abandoned me?"

Brianna stood up and looked down at Edward. What a powerful presence he had. Their closeness lulled her into a sleepy euphoria. Was this the false sense of comfort that had fooled her before? She rested her hand on a tree branch for support.

"Now, there, there." He passed up a freshly ironed handkerchief, monogrammed with an S. "No tears, Miss Baird. I see I've upset you."

Brianna dabbed her eyes and blew her nose. Although employed in the devil's work by Father's standards, this man's eyes shone with kindness. He reminded her of Teddy from Fells Point, a dark-haired boy she'd befriended in childhood, who had died of yellow fever. He, too, had looked out for her, even guarded her from a boy who had bullied her each day after school. Yet, this man was not Teddy. All the more reason she must keep her wits.

Brianna settled back down on the bench; her hand fingered a hole in her wrinkled skirt. Her eyes and throat were as dry as the dusty path under her feet. "What about you, Mr. Spina?"

"Born here . . . Italian family from Genoa. Shipbuilding by trade. My father wanted me to join the business here like my eight brothers, but I had a talent with cards."

Brianna concentrated on the soft southern cadence of Spina's voice, and Annie's face came to mind. What would Annie think of her predicament? Of this man who took an interest in her? Annie may tell her to do the next right thing in order to survive—Brianna struggled to grasp what that might be.

Edward broke the silence. "I have an idea, Miss Baird. Jacob's is my favorite seafood restaurant in New Orleans. He will set you up with some fine gumbo. After some refreshment, you'll feel better."

His eyes wrinkled when he grinned, and his moustache curled against his lip. Yes, he did resemble Teddy. The same generous mouth and twinkling eyes. Was it hunger that made her think that?

Brianna said, "I am ready to eat again, to be sure. Mr. Ginn's brioche did not fill my empty stomach." She patted her skirt. "I should eat in the kitchen. Not a proper day dress for dining."

Edward tamped out the cigar on the bricks below, and squashed it with the heel of his boot. His finger tapped the bench seat between them. "Come, you'll feel peart in no time, my dear." He sized up her appearance. "Your dress? No matter. You're my companion, and I don't mind. Anyone who makes a fuss will have to deal with me."

His gentle hands wrapped around hers and he lifted her up off the bench. Brianna stepped back, pulling her hands away. "I'm not your companion, Mr. Spina." Her words chopped the air.

He dropped her hands and sighed. "Very well, you're not even my acquaintance." Edward turned on his heel.

Brianna stepped behind him. "But I wish to go to Madame DeSalle's for déjeuner. You promised." Her voice wavered, her mind confused.

He looked over his shoulder at her. "Mademoiselle, the Maison takes lunch at the noon hour, not a moment later. It is now 12:45. See the clock up on the cathedral?" Edward pointed up with his walking stick.

She peered around him at the church façade. One iron hand faced due north, the other west.

With her arm looped under Edward's elbow, Brianna brushed aside her misgivings while he guided her into the crush of the Vieux Carré.

Twenty-Two

YOUR NOBLE CAUSE

A full Louisiana moon shone down that evening on Edward Spina and Nancy DeSalle as they sipped from a bottle of Spanish sherry. Palm fronds waved over them in the interior courtyard of the Maison DeSalle on Decatur Street. Edward knew theirs to be an unusual meeting in the annals of New Orleans brothels. In the adjacent gambling hall, faro games and banjo music underscored the shadowy encounter.

A single candle flickered on their table among the trees. The crescendo of men's shouts and women's laughter filled the air, marking wins and losses. Edward imagined Miss Brianna Baird slumbering upstairs in a canopy bed, mosquito netting draped over the top and sides. Her hair spread out behind her on the pillow, her soft rose lips slightly opened as she dreamed. If only he were there holding her.

Down in the garden, a tiered fountain trickled water into a slimy pool filled with lilies whose pink buds tightened in sleep. The screech of a barn owl carved into the night.

"So, do I make myself understood?" Edward reached for the bottle and gave himself a second pour.

"Of course, Monsieur Spina," DeSalle breathed. The candlelight reflected the deep folds of her breasts. "You wish Miss Baird to be yours alone to do with what you'd like." She licked her lips.

He raised his glass and sipped. "To make it clear, Madame, I wish you to provide her room and board, and keep her free from entertaining any other customers."

"Ah, but she would be the envy of the other girls. They would work and she would lie about idle? That would create disharmony, Monsieur." Her frown formed a half-moon across her lips.

"She will hardly be idle. You yourself have told me she excels at needlework. She will be engaged in sewing dresses for the courtesans, won't she?"

DeSalle's voice tightened. "I will have to consider, Monsieur." She fingered the glittering rings on her right hand.

"In addition to the sum we have discussed, I promise she will produce exquisite needlework." Edward reached into his jacket and pulled out ten fifty-dollar banknotes from the Citizens Bank of Louisiana.

Nancy eyed the money in his hands. "Ah, oui? I would hardly expect such a simple girl to rival a Parisian fashion designer."

Edward fanned the dollar bills. "At dejeuner, she described her work to me at length, Madame. I am willing to take a chance in buying her from you."

"So much extra trouble for me," DeSalle grumbled, then downed a glass of sherry and licked her lips. "If her needlework proves unpopular, I prefer to let other men . . . well, have their way with her, in order to make up the difference."

"I will make it well worth your while, Madame." Edward thwacked an extra five bills on the table.

"How?" She tapped her fingers together, her eyes glittering in the semi-darkness.

"Her work will be equal to the best fashion house in Paris."

DeSalle tented her elbows on the table. "Why should I believe this promise? I have known you many years, and never before have I seen you make such a risky proposition. After all, you have only just met the girl." The red rouge spot on one of her cheeks stood out against her tan skin as she leaned toward him in the candlelight. "She has never trained in Paris. Besides, you have never seen a sample of her work. How do you know she tells the truth?"

"I must take it on faith. She speaks with such sincerity. Something you have long ago forgotten. There are still innocents in this world . . . of course, you wouldn't know any of them. You've chosen to inhabit a den of dark pleasures."

"*Phh* . . . my girls are dedicated to their work and to the men they serve. We are creatures of the night, and ours is a noble cause."

"So what I am proposing has a definite benefit to your noble cause, Madam. If you hire Brianna, your girls and their gowns will summon more attention in the Vieux Carré than you have ever dreamed."

"Ah, oui?" DeSalle purred, her chest rising and falling. "Why this particular girl? I have many other women who long to be by your side. This one is unschooled, ragged. She will take some time to train."

Edward's voice rose. "I fail to see why I should have to explain my inclinations to you, Madame. Suffice it to say, I find her captivating in her freshness, her relative innocence. I tire of those painted dolls who throw themselves at me. They have not a brain in their heads, yet here is a maiden with spirit and beauty. In your house, she will be cultivated and groomed to be by my side." He sat surprised at the strength of his conviction.

DeSalle nodded, unfazed by his strong tone. "I have seen many purchases of the flesh in New Orleans, Monsieur. Yet few trades involve changing a person for the better. Perhaps you do have good intentions. But I have a business to run, my friend."

His tone became chilly. "I am well aware of that, Madame."

"I need to protect my house, Monsieur. I must make another proposal . . . that is, if I accept Brianna into my house."

"Go on."

"Should her needlework not prove satisfactory, I will open her services to the other men at the house, and you will not be her exclusive . . . shall we say . . . patron."

Edward swept the money back into a pile before him, his face glowering. "Yet, mark this. Should you or any other member of the establishment coerce, threaten, or abuse the said Miss Baird in any way, I assure you another gentleman will never cross your threshold in the Crescent City."

"Of course." She twisted her rings.

He leaned toward her in the darkness and hissed. "Your name will be as low as the mud from last year's Sauvé's Crevasse. Recall when the floods buried the streets of New Orleans."

DeSalle broke into a nervous, slight cough. "I do remember the slime and filth on the walls of the Maison. *Quelle horreur.*"

Edward bent over the table toward her, his hands resting on the money pile. "So . . . do we, or do we not have an agreement, Madame?"

She arched her eyebrows. "Very well."

In silence, Edward turned over the stack of bills. DeSalle kneaded them with her bony fingers, then thrust them into the recessed pocket of her skirt. Her eyes blazed like a pair of glass lanterns.

Her crinoline rustled as she rose from her seat. "*Merci,* Monsieur." After a low curtsy, DeSalle spun and vanished into the lights and noise of the bordello.

Edward warmed to the vision of Brianna's face as it hovered before him in the candle flame. *Madonna of the Pomegranate.* Her heavy eyelids would be closed in dreams, sheltering those golden-hazel eyes flecked with green. A trace of blush would play upon her cheeks. He felt a strange satisfaction. He had done it: Brianna would be his alone. An owl hooted in the trees.

Twenty-Three

THE OPEN DOOR

New Orleans, Louisiana
June 1850

The next morning, Brianna regarded the veil of mosquito netting suspended from the canopy above her bed. When little Ambrose was born, the biting bugs nearly maddened her without such protection. Another surge of pain cramped her stomach. Would they ever go away? She rubbed her eyes and snuggled into the nest of cotton sheets. A light blanket created pink patterns where she'd kicked it aside during the hot night. She nestled in her cocoon, safe and cool, a refuge from the struggles of yesterday in this eccentric town. Brianna visualized New Orleans, a web of Creole cottages, chaotic marketplaces, and secretive balconies, simmering outside her window.

Arching her arms above her head, Brianna stretched her legs out over the sheets and blanket. She was lazy as a lizard taking a sunbath on the pier. The aroma of chicory coffee tickled her nose; women's words murmured down a distant hallway. Time to get up.

Brianna sat up against the pillows and peered out through the mosquito net. Palm fronds waved in the speckled light outside the French doors opening onto her balcony. A flying roach clattered against the wooden screen where light filtered in from an open window. Someone had forgotten to close the shutters. Where was the dress she'd worn to bed? She was now in a cotton nightdress, but had no recollection of changing into it. Brianna thought she'd left it on the chair, but it stood empty under the window.

Then more sounds joined with the voices. Pots clanked, followed by the tinkling of glassware. The kitchen was preparing breakfast. Brianna's stomach grumbled—what wouldn't she give for another sugar-topped *beignet*? Was that yesterday, or the day before? Edward's face hovered in her mind. He'd seemed kindly, and yet his presence was unnerving. He'd soothed her, yet she had been betrayed by such soothing. Would he do as he had promised and come and see her again? Edward's promise excited her, but she caught herself—she dared not hope. She'd dined on hope and found herself near starvation.

Brianna parted the mosquito netting. She licked her dry lips, then swung her feet over the edge of the high bed. This bed was like the crow's nest on a sailing ship at the Inner Harbor; she peered over the side at the wooden floors and scattered, woven-grass rugs. Why were the beds so high? She had one answer, at least—a cockroach scurried across the floor and disappeared under the bed.

Her fingers raked through the tangle of gold-red hair spilling over her breasts. What a mess it was. A soft knock sounded at the door and an aproned maid appeared, holding a yellow gown and a sewing box.

"*Bonjour.*"

The maid lowered in a half-curtsy. "*Bonjour*, Mademoiselle." The woman's silver hair gleamed against her chocolate skin. She placed the dress and box on the chair.

"What's your name?"

The woman turned and faced Brianna. "The house calls me Emma." Her tone was deep and rich.

Brianna nodded. "Yes, I see. Emma, where are you from?"

Emma fingered her apron. "I am not allowed to give personal information. Madame's orders."

"Why not?" Brianna's eyebrows rose. Was this a sign that the women in this house had lost their right to talk to one another? In Fells Point, the slaves she knew were on familiar terms with others in the house. She had not expected silence here in New Orleans.

Emma stepped away, her face a mask. She smoothed the yellow-striped gown where it lay over the chair.

Brianna eyed her scuffed brown shoes. "Oh, I think I understand. Back in some Baltimore houses we treat slaves in a less formal way, but I see things are stricter here in New Orleans."

"Oui, I am a freedwoman but Madame has her rules. I could be punished for being friendly with you."

Did Brianna catch wistfulness in the maid's expression? Something compelled her to exchange words, despite the threat. She said, "I would not want to trouble you. I am so alone, you see. My name is Brianna." Sadness gripped her throat.

The maid backed toward the door, her weathered hands clutching the edges of her starched white apron.

Brianna tried again, lowering her voice. "Please Emma, I need you to trust me. I do not know anyone here."

Emma whispered, "Oui, but here in New Orleans we abide by *Le Code Noir*."

"I . . . I do not understand. The Black Code? What does that signify?" The term sounded mysterious and forbidding.

"Long ago in Louisiana, the French established a code governing how we Negroes are treated, slaves or free."

Brianna heard the unspoken pain in the woman's teaching. "Please tell me more."

In seconds, Emma's soft face hardened into a stony façade. "Perhaps later. Now, Mademoiselle, please let me run your bath and dress you in this morning's gown." She placed a wooden footstool under Brianna's feet, and helped her off the high bed. Then, Emma picked up the yellow dress where it was draped across the chair, and she held it up against Brianna's chest.

Silk bows were trailing from the sleeves. The material was soft to the touch and it smelled of lavender. Brianna said, "Oh, that is for me. I wondered about that. Yet I have such hunger I would faint before I dress."

Emma leaned back and looked into her eyes. "I work fast, Mademoiselle."

Brianna said, "Very well, if you hurry." Her mouth curved into a smile. "No matter the code, please call me Brianna."

Emma shook her head and sighed. "*Bien sûr*, Mademoiselle Brianna."

She lugged in a heavy pot of sloshing hot water, then carried in cotton towels over her arm. Emma's mouth set in a firm line, and she got to work undressing and washing Brianna. The maid's gentle hands worked the soap and water over each part of her body. The white cloth in the water took on the pink cast of menstrual blood, a familiar sight in the parlor house.

Emma worked so fast that Brianna forgot to be embarrassed by her nudity and her blood. Out of modesty, she put her arms over her breasts and stepped into the drawers held open by her maid, who then tied them in place. Next, the maid pulled the knee-length chemise over Brianna's head, and she felt the soft cotton fall over her face and down onto her shoulders. Its scent spoke of fresh air and gardenias. She stepped into her white stockings, and Emma pulled them up to her knees, tying narrow ribbons under each knee to keep them in place.

The maid's quick fingers then placed Brianna's corset around her midriff and laced it up in the back. For a moment, Brianna had to get used to less breathing space and constriction in her ribs and waist. Emma held out a petticoat, drew it up, and tied it in the back. With gentle fingers, Emma lifted and tied the horsehair crinoline around her waist, which bounced around her hips. A final hand-embroidered petticoat added a soft layer to hide the stiffer crinoline under her dress.

Emma eased the yellow-striped day dress over Brianna's head.

Brianna couldn't believe her eyes. Even though she'd worked on such a lovely dress for Miss Osborne, she'd never worn one as fine as this. Such puffy sleeves, such fine lacework trimming the waist.

Once the gown was buttoned, Emma took a couple of steps away and regarded Brianna through narrowed eyes. "The dress is too large, so we'll have to make some temporary alterations for now. You have a very tiny waist. Turn around, please."

"I'm a seamstress. I may alter the gown after I wear it today," Brianna said. A small cross dangled from a chain on Emma's neck.

"Oui, Mademoiselle." Emma's fingers pulled pins from a pincushion on the table and attached them to the gown.

Brianna pulled in her stomach as the maid tightened the waistband.

Then, after a thorough combing of Brianna's copper, waist-length hair, Emma styled it into a chignon, then placed delicate ringlets over each ear. She dabbed some pink rouge on Brianna's cheeks. Under each ear, she patted *Eau de Judée* perfume from a crystal bottle marked *Guerlain, Paris.*

Brianna breathed in the soft scent of roses and jasmine. She loved this Emma, the maid with no last name. Mama had never pampered her this way; she was always either too tired or too sad. She could see her mother snoring now at the kitchen table, Louie the Labrador snoozing beneath her chair.

The maid's words fell like soft rainfall on the forest of Brianna's thoughts. "Mademoiselle, now you must go down to breakfast, eat ladylike, and be sure not to soil this dress. You will wear this morning dress many times for days to come."

"Oui, Emma." Brianna smiled. "*Merci beaucoup.*"

The woman bent over her and murmured, "You are most welcome, Mademoiselle."

Brianna's mind fluttered away in anxiety, but then she sensed Emma's continued presence; she heard Emma's soft, insistent breathing next to her.

A hand pressed on her shoulder. "There, there, Miss Brianna. I know, I know." Brianna looked up into her face. Emma's dark eyes cast a shadow. This woman recognized her own silent grief.

A few moments later, a colored butler seated Brianna in the dining room as if she were royalty. He placed a lace-appliqué napkin on her lap. An aproned waiter poured *café au lait* into her fine china cup. Gold plating shimmered on the rim. From one pitcher, the waiter poured the *café*; the other, the milk. The two streams cross-splashed into the cup where they created swirls of white and beige.

"*Sucre?*" The waiter offered, holding tiny tongs over brown sugar lumps in a bowl.

"Oui, *deux.*" Two lumps plopped into Brianna's cup.

Across the blue tablecloth, four girls sat, their navy day dresses neatly pressed. Their ringlets bounced while they worked silverware across their plates, buttering bread, slicing bacon, pouring caramel on their couscous, then raising spoonfuls to their mouths.

Madame DeSalle held the regal position at the end of the table. In place of the former parrot feathers, her hair was coiled in a crown of braids. She set an elbow against the table and gestured with a limp wrist. "This morning we are greeting a new member of our esteemed house."

The girls put down their silverware in anticipation. "*Bonjour,*" they said in chorus.

DeSalle continued. "Mademoiselle Brianna Baird comes to us from Baltimore, Maryland."

Brianna nodded. A hot flush was creeping up her neck. She hated it when other girls stared at her, girls she did not know. What did they think of her? She remembered Miss Osborne forcing dreaded introductions among the seamstresses when they began working for her. It had always seemed strained, embarrassing.

DeSalle's tone shifted from welcoming to reprimanding. "No, no, Mademoiselle Brianna, we do not nod our heads when introduced. Instead, girls, what do we do?"

The youngest girl, looking to be around thirteen, chirped up. "We stand, introduce, then curtsy, Madame."

She peeped like the wind-up doll Brianna had spotted at the French Market yesterday. A mere child. What was such a young girl doing in a parlor house? She'd never seen girls this young on Thames Street.

"Thank you, Rosa," DeSalle said.

The other girls rose in turn to introduce themselves: Rosa from Italy, Celeste from Paris, Chantille from New Orleans, and so on down the row. All fallen angels. Their skin looked fresh and untouched, their cheeks rosy, their necklines low. The youngest named Rosa was undeveloped, her *bustière* flat, whereas the other girls filled theirs with perky curves.

Brianna scanned their wide eyes. The table sat in tense, expectant silence. It was her turn now. She stood, her legs as wobbly as sticks. "Brianna Baird, Baltimore." She curtsied and sat down as fast as possible.

She couldn't help wondering about these soiled girls. They must all be under sixteen. In Baltimore, that was the legal age for parlor house courtesans, according to Miss Rose. How did such girls end up here? She was by far the oldest at seventeen, but she wasn't one of them—she was the seamstress. Brianna struggled with the uncertainty that was rising in her. Why did she have to sit with them? Wouldn't a seamstress sit with the better servants?

She ran a hand over the lace tablecloth and gazed at the brass candlesticks lit for breakfast. Louisiana morning light filtered through the tall dining-room windows and cast a prism on the walls. What a contrast to the bleakness of her Baltimore home. Brianna visualized the shards of china that speckled the kitchen wall where Father had thrown the last soup tureen.

She stole a sideways glance at DeSalle. The madam's rings glittered as she raised the cut-glass goblet to her lips, then drank her orange juice. Every now and then, the waiter would pour from a rum bottle into the madam's glass. The customary kitchen clatter interrupted this morning's speech, so the waiter left DeSalle's side to close the swinging door. Through spectacles perched on the end of her nose, DeSalle studied a sheet of paper. The madam's eyebrows hovered over her glasses; she pursed her lips.

The madam clanged a spoon against her orange juice glass. "*Attention, s'îl vous plait, attention Mesdemoiselles.*"

The chorus answered, "Oui, Madame DeSalle."

Brianna's voice trailed after the others. She held up her fork and knife, imitating their manners. How ridiculous could they be? Oh well, she would go along anyway, trying to fit in. What other choice did she have? At least here, she would have food in her stomach and a bed to sleep in.

Madame DeSalle's eyebrow arch reappeared as she called out the day's events and assignments. "Rosa, you will greet the gentlemen callers, offering them cigars and making sure their brandy glasses are filled. Celeste, what piece have you practiced to play today on the melodeon?"

Celeste frowned, a wrinkle etched into the smooth skin between her eyes. She had a marked French accent. "I cannot decide, Madame, whether to play a waltz or a march."

"A waltz, Celeste. Less formal. Much more lively on a summer afternoon, don't you think?" DeSalle's dark braids glistened with pomade.

Brianna cut her ham into small pieces and brought them to her mouth, full of questions. How did such girls know the differences among types of dances? If she hadn't met Spenser, she'd never have known a waltz from a polka.

A hand on Brianna's arm startled her. "What is the matter, my dear? You look unhappy with our choice." Madame had reached over to

Brianna, her rum breath filling the space between them. "Do you prefer another piece?"

Brianna blinked away a tear from the corner of her left eye. "No, no. Mere dust, Madame. Oh, no, a waltz is just fine." Brianna shook her head.

"And, Chantille, you will wear *le combinaison* . . . the slip . . . today, and invite the first man to dance with you, just to warm things up."

Madame turned to Brianna. "*Le combinaison* is a lovely lace negligee that allows the customer to see all of a woman's charms."

Brianna swallowed. "Oh. I see."

Chantille's voice hardened. "Oh, Madame, must I wear that tonight? The men pinch me hard. Last time Monsieur Hebert, the old fat man, was rough with me, and I bled for a day after he took me to bed."

"Chantille, must you always be so outspoken?" Madame's brilliant black eyes squinted at her.

"Yes, Madame. I . . . I mean no, Madame." The girl's face reddened.

Brianna reached for her coffee cup and held it up to her lips. Maybe Madame would ignore her today since she was new. Before she could take a sip, Madame called, "Baird." She cringed and set down the cup.

"Your last name is too hard for me to pronounce each time I say it. It sounds too much like a sailing ship. Wasn't one of Columbus's ships called The Baird? Ridiculous. From now on, we will call you Brianna." A dark contempt twisted the madam's smile.

Brianna broiled in lonely silence. Although grateful for DeSalle's shelter, she was not to be a stud horse or a brood mare readied for a sale. A seamstress attached to any house never went by her Christian name. Miss Osborne's staff in Baltimore took great pains to treat seamstresses in a professional way, always addressing them formally, even though they were mere working girls. Without being called *Miss Baird*, she was reduced to the status of strumpet, and she shut her eyes against it, seething.

Madame continued. "Brianna, this afternoon you will bring in a box of mending to do in the parlor, and then you will work in the corner after greeting our guests. A special gentleman caller has asked for you today."

"Which gentleman caller, Madame?" She held her glass in midair.

"Monsieur Spina, of course." Madame's dark-eyed squint silenced further questions.

Brianna sipped from her water glass, but marbles lumped down her throat. Why was he calling on her? What did he expect?

"That will be all for today, girls." Madame puffed herself up to her full height like a mighty hen. When she stalked out, her sharp heels scratched like talons on the wooden floor.

Shadows gathered across the street. Emma washed Brianna's thick, abundant hair in a bowl. After a thorough towel drying, she twisted it into plaits in her room. Knuckles tapped against the door. Brianna searched Emma's face. "What do I say?"

Emma said, "The word to use is *entrez*, or *enter*, Mademoiselle." She spoke in a slow, patient way.

"Very well, *entrez*," she said. A squeaky hinge complained as the door opened, then swung shut behind Celeste, the young French girl from the morning table.

Emma continued plaiting the gleaming red hair, winding the strands up on her crown, then securing them with pins.

Celeste said in a heavy French accent, "I'm glad you are here, Brianna. We need an older girl in the house. The young ones cause such a row."

"Yes, I feel really old around them." Brianna appreciated the girl's remark—it meant she'd noticed her at the table.

Emma pulled Brianna's shoulders back into position. "Mademoiselle, keep your head straight as you talk, oui?"

Brianna obeyed, yet she wondered. Emma's cultured mannerisms, her perfect French, her polished English: This was not the usual behavior of a typical freedwoman in Maryland. Was it different here in Louisiana?

"Emma, how do you know such expert French and English?" Brianna asked.

"Master LeComte at Halldown Plantation insisted all house slaves learn to read and write to better serve his guests."

"I see." Brianna pictured Emma serving gaily-dressed women on a porticoed gallery she had once seen on postcards in Baltimore.

Emma's velvet voice soothed her. Brianna wished her mother had spoken to her that way. Instead, Annie had been left to raise her. Maybe if Mama had guided her, she would not have ended up here, of all places. Annie had arranged her hair since childhood. She saw the scissors and remembered her sister's curls.

Out of the corner of her eye, she saw Celeste settle, facing her on the dainty cushioned chair next to the dressing table. Her fingers arranged the flounces on her skirt. "I am dressed for tonight, so I thought I would come see you. Our rooms are next-door to one another." Her voice echoed kindness. "So, what is your *spécialité*?"

Brianna hesitated. "What is a . . . a *spécialité*?"

"Something you do to entertain men? We all have a talent, *non*?" Celeste's pearl earrings dangled as she spoke.

Brianna struggled with her response. "I do not have that kind of ability. I do not even play the melodeon. I only just learned how to waltz and I am not a good dancer." Emma's hands tugged strands of her hair.

Celeste continued to probe. "Surely you have a specialty you use *au lit*? In bed?"

Brianna gasped. "Oh, no . . . never. I do not know about such things." What was this girl up to?

Celeste persisted. "Perhaps you don't understand, Mademoiselle. My English is not good. For example, I am skilled at *tour du monde* . . . that is, I use my tongue all around the world, of a man's body, you see."

Brianna sprang up, horrified, and Emma leaped back, avoiding an elbow in the face. "I do not want to talk about these matters. You do not understand. I am the seamstress. I sew. I make dresses, long beautiful gowns. With ribbons, satin, silk, lace. That is all I do." A spurt of anger rose inside her. "I . . . I am not a har—"

"A courtesan, Mademoiselle?" Celeste regarded Brianna. "Ah, *bien, c'est étrange.* Strange. You are most beautiful. You would be *exceptionelle*, even in France. And Madame's girls are without equal. In the years I am here, I never see a seamstress with her own maid, only the courtesan. In fact, Madame DeSalle already has a seamstress in the house . . . Madame Garnier from Paris. Why would she hire another?"

Brianna bit her bottom lip. "She must need one."

"I am young and foreign, but even I do not think that. Besides, Madame says you will receive a visitor tonight, a Monsieur Spina, non?" Celeste winked.

Tears pricked Brianna's eyes. Had she been wrong to trust people again? There could be some truth in Celeste's words, and she worried that she had been tricked again into believing a lie that she'd be serving as a seamstress. What made her believe people like Spenser and Madame DeSalle? She'd never trusted her parents; why put her faith in these strangers? She chilled at the realization that she could not even trust herself.

Emma's hands braced Brianna's shoulders. "Mademoiselle Celeste. Be quiet. See you are upsetting Mademoiselle Brianna? Go back to your chamber. I must change Mademoiselle Brianna's gown now." She unbuttoned the back of Brianna's dressing gown.

"Ah, oui." Celeste lifted her crinolines, and rose, hands on her hips. "Good-bye for now. See you downstairs."

Celeste's door clicked open, then shut next door.

"*Merci*," Brianna whispered in Emma's ear.

Twenty-Four

A SAIL BLOCKING THE LIGHT

The notes of a lilting waltz resonated at the top of the stairs where Emma delivered Brianna to the public for the first time, dressed in a shining silk blue evening gown, her hair done up in plaits adorned with orange hibiscus, her ears glittering with long lapis earrings.

Before releasing her, Emma glowed at Brianna. "You are the most lovely girl I have ever prepared for Madame."

"Give me courage, Emma. I need it tonight."

Emma wiped a solitary tear from Brianna's eye. "Your strength lies inside of you, *ma chérie*. You have only to act with your heart."

"Yes, yes, my heart." This same strength could also see her out the door.

Sam, the little kitchen slave, raced up the stairs, and handed Emma a wooden sewing box embellished with lily flowers, the symbol of New Orleans.

Emma passed the sewing box to Brianna. Brianna balanced in pointy new shoes and steadied herself on the stairs. She navigated the fifteen downward steps and survived a near tumble after she caught her heel in one of her voluminous skirts. Emma watched her from the top of the stairs and made the sign of the cross.

The house parrot in a gilded cage greeted Brianna as she entered the high-ceilinged drawing room. He screeched "*Bonsoir*, my beauty!" His feathers floated in the air, crimson and yellow, mingling in clouds of cigar smoke. Celeste worked the keys of the melodeon. Men in various states of drunkenness languished on the couches and chairs, their cravats askew, sleeves rolled up, revealing tattoos. Tobacco wads pinged as they landed in a spittoon. Madame had advised Brianna that many of the men were upstanding members of New Orleans society, but their lusty behavior was no indicator of rank. How many of them had lied to their wives about their whereabouts, the way Spenser had lied to her?

Peering through the smoke, Brianna strained to recognize the fallen angels from this morning's breakfast table. Layers of makeup and smudges of charcoal smothered their fine features. Gaudy red lipstick stained their lips. Their small breasts emerged, pushed up under corsets underlying their low-cut gowns. On the couch, Chantille perched on a blond man's lap, his hands fondling her breasts through a filmy slip. He wore a wedding ring similar to Spenser's.

"You luscious piece of fruit," the man cooed, kissing her neck. Chantille's morning smile had vanished; in its place, Brianna caught her wan expression, her vacant eyes. She'd seen that same blank look on the faces of the slaves yesterday. Rich red threads of the Belgian tapestry on the wall behind the piano contrasted with blue velvet curtains lining tall windows. A candelabra smoked and sputtered in the middle of the ceiling.

Brianna wheezed. How the fumes irritated her dry throat. Could she find a place to hide herself from these men? There. She tiptoed to a horsehide chair with a stiff back in the corner. These chairs were not made for long sittings. She remembered Madame DeSalle's stern lecture: the girls were to be up and around, mingling with men, and not seated, drinking tea.

Celeste was an accomplished musician, Brianna noticed. She played the melodeon with a good sense of tempo and style. She had trained in Paris, of course.

Brianna pulled a thread and needle from the sewing box, but the soot sent stinging drifts into her eyes. They burned and watered. How disappointing: Emma's eye powder would soon smudge. Then, a motion drew her attention to a display in the center of the room.

Rosa, the little one, meandered about in striped pantaloons, lighting cigars and refilling brandy snifters. Every so often, a man's hand would reach out and pinch her bottom or squeeze her little pink breasts. They called her *nymph*, and the more they drank, the more of her they fondled as she strolled from man to man. She acted the part of their little doll; she perched on their laps and whispered in their ears.

How revolting. Nausea rose inside of Brianna as a pock-faced, jowly man of advanced years grabbed Rosa and engaged her in a waltz. He wore a diamond stud in his cravat. Disgusting. She could not bear to watch this old lecher, a scarred remnant of venereal disease, use the young maiden as a piece of trash. Gonorrhea had left its tracks on his face—reddened ridges and purple valleys. Impossible to erase, Annie had told her. This illness rendered the victim a ravaged testament to his own excessive lust.

This hideous man whirled tiny Rosa around the room as though she were a puppet. In the humid stuffiness, Rosa's perfect ringlets drooped like wasted tears. Poor girl—the sight of the grotesque and the perfect sent a shock through her. Thank the Lord no one noticed her here in the corner. Where was Monsieur Spina? Madame DeSalle had sounded so confident he would come tonight. The music silenced when Celeste turned the pages in her music book and looked for another waltz. As if on cue, all action stopped, and one man cleared his throat. The clock chimed on the mantel.

In the following sliver of silence, Brianna sensed the men's eyes penetrating her secret corner. Her heartbeat was so loud. Could they all hear it?

A male voice challenged, "Hey, Galsworthy, there's a match for you. Think you can handle a spinster seamstress?" Brianna angled over her mending like a bent pin. Fear rose inside of her first as a small wave, then larger, then very large. She pressed her elbows into her sides. *Please God, make me disappear.*

"Whatcha doin' there, Missy?" A deep gruff voice blew tobacco juice into her ear.

Brianna recoiled, then shuddered in her chair. The needle slipped out of her damp fingers onto the carpet. A tall, gangly brute hung like a sail over her, blocking the light. Two beady eyes pierced hers in the darkness. The yellowing whites of his eyes were the only light visible in the thick blue haze. The man's heavy hand pressed down upon her shoulder. She flinched. No way she could get away now.

Then Celeste performed a cheerful waltz, the one-two-three rhythm enlivening the drunken crowd.

Brianna was about to cry for help but she knew it was fruitless; the other men had turned away and resumed their drinking, each awaiting his turn to grope the unfortunate Rosa.

The man's grip was harder now, his fingers digging into her collarbone. "I am sewing, sir." Brianna's voice was firm, but his hand continued to press her down. An anchor in the Inner Harbor would weigh about as much.

"Hmm."

She gazed up to see the giant lick his lips, then gulp down two fingers of rye from a tumbler in his other hand.

His voice rasped. "Why on earth would a beautiful creature like you be sewing in the drawing room of the famous Maison DeSalle? You are but a tantalizer . . . and for that, I would give you a spanking." The man pulled her roughly to her feet and held her up with one arm, his other hand taking her face and peering into it. He bared his teeth, his canines long and yellow.

On his foul breath, Brianna caught a whiff of alcohol, cheap cigars, and rotted teeth. She swooned against his arms and fainted away.

The towering Galsworthy laughed. "Must mean the snatch likes me. They all want a good, long ride. Well, she's got that and more in me. Then, by jigger, a good lashing for more fun."

With that, he hoisted Brianna's delicate frame over his shoulder as though she were a sack of potatoes. The men broke into a cheer behind him, and he gave them a triumphant wave. He strode into the hallway. Now he would carry the seamstress up to her private chamber where he could unbutton her layers in his own sweet time.

No matter she was insensible. Better that way. Lust rose in his loins, and he salivated. He forgot his manners and spat on the wooden floor on his way out of the elegant parlor.

Twenty-Five

THE FOUL MESS

Madame DeSalle heard heavy footsteps mounting the stairs a bit earlier than usual, for she had planned an elegant repast for the gentlemen and their girls. She left her office chair and entered the foyer in time to see Brianna's red braids bounce against Galsworthy's back as he toted her up the stairs. She stopped short, fearing the man's rage.

New Orleans knew him as the contemptible overseer from Halldown Plantation. What would Mr. Spina say? Drops of sweat itched her upper lip. Where was Sam? He'd be washing the pots and pans by now. She scuttled down the hallway toward the kitchen, holding down the beads that were flapping on her chest. Throwing open the kitchen door, she found Sam drying a colander, drops of sweat on his forehead.

"Sam!"

He faced her, his eyes narrowing with concern. "Yes, Madame."

She took a moment to catch her breath. "Follow me. We must put a saddle on Muley. Hurry! We may already be too late!"

Out in the yard, Sam heaved a saddle on Muley's bowed back. The old horse eyed him and Madame DeSalle with a pained expression.

Sam rose up onto the saddle, his feet in the stirrups.

"Go to the Bourbon Orleans. Tell Mr. Spina he must come immediately," she said. "It concerns his personal property." She gave Muley a slap on the hind quarters to get him going.

Within a half an hour, a gust of wind slammed the door behind Edward Spina as he stood in the grand hallway of Maison DeSalle. He watched as Pierre the bouncer removed his kid gloves and top hat. Pierre brushed the dust off the back of Edward's riding jacket, and deposited his whip in the nearby stand. Edward sat on the bench while Pierre worked off his boots and slid the usual red velvet slippers onto his feet.

Pierre asked his usual question, "How were the tables today, Monsieur?"

Edward watched the bald spot on the servant's inclined head while easing the pair of velvet slippers on his feet. "More than generous, Pierre, for a day in the Garden District." Then the gambler checked himself in the wavy mirror at the coat stand, and he tidied his mustache. Turning to Pierre, he demanded, "A glass of DeSalle's best French Bordeaux. In fact, make it two! This is a cause for celebration." What would Brianna Baird look like, sound like, and act like tonight? Jubilation rose within him, a feeling he had nearly forgotten. This auburn-haired nymph had captured him in her net filled with stars and moonlight.

Madame strode into the hallway and curtsied. "Good evening, Mr. Spina. What a pleasure . . ."

Edward noticed the way her mouth twisted into a knot, and a wave of uneasiness engulfed him. "Where is my Miss Brianna Baird?" He took in the smoke-filled salon and the girls engaged in foreplay with the drunken men. That scene was not what he'd had in mind for Brianna.

Madam DeSalle's billowy chest sank like pinpricked balloons. Words gurgled in her throat. "Did you not see Sam? He rode Muley to the Bourbon Orleans to find you. Something's happened to Miss . . ."

Spina's smile vanished faster than lightning into the ground. If only he could shoot daggers at her out of his eyes. "What have you done?" Not willing to wait, he insisted again, this time with more force. "Where is Miss Baird?" He clenched his teeth, his heart thumping a fierce rhythm in his chest.

As if on cue, the parrot mimicked him. "Waaalk! Where is Miss Baird?"

DeSalle's mouth opened into a soundless cave, then she groaned in terrible pain.

"Useless woman! Out of my way!" He gave her a push, then backed her toward the staircase. She lost her balance, then recovered, twisting the heel of her button shoe.

He glanced up the stairs. "Oh, no, you didn't . . . you haven't. So help me God, Madame, I will ruin you. Where is she? Where is she?" His voice thundered through the house, and he hoped the passersby could hear him. In dismay, he saw the men and girls paused in their embraces as they heard the storm, although so drunk with laudanum-laced whiskey, they took little note. Bastards, all of them.

The parrot said, "*Mon Dieu*! Where is she?"

"In her room." DeSalle's voice was barely a whisper. "Upstairs, second on the left."

After grabbing his whip from the coat stand, Edward leaped upstairs, two steps at a time.

Over his shoulder, he saw Madame gape after him, her gold teeth glinting. Pierre froze by her side.

Edward stumbled over a woman's body lying face-down on the landing, her white apron stark against her gray dress. "Emma, oh Emma, are you all right?" Edward knelt down next to her and turned her over. A slash of red blood trickled into her black and gray curls.

Her eyelids flickered, and she mumbled into his ear. "Monsieur, I tried to protect . . ."

He rose, then flung open the door to Brianna's room with such force the doorknob knocked a hole in the wall.

A shirtless Galsworthy sat astride the insensible girl as though she were a prize pony. The palms of his hands roamed over her bare breasts. Sweat and drool coursed down his pocked face.

Edward did not wait for explanations. He grasped his whip in both hands, looped it and slipped a garrote over Galsworthy's head and around his neck, then pulled back with all his might, twisting the handle, all the while yelling at the top of his lungs for Pierre. He heard Madame's voice in the hallway shout, "Pierre! Come quickly!"

Filled with surprise and rage, Galsworthy choke-gasped, so Edward pulled tighter, not intending to kill, but to disable the man. Many years of practice told him that with any luck, he'd not have to wait long. The key was to surprise the opponent. The man was a brute, but this would work as it had many times before at the New Orleans shipyards. Galsworthy flailed his arms, kicked his legs, and sputtered. All the while, his dull weight pressed back and forth, a rolling pin crushing Brianna's body. After clawing at the whip, Galsworthy went limp and collapsed against the bed.

Edward paused in wordless contemplation of Brianna who lay in oblivion, her pale skin a palette of red scratches and plum-colored swellings. What kind of monster would do this?

Footsteps pounded the landing outside, and Pierre burst through the doorway. "Come, give me a hand with this brute," Edward said. He lugged the giant off the bed, and Pierre grabbed his feet. Together they dragged him out of the room and into the upstairs hallway.

Madame posed on the landing, her cleavage a tide that rose and fell with her panic. She said, "Be careful to go around Emma. There, two more steps and you'll be at the top step of the staircase."

Edward couldn't help but snap, "It's about time you helped. Look toward Emma. She needs a plaster on that forehead." Madame's shoulders drooped and she disappeared into her bedroom at the end of the hallway.

Meanwhile, Edward dragged the bulky man to the top step of the staircase. Avoiding the dangling arms, Pierre shoved him down the stairs.

Both men hustled after the tumbling body, and stood watching as it hit the bottom floor with a thump. Edward kneeled to get a closer look at Galsworthy, splayed out across the floorboards. A pinch of crimson stained the man's neck where the whip's leather had burned into his flesh. His eyes rolled back and forth under closed lids. Edward lifted the man's wrist and felt for a pulse. It was strong—the man had shown unbelievable resilience. Edward rose, standing over the man, staring at the red line on his neck.

Madame's voice mixed with Emma's on the landing. DeSalle helped her sit up and was now pressing a chartreuse silk scarf on the head wound. About time she did something useful.

Edward's throat tightened with a sickening sense of betrayal. What had made him think he could leave Brianna alone for a moment in this den of depravity? Then truth struck him. He'd been the betrayer. How often had he been the one to fondle young women in lust and take them against their will? He was no innocent. His own miserable acts came back to haunt him, but now he saw for the first time what he must do. He would protect Brianna from all that was rancid in this town, like the rotten refuse lying there on the floor.

A couple of hours passed. Edward and Pierre sat in somber silence on the bottom step of the stairs, holding the same steady vigilance that one would hold for a corpse. When Galsworthy stirred, Edward tapped Pierre's arm and got up.

Holding his head, Galsworthy rose onto his knees and sneered up at Edward. "She ain't worth all that much. Nothing but a tramp! You can have her . . . she's all dried up . . . that's why she can only be a seamstress! Stupid twat!"

Edward's pulse beat double time. "Still wrathy, are you? Get the hell out of here, disgusting gizzard." If not for the hangman's noose, he'd relish killing the man then and there.

Pierre, prepared for any unruly occasion, opened the door just in time to watch the bootless Galsworthy limp out the threshold. The scoundrel spat a parting "Fuck you all!"

Pierre threw his shirt and boots out to him. When Pierre opened his mouth to yell back, Edward elbowed him in the ribs, so he stayed silent.

Edward watched the overseer rage at them from down on the muddy sidewalk. What an incoherent, foul mess.

Galsworthy said, "And as for that slave-chattel woman up there, wait and see. I plans to pile on the agony to her worthless slavin' son and husband, that's what I do to her. That seamstress will have her day yet in my arms, mine to keep."

Pierre grinned, then locked the door behind him. He faced Edward who still held the whip in his hand. "Pretty fast work with the whip, Mr. Spina. Never seen such a smooth garrote before."

Edward took a perverse pleasure in the compliment. "I shall take that kindly, Pierre. My Italian cousins would have killed the man, but I do not wish to bring further scandal to the house. It is enough that Mademoiselle Brianna had to suffer such indignities at the hands of this rogue."

He handed Pierre the whip and watched him drop it back into the stand.

Twenty-Six

THE PROMISE

Some hours later, Brianna awoke with a start to smelling salts in her nose. Two candlelit faces peered at her, in and out of focus. She looked over at her blue evening gown that lay in tatters about her, and then to the modesty sheet across her chest. Hibiscus flowers crushed cold against her cheek. A pain jabbed her earlobe, torn after her long emerald earring caught in the attacker's sleeve.

"Brianna?" A man's voice sounded far away as if in a dark tunnel.

"Mademoiselle," another softer voice said. She recognized Emma's cheekbones, highlighted in the flickering light, and she worked harder to open her crust-laden eyes.

"Yes," she answered through dry lips. "Water . . ."

Again, Brianna heard the same man's voice. "She wants water, Emma. There you are. Here, my dear." A glass pressed against her lips, and she drank. Her tongue moved thick and swollen. Two brown hands held her own, and she sensed a wet towel on her lips.

She heard Emma. "There's some blood on her gown, Mr. Spina. I must get her out of this dress."

"Let me help," the man's voice said.

That was all Brianna could recall days later as she rested under the filmy splendor of mosquito netting. She eyed the sleeves of her white embroidered nightgown, and as she turned her head, she could see her abundant hair fanning across the pillow. A man's hand offered her a tablespoon of chicken broth.

"Where am I? Is that you, Teddy?"

"My dear Brianna, you are with me, Edward, of course." The mustache grinned. Deep dimples accented the angular face.

"No . . . not Teddy?" She propped herself up against her pillows, and peered into his eyes, then past him. As she surveyed the room, shreds of memory came together.

"What day is it?" she asked.

"It's the eighteenth of June, 1850." Edward flipped open his pocket watch. "Eleven o'clock in the morning, to be precise."

"New Orleans?"

"Nothing better," he said. "Now, my darlin', do take some of this *potage*. Emma does not trust me with feeding you, but I'm bound to prove her wrong."

She opened her mouth and warm liquid eased down her throat.

"How did I get here?" A dull pain throbbed in her temple.

"You were attacked, Brianna. By a certain Galsworthy . . . a scoundrel who is no better than a dog. Your bruises came from the very villain who tried to steal your virtue."

"Virtue?" she asked.

"Yes, and he's quite lucky I didn't get a few rounds of shot into him before he left. Lucky cuss." He dabbed a napkin against her lip to catch a drop of soup.

Brianna's eyes wandered from his face to an engraving on the wall above the gilt chair holding Edward's jacket. She'd noticed it before her illness when Emma had fixed her hair.

"Is that Napoleon's Tomb?" she asked. Emma settled a cool rag on her forehead. A chill coursed through her and set her teeth chattering.

He turned to look. "Why, it is indeed. How did you know?"

"My mother has postcards of Paris. Have you been there?" she asked. Her teeth tapped together.

"No my dear. Perhaps someday. Is that a place you would like to go?"

"Yes," she said, peering out from under the cloth. "I've always dreamed of going there. They say the women and men are elegant and the city has lovely trees."

"Perhaps I'll take you there someday," he said, brushing a lock of hair from her cheek. She gave a wistful sigh. "I've seen a drawing of Versailles and the Tuileries Garden in Paris." Her mind drifted. "We studied it during French class in Baltimore. We have to learn French to advance as seamstresses, as we have to read directions on French patterns at Betsy Osborne's shop in Baltimore."

Her eye caught Emma and Edward exchanging worried glances. "Is something wrong?"

Emma's rich voice came from the end of the bed where she sat, her brow wrinkled. "*Non*, Mademoiselle, nothing is wrong, but you must have some more food to build strength. You are not yourself yet."

"Emma. That is true. I do not feel my old self. Thank you . . . both of you . . . I fear I was in mortal danger and you have—you are—nursing me back to health."

"Oui, Mr. Spina has been most helpful. He has been by your side all during your ague. Mr. Galsworthy gave you an awful fever." Emma's black eyes shone.

Edward's warm hand patted her cold one. "And Emma saw you through your fits during several long nights."

Brianna took another tablespoon of soup. She licked her lips, her mind back in Baltimore. "I must go to work after this luncheon. Miss Osborne will be angry that I am late. She counts on me to do the finishing work on the gowns. It is a summer dress—the ladies are preparing for their outdoor galas."

She pushed away the soup bowl and Edward's hand. "Let me get up," she said. "My sister Annie must be waiting for me. I will go and put on my day dress. And my apron." She turned her head toward the armoire in the corner. "Where is my apron?" Her sudden movement sloshed soup over the sides of the bowl.

Emma used the rag from her forehead to mop up the spill.

Brianna sat upright, then slid her legs over to the edge of the high bed where she dangled them over the side. Her mind was whirling like the wooden top she and Annie would play with as children. Emma whispered to Edward, "She may be going into one of her fits again, Mr. Spina."

"I hope not," he said.

Edward settled next to her on the side of the bed and then arranged the wooden stepstool under her feet. The mattress sagged a bit under his weight.

"Now, Brianna, I want you to listen to me." His tone was soft and it pacified her.

Yet she felt a sense of urgency, as though she was late for something. Was she supposed to be at Miss Osborne's? "I must get to work . . . Father will beat me if I don't come home with money." Brianna trembled, her nightgown exposing her naked legs to the morning air.

"Listen, that is all in the past. I am here. Do you trust me?" Edward's dark eyes appeared luminous, and she searched his face for the familiar dimples in his cheeks.

Edward's gentle hands pressed her back down against the pillows. "Rest there and breathe in, and out. I have to do the same during a card game when I am about to fold. In and out." He took her hand and placed her palm against his chest. "Now, follow me. In . . ." He inhaled as she followed. "Now out . . ." And she exhaled.

Brianna calmed, wrapped in an invisible warmth. His hands, his face, his voice gave her a new sense of security, like being up in her bedroom with Mercy, the cat. Edward folded her into the blankets and Emma reached over and fluffed the pillows under her head.

Then, in the midst of her tranquility, Edward told her what had happened the night she took ill. He explained Galsworthy's attack and the ensuing fight. So that was the missing piece of her story. There it was again—the ache that came when she thought of Ambrose.

She studied Edward's face. "After that man hurt me, what then?"

"Galsworthy is full of infections. A raging fever gripped you, body and soul. Dr. Dufilho came and cupped you."

"Where?"

"On your stomach and leg. A splendid lot of blood you let, forcefully too. Best leeches from his pharmacy, weren't they, Emma?" Edward reached over and patted her ice pack into place. "Only but the best for such a beautiful girl."

Emma broke in. "Oh yes, Mr. Spina took great care to choose them with the pharmacist, and Mademoiselle, you looked so much better afterward. Delightfully pale. You had suffered a strange fever, and you were still ill . . . *pardon*, Mademoiselle." She held a finger to her lips.

"Yes," Brianna said. Her eyes drew away from Emma and fixed again on Napoleon's tomb. She pictured little Ambrose cradled in the arms of the great Emperor. He would guard her secret.

Edward rose from the chair. "Thus, Mademoiselle Baird, I am at your service." He made a short bow, and took his jacket from the chair. He was short of stature, yet solid and strong, resembling drawings of Napoleon.

"Must you leave so soon?" Brianna said. He gave her an easy companionship and the way he stroked her hand was like a brother . . . a friend.

What was all that on her bedside table? She eyed the collection of tonic and herbal medicine bottles arrayed in brown and green bottles of varying shapes and sizes. An amber bottle labeled GRIS-GRIS POTION sat among the collection. Her relief changed to suspicion.

"Did you use all those medicines on me, Mr. Spina?"

"You took them to recover, my dear. We used voodoo medicines to bring you out of the stupors. Please, call me Edward."

"Voodoo, Mr. Edward? Then I must be lucky to be alive."

"Yes, my girl. After the New Orleans fever, anyone is fortunate to live. Many a poor soul does not survive and the flushes run rampant in this city. So many mosquitoes and biting insects. Folks say the critters come over on the slave ships from Africa."

Edward lifted her hand to his lips. The fuzziness of his mustache awakened a familiar sense of pleasure as he kissed her palm.

She laughed. "That tickles."

He leaned back, looking her over. "Although I find your companionship enchanting, I have a table waiting at the gambling hells. Luck tonight will deliver you a new ballgown, my dear, in the same way fortune brought you to me." His clothes carried the aroma of chicory and pipe tobacco.

Brianna followed the outlines of his face, but her breath came in shallow bursts. "That is very sweet, Mr. Spina . . . I mean, Mr. Edward . . . but what is to become of me here at Madame DeSalle's? Surely I cannot stay here for long. I will not be prey to such leering men. I would not even call them *men*. In fact, they are beasts." Her face grew hot, and she pulled off the rag from her temple.

"That is not something you need worry about, my Brianna. Rest assured your situation will sort itself out. You are safe here under my protection." His eyes were stern, watchful.

Brianna lay back against her pillow. "Poor Mama, she would jump into her grave and close the lid over herself to know I was safe in this sisterhood of misery."

"Be that as it may, Mademoiselle, I am at your service." Edward gave a deep bow. Emma walked him to the bedroom door and then it clicked behind her, leaving Brianna alone to imagine little Ambrose, floating in the starry sky above the sights of Paris.

Twenty-Seven

CAUTION

New Orleans, Louisiana
July 1850

In July, Brianna's health returned, and life interested her again. No longer did she struggle to walk from her bed to the window. She gained strength to go up and down the stairs without Emma's arm guiding her. Her appetite returned, and she had the energy to plan the seamstress room DeSalle had set aside for her downstairs. Men had proven they were not to be trusted, but did Edward truly mean to protect her? Something about his soothing manner cut through her confusion. One day when he asked her out on an expedition, she gave an enthusiastic reply. Was that her own voice that said yes? It was lively, not like before.

On a sultry morning the following week, their arms full of parcels and one giant hatbox, Edward guided Brianna down Royal Street through the Vieux Carré. The familiar fragrance of beignets wafted through the streets, and carts and carriages of all sorts stirred the dust.

Although she continued to experience faintness from time to time, her bruises had turned from navy blue to light green, and her energy had returned.

Blended voices echoed from wrought iron balconies above the shops. Who were they and what were they doing? She peered up to see men and women seated behind Spanish balustrades. They drank coffee from china cups, slaves fanning them.

Brianna beamed over at him as he matched her stride. "Thank you for all your kindness, Mr. Edward."

"Watch out, ma chérie." A bucket of water rained down on them from a vine-laden veranda.

"Thunder!" She gasped, dropping a brown-paper-wrapped package in the muddy street. As Brianna reached over to pick up the bundle, she caught Edward's eyes scanning her graceful figure. An unwelcome surge of excitement filled her. She'd had this feeling before. Images of Spenser, the waltz, reeled before her. *Be careful, go with caution*, she told herself.

"My instincts about you were correct from the first moment I saw you." Edward's voice was slow and easy.

"Oui?" She inclined her head, gripping her belongings to her chest.

He stood back to look at her as though examining a painting at an artist's easel in front of the Cabildo.

"Emma has taken great care of you. How tiny your waist appears in that flowing summer dress."

Brianna looked down at the red rosebud print of her cotton skirt. "Yes . . . she did pick this out for me." Despite some misgivings, she warmed to his enthusiasm.

He tipped the brim of his top hat back with his cane. "The poet would write about you, *Cascades of gleaming red-blond hair reflected sun like autumn leaves in the bayou. Her hair framed her face and breasts . . .*"

"Do stop, Mr. Edward. You are making me feel ridiculous."

"Ridiculous or not, I know I will be able to make a great woman of you." His voice carried pride and passion.

Brianna should have been flattered and pleased at his attentions. It was true she found him attractive and his words caused her to quiver. But, she'd been down this road before with a man. A deep familiar pain throbbed inside her, and she prickled at his words. "Mr. Edward, do you think you own me? I am not a slave of New Orleans. I have seen the auction blocks in front of the slave pens. I am not a woman to be bought and sold." She held her shoulders back. "I am a seamstress."

Edward murmured into her ear, "What I mean is I would like you to be a slave to my love."

Packages balanced precariously in her arms. She shook her head. "Mr. Edward, I am still . . . that is, I am . . ." Afraid to look directly into his eyes, she focused on his lips. She needed more time to erase the mistakes of the past.

He stood expectantly. "Yes?"

"Mr. Edward, I am not able to love you in that way." A group of schoolchildren were running a hoop along the sidewalk and she stepped into a shop doorway to avoid them.

The proprietor came out with a ladder and jostled them.

Edward followed her back onto the sidewalk. "I am aware of that, ma cherie. Emma told me of your frail condition."

Didn't he know the last thing she needed right now was another man to drop her on some church steps? She stepped toward him. "Besides, I don't have those sort of feelings. You are some years older than I."

His voice sounded vibrant, hopeful. "Time will heal you, Brianna. And I can wait. I am only a few years older and I am quite young when it comes to love. You are worth waiting for. You are my lucky coin, my double eagle."

She stepped back, filled with a guilty regret. "But I would not want to disappoint you, after all that you have done for me. I have no way to repay you. You have nursed me back to health, and now these clothes?" A rising panic amplified her voice.

"You owe me nothing, Miss Baird. Just promise me one thing." He smoothed the paper on the side of his package.

"That sorely depends, Mr. Edward. I know not to make vows since I have been hurt mortally in the past." A line of sweat trickled down her spine, soaking her chemise.

Edward's hand reached out, took one of her bundles, and he added it to his own load. He strode ahead of her through the throngs of passersby, leading her toward the source of heavenly seafood smells. He glanced over his shoulder, speaking while he walked. "Promise you will give me a chance. When you lay recovering from your illness, I watched over you every day. I realized I could not lose you." Did his mouth curve with tenderness? Was she more drawn to him than she cared to admit?

They emerged into the sunny intersection of Royal and Toulouse where they waited to cross. Brianna sighed. "Very well, I will give you a chance to be a friend." She smiled up at him. A horse-drawn fire wagon passed, creating a blur of red and brass.

Despite her earlier sadness, she did want to be there on that street corner with him. In the midst of dust and noise, Edward put her at ease. Yet her sister Annie's voice whispered through the tendrils of spider ferns flowing from porches above her, *Guard your heart, sister, guard your heart.*

As they followed the pedestrian stream moving across Toulouse, Edward spoke. "Someday you will know the difference between real love and love you thought was real. But for now, my dear girl, let us dine. If we are to be as cousins or friends, I am content with that for now. It would be my pleasure to introduce you to the sights and sounds of my native city. I can think of nothing finer to compliment this moment than roast duck washed down with a hearty bourbon."

Edward's voice revealed experience, maybe even maturity. Even though Brianna appreciated his courtesies, she'd learned that men could come and go. So, she needed to think of preserving herself in the middle of this new town and establishing a new role as this gentleman's friend, if that was what she was.

Brianna ran her tongue across her lips. She considered her role at Maison DeSalle. Maybe she'd see the latest season's gowns on women diners at Alciatore. Wealthy Creole women had Parisian designers; she'd copy whatever she saw. Madame DeSalle's girls would wear the latest patterns and new designs. That would give Edward even more reason to be proud of her.

The gloved footman at the Pension Alciatore opened wide the wooden door, greeting Mr. Spina. The maître d' led the couple into the dining room, taking their boxes, hats, and gloves. She and Edward melted into a world of white linen, chandeliers, and lavender roses.

Three waiters in white suits surrounded the couple. Brianna had never seen such grandeur. One man lit candles on the table and another removed china plates and arranged silverware at their place settings. The scents of garlic, olive oil, and fresh herbs from the kitchen aroused her appetite.

The meal service was swift and efficient. In less than half an hour, their trio of waiters wheeled out an elegant cart featuring a silver casserole. One server lifted the lid and steam issued upward in gusts of onion and peppers. The second server ladled chunks of white meat, carrots, onions, and chilies from the casserole into a bowl, drizzling broth over the mixture. Moments later, Edward glanced up from his dish. He held his spoon out to her. "Care for a taste?"

Brianna shrank into her chair. "This food in New Orleans is rich . . . I'm not accustomed to it."

"Your stomach is tender from your illness. Try a sip. It won't hurt you," Edward said.

"Um . . . is it a chicken soup?" She sniffed the steaming broth.

"No, it's alligator," Edward said. He took a small taste from the spoon and held it out to Brianna.

She took a sip. "And to think I'm eating part of a reptile. I understand they have large jaws and many teeth." Her unease tiptoed out with the waiter.

Edward gave a broad smile. "Do you want to go into the bayou and hunt them, right outside of town? My family has a boat."

"No, thank you. I'm satisfied with my oysters, though the sauce is much spicier than I've had in Baltimore. We only ate oysters on a rare occasion when Father stopped drinking whiskey for a spell. Otherwise, it was potatoes and moldy bread."

"Prepare your appetite, ma cherie. The next course is Shrimp *Remoulade*—Chef Alciatore's famous dish."

"I guess that is why all the tables are full today at the dinner hour," Brianna said.

She glanced around the high-ceilinged room, noting men and women in their finest light silks and brocades, their heads bent in conversation. A stout matron sipped from a crystal water glass. The green glow of her chine floral silk accented bell sleeves piped with Chantilly lace. Brianna marveled at the variety of fine French cloth; indeed, the airy nature of summer dresses lifted the room, suspending it in cool clouds of ruffles and taffeta.

"What are you looking at, my girl?" Edward put down his spoon.

"Their dresses." She blinked.

"You shall have those gowns, and more, you will see." He patted her hand.

"It is not that I want their dresses, Mr. Edward."

"I do not understand." He shrugged.

"I want to *design* their dresses."

"Women's trifles, my dear."

Brianna stiffened. Maybe he expected more of her than she did. Or was it less? She fumed in silence.

Edward took a sip of bourbon, and looked out the window for a moment at a passing carriage.

Brianna leaned forward toward him. "At Betsy Osborne's shop, the design of fine apparel was anything but a trifle," she said. "We studied French designs for hours on end in order to memorize them."

Edward's eyebrows raised. "It's not important how much you work with needle and thread. You belong to me now." He wiped his lips with his napkin.

"What do you mean? Belong to you?" Brianna's teeth clenched. Former fears paraded through her mind. Father had treated mother as his possession. A tree of scars had glared on the back of a slave she'd seen at auction, reminding her of Mama's beatings. Was her condition, and that of women like her, no more favorable? She should never have trusted this man. How could she have fallen into his hands so easily when she knew better? He was no better than Spenser, just different.

"Yes, you are part of my estate." He fingered the lip of his bourbon glass.

"But surely I am not a slave. I have already made that quite clear. I am a free woman from Baltimore. A seamstress. I design gowns."

"I do not jest, ma cherie. You belong to me. I paid for you."

"Who did you pay?" Her jaw tightened.

"Madame DeSalle."

The words burned into her mind like the imprint of a red hot poker. Brianna would not be bought and sold. She rose from her chair and slapped Edward across the face with all her might.

Twenty-Eight

STAMPED IN PARIS

Brianna waited for Edward 's reply—for him to rise and hit her, to make a scene, to drag her out of this fine establishment. She glared at him until the clatter of plates and murmur of voices resumed. There was always the anger of her father, followed by a volley of blows. He'd cast her out onto the street and send her packing. Then where would she go, what would she do?

But Edward did no such thing. Instead, he rubbed his cheek, took another mouthful of bourbon, and snapped his fingers for the waiter. "Philippe," he said, "a bottle of your finest champagne."

"Yes, Monsieur Spina, right away," the quadroon waiter said. "May I ask the occasion?"

"Yes, surely." Edward beamed his eyes on Brianna. "I am in love."

Several days passed without any sign of Edward at Maison DeSalle. Though she missed the glow of his smile, Brianna grew accustomed to life in a parlor house. At any hour of the day, she swept her skirts around men and women scrubbing Italian marble floors, polishing brass lamps, or replacing spent candles. Heaven help the slave who did not follow DeSalle's directions. Now and then, Brianna wondered how Edward was occupied, but she busied herself buying materials and supplies for her sewing room at the house. She couldn't afford romantic distractions. A man would never be at the center of her world again.

One day, Edward came to see her in her sewing room. He guided her out into the garden and seated her on a bench across from him. He carried a pouch under his arm. His eyes were round and serious.

"I have brought something for you, Brianna." He passed her the pouch.

"What is it now? Shackles?" She regretted those words as soon as they had left her lips.

He continued, tapping the package with his hand. "Go ahead and open it."

Brianna untied the leather straps, and pulled out thick, white vellum envelopes. She broke the seal on the first one and tugged out a sheet of paper with the drawing of a woman's ballgown. She drew out the delicate tissue-paper sections familiar to all seamstresses. These were marked IMPRIMÉ À PARIS. She was caught off guard. "They say *Printed in Paris.*" She looked from the designs to Edward, then back again. "They are marvelous."

He smoothed his brow with his left hand. "I realized so much after you . . . that is . . . after our luncheon at Alciatore's."

"I am sorry I slapped you, but I am not another's property, you see." Her eyes brimmed and she gathered her strength.

Edward sat forward, his eyes on the designs. "I must have needed reminding, Brianna, and you taught me something." A slight tinge of wonder played in his voice.

Her words tumbled out. "They are just what I wanted. I can make many other designs once I have these pieces at hand—frocks and gowns for all occasions. They are *à la mode*; that is, they are what is seen today on the streets of Paris."

He broke in, "And soon to be on the streets of the Vieux Carré."

A niggling concern rose inside of her. What did he want in return? For now, she tucked her fear back inside the pouch with the drawings. Her mind swam with ideas for new gowns.

"I am glad you like them." His voice disturbed her imagined designs.

"Where did you find them?"

His eyebrows arched. "My father's friend at the wharf is an importer-exporter."

Brianna turned to him, and bowed her head in a formal way. "A professional seamstress from here to New York would be grateful to have these precious patterns. I will use them well."

"You see, Brianna, I do want you to succeed with your seamstress work. But I also have another motive."

There it was again, the spurt of anxiety.

Edward reached out his hand to hold hers, but Brianna cast him a wary look, so he rested his hands in his lap instead.

"What motive might that be?" She put both hands in her pockets.

"One pattern is for a ballgown. I wish you to wear it when I take you to the frolic at the Orleans next month."

"When you take me? You haven't asked me yet, Monsieur." Heat rushed to her face.

"Brianna, then will you go with me?" His question held a simple longing, full of desire.

She sat in silence for a moment, watching a hummingbird sip nectar from a trumpet flower over them.

Edward waited in the quiet for her reply.

Her words came slowly. "Very well. I will go as your companion if that is what you wish."

His deep voice simmered with yearning. "When you have it in your heart to forgive me, my dear, please let me know. I shall be waiting for you."

Edward arose, took her hand in his, and kissed the back of it. His lips were tender against her skin. She found it hard to control the urge to leap up, hold him close, and smother his lips with fervent kisses. Yet now she held herself in check. No more girlish mistakes with men. She was a woman now.

He patted on his top hat. "*Au revoir*," he said.

She was glad of that. An involuntary tremor of desire ran through her. "I will see you again." Brianna followed him to the front door. He skirted the flower beds and locked the back gate behind him.

Twenty-Nine

MADELEINE

New Orleans, Louisiana
September 1850

During the following months, Brianna developed a close friendship with Celeste. They kept confidences, a rare quality among parlor house doves. Each day, the two would share their reactions to goings-on at the house, and Brianna's bond with Celeste grew strong and true. Celeste showed genuine interest in Brianna's past, and she laughed at the stories about Louie the Labrador and Miss Osborne's shop. In return, Brianna listened to Celeste's stories of growing up in Paris and her daily life in Faubourg Saint-Germain. They shared hopes and dreams for the future husbands and children they wanted and the grand houses they would inhabit. They also remarked that none of their dreams included a parlor house.

One morning after Edward's visit, Brianna laid out her ballgown pattern on the long table in her sewing room.

Celeste wandered in, her petticoats swishing back and forth as she walked. The girl ran her fingers over the lace collar and sleeves that rested on the side table. "Your work is lovely," she said.

"Thank you. Please tell me more about Paris." Brianna was pinning her pattern to some slippery yards of iridescent satin material. "I have always wanted to go there. Before my mother became so sad, she told me all about the city, and we would look at pictures in the broadsheets." She bent over the fabric, intent on her work.

Celeste stood by her side and looked on, carrying the scent of maple and cinnamon. "Was your mother from Paris, too?" She held a swath of material for Brianna to pin.

Brianna flattened out the garment. "No, but she longed to go there, too, and she talked so little. I loved to hear her stories about Paris. I want to hear you tell about it." She glanced at her friend.

Celeste's blue eyes widened with hope that someone would finally understand her. "Certainly, Mademoiselle." She drew out a tattered daguerreotype from her apron pocket. A weary-looking woman stared out at the world.

Brianna studied the brown and beige image. "What was her name, Celeste?" Brianna noted the same high cheekbones and heart-shaped lips in her friend's face.

"Madeleine." Celeste brushed the corner of her right eye to stop a tear.

"May I?" Brianna lay the daguerreotype down on the table in a shaft of light. "I haven't ever seen a coat designed that way."

Celeste touched the image. "*Maman* loved this long woolen coat with black braid. A Parisian style some years ago."

"This picture is expensive . . . how could she afford it?" Brianna held her scissors mid-air.

Celeste pocketed the picture, then patted her skirt. "She served as a maid for a wealthy banker in Paris. He bought the picture for her. She saved for me to come to America . . . to *Louisiane.* She wanted a better life for me." A tired resignation emerged in her voice.

"Whatever happened to your father? You never mention him." Brianna saw Papa's mottled red face as he threw plates against the kitchen wall.

Celeste shrugged. "He abandoned Maman when I quite young, so I never knew him." The girl stared into the distance, her eyes vacant.

The memories continued to flicker. Spenser had played the violin on the altar that night. Ambrose would never have known his father either. Brianna blinked them away and continued. "So, managing in Paris was difficult?" She searched her basket for a strip of lace.

Celeste sighed. "Under Louis Napoleon, the people starve." Her voice hardened. "The women of the court strut about in diamonds and change into a new dress every hour. The royals sit at banquets eating course after course, yet the children of France die from lack of food."

"Ah, I see. So it is dangerous to live there now." Brianna measured the lace against the cuff.

"Oui." Celeste swallowed. "My uncle died at the barricades in 1848. Shot down like a dog for simply asking for food. Soldiers left him to rot as an example to the neighborhood."

"How horrible." She pictured a gray corpse peppered with flies.

"And now, Maman, she has the . . . how to do you say it? Her lungs are weak, and she will die alone without me. She is so far away. I doubt I shall ever see her again." Celeste's voice grew thick with sadness.

"You must mean she has consumption. Such pain," Brianna said. She put down her measuring tape and hugged her dear companion.

Celeste pulled away. "But I am much better to live here than in France. Even though disgusting men paw me every night, I am alive. In the stench and filth of Paris, I would die of cholera." She looked up at her.

Brianna caught the girl's upward glance. "I know, I know," she said. "At least here, we have a roof over our heads and three meals a day." The pinch of near-starvation lingered in her dreams.

Celeste fingered a spool of thread. "We are companions of men, but better off than corpses."

Brianna trembled, remembering. "I was almost a corpse once. Do you remember how sick I was when I first came here? After that fiend Galsworthy attacked me? I had just lost . . . everything," she said. She pulled the tissue paper pattern off her trimmings.

"Oui." Celeste paused, her eyes narrowing. "One of the colored susans told us she has seen Galsworthy prowling among the brothels on Gallatin Street. Do be careful. I have heard he killed a frail sister."

"I didn't know." Brianna held up her unthreaded needle. Her throat tightened. Without Edward's intervention, she could have been that girl.

"New Orleans is full of evil men." Celeste frowned. "So is Paris. There are many women even younger with babies," she said. "They squat in the gutters, clutching the infants to their breasts. The babies are too weak to suckle, and so they die in their mothers' arms."

Anxiety gnawed away at Brianna's self-assurance. She murmured as she stitched, "But lucky for you, Paris is in the past, just as Baltimore is for me." She turned the garment over and tied a knot in the thread. She fell silent, wondering. Who was the more dangerous? Galsworthy, the man who had attacked her, or Edward, the man who had bought her for his own use? Although Edward had not insisted on physical relations, someday he may demand it. How could she love someone who had traded for her very person? She exhaled sharply. He was a complex man. Yet he bought her the patterns and encouraged her work. He humbled himself and asked for her forgiveness.

The bell rang out in the dining room, calling them to the noon meal. Brianna repeated Nancy DeSalle's rule out loud to herself: "No one comes late to the table. A skipped meal is a missed meal."

Brianna folded her fabric, placed her scissors on top, and turned to Celeste. "Let us enjoy the meal, thanking God we are here and not in Paris. When I passed through the kitchen this morning, our cook was fixing up chicken with peaches. My favorite."

"Oui. And tonight with the men, I do not have to wear le combinaison." Celeste brightened. Again Brianna watched her friend kiss, then stow, her mother's picture back into the folds of her skirt for safekeeping.

She saw her own mother's face and mouthed a silent prayer.

Thirty

RESISTANCE

As she ate with the girls that afternoon, Brianna considered her own lack of freedom. As in Paris, American society condemned women fallen from grace. Brianna knew that outside the protection of their families, streetwalkers led short, miserable lives. They passed her in the streets, their eyes blackened, their faces pocked with scars. The young and abandoned often died in the streets from starvation or venereal disease. No one came to their rescue.

Brianna would step around their bloated corpses on Bourbon Street during her daily errands for needles and thread, holding her handkerchief against her nose to block the fumes of decay. She could not help but notice the naked girls in brothel windows observing her throughout the Vieux Carré. The painted ladies tantalized men, exposing their breasts, and the men responded by leering and licking their lips. Though she continued to seethe about Edward's claim on her, she realized that without him at her side, she would be among those wanton girls, her future numbered in days rather than years.

Brianna participated in the daily routines of the parlor house with the polished mirrors, high ceilings, and red-and-white-painted walls. She kept silent during breakfast and dinner each day. The chattering doves told stories of violent, disruptive brothels, especially those on Gallatin Street. In time, she learned that the girls at DeSalle's earned a decent wage compared to most prostitutes. Nancy would never tolerate nonsense among her girls; she would cast them out into the street to fend for themselves.

Of course, Brianna earned her room and board through her needlework. Edward kept her as his own woman. He continued to call on her every day, and he made it no secret that he arm-twisted Madame to keep her safe. Every now and then, she overheard him use stern language as he spoke to Nancy about Brianna's care. She noticed DeSalle shrink in his presence, then expand in his absence.

Brianna's own resentments began to fade, and she understood in time that this house offered the best place for her to live, since she was Edward's courtesan, at least in name. As time passed, Edward never made physical claims on her of any kind, and he went to the gambling tables every night.

When she asked Edward why he kept her at Madame DeSalle's and not in his own home, he answered that he lived elsewhere in a spare room, no house for a woman to inhabit when he was gone at night. Many men in the gaming trade had threatened him over time, and Brianna was free from danger at the parlor house. She was content with their arrangement for now.

Thirty-One

⁘ EL DORADO ⁘

New Orleans, Louisiana
September 1850

As one humid Sunday afternoon folded into sleepy dusk, Brianna gazed enraptured at her new puppy. A long-eared Spaniel with black and white patches, he was only two months old, and he slept in Brianna's lap as Edward's open cabriolet bumped over the cobbled streets on its way to Tivoli Gardens. Brianna and Edward would often stroll there under the spreading oaks after savoring ices and riding the carousel. Every now and then, when the driver cracked his whip, she could hear the pup whimper in his dreams.

"What should we name him, Edward?" If only she could control her excitement.

"Well, how about Andy?" An indulgent glint appeared in Edward eyes.

"Why Andy? Is that your friend's name?" Brianna asked.

"For the famous Andrew Jackson who led the Battle of New Orleans, of course."

"You are patriotic." Her mind filled with the vision of their first meeting at Place D'Armes and how dizzy she had been. How long ago her pains of childbirth seemed to be, the tide of memories ebbing, then flowing away into the past.

"I love my dog," Edward said, and winked at Brianna.

"He's not your dog, Mr. Edward! He's *our* dog. Just because you gave him to me doesn't mean you have a right to say he's yours. He is not your slave, too." Why had she said that? She cringed as soon as the words left her mouth.

"You will never forgive that in me, will you?" Edward's jaw clenched.

She leaned against him. "No . . . well, maybe." Was she forgiving him? Or was she just surrendering, tired of fighting her anger? The spaniel yawned, and curled up into a tight ball. Brianna stroked his velvety ears. "This dog likes me," she said. "You know, we had a dog in Baltimore we called Louie the Labrador." She nuzzled the top of his head.

Edward held down his top hat as they went over a rut in the muddy road. "My big Italian family always had dogs. They roamed around and picked up extra bones from the floor. Mama said we did not have to sweep as often since we had them."

Brianna's gloved hand rested on Edward's arm as he slapped a rein on the horses. "Louie heard all my problems growing up. It pained me to see my father kick him when he was angry. The dog would lick any wound inflicted on us." They flew by a lamplighter perched on a ladder at the side of the road. The waters of the Carondelet Canal shimmered alongside their route; fishermen cast their lines from its banks.

"Your family stories are all so sad." Edward shook his head.

He gazed with longing at Brianna, and at times his face warmed with desire. She had grown aware that he found her hard to resist, and each day his attentions increased. Over the months he had told her she was different from any other woman because she embodied the ethereal and the natural. He continued to call her his Madonna. He had frequented many women, painted ladies and demure maids, yet none attracted him the way Brianna did. He told her she made an everyday outing into an adventure with her curiosity and enthusiasm. Each time he told her sweet things, the veil of resistance toward him began to shred, and once again she found herself missing his company when he was gone.

The horses clamped down at their bits. They snorted into the cool air when Edward clucked them over to a hitching post in the park. Brianna bent down to put a red ribbon around the small puppy's neck. Edward cleared his throat, a sign he was getting serious.

She glanced down at him while she stepped down from the carriage. "Whatever is the matter, Edward?" Her green eyes watered; her old fears quickened.

"Brianna, I am going to be gone for apiece. I got Andy here to keep you company." He passed the reins over to a hostler and dropped a coin in the man's palm.

At his word *gone*, her neck stiffened. "You're leaving? When?"

His arm tucked under her elbow. "I am to leave not long after the masked ball to be gone a year or two. I will send you money by Wells Fargo express so you remain safe at Madame DeSalle's. You may continue your needlework while I am gone."

Brianna swallowed hard. Only Edward stood between her and the streetwalker's existence—what would become of her without him? "I don't understand. Why ever would you leave?"

"My friend Giorgio is making it big in the gold fields of California."

"You always talk about how profitable the gaming tables are here in New Orleans, and how you know the territory where you have grown up."

"His latest letter says the tables are hopping in San Francisco."

"Hopping? What does that mean?"

"My largest take of an evening's game in New Orleans would equal an hour's play in the El Dorado." Brianna gripped the dog's leash, her hands hard as iron. For a long moment, she absorbed the enormity of his prospects and the enthusiasm on his face.

"But, Edward, I can't do that. I'm not safe anywhere in New Orleans without you. Besides, I'm not to be kept like an insect in amber." Her stomach knotted.

Edward's brows knit together. "You may be right. I do not own you as you have continued to remind me. Yet I have made a firm decision."

Brianna searched his eyes. "Mr. Edward, is it because we have not been together, you know, in that way? Is that why you would leave me, because if that is the only reason, you know I will always . . ." She moved a step closer to him.

He fingered one of her stray curls. "No, my Brianna. I have been a patient man. And a man who loves a woman is willing to wait. The time will come when you will love me with your body and your soul the way I love you." His lower lip trembled.

An unfamiliar desperation rose in her throat. "But Edward, I cannot live without you. I have gotten used to our times together every day. I love . . . that is, I find pleasure with you. You make me laugh, and sometimes you make me mad."

"It is true. But, Brianna, I cannot wait around for the gold rush to be over. The boom times are happening now. Do you know they pay winnings in gold dust, not in coin? California is brimming with gold. A gambler will win big for life. Do you not see? I will return to you so wealthy we could travel at our leisure for the rest of our lives. I will take you to Paris." His eyes shone, his mood buoyant.

Brianna grasped his arm. "So what shall I do? Where shall I go? I cannot live a day without you. Please . . . please, do not go!" Her chest ached with fear.

Edward reached into his vest pocket and plucked out his white linen handkerchief marked with an *S*. He dabbed her eyes, nose, and lips. Then, he kissed her in front of the New Orleans society out for their late afternoon stroll in the gathering darkness of the evening.

No man had ever embraced her before besides Spenser. Brianna had never had a kiss that carried her into another world as did Edward's embrace. His tender mouth probed the outline of her lips. She felt the soft caress of his mustache, and as his tongue searched for hers, the heat surged from deep within her. She lost track of time and place. Each wave of pleasure led to another, and she wanted him as he had so long desired her. True, he was a different man than Spenser Brown. Where Spenser was tall, Edward was short; where Spenser played music, Edward played cards; but most importantly—where the other had abandoned her, this man yearned for her.

Men had never wanted her before. Father saw her as a burden. Spenser viewed her as an object to be discarded. A sudden realization filled her—this man in her arms gave and received love. Edward showed her what it was to need and be needed in the same way. A thrill coursed through her, followed by an urgent stab. He must not leave her behind.

"Please." She nuzzled his ear. "Take me with you to San Francisco."

Edward cradled her face between his gloved hands. "Let's say I'll think about it." He bent and brushed her cheek with his lips.

"You shall?" she cried, forgetting little Andy at her feet.

"Yes, I will. But don't be surprised if the answer is no. The Panama journey is dangerous and I hear the life in California is unseemly for the delicate flower you are. But I am happy you would like to go with me. I never dreamed you might."

In silence, she pressed her lips on his eyes, nose, and forehead, then settled her head against his chest.

Fine gentry strolling by shook their heads, wondering when this public debauchery among the lower classes would end. A matron glared at them, her plaid crinoline skirt bouncing along around her. Her top-hatted husband snorted in disgust, then lit a fresh cigar. Used to these common sights in New Orleans, they moved on to the next gathering of elites in the evening twilight.

Andy yelped and Edward laughed to see him tangled in Brianna's leash.

Brianna looked toward the variety of cafés nestled under the live oak trees. "He is hungry," she said. "Let us buy some meat on a stick. And Edward, I would like a pear tart with cream in the gardens." She smiled up at him.

"So would I," Edward said. "But my real hunger is only for you, Brianna."

Thirty-Two

LONGER THAN USUAL

Later that evening, Edward stood in the hallway facing Brianna's room, holding her straw bonnet. He rested his hand on the door jamb which was his usual custom during the evening farewell. Tonight their goodnight lingered longer than usual. Ordinarily, she would peck him on the cheek and close the door, listening to his whistling as he left for his next hand of poker. But this time, she stood facing him on tiptoe, and he held a strong arm around her waist. Edward kissed her softly, then with more rhythm and force, thrusting his tongue deep into her mouth as she answered his passion with her own sighs.

"I must put Andy in his bed." Brianna broke away, breathless, leading Edward into her room, and closing the door behind them.

Edward chuckled and followed her. "Andy, time for sleep," he said.

Brianna whistled the dog into his wooden crate, then covered it with her homemade calico quilt.

As Brianna and Edward stepped away from the dog's bed, a shy silence hovered between them. She had always put distance between them as of way of protecting herself, but now she wanted nothing more than to be sheltered in the airless space against Edward's chest, to sense his heartbeat as their lips melted together. She looked into his chocolate eyes, rimmed with black lashes, and said, "I think I love you, Edward."

His eyes grew round, and he drew her to him. He clutched her gently to his chest. "I love you, too, Brianna. I have ever since that first day I saw you when I flipped the double eagle for you. You have spoiled me for anyone else. You have me. All of me."

Brianna unwound his cravat and unbuttoned his vest, his bare chest warm against the palm of her hand. He guided her hand down to his manhood, and she felt it throb and grow larger. He turned her around, facing away from him, and he planted tantalizing kisses on her neck and shoulders, unbuttoning her gown. "I never know which buttons to unfasten." His words glowed with an intense fire.

Edward eased down her garment, untied her petticoats and crinolines, and unlaced her corset, which he pulled off and cast onto a chair. He stood for a moment behind her, his hands smoothing her chemise over the surface of her breasts, then cupping them for a moment.

With a gentle twirl, she faced him, then rested her body before him on the bed.

She watched him undress. She lay with her hands behind her head, waiting with a burning desire for another kiss, his hands on her breasts, her thighs.

She smiled and guided his hands to the proper hooks and laces, then felt him stroke her body slowly and gently, exposing more of her skin as he folded back her chemise, then lifted it over her head. She envisioned herself as a rose and Edward as the sun's rays exposing her petals, one by one.

Edward lay down beside her, his breath coming faster now. "I want to look at you, my love, before I make you my own." He traced her eyes and lips with his index finger, then kissed her deeply. His expert touch and loving hands massaged her breasts, and desire rose in her like a flame. He lay on top of her, and she felt the warmth of his naked skin covering hers.

Brianna looked up to see his eyes dilated with desire. Her fingers disappeared into his thick dark hair. He opened her legs wide with his thighs, and she felt his manhood etching circles into her, delightful circles, playful circles. He held her shoulders, his breath coming faster. He was mature, not childlike. He was a man, not a boy. His fingers found her softness and caressed her sweet spot, then worked slowly into her until she moaned. Then he opened her legs wide and sank into her softness.

"Come to me," she murmured. She drew his hips into her, his thrusting soft at first, careful, then stronger and stronger. She drifted into the river of music, her sighs an echo to his moans as she held his back, allowing his thrusts to take her downstream with him. His kisses were deep, insistent, penetrating. He led her slowly to the peak of desire, pausing now and then to smile at her satisfaction. Then he burst inside of her, unleashing a great flood of warmth, followed by an explosion of colors only she could see.

He remained inside of her, rose onto his elbows, and smiled down at her in silence. "My lovely Brianna. You are mine. All mine. And I am yours and ever shall be." With that he lay down on top of her, careful not to crush her. "I could die right now in your arms." He buried his face in her soft, red-gold curls.

She held him close, allowing his warm body to fill all the empty spots in her darkened heart. "Dear Edward," she said, tears of release wetting her cheeks, "you will never die without me."

He gave a muffled moan. "Oh, by the way, Edward," she whispered a moment later.

"Yes, Brianna."

"Your boots are still on your feet, and I have lost one of my leather pumps."

They shook with laughter and held each other tight.

Past midnight that evening, the curious creaking of bedsprings awakened Emma who slept in the room next to Brianna's. She was well used to hearing a variety of noises from the girls' rooms as they entertained men. But this sound was different. Curious, she grabbed her candle and padded down the hallway to check on her mistress.

Emma frowned. "God forbid she is ill again." She rested her hand on the doorknob to Brianna's room. The moment she turned it she heard a man and woman whispering. She lifted her hand away from the door. "No, Brianna is not sick . . . lovesick maybe, but not ill." She grinned, thinking of Richard's body entwined with her own.

As Emma turned back to her room, she stared into the dancing light of her candle. She had seen that flame in Edward's eyes that same afternoon as he watched her fit Brianna into her finished ballgown. His eyes studied her body, captivated. And Emma observed the flush in Brianna's face each time Edward complimented the dress.

Now seated on her bed, Emma continued to think of Edward and Brianna. There would be time for their love to develop. Brianna had some growing up to do. She had yet to understand the nature of true love and sacrifice. No doubt that in time, Brianna would realize what a special man Edward was, and appreciate the gift he had given her. Patience was a blessing according to her Richard.

Emma crawled under the covers and lay smiling up at the mosquito net. She patted the place inside the mattress where she hid her *piastres* from Madame DeSalle. In a few more years, she would earn freedom for Richard and her son Moses. She had promised them that. Her candle painted lights and shadows on her bedroom wall. Once free, her family would be together forever. She wished that for Edward and Brianna. Freedom to love. The candle wax sputtered as she blew out the light.

Thirty-Three

AN INTERCESSION

The next morning in the darkness of the bricked archway, Brianna missed a step slippery from moss and dampness. She caught herself before running into a laundress lugging up piles of pillowcases, sheets, and towels. A few minutes before in the garden, she'd looked over to see Emma waving to a muscular colored man from the first-floor balcony. This hadn't been the first time. At least twice a week, Emma's signals coincided with the man's visits to the back stoop where he would deliver a vegetable crate marked HALLDOWN PLANTATION. Although Emma's face had been partly concealed behind the shutter, Brianna spied the blown kiss sent his way. Another day when she'd looked for Emma, the maid was nowhere to be found. The time on the grandfather clock in the parlor had said two o'clock, the same hour when the vegetable crate arrived.

Today, she was bound to find out what was going on between the two. She lifted her skirts to avoid tripping, and followed at a distance behind the man through the adjoining courtyard.

The man stepped into full sunlight, turned, and Brianna saw that his left eye was swollen nearly shut. If only she'd worn a hat out there—the sun was too bright, the air too hot and languid. On seeing her, the man tapped his hat with a white-bandaged hand and limped out of the courtyard; his bent burly figure sidestepped the white wrought-iron chaise set out near the fountain.

She struggled to catch her breath. "Sir, please, I am Brianna, the seamstress. May I share a word?"

He turned, sweat pearling on his dark forehead, a wrinkle of concern deepening between his eyes.

"Yes, Ma'am," he said in a low tone. He stood facing her, holding his head down. He clutched his sweat-stained hat in one hand. She noticed a deep scar around his wrist where a chain's link had bitten into his flesh.

"Let us retire to an alleyway where we may speak unobserved," she said, drawing near to him.

"Yes, Ma'am," he repeated again, this time so softly she strained to hear him. He followed her through a narrow passageway. Together they brushed aside the green vines and tendrils opening into a nook in the bricked alleyway where many brothel girls went to smoke and engage in a private conversation.

Brianna ushered Richard behind a brick column supporting an archway. Water dripped from the fountain and laughter rang out from the parlor house. Droplets of air lay damp and clammy on her skin.

A tendon pulsed in his neck, his one large brown eye wide, expectant, the other scab-crusted shut. His back angled forward like the top of a fish hook.

She wanted to calm his worries. "Do not be afraid, Sir. Emma is my maidservant, and I am most grateful to know you as her friend."

He backed a step away. "I . . . I don't understand." He shook his head without looking at her face, almost as though she were invisible.

Brianna took a half-step toward him. "Please, I only want a word. I am Emma's friend and she is an angel to me. You see, she rescued me when I was terribly ill, and she nursed me back to health. If it had not been for her loving care, I would be with God right now instead of here with you." She rested her hand against the column to steady herself from the dizzying effect of the heat.

He plucked a blue tattered rag from his pocket and swept it across his forehead. A loud bang ricocheted beyond the wall between them and the street, and he flinched.

Brianna persisted. "I want to help. Master LeComte of Halldown Plantation. "

"What about him, Ma'am?" He shuffled back an additional step, his eyes wide.

"He had a teacher train Emma to read and write. She told me the story."

Richard's jaw clenched. "Ma'am, I know you mean well, but we're happy the way things be. I see my wife once a day, and that is the most I can hope for in this lifetime.

"So you are Emma's husband?" She'd guessed as much, but now her suspicions were confirmed.

His eyes darted back and forth. "I won't tarry, Ma'am. Must get back to the plantation. The bossman, Mr. Galsworthy, he's a cruel man." He shook his head as though ridding himself of the unpleasant thought.

Now it was Brianna's turn to be surprised. "Galsworthy? Can you tell me more?" She tipped her head to the side.

"Galsworthy. My overseer. He's in love with the lash. I fear not only for myself but for the life of my son, Moses. He kills men for sport, that man." Richard turned to go, sweat forming on his upper lip.

Galsworthy. The scum who had attacked her. Here was another victim of his rampage. She stepped closer, speaking in a whisper. "What if I could help Emma buy your freedom?"

Richard ran a free hand through his damp gray curls. "I've got my son Moses with me. Besides, I got stripes on my back from white folks like you . . . folks who promised good and then turned their backs and watched me take the blame for what they'd done. Why should you be any different?" His tone turned bitter.

"You do not know me, Richard. Yet in time, you will. I will earn your trust. I care for Emma as though she were my blood sister. She is better than a sister to me, for she gives me wise counsel and keeps me from harm. I want to help her . . . you . . . Moses . . . out of love."

A husky voice interrupted them. "Brianna? Brianna?" The voice of Madame DeSalle streamed over from the adjoining courtyard.

Richard winced, his face a web of pain.

Brianna lowered her voice. "I must go. Please do not despair. I would never betray you. Will you promise me one thing?"

Richard leaned forward; his face looked down into hers. "Ma'am, I cannot promise. I do not even own my own body . . . I'm property. Mr. Galsworthy . . . he's been worse lately. He's in a mighty vengeance toward Emma ever since she saw him when he attacked yourself."

"Is that where your bruises came from?"

"Yes Ma'am. He figures he cannot touch Emma, so he's a right to take revenge on me and Moses without Master LeComte doing anything about it."

"Brianna." Madame DeSalle's voice swelled like a balloon.

Startled, Richard's arm grazed hers as he pushed past her and headed out under the arched passageway leading to the street.

Brianna stepped aside, yet she could not let him go without a promise. She matched his quick steps. "All right. At least agree that I may speak with you again when circumstances are safe."

Richard backed away. "It must not be here, Ma'am." More sweat speckled his forehead.

She touched his arm. "Where, then, can I contact you without fear of discovery?"

He chewed his thumbnail, thinking. "Congo Square, the night of the masked ball."

Thirty-Four

THE PRIESTESS

Later that afternoon, Brianna and Emma ducked into the cool shadows of Pirate's Alley as they made their way toward St. Louis Cathedral and the Pontalba building, a new center for shops and restaurants. Brianna had spied a hat shop there once on a previous outing with Edward. Andy pranced alongside her, his blue embroidered leash sparkling in patches of sunlight.

Brianna and Emma lingered a moment in front of the Cabildo, the City Hall, where a wrinkled cake lady offered a bite to Andy. The bells from the Cathedral rang the quarter hour. Brianna couldn't believe her eyes—five or six magnificent white steamboats were churning up and down the river, their red paddlewheels bright against the brown river waters. Two serious-looking bankers in gray topcoats and red cravats crossed in front of them, one checking his pocket watch.

Over the noise of a coach rattling by on the cobblestones, Emma said,

"Miss Brianna, I wish to say a prayer at the cathedral on our way, if you do not mind my doing so."

"Of course I don't mind. I'll light a candle for my . . . uh . . . sister Annie." Her chin quivered as Ambrose's tiny apparition wavered in the ether before her.

Emma said, "Maybe Madame LaVeau will be in church today. We have missed her during our prior visits. You could ask her for a Voodoo cleansing prayer. She may even give you a charm."

"She sounds like a fascinating creature," Brianna said. She would add the woman to her secret catalogue of the weird and strange people in this town. Yet she had no fear of them, like Annie who was never afraid of protecting her from the odd predator.

Outside the cathedral, they stopped to examine the brand new façade, which gleamed a creamy white in the late afternoon sun. Brianna folded her parasol, then shielded her eyes from the glare. A carpenter on a ladder slathered paint onto a wooden beam.

Andy padded next to Brianna into the cool interior, his toenails making a *scratch-scratch* noise. Once inside, Brianna searched the high ceilings for pictures of the saints and the stations of the cross. How she'd grown fond of Emma's trips into the cathedral; there was such peace within its sheltering walls. Every so often, she would hear whispers from the upper galleries, but today her eye focused on the magnificent altar and the many stained-glass images of King Louis of France, which lined the walls.

Where was Emma off to? Brianna followed her to the holy water font, and watched her make the sign of the cross. Together their soft voices repeated, "In the name of the Father, the Son, and the Holy Spirit, Amen." Alongside Emma, she genuflected before the altar.

Today, a Creole woman with deep-set eyes and a heart shaped mouth sat under the gallery to the right of the altar. The many folds of a red and white turban piled high atop her head. A giant statue of Christ on the cross covered the wall behind her. A Creole man perched on a chair before her, and from a distance, Brianna saw her whisper and the man nod at intervals.

Emma spoke in a tone filled with awe. "See, Mademoiselle, Madame LaVeau is giving him spiritual counsel."

"But what is a Voodoo priestess doing here in a Catholic cathedral? Surely the bishop doesn't allow spells and incantations inside a sacred place." She heard an edge to her own voice.

"We are in New Orleans. Our beliefs are ancient. We practice the Catholic religion mixed with West Indian beliefs and practices. They intertwine. The system is peculiar to outsiders, but it is our way. In times past, Madame LaVeau's spells and incantations brought fear to white folks, but now she devotes herself to good works, helping yellow fever patients. All kinds seek her counsel, especially those in painful circumstances."

"Ah, I see. Your city does amaze me. A mix of angels and devils." She made the sign of the cross again for good measure, remembering Father's upright hand as he would complete it.

As the man rose, Brianna noticed a yellow bag and a large Catholic rosary dangling from his hand.

Marie LaVeau's deep voice rippled across the church transept. "Emma, please come. I am bereft we have not been with each other for such a long time."

Brianna let Emma lead, and they threaded their way through the pews over to the side altar. Andy's paws clicked on the marble floors.

When they arrived, Emma leaned down, and the women kissed each other on both cheeks, the French custom.

Brianna lingered behind Emma. She'd never seen such a glorious Creole woman. Marie LaVeau posed in regal splendor on a large seated armchair. Whenever she turned her head, Brianna saw her large looped earrings, multicolored headdress, and white gown capture the angles of the light. The woman's high cheekbones and luminous eyes added to the impression of an African priestess, and Madame LaVeau breathed power and majesty akin to queens Brianna had learned about in the Baltimore grammar school.

LaVeau glanced at Brianna. "Who have we here? Such a crown of auburn hair. And what a charming dog." LaVeau arranged her blue shawl about her shoulders as though it were a royal robe.

Emma curtsied. "May I introduce my mistress, Mademoiselle Brianna Baird."

"*Enchantée*, Mademoiselle," LaVeau said, bowing her head.

"She works as a seamstress for us now at Maison DeSalle." Emma spoke with reverence.

LaVeau's dark eyes gleamed. "Ah, Nancy has taken on another needleworker. Let us hope this young one has talent. That German *frau* from two years past had no sense of design, and the girls wore cargo boxes rather than dresses as of late. Well, I am glad to meet you, Miss Baird. Welcome to New Orleans." She extended her jewel-bedecked hand toward Brianna.

Madame LaVeau's giant palm enveloped her hand, much as a leaf would enfold a lost insect. Those eyes harbored deep chambers, locked, mysterious, a bayou of other worlds.

"Thank you, Madame LaVeau," Brianna said. She sensed danger yet kinship in the woman whose soft eyes beguiled her with their intensity. This woman embodied elements she admired—vision, rebellion, power. She belonged here, now. Brianna relaxed into her presence where she found a tranquil haven.

Emma wandered away toward the central altar, and a kneeler creaked in a pew where she knelt in prayer.

"What is your petition today, little one?" Madame asked. "Sit." Brianna drew a chair next to her, and extended a hand toward Andy. He licked her fingers, and a smile crossed her face.

Brianna sat, the wooden chair wobbling under her. "Madame, I would ask you to pray to my Ambrose for me."

Madame tipped her head back for a moment, then closed her eyes.

She said, "Ah, an intercession. Let me guess . . . is Ambrose a relative whom you have lost?"

"Yes, Madame, he is my lost child . . . a baby . . ." Brianna's hesitated, and she thought death at that moment would mean deliverance from this memory. A hot tear escaped her eyelid and meandered down her cheek.

Madame's eyes opened, and Brianna looked into their dark realms. "Tell me of the story of your loss, my fragile girl." The woman's voice soothed her.

Words poured out of Brianna, water through a broken levee. "I was sent away here, to New Orleans, and when it came time for the baby to be born, my landlady, Mrs. Goulet, helped me. I was in such pain for so many days I lost count. Then, I had the most crushing pains and Mrs. Goulet said he was crowning, and she told me to push hard. I pushed and . . ." She lost her courage and sobs rose inside of her and took her tongue. Andy whimpered as though he understood.

Madame lingered in patient silence. After a few minutes she said, "When you are ready, do go on."

Brianna's words returned. "I saw Mrs. Goulet lift him out of me. She cut his cord and lay him on my stomach. But he didn't move. She swiped her finger in his mouth to clear his airway, but he never breathed. She slapped his back get him to breathe, but he was silent. So perfect, but the life had gone out of him. Mrs. Goulet said he died in the birthing. I knew this to be true since he'd kicked inside the day before." She shielded her eyes behind the arc of her fingers. No one knew the agony she carried, the shame.

A hand patted her arm. Madame said, "You are not alone, Brianna. We are many who have lost a babe . . . some of us more than one as we left the birthing bed. During our many yellow fever epidemics, many are the infants lost to us."

Brianna thought the weight on her own chest was more than she could bear. She lowered her fingers from her eyes. "I want to pray with you. I thought I could find some relief, since the burden is so heavy to carry alone. Emma told me you ease people's pain."

"Yes, and God and his angels are listening, along with your little Ambrose. He is now at home in heaven. Look at the red carpet beneath the altar." She stretched a ring-laden finger toward the sanctuary. "Go on, take a good look."

Brianna stepped over and examined the contrast of the red rug against the white marble flooring. "Madame?" She turned back to LaVeau.

"The red symbolizes the blood of Christ spilling to save the innocents. Underneath the carpet lie the bones of many saints of New Orleans, dating back years to the city's founding."

"Oh?" Brianna's troubled spirits quieted and she resumed her seat next to LaVeau.

"Yes, and many citizens from the last century." The woman's earrings clicked as she spoke. "One is a baby. *Male child Bosque*, say the records."

"When did he die?" An upwelling of tears stung Brianna's eyes.

"All we know is the year, which is 1798. The records in the Cathedral's archives are incomplete. The French and Spanish buried their dead inside the Cathedral walls as a tradition. They continued that custom here in *Nouvelle* Orleans." LaVeau rested her elbows on the chair and steepled her fingers. "The baby's bones are sacred. They rest here in the bowels of the Cathedral to bless all mothers who walk upon its floor. I feel his presence around us, a blessing." She closed her eyes and swayed her shoulders back and forth.

Brianna shivered. A baby . . . alone like Ambrose.

"May I come nearer?" the woman whispered.

She had nothing to lose, so she nodded.

The Voodoo Queen eased to the edge of her chair, her knees touching Brianna's. Her large hands cupped Brianna's face and the warm air from her sweet breath surrounded her. Rather than pull away, a strange force held Brianna there as Madame LaVeau traced her eyes, lips, and mouth with her index finger. Brianna felt her pull a strand of hair off her shoulder where it rested. LaVeau smelled, then tasted it. Then, in low tones that grew louder, the woman moaned a tune Brianna had never heard, its rhythms and cadences mysterious. Yet she knew this song would give her comfort.

Oh my daughter,
The love of the Mother sings for eternity in your soul,
And the love of the lost child echoes in your heart.
Your soul vibrates with the cries of your child,
And with the help of Man God you shall meet and comfort him.
Look around you.
Your babe sings in the treetops on a windy day.
Hear his song in the steam whistle on the Mississippi,
Feel his warmth in a bowl of steaming gumbo.
As you waken in the morning,
The first light through the window carries his little smile to you.
Let his light carry you through life,
Guiding your footsteps into the moments of eternal unity with your son.
Be open to love.
Other loves.
Your man's love.
So Be It.

Madame rested, eyes closed, limp hands in her lap.

Brianna thought she slept. "Oh, thank you, Madame." She made a move to rise.

LaVeau jerked awake, her eyes luminous. She pressed her ring-laden hand on Brianna's knee. "Stay for a while. We are just beginning, little one. Now, we must work harder to ease your pain. The deeper your pain, the deeper the effort. I sense your essence, and that core is deep and dark, full of hidden longings. There is a man who loves you, or is ready to love you very much. You must tell him everything of your pain, the child, the loss. Spare nothing of your story. Only then will you be healed in unity with all living things."

Brianna breathed deeply, measuring the woman's words.

"Now we must bow down to our Creator."

Brianna followed Madame and she knelt by her side on the cool stone floor of the Cathedral. Andy lay down next to them.

LaVeau's voice lowered to a sing-song drone. Soon her voice became almost lullaby-like in its sweetness. She moved her hips; her long arm held Brianna's waist. They wove side to side, their movements like an evening's butterfly flitting among the trees. Their faces inclined upward, their eyes sealed tight.

"Let us pray."

Brianna repeated after her, the marble tile hard against her knees.

Madame's voice echoed within the sanctuary as she continued her petition.

"Man God, reach down your loving arms and comfort this young lost mother, wandering in her bereavement. Pull your saints around you and hover with your angels to make a rainbow that surrounds our lost little mother. Cast your heavenly light into the Vieux Carré and everywhere she walks in your glory. Bring her peace and harmony until you choose to have her join you for all eternity. Amen."

Brianna gazed up at Christ hanging on the cross. She went numb, like that figure on the crucifix, waiting for relief from God. Why would Christ not open his eyes and talk to her? She must be as patient as Ambrose must have been when he died without a sound or a cry.

Madame's fingers pressed a soft object into Brianna's hand. She muttered words over it in a foreign tongue, then sprinkled it with water from a holy water font. Brianna looked down to see a small black bag, held together by string. She guessed it contained lumpy objects, maybe roots and bones.

"Wear this in your left pocket always, until you no longer need it . . . and keep it beside you at night."

"How will I know I don't need it anymore?" A sob gathered in her throat.

"When you no longer feel the emptiness consume you. When you are strong and powerful within yourself. When the loneliness does not take and shred you like a snakeskin. When you feel whole and at peace with God. Above all else, when you are patient with others, yourself, and with love. You are still young. You do not know what lies ahead, just as you never knew what lurked behind when you were a child."

Marie LaVeau held the young woman to her breasts, chanting softly to her in a soft rhythm, a gentle flow that nurtured her and took her deep within her soul.

Sometime later, Brianna heard a voice whispering in her ear. "Brianna, we must go, it is late, and Madame DeSalle will be angry if we do not return to dress for supper."

Brianna blinked up into Emma's downturned face, now darkened by the fading light inside the cathedral. Madame's seat was empty. She rubbed her eyes. "Where is Marie LaVeau? What's happened to Andy?" she asked. A priest with a taper padded about, lighting candles on the altar. Voices muttered from a distant confessional.

Emma said, "We both of us fell asleep. She must have left us a while ago. Andy's here by my side. What is that in your lap? Ah, a *gris-gris*. How fortunate to have it specially blessed by her hands. Come, let me help you up."

Brianna gathered her shawl and parasol, then put the gris-gris in her pocket. "Right or left?" she asked. "I don't remember."

Emma gave her a sidelong glance. "It is always the left."

Thirty-Five

REVELATIONS

The following day, Brianna swept her plaid skirts into Moreau's Hat Shop in the Pontalba as the afternoon sun lowered in the sky. The exclusive shop catered to the upper-crust families and plantation owners of Louisiana. Brianna and Emma eyed men's bowlers and top hats perched on displays in the street's bow window. Behind a counter, flanked by a brick wall in the back of the shop, hat makers glued bands and sewed brims onto top hats.

A short, skinny man in suspenders and a frock coat ambled over from a display table, and bowed down with a cordial smile. "*Je m'appelle* Moreau. May I be of service, Mademoiselle?" He averted his eyes from Emma.

Ignoring his rude behavior, Brianna said, "Well, in fact, I am seeking a fine summer hat for my brother. One that will endure through a southern sea voyage." Edward had told her about the blistering heat and large bugs. Would a hat be enough protection for the Panama crossing?

"Hmmm, Mademoiselle, let me show you several items you may wish to purchase." He guided Brianna to a chair on the red Persian carpet. Emma stood next to her, her hand resting on the back of the chair. She saw Moreau sneer at Emma, his eyes darting up and down her person, then fixing on her scuffed shoes. "Slaves wait out on the sidewalk." His curling upper lip revealed a row of tobacco-stained teeth.

"She is no slave, Monsieur," Brianna said, rising to her full height in the chair. "She is a free woman and my maid." This man needed reminding, no doubt.

"Of course, of course." Moreau's eyes slitted and he fluttered around like a hungry bird. "How could I be so mistaken? Please do sit down."

His high heeled boots scratched at the wooden floor, then vanished through a green velvet curtain into the stockroom.

Emma dragged her own chair over, then settled into the cushions.

Brianna observed Emma staring at her own scuffed shoes. Brianna touched her arm. "What an unsavory man. I . . . I am sorry, Emma. Have hope. California is much more civilized than this." She shook her head in silence. This system of Louisiana laws endorsed cruelty. Even dogs were not safe from kicks on the streets. Slaves' rights vanished with their births.

A bitter silence united the two women. Brianna whispered, "I am saying this hat is for my brother so as not to alert the city as to Edward's intentions of going to Panama. Some of his gambling partners may be willing to play some bad hands if they know he won't be around to collect from them."

Emma nodded. "Men are desperate in this town."

Several hat makers in black aprons pounded top hats and flattened brims at a distant table. A shop assistant wearing a black mourning armband counted coins in the till. Behind the green curtain, boxes shuffled and men muttered. Brianna shifted in her chair. What was taking so long?

Emma's head bowed as though she were deep in prayer. "It is no matter, Mademoiselle Baird. I am quite accustomed to this treatment. Some shop owners dismiss me before they find out why I am there. I carry my papers with me now. I never had to do that before. They say more whites are moving into New Orleans, kidnapping Negro freedmen. Times are changing toward us coloreds." She reached over and tidied a lock of hair on Brianna's collar.

Brianna put a hand on her arm. "I am glad we are here together, away from DeSalle's. We are never able to speak freely together there. Please permit me to ask, have you ever thought of leaving New Orleans?"

"No." Emma's eyes welled with tears. "Where on earth would I go? New Orleans has always been my home. And besides, I could never leave my family."

Brianna envisioned Richard's dark eyes and imagined Emma's son Moses she had yet to meet. She nodded in sympathy, then she murmured to Emma, "What if we were able to take your whole family with us to California?"

"I find that quite dangerous to consider, Mademoiselle. Besides, has Mr. Spina agreed to take you with him?" Her eyes darted around at the clerks and their customers.

"Not yet, but I am working on that. If I were able to convince Edward, why would it be dangerous to take your whole family?" Brianna pulled her chair close so their skirts touched.

Emma continued. "Both my Richard and our son Moses belong to Pierre LeComte of Halldown plantation. I have saved some money to buy them. After that I will petition the court for their freedom, but I am a long way from being able to purchase them both."

"I am sorry." Brianna thought of the pain of leaving a son behind. "Doesn't the son always take on the status of the mother? Since you are free, I think Moses should be, also."

"He is only eighteen years, Mademoiselle."

"I see," Brianna said. "Would you consider taking Richard first, then returning for Moses when you can afford his purchase?"

Emma took in a sharp breath. "I would never take one and leave the other behind."

"Why not?" The green curtains moved between them and the stockroom, yet she paid no mind.

Emma frowned. "Louisiana law does not allow Moses his freedom until he reaches the age of thirty. Twelve more years in captivity."

The stockroom curtains shifted again. This time, polished boots appeared on the other side of the curtains. Moreau was sure taking his sweet time finding their merchandise. Could he be eavesdropping? Brianna chided herself for being suspicious—not everyone in New Orleans was an enemy.

Emma's lower lip trembled. "Galsworthy is their overseer, and he would surely kill whomever remains out of spite." She lifted her chin. "Galsworthy is a vengeful man who has gotten away with many a murder and rape of innocent girls. Mademoiselle, you were not his first victim in New Orleans."

Brianna closed her eyes. "Richard had bruises on his face when I saw him. Was that Galsworthy's doings?"

Emma rubbed her forehead. "That and more torture. Richard tells me of unspeakable acts to him and Moses. I know it is out of revenge for my presence the night of his attack on your person."

The green curtain shuddered again, but this time, no boots.

Emma continued. "I beg your pardon, Mademoiselle. I did not mean to upset you."

Brianna stared into mid-space. "I fear I shall never recover from that night." The Galsworthy attack had been added to her mental list, along with the night she lost Spenser and the night Ambrose passed away. A flutter rose in her belly. If Edward had not beaten the man, Galsworthy might have killed her.

At last, the green curtain parted. Monsieur Moreau and his shop assistant balanced several boxes while they walked out to Brianna and Emma. They bent down and up, stacking the merchandise at their feet.

"*Et voilà, Mesdames.*" The hatter's smooth voice reminded Brianna of the funeral director in charge of her grandma's coffin. Tissue paper rustled as Moreau's thin fingers dug into one of the round cartons. "Here are some selections we might try for the gentleman. Of course, it depends upon the type of sea voyage your brother will take, and his particular taste in hats. May I ask his occupation?" Moreau's nose wrinkled.

"Yes, he is a businessman. He plans to go to San Francisco via Panama," Brianna said.

"In that case, he needs a sturdy, but light headwear that will protect from the wind and the sun. May I suggest this one for Monsieur?" He pulled out a large off-white hat with a wide brim from a red box. The design featured a crisscrossed star pattern within the weave.

Brianna's eyes widened. "I have never seen a hat such as that. Have you, Emma?"

"No, on the streets of New Orleans it would appear a novelty." Emma said.

The hatter whirled away, turning his back to Emma. He leaned toward Brianna and she saw his upper lip curl with an arrogant twist. "Yes, exactly, Mademoiselle. This is a very new hat, quite unique. We in the trade call it the Panama, the *Paja Toquilla*, from Ecuador. We only carry two in stock." He sniffed and blinked twice. "They were very difficult to acquire since most of them are going directly from Ecuador to San Francisco to be worn by the miners during the gold rush." He puffed his chest and massaged his thumbs, first one then the other.

What an insufferable buffoon, yet Brianna was intent on buying this for Edward. She held the hat and flexed the brim. "Well made."

"These fine hats are woven by hand and some take six months to a year to finish, depending on the intricacy of the fiber and design. It is an old, very traditional process, I'm told." He cupped his elbow with one hand and tapped his lips with the other.

Brianna wrinkled her nose. "Are you sure it is sturdy enough to withstand the sailing? And the overland journey?"

His eyebrows rose into points. "Yes, of course. One of the finest he will ever own. The most beautiful. A favorite with my plantation owners. Do you have his measurements?"

Brianna hesitated, searching for an answer. In truth, she'd never thought about measuring Edward's head. It would ruin the surprise. After a moment she said, "Although the hat is for my brother, perhaps you could use Mr. Spina's head measurements. I know he shops here frequently." She stiffened, her corset digging in to her middle. This little man was not only ignorant but irritating as all giddy-up.

"Mister?" He tilted his head.

"Spina." She coughed.

"Mademoiselle, are you referring to *the* Edward Spina?"

"Yes, the very same. After you measure, you may wrap it and charge it to Mr. Spina's account."

"Edward Spina?" he asked.

"The very same." Brianna handed him Spina's calling card. She turned it over and pointed to his permission to purchase, handwritten and signed on the back.

His face brightened. "Ah, oui." He snapped his fingers at the shop assistant standing beside him. "Trigg, bring me my ledger."

"Oui, Monsieur." The young man wrestled the big book into his arms, and carried it forward.

Brianna and Emma followed as Moreau stepped to the back counter. They stood observing him as he ran his index finger down the elegant scrawl of the account book.

"Mademoiselle, I see that Mr. Spina is a customer, and yet I would dread the thought one might take the hat upon pretense of knowing such a fine gentleman."

"I assure you, my word is sound, Mr. Moreau." She inched her fingers forward on the counter.

He bent toward her, his eyes squinting with suspicion. "So I am sure, Mademoiselle, would you mind offering me his billing address? I must see that it matches this one in the ledger. I keep my accounts secure, you see."

Emma whispered the address into her ear.

Brianna leaned back. "Of course. Six twenty-two Conti."

Moreau's face brightened. "Ah, yes, of course, you are correct. Well, then, that is where I shall send the bill." He turned and snapped his fingers. "Antoine, would you wrap the hat please?" He backed away, then turned back to the counter and bent once again over the ledger.

Brianna and Emma trailed him to the main counter, their crinolines waving and bowing against the low display tables as they walked. If only Edward knew what she had to endure in order to purchase a simple hat, he'd be extra grateful for this gift.

A bell tinkled at the door. A well-dressed family poured into the shop. A young girl skipped over to the front table display, at which point her mother called her back to the door. The woman pointed her closed fan at Brianna, blushed, and her husband nodded. They vanished before the apprentice could reach them. The bell resumed its chime.

Brianna stared after them. "Why did they leave in such haste, Emma?"

"Mademoiselle, they know we are irregular."

"But how? They never spoke to us."

Her eyes brightened. "Natives of the Vieux Carré know their own kind. Their families go back centuries, Mademoiselle."

Brianna's throat thickened. She was now a member of the fallen class, no longer of churchgoing society, no matter how much she pretended otherwise. She would forever live outside the bounds of polite company here in New Orleans. Perhaps in San Francisco, no one would care. Please Edward, take her—take them all. She dared to hope.

Moreau broke into her thoughts, pointing to his book. "I have located Monsieur Spina's account. And this is for him?" Moreau scrutinized her from an angle. He ran his red tongue across his lips. Something about the man gave Brianna pause. He was cunning, this one. He reminded her of Betsy Osborne. She guessed he gained business by learning the latest news, then spreading it like a wave across New Orleans. She guessed he possessed more up-to-date gossip than today's edition of *The Picayune*.

"Mmm . . . actually, no. It is for Louie, my brother from Baltimore." Her voice rose as it usually did when she lied. She'd never say it was for Edward. It was meant as a surprise. Besides, the whole town would talk if they thought she was his mistress. Or did they talk already?

Moreau flapped the receipt between his fingers. "Oh yes, yes. My memory is not quite what it used to be."

Her eyes met his. They had the look of black ice on winter's slippery byways in Baltimore.

Moreau's nostrils flared. "How nice of you to choose such a fine hat for his sea voyage. He will appreciate a hat such as this to protect against the intense sun at the equator." A green vein throbbed on his forehead. "Is there anything else for which I can be of service?" His index finger flicked the end of his nose.

"No, *merci*." Brianna tugged the receipt from his hand and Emma secured the hatbox. He bowed them out of the store, and Brianna glanced back. Was he watching them walk away from the shop? His gaze sliced into hers. Between them fear hovered, sharp as a knife's tip.

Thirty-Six

THE SECOND LINE

Brianna and Emma wove their way across Bourbon Street, threading through crowds of colored men and women in a funeral procession, their second line singing and dancing for the dead man carried on shoulders in an open wooden coffin. The bloated corpse, its head melting into a white cushion, led the procession under the hot sun. Deafening trumpets, drums, and crescendos of African chants filled the balmy air. Brianna imitated Emma's footsteps that moved to the beats, two back, then one forth.

No use hurrying across; the faster they walked, the slower the crowds moved around them. Even the tiny children gyrated and leaped to the music. And there was something comforting about the second line. She remembered the cold church funerals in Baltimore, her grandma's lonely coffin sitting between candles on a bier. This was different—a sendoff filled with affection, song, and life.

Once the line released Brianna and Emma onto St. Philip Street, the noise quelled. The tail of the procession veered toward the Saint Louis Cemetery. Brianna put her arm through Emma's and drew her closer as they walked along. "I have one question, Emma. How is it that you are emancipated, but your husband is still a slave?"

Emma shook her head. "I should not have revealed this much, Mademoiselle. God bless me, I have never told my story to a living soul; that is, except Madame DeSalle. She knows. The rest think I am a spinster. If the others discovered I was married to a slave, they may tell LeComte about Richard's visits to me, and then he would never let him off the plantation." Her voice faltered. "Then I would never get to see him."

Brianna stopped on the sidewalk. "So even though you are free, your husband has no rights to his freedom through marriage?"

"Correct. Richard must be purchased, then freed by the court along with Moses."

"So terribly complicated. Emma, California is not slave territory, at least for the time being. With us, you would arrive there with your family intact, and you would have an empty slate. Complete freedom to start over fresh. To build your lives there with our help. No one would know us."

Emma pressed a gray handkerchief to her eyes. "I do not know. I am saving to buy my men their freedom, Mademoiselle. Taking slaves out of Louisiana is a hanging crime. I want them to be free."

"I know you do," Brianna said. Sympathetic tears burned her own eyes. "Please go on."

"I visited Halldown last year to make an offer. Pierre LeComte laughed in my face. He shamed me as I stood below him on his porch steps. At first he agreed to one thousand piastres for the both of them, but now since Moses is eighteen and good-sized, he has upped the price to fifteen hundred. And I have only saved five hundred." She halted and blew her nose.

Brianna looked over her shoulder to make sure there were no listeners. She drew Emma into a doorway of a closed shop, its sign marked AT THE FUNERAL.

"How did you get your freedom? I need to know."

Emma said, "From Master LeComte's father, Auguste. He was a just and fair man, unlike his greedy sugarcane-planting son, Pierre. Auguste let me buy my freedom, so I started making payments in 1835. I think he was grateful to me. You see, I saved his daughter one day after she slipped into the bayou on a fishing expedition. I jumped in and pried her from the jaws of an alligator. He was filled with gratitude, and I was assigned to work in the main house instead of the fields. My master insisted all house slaves learn to read and write to better serve his guests. By 1845, he set me free. I will never forget the day he gave me my freedom paper. We both cried. I was one of the lucky ones. Other women shared my cabin. They were mistresses and mothers like me, but he never freed them."

Brianna said, "One thing I do not comprehend."

"What is that?" Emma tucked a stray hair under her headrag and clutched the hatbox to her chest.

"If the old master let you earn your freedom, why not Richard? Or your child Moses?"

She shook her head "Not so simple. My men were too valuable to let go come planting time. Richard and Moses were to be freed in 1846, paid off by the money I'd given the master. But then old LeComte passed away, leaving my men as part of the plantation's inheritance, rather than noting they were to be granted their freedom.

"He did?" Brianna guessed the outcome. "Do go on."

"So later on, my Richard approached Pierre the son, only to learn that scoundrel had taken all the freedom money I'd given Auguste. Eleven years of my hard-earned piastres washed down the river. Do you know that that rascal Pierre lied and said he had never received the payments from his father? Auguste instructed his son to fill out the deed that would free my men, but he never did do so."

"And I suppose a judge would never hear your complaint?"

"Like I said before, things are tightening up in New Orleans against slaves, freed or not. Many judges are in league with plantation owners."

"Sounds like I have work to do," Brianna said. She set her lips in a resolute line.

Emma gripped Brianna's arm, then loosened it. "Mademoiselle, do be careful. This city is mighty dangerous. And we women have no standing. You are a kept woman and I am a maid. We have as many rights as an alligator without teeth. Many women talk too much and disappear into the Big Muddy. We must keep to our place."

How different Emma sounded when she spoke with the wisdom of a freed slave. Brianna vowed to contemplate the dangers she faced. "I will remember that," she said, blending alongside Emma in the flow of shoppers on St. Phillip, their dreams carried along with their footsteps.

Thirty-Seven

THE LOWER DECK

The next day, the aromas of nutmeg, brown sugar, cream, and morning coffee drifted in the wharf-side air. The clang of bells and shouts of stevedores blended with stomping horses' hooves. New Orleans was waking up. Seagulls stretched their bills as the sun extended its rays down to the riverbank.

Edward grinned at Brianna over his *café au lait.* "All right, you may come with me to the steamboat if you must insist."

"I promise I'll be quiet and look interested," Brianna said. His arm was firm under her laced gloved hand.

"I say, Mademoiselle, sometimes you do turn my heart upside down." He exhaled, then a smile crept across his face.

"I am allowed to ask one question, though, am I not?" Brianna bit her lower lip.

"Yes, I suppose. What is it?" He put on his new Panama hat and turned the brim around just so.

"Why are we going to see Captain Leathers?" She toed a pebble on the ground.

His faint smile spoke of amusement. "I must finalize the bill of lading for the cotton I am shipping to Natchez. He is charge of my inventory."

"So, you do more than gamble?" She smiled.

His voice was firm, guarded. "I have my hand in many things in this town, and I must tie up all loose ends before I leave for California, my dear."

Edward extended his arm for Brianna as she gained her footing. They stepped out from under the cool veranda at the Pontalba, and the tropical sun pressed onto their heads.

"Your walking stick, Edward." She looked around.

He said, "Oh yes, it is no longer by my chair. I wonder if—"

They looked up to see a little Creole girl running away down the street with it toward the Cathedral.

Edward ran a few paces, then yelled, "Stop, thief!"

A policeman on horseback saw the snatch and galloped after the child.

He turned back to Brianna, his eyes wide with outrage. "My best stick. Rather brazen to have grabbed it from right under a man's nose."

"Quite bold, I agree." She followed his gaze down the street. The running child and policeman disappeared around a bend. The heat made lazy waves shimmer through the sunlight. Brianna pulled out her fan from her sleeve and moved it slowly back and forth in front of her. The bit of breeze provided some relief from the suffocating humidity that rose from the steamy cobblestones under their feet. Although the heat in Baltimore slowed her down, the dampness of New Orleans sapped her strength.

Edward continued to peer down the street, then exhaled. "The policeman knows me, so we need not tarry." He pulled his pocket watch from his waistcoat and clicked it open. "Captain Leathers cannot be kept waiting . . . he sails at 1400 and it is 0900 now. Let us cut across the square, my dear, and make haste as we go."

A stevedore steered a horse and cart in front of Brianna and Edward as they stepped onto the gangway of the sidewheeler. Around them, the noise of the wharf was deafening. Captains barked, sailors yelled, lovers cried, stevedores grunted, and horses neighed. The smells of oil, fish, wood, and fresh paint blended in the smoky air.

Brianna heard a voice call out from above, "Well, if it isn't my good friend, Eddie Spina!" She looked up to see the white-coated Captain waving down at her and Edward from the texas.

A few moments later, he joined them on the lower deck. At over six feet tall, white-coated Captain Leathers towered over Edward. Brianna noted his long beard and ruddy cheeks. Extremes of wind and heat, and the battering of hurricanes had left their mark on the sailor.

They shook hands, and the captain bent over and kissed Brianna's gloved hand. "Pleased to meet the lady." His blue eyes twinkled as he removed his gold-braided hat with a blue insignia.

It was hard not to smile in his presence. What a joyful man.

A hand clutched her arm. "This is Mademoiselle Brianna Baird," Edward said.

The captain offered her the crook of his elbow. "Welcome aboard, Mademoiselle; *enchantée.* Let us share luncheon as we oversee the loading of the last bales of cotton. We are bound for Natchez at 1400 hours." He passed a paper marked THE BILL OF LADING to Edward and watched him sign it.

After he put down the nib pen, Edward regarded Brianna and raised his eyebrows. "Luncheon with the captain is not to be missed. What is Giovanni serving today?"

Brianna liked the way Edward took charge and always included her, particularly with new people. A glow filled her as she stood gazing back at him.

The captain smiled. "Today's fare includes smoked oysters, Russian caviar, and French champagne." He led them to the upper hurricane deck where a white cloth and red rose decorated a table. "Please, do sit down while I finalize departure preparations." He disappeared down the ladder to the boiler deck.

The last of the captain's retreating steps left an electric silence between them. Brianna's heart hammered with incredible beats.

Edward's deep, rich voice broke the quiet. "Come here." His full body pressed against hers. She quivered, aroused by the scent of his skin. Then he pulled away, leaving her breathless, and held her out at arm's length.

His gaze raked her from top to toe. "You do look lovely in the green dress I bought you last week. And I do like the extra ringlets scattered about your face these days. A new style?"

Brianna flushed at his attentions. "Edward, I am always beholden to Emma, for she knows how to complete all the parts of my dressing table. I owe it to her."

Edward set out a chair for Brianna, and she half-sat, resting an elbow on the table, the other hand on the knob of her parasol. Now that he had aroused her senses, she struggled to control her own trembling hands. What a marvel. She found herself more attracted to this man with each encounter. He was kind and passionate toward her. His deep, sensual kisses came back to her in memory and she sat mesmerized in the lazy heat, waving her fan back and forth.

A steamboat whistle blasted from the wharf, startling her. Two boats passed by, their passengers waving up at them.

Brianna fluttered Mrs. Morgan's handkerchief in response, then rose and stepped over to the starboard where she had a clear view up and down the river. The boat rocked on its moorings. She held onto the railing and peered out. In addition to the passing boats, three sidewheelers named the *Louisiana*, *Hibernia*, and *Canada* pumped smoke and steam into the air, a mixture of black, gray, and white trails drifting in parallel streams up the Mississippi. Two tall-masted sailing ships caught a breeze and thrust downriver, flags soaring from their crow's nests.

Three figures were hurrying along the wharf toward their ship. Brianna leaned over the side of the boat to concentrate on them. As their blurry images grew closer to her, the outlines emerged: two white-uniformed Ursuline nuns strode toward her, their habits flapping about in the river's breeze. They dragged a small mixed-race girl along between them. Their faces came into focus as they reached the dock. Two holy sisters, red-faced and serious; one mud-streaked girl, squirmy and rebellious. Who were they and what were they doing at this ship?

Edward's voice called out to Brianna, "Have you looked at the opposite bank yet?" He stretched out his long legs and tipped his hat over his face.

"No, but I will." She crossed back to the other side and scanned the riverscape. Many more ships had docked on the opposite shore and on the distant levee; they resembled the wooden toys she and Annie had played with as children.

Dear Annie—she'd be worried sick about her. Brianna composed a mental letter to her sister. She was fine now, nothing to worry about. Annie would wonder about the baby. Best not to lie about Ambrose—she'd tell her the truth someday when they reunited on earth or in heaven.

Brianna rejoined Edward at the table and he leaned over and kissed her cheek. It was hard not to stare at his muscular body, his handsome expression.

He yawned. "I hope the captain comes back soon. Getting hungry." With his elbows resting on the side arms of the chair, Edward fingered the Panama hat in his lap. "We're soon to leave the Crescent City. In two weeks, we sail to Panama from this wharf. Then we cross the Isthmus to the Pacific. At that point, we pick up another ship for the Golden Gate."

"We?"

"Yes, we, my love. You and I."

"When did you decide?" She twisted the tassel on her fan, a wave of excitement coursing through her. Though she was thrilled, she was also frightened. In a way, she had prepared for the worst, but now . . .

"I knew it was *yes* the moment you asked. I merely had to make sure I could book another passage. Otherwise, I would have to send for you, and that would be very dangerous."

"We leave in two weeks? So soon?"

He glanced toward her, his eyes sparkling. "We must not waste time, my dear. Money awaits at the golden tables in Yerba Buena. The amount of riches would make a fool blush, I'm told."

She reached over the table and fingered a rose petal from a bouquet in the vase. "I have hesitated to ask you, because I would not have you think me forward or presuming, but I . . ." She opened her mouth but nothing would come.

He brushed a piece of dust from his lapel. "You may say it without fear, Brianna. I will not have you keep silent when you are bound to reveal your thoughts. If it's about bringing our dog, Andy, of course you may, although the voyage may be harsh for a little animal. Nevertheless, he will be welcome with us."

She gazed into his beaming eyes. "No—although I do want Andy to come, this concerns our dear Emma. She has a husband and a son. Richard and Moses. Slaves on Halldown Plantation."

"Yes, I am familiar, indeed, with Halldown." He brightened. "Old man LeComte was a traditional Creole planter. He spoke only French and harked back to the last century. He had a kind heart, he did. Treated his slaves well, I heard." He paused. "In fact, I remember when he granted Emma her freedom."

"You do?" How fortunate he knew all this—her mind embraced a slight hope.

He nodded. "Even though she was legally married, he gave manumission only to her in thanks for rescuing his little girl Alice after she fell into a lake on the property. Since she was free, she could no longer stay at Halldown. Madame DeSalle knew old man LeComte, and he suggested she hire Emma at that time so she would be gainfully employed."

Brianna searched his face. "Richard and Moses were not so fortunate."

"Ah, they had to stay on under the new master, the younger Pierre LeComte. Not so kind, I have heard. Mean as the devil to his slaves." He gave her a hard smile. "The son of a combunction Galsworthy is the overseer. A cruel pair . . . two peas in a pod." He crossed his arms, a frown darkening his face.

"I fear the *Galsworthy* name, Edward." Her chest tightened. She batted away a fly buzzing around her head. She could still feel the scoundrel's weight on her belly.

Spots of color appeared on his cheeks. "As well you should after what he did to you. He knows he risks a duel should he cross paths with me again, so I have not seen the cussed devil since that day." His lips flattened into a thin, straight line.

"Edward, Emma is saving to buy their freedom, but—" A passing ship's horn cut off her words.

He raised his voice. "Let me guess, she is short of money."

"How did you know?" She rested the edge of her fan against her lips. She'd made an inroad; now would he help?

His eyes focused away on the wooden scrollwork on deck. "I have observed her downcast face the past few years, and I am skilled at reading minds, remember?" He turned and put both elbows on the table facing Brianna. "How much does she need to buy their freedom?"

"One thousand piastres." She picked at her open fan. She regained his face and studied his reaction.

His eyes closed tight, then opened wide. She waved the fan back and forth in silence.

He pressed her. "And . . . another guess . . . you want me to help her buy their liberty so they can all come to California with us."

She snapped her fan shut. "Oh, please . . . could they? It would be beyond our wildest dreams and . . ." Her voice faded into the harmony of voices that composed the music of the river—chants and cries of captains and crew easing in and out of the loading docks around them.

Thirty-Eight

URSULINE NUNS

Within a few moments, Captain Leathers' footsteps pounded on the ladder up to their deck. He doffed his hat, folding his long form into a deckchair next to the table. "Missing your cane? These nuns say they recovered it from some runt who made off with it. Giovanni!" he said.

"Yes, Captain." His cook huffed up the stairs in a long white apron. Behind him, the portly Ursuline nuns hefted a muscular child-ruffian in dirty skirts. The cook's bulbous red cheeks matched the streams of dried blood etched on his smock. "Captain, sir."

Brianna stared, transfixed. Wasn't this the trio she'd seen trudging toward them earlier on the wharf? Whatever were they doing up here?

At the sight of the nuns, the captain sprang up from his deckchair and made the sign of the cross. He bowed. "Bonjour, Sisters, how may I be of service?" His words skittered through the rafters of the wooden canopy over them.

Giovanni wiped his hands on his apron, his bug eyes resembling a Louisiana bullfrog.

The taller of the two nuns took charge. She spoke in French-accented English. "I am Sister Francoise and this is Sister Claire from the convent school on Chartres Street. Our student, Marie, has been brought back to us by Officer McAllister of the New Orleans Police Department."

The little girl ran a grimy hand across her runny nose. She looked up at the nuns, then at Edward. Stiff, thick braids hung down her chest, and twine, rather than ribbon, fastened her hair.

Edward gained his feet and addressed the group. "Yes, indeed, that is the little rounder who stole my cane and was playing a game of mumblety-peg by aiming it at holes in the street. Quite so."

The other nun produced the cane from under the white folds of her layered habit, her rosary beads clacking as her pleats dropped back into place. As though prearranged, she placed the walking stick into the grubby hands of her charge.

"Come here, young one." Edward reached for the little girl's arm while the nuns propelled her forward. He kneeled in front of what appeared to be a child of eight or nine. After fingering the girl's hair out of her eyes, he took her hand in his, removing the cane.

Her brown eyes gleamed round and large, reflecting the river water's light.

"Go ahead," said Sister Francoise. "Tell the gentleman you are sorry for what you did."

"I am very sorry, Monsieur. I have prayed to Mary and Jesus for forgiveness, and now I shall wax the convent floors for three days as a penance. I . . . I only . . ."

"What? Go ahead." Edward nodded encouragement.

Marie sighed, her grubby hand itching a patch of hair. "I wanted the cane to play with. I have no toy, you see, and your cane would come in handy for stickball, or javelin games."

"Yes, it would," Edward rose and looked down at her, his hand remaining on her shoulder. "But unfortunately, it does not belong to you. Someday after you have waxed enough floors and listened to your teachers at the convent, you will have your own house and your own toys."

Her voice grew louder. "My house burned in a fire, along with my parents. On Lake Pontchartrain. I lost my brother and sister also. My dolls and toys are gone." She shivered, even though the sun made gumbo on the river.

Brianna, the captain, Giovanni, and the nuns encircled Edward and the child.

Was there more Brianna would learn about this complex man? There was an eagerness in his eyes that told her he truly enjoyed being with children.

Edward pulled a gold coin from his vest pocket and slid it into the urchin's hands.

He spoke with mock severity. "Do you know what they call this coin?"

The little girl shook her head; a halo of greasy hair framed her cheeks. She could use a lice comb and a long bath.

Edward grinned at her. "The double eagle. It is a special coin made at the Old Mint. Only very important people carry this coin. It has special importance to me since it brought me to someone I love very much. Do you understand, little one?"

She nodded, then cast one braid over her shoulder.

He pressed the coin into her hand. "Now, I want you to give this to the Sisters for safekeeping. I will ask them to buy you a doll or bat for your games. No child should grow up without a toy, for childhood is brief and yours has been sad, my dear."

Brianna caught the captain wiping his eyes with his red neckerchief. Giovanni cleared his throat and squeezed his eyelids together. The nuns kissed the crucifixes on their rosaries.

Little Marie ran her index finger over one side of the coin, then the other. She turned to the nuns. "Look what the nice man gave me, Sisters. Did you hear?"

"*Oui, ma petite.*" Sister Francoise held the child against the folds of her skirt. She turned to Edward, then to the group. "Your generosity will be rewarded in heaven, Monsieur. This money will buy our Marie a toy, and the rest we will deposit in her account at the orphanage."

The nuns turned to the stepladder to descend to the lower deck.

Little Marie held out the coin and examined it again. "You have made me very happy." A smile broadened her sooty cheeks.

"*Au revoir, merci,*" the group chimed, and the tops of their heads bobbed down the stairs.

The captain whooped. "We must celebrate your generosity, Spina." He gestured to Giovanni. "Bring up champagne, and the oysters you've been roasting in garlic. Also, some of that Beluga Caviar from Boris Tkachoff, captain of *The Volga.* Oh, and have Lapham polish up that cane."

"Aye, aye, Captain," Giovanni said. He waited, seeming to know there would be more.

The captain surveyed the ships tied up on the wharf before them. He pointed to a vessel whose sides rubbed against the dock. "My friends, that is the Russian ship docked here all winter. He savors our pickled pig's feet, so we must delight in his caviar. Giovanni, also bring up some hard bread from the galley, and we'll be set."

Giovanni's throaty voice sounded. "No crawfish? I have them boiling just the way you like them."

"Very well, Giovanni. Bring it all. We will give the lady a feast. From the looks of it, she could use some fattening up." He winked.

Brianna did not take offense. She grinned at his grandfatherly ways.

The cook's fleshy form struggled down the ladder.

The captain watched, grinned, and scratched his beard.

Edward asked, "Giovanni has been faithful to you for how many years, Captain?"

"Ah, I would venture twenty years. We met fighting pirates off Florida, and since then, we have been in business. Could not be without him. He keeps me sober . . . too much rum and I would fall overboard. He and Lapham the engineer work like well-oiled pistons." He crossed his leg and looked toward the ladder. "I'm getting hungry." He scratched an armpit. "So, when do you leave for *Californie*?"

"Two weeks, Captain. No sooner, no later." Edward said.

Brianna's stomach fluttered. Only two weeks before their big adventure. Could she wait that long?

The captain's broad face brightened. "How many in your party?"

Edward flashed a smile at Brianna. "We aim to be five of us and a dog."

The next day, Edward whooshed into his father's office marked FOREMAN at the Algiers Point Shipyard. The wind slammed the door behind him and panes rattled in the windows. "Santa Maria, going to pour down any minute, Papa." Edward slicked back the hair that had fallen into his face during his trip over from the wharf. This visit filled him with dread and love. Dread that he would need to reveal more than he wished of his private life, and love that continued to grow as he reflected on life without his father.

"Those waves." His father pointed at them with a pencil, pausing from his ledger. The mud murk of the turbulent river rose up into the flowing current, alternating waves of sepia and ochre. Out the window, a flash of lightning pierced the black sky, followed by thunder bellowing a resounding complaint. He reached over and lit a whale-oil lamp.

Edward's voice rang tender. "I see by the dark circles under your eyes, you have been working too hard, Papa." He put his hands on his father's shoulders, then bent down and kissed the top of his balding head.

His father's coal-dark eyes brightened. "How are the tables treating you, my son? I want you here to work with your brothers, but by your dress, I see you have been doing well at your games of chance." He shook his head and tucked the pencil behind his ear. "Even as a lad, you beat us all at our card games." His gaze moved out to the river. "I had always hoped you would take your talent for strategy to help me here at the shipyards. A master builder uses those talents, and sometimes the risks are even greater, my son." He sized up Edward. "Perhaps you have had a turn of mind and are here for a position?"

Edward chose his words carefully so he would not hurt him. "Papa, I am here to ask a favor; actually, to make a business proposition. You remember the extra marine steam engine you told me you had on hand during the summer?"

"Yes, the yard clerk has stored it away in the building over there." His father removed the pencil from his ear and pointed out a low, squat building now drenched in the pouring rain. Men in slickers and boots covered the sawpits with a tarp, after which their yellow coats disappeared into a door marked MESS HALL. "I have run an advertisement for it nigh on three months in *The Picayune*, with no takers." He swiveled on his stool and regarded his son. "Have you a buyer for me, Edward? If so, you would do me a great kindness to relieve me of the burden. We are short on construction space, and the master builder has a mind to enlarge the storage building to include space for a blacksmith's shop."

Edward anchored the tips of his fingers on the edge of his father's desk. "As a matter of fact, I am the buyer." He watched the raindrops pelt the neighboring roofs, bouncing off them onto the ground. He gave his father a sideways glance.

The elder Spina chewed the end of his pencil. "Son, you've said some strange things, but this is puzzling. What on earth would you do with a steam engine in a gambling hell?"

"I want to use it to lure another buyer into making me a trade. I know that he is . . . or will be . . . prepared to negotiate."

"Aren't you a bit hasty?" His father scratched his head with the tip of his pencil. "Who is this . . .er . . . second buyer you have in mind?" His thick eyebrows knit together like a wool sock.

Edward shifted his gaze from his father out to the waves. "Let us say he is a large property owner."

"A plantation owner? Do not lie to me, son. What would a plantation owner need with a marine engine? Why this sudden urge to make this trade? Trade for what?" His father shifted in his chair. "Besides, you told me upon our last meeting that you were bound for San Francisco. This sort of business seems a bit out of your league." He tapped his pencil on the ledger.

Edward peered down into the coal-black depths of his father's eyes. "I am to sell the machine so he may use it to press cane. In return I will gain two of his slaves. I plan to free them and take them with me to see the elephant."

"Ah, I see." His father gnawed the end of his pencil. "So these slaves, I take it, are to assist you with your endeavors in transit?"

"Yes, Papa." He remembered many of these conversations from childhood when his father would pick apart his requests for new toys, then buggies, then money for trips away. Edward paused, waiting for his father's next probe.

"And there must be a young lady involved. In my experience of raising nine sons, there has always been a woman involved. Eh . . . it's always love, they say, in Genoa."

Edward grew warm as he imagined Brianna's light freckles, her upturned nose. "Yes, Papa, I am in love. She rivals the beauty of the *Madonna of the Pomegranate*." He would never forget a single detail of that face.

"Ah, I see." His father leaned back and put his hand on one knee. "It is your business, my son, for you are thirty-two. Yet it is my place to urge you to act on your behalf, not the young lady's. Make sure you will not be taken for a fool in these matters.

Edward fingered his damp lapel. "Papa, I truly want this, and I have no fear that the man would give me a bum trade."

His father nodded, then rose and reached out a hand. "Then, son, you have my ultimate blessing in the matter. By the way, is matrimony in store? You are, after all, of an age to start a family." His gaze was calm, expectant.

Edward absorbed the generosity his father's eyes and a longing came over him. This man had guided him all of his days. In a lifetime away in California, chances were high he may never see him again. He swallowed hard.

Papa walked him to the door and they kissed on both cheeks as was their Italian custom. The rainstorm stopped as suddenly as it had started, so typical in the Crescent City. Black clouds washed away; now light-blue skies and palms and magnolias set free the raindrops in light winds that gave breath to the city below.

Thirty-Nine

PROFIT AND LOSS

New Orleans, Louisiana
September 1850

A week later, late evening draped the French Quarter in hues of dark blue and gray. Celebrations were winding down after the masked ball. Masks of red, gold, and bronze festooned shop windows. Heavy rains left giant puddles in the dung-laden streets, and as Brianna and Emma wended their way through the neighborhood, Brianna's day dress grew damp and Emma shivered in her thin, apron-covered maid's dress. Water soaked their thin-soled ankle boots.

Brianna followed Emma's gaunt form, and she was grateful to have a guide into the exotic world of African-Caribbean custom and practice that laid sway in Congo Square. Drunken sailors leered at Brianna on the street, and she batted away one pesky youth who reeked of whiskey. Small boys and girls ran the byways, picking up sticks and swinging them at one another, imitating Punch and Judy. A lamplighter frowned down at them from a rickety ladder in the road. From time to time, a husky matron appeared at a window and her French patter summoned a wayward child home.

Emma's breath came fast as they walked. "Does Mr. Edward know you are away in the streets?" She ducked under a low palm branch hovering over the sidewalk, and she lifted it up for Brianna to pass behind her. They stepped around a dead dog embedded in the mushy ground of Dauphine Street, passersby oblivious to the smell and the crown of flies nursing on the swollen corpse.

She held onto Emma's arm. "No, I have chosen to tell him at another time. Right now, he has enough to do with our departure coming nigh. He must tie up the loose ends of his many affairs in the Crescent City. I do not want to worry him further. Plus, I consider it somewhat an adventure. After all, we must get used to taking risks, Emma."

Brianna paused and looked up at her. "We shall certainly be in a stranger's land in Yerba Buena. The town is dust surrounded by water I hear, and there are very few women there. You and I must gain our strength before the journey."

"Let us hope we are up to the task. Ah, here we are," Emma said.

As they rounded the bend onto Orleans Street, the public square loomed across Rampart Street. Brianna had expected a prim park with box hedges like those in Maryland. Instead, the tangled silhouettes of live oak branches sheltered shapes that moved and swayed to drum beats on muddy ground. The flambeaux and torches held by the colored people in the square gave an eerie glow to the proceedings, and Brianna crossed herself as she had seen Emma do.

Father would not approve of this Catholic tradition. He considered it heathen, but then again, she was free of Father now, wasn't she? That was what fueled her distaste for Richard and Moses's enslavement—she had burst through her own shackled life. Of course, she'd lost Ambrose in the process, but he would always be with her. She felt for her gris-gris bag in her top petticoat pocket. Taking it out, she held it to her chest and prayed for her baby's safety as he crossed through the gates of heaven and met God.

The humid air smelled dank and putrid. The scent of decay permeated the air after the rain—the rot of garbage in the streets, the rot of feces laid waste, the rot of the dead and bloated drunks lying in the road. Her heart beat faster. Congo drums resonated in her ears and vibrated in her soul. The drums hypnotized listeners, and the closer she and Emma advanced, the more powerful the pulsating thunder. Crowds surrounding them bobbed their heads and moved their hips, absorbed in the chants and rhythms of the percussion. *Bo, bo, bo, bo, bum, bah, bah, bah, bah, oh ya, oh ya* resonated through the air.

As they approached, men and women of all shapes bowed and rose; their bare arms floated up and down in time with the music. Small children in their mothers' arms bobbed their heads in harmony with their mothers, wearing multi-colored headrags. An old wizened Creole, with wrinkled slits for eyes, sang and jerked to a strange music all her own. To her right, Brianna spied Richard playing a large drum, eyes closed. His large hands tapped the drum skin in soft beats, then pounded loud, powerful center beats. As Brianna adapted to the rhythms and the movements, her spirit flowed with the harmonic sounds.

Emma danced her way over to Richard and murmured into his ear. His lips moved, and a grin spread across his face, his white teeth flashing a laugh in the darkness. He handed the drum over to a young man standing behind him who continued the same persistent rhythm in his place.

Richard guided the women a distance away from the dances. In the contrast of a quiet palm grove, the call of bullfrogs signaled the night beyond the trees. He took a red handkerchief from his pocket and wiped the sweat from his forehead.

"You came, Mademoiselle Brianna." He glanced at Brianna's skirt rather than at her face. Slaves kept to their place.

"Oh, yes, I would not let you down." Brianna stepped toward him. "Are we safe here? I mean, are you safe here . . . this far from the plantation?" She noticed a crimson gash on his neck. The wound looked to follow the path of a whip. This had to be Galsworthy's work, sickening in its familiarity.

Richard's spoke his soft, measured words in the darkness. "We slaves are allowed to drum and dance in Congo Square. It's the only place in New Orleans where we congregate. It's an ancient tradition here, and the night watchmen don't meddle with us. Plantation owners know we're here. We're free here to speak as we do."

Brianna continued. "Richard, Mr. Spina has agreed to help Emma buy your freedom . . . that is, for you and Moses." A bat's wing cut into the darkness above her, and she cowered for a moment.

His eyes narrowed, his voice lined with terror. "Like I told you before, Mademoiselle Brianna, I fear the master and his overseer. They're up to no good and we're lowly to them, something like a grain of salt."

"Richard, Mr. Spina and I will be at the plantation soon, sometime next week. You and Moses must be ready to leave. We will pay Monsieur LeComte your bond, then we will fetch you and Moses. We must then hasten to the Presbytère, where we will submit your freedom papers to the judge."

Richard put his hand on his wife's shoulder. "Emma, is this true? 'Cause if it's not, Mademoiselle, you're more cruel than Mr. Galsworthy who carries the whip in his hand." His eyes reflected the torches in the distance.

Emma focused moist eyes on her mistress. "Mademoiselle Brianna, I need a moment alone with my husband."

Brianna tiptoed away and settled on a stone bench illuminated by the distant light. It was up to them now. A large flying beetle brushed her cheek, and she swatted it away with her fan. Through the trees the lights of the Creole cottages shone in the Vieux Carré, and the streams from torch flames illuminated the revelers.

Nearer, the percussive beats continued in Congo Square, and her heart kept time. Her hand reached up to feel the vein pulse in her neck. The drums reverberated in her bones. She wanted Emma and Richard to be happy, to be joined as one. Every couple deserved that one chance.

Emma and Richard conferred in the shadows, their hands entwined. Brianna's heart fell as Richard shook his head. She feared he had decided not to take the risk. Then he stretched out his arms. Emma drew him near and they hugged and danced a waltz of their own making.

After a spell, they returned to her, and Brianna stood, fearing the worst. "What have you decided?"

Richard's wide smile gave his answer away, followed by a long sigh of contentment. "I'm about to give it a try. For Emma and for Moses. It's worth risking my life, just to see my son taste his freedom. And California. Well, Mademoiselle, that's a dream my old soul would like to see." His cheeks caught a glimmer of light.

She sighed and clapped her hands. "Good. Richard, when I saw you shake your head, I figured you were saying no. I cannot be more pleased you are willing to take the chance for freedom. Now, I must return to Madame DeSalle's to commence packing my trunks for the journey. Emma? Say goodbye to Richard. Remember it is not farewell, only goodbye for now. We will see you within a few days' time."

Their footsteps carried the rhythms of Congo Square back to Madame DeSalle's and into the ether of sleep.

Forty

MINT JULEP

Four days later, Brianna straightened her wind-swept bonnet. Edward guided the mare leading their trap off the river road into the shady groves surrounding Halldown Plantation. They stopped for a ribbon snake undulating across the road, its black and white stripes lending an elegant formality to the otherwise dusty byway. She turned her head in time to notice a brown marsh rabbit sit up, alert, in the deep grasses of the adjoining field, its small, mouse-like ears pricked in her direction.

A dark thought intruded on the beauty of their surroundings. "I am nervous about the possibility of seeing Mr. Galsworthy on the estate. Aren't you?"

Edward's lips formed a grim line. "Galsworthy wouldn't dare do anything to us. From what I know, LeComte is a harsh master, and he would frown on Galsworthy's bringing scandal of any sort to his plantation."

He pulled in the reins, letting them out slowly to guide the horses around a cypress rooted in the middle of the road.

She brushed aside the Spanish moss that hung in silver strands from the tree. "I still don't trust him after what he did to me and Emma. And after all the other stories the girls have told me."

"Stop, my dear. You're preoccupied with matters that are either rumor or in the past. I'm here now." She felt his gloved hand enclosing hers.

A carriage house emerged on the left. Edward lifted Brianna out of the coach and set her feet on the graveled path. He gave her a light kiss on her forehead. A tall slave appeared in high boots, and took the horses' reins, unhitching, then leading them into the barn for water. Pushing back the brim of her bonnet, Brianna stared upward at the two-tiered white columns bracing the floors of Halldown's grand mansion. Then she surveyed the avenue of live oak trees, their moss-draped branches shrouding a wide path down to the river landing.

In the distance, miniature steamboats plied the riverways between other Louisiana ports, cities such as St. Francisville and Natchez. The sunlight sprinkled a soft glow on the scene, as if filtered through Battenberg lace. Edward took her elbow and led her up the brick stairs onto the lower portico where Pierre LeComte and his wife Mathilde met them in solemn stiffness.

After LeComte shut the plantation doors behind him, the portly gent extended his hand in greeting and Brianna returned the handshake. She drew in her breath and let it out, bit by bit. LeComte guided them out to the porch. She had a powerful realization—of course they would not be invited inside. A plantation owner could not afford the scandal attached to a dalliance with a gambler and a prostitute under his own roof.

As was customary for southern gentility, his wife Mathilde offered them a mint julep. The lady of the house waved her hand at a white-aproned colored girl who curtsied and went inside. Tall and gaunt, she drew an ornate Chinese fan from a loop on her wrist and flapped it open, her hazel eyes steady as she stood with prim serenity by her husband's side. Brianna gauged the woman. A plantation mistress would endure their low company but for a moment; to engage further would tarnish her society.

The straw chair creaked as Brianna nestled into it. Bees buzzed nearby, and a sweet scent wafted from the spray of red roses cascading along the railing. An ivy tendril wound itself around a Greek column in the corner of the porch. The moist air lay heavy under the live oak branches. Brianna perspired; the wetness sheathed her back. Soon the usual drip of sweat streamed under her laced corset. Yet she held still, her back straight, her eyes alert. Brianna sensed that every movement and word mattered here. *Hold yourself close*, Edward had told her. And that she did.

Pierre LeComte nestled back in his straw top hat and blinding-white suit. then crossed his legs. "So, Mr. Spina, to what do I owe the honor of your visit . . . that of you, and the lovely . . . er, Mademoiselle . . ." He shifted on his heel toward her, a wary gleam playing in his eyes.

"Baird," Edward said.

"Ah, so this is Miss Baird?" His eyes remained transfixed on her face until she looked away in discomfort.

Why did he look at her with suspicion? Or was it disgust? Her stomach constricted, but she held her gaze steady and her face matter-of-fact. LeComte's disdain would only strengthen her courage. Besides, was it disdain? Plantation owners often frequented brothels—Celeste had told her so.

The mint juleps arrived, and she sipped the fragrant liquid. Grains of sugar pearled at the edges of her fluted glass. Something told her to be attentive; she was no match for strong drink on a hot day. Father's whirling and dipping figure appeared in her mind.

The men got up, lifted up their drinks, and strolled away down the length of the open porch. They slid into two chairs in the distance. She resisted the urge to get up and go with them. If she stayed here, alone with the mistress, she'd lose her protection. The thought gnawed at her confidence.

Mathilde LeComte settled into a white wicker chair across from Brianna. What now? The mistress extracted a ball of yarn from a basket sitting there. She wound wool strands around her knitting needles, at work on the pink sweater in her lap.

Their strained silence spoke of distance and class. Brianna eased her fan from her pocket, and her eyes followed its painted red flowers as she waved it back and forth through the humid air.

Brianna disturbed the silence. "What does one do to stay cool on a day like today?" she asked. Might as well be amiable in the situation. The men would finish soon enough.

Mathilde sighed, and rolled her eyes. The prospect of conversation with the wretched appeared a trial too difficult to bear. The needles clicked as she knitted, then purled the yarn.

Brianna crossed her legs at the ankles, and having nothing better to do, sipped from the mint julep. She took a risk, fully expecting Mathilde to ignore her. "I see your husband is wearing a handsome hat in this weather."

Mathilde did not look up. "Ah, yes, but I can't get him to adapt to the latest style, like the Panama your . . . er . . . Mr. Spina is sporting today."

Since the woman was interested in fashion, Brianna probed. "Where do you buy your husband's hats?"

"Moreau's Hat Shop." Mathilde's clipped words emphasized her prominent social standing.

Brianna swallowed to quell the excitement building in her voice. "In the Quarter?"

Mathilde raised the knitting needles an inch. "Yes. Moreau was the hatter to Pierre's father as well."

Brianna continued. "So, you have known him for many years?"

She gave Brianna a sideways glance. "As long as I've known Pierre, which goes back to childhood. I think Moreau's family establishment was founded the eighteenth century. The oldest hat shop in New Orleans, without a doubt." Mathilde reached down for another ball of yarn.

Brianna's eyes followed the woman's fingers as she unwound the yarn. "I recently purchased a hat for my brother at his shop." Might as well continue the white lie.

Mathilde tilted her head. "What kind, may I ask? He trades in very high quality." Her eyes flitted over Brianna's attire. "I'm a bit surprised he would sell to your sort, my dear."

Brianna flinched, but went on. "He sold me a Panama hat." Brianna imagined Edward under a palm tree wearing that hat.

The woman's eyebrows climbed a half inch. "An excellent choice." She sniffed as if to purify the air she breathed.

Brianna considered her situation. If she touched the gris-gris bag in her dress pocket, would the woman go away? She slid her hand into her pocket and wrapped it around the soft silken material. The delicate bag gave her a strange sense of hope that transcended this petty woman's beliefs. Suddenly, it no longer mattered that she was a seamstress from a brothel. She and Edward were here on a mission for freedom. Her own discomforts were not important; instead, she needed to use her head.

Mathilde knitted on in stony silence, marred only by an occasional snap as a flying beetle bounced off a windowpane on the side of the house.

Brianna shifted in her chair and looked down at her own kidskin bottines. She'd keep mud from soiling the Turkish satin laces and bow. The little dirt under the heel would come off as she walked. The heat was paralyzing in its intensity. With her free hand, she lifted her fan from where it lay on her lap, and resumed sweeping it back and forth, her slow, languid movements fruitless against the heavy air.

After those few moments of strained calm, Mathilde stopped her work and stood. The yarn basket creaked inside her arms. "I must attend to some letters. Please forgive me." She brushed her buoyant yellow skirts into the house, her maidservant following close behind.

Brianna whispered, "Thank God and Madame LaVeau." She released her gris-gris bag and set it back into her pocket. She wouldn't know what else to say to Mathilde LeComte, even on her deathbed. Sakes alive. The woman's cold demeanor gave her shivers, even in the bayou's heat. She inspected the depths of her julep. The pastel swirls reminded her of St. Paddy's day in Baltimore, where she had marched in the parade with Annie. Bright green—summer green. After a few sips, her head swam. A few more gulps made her sleepy in the heat. No matter now. No one to impress.

Forty-One

A GRAND SCALE

In the distance, Edward engaged in heated conversation with LeComte. At times, Brianna overheard mention of *Miss Baird*, but she paid no mind. She tucked her fan back into her pocket, got up, and left the half-empty glass shimmering on the side table. Leaning on her parasol to keep steady, she aimed for the porch railing where she had a good view of the men. She strolled from bush to overhanging bush, pretending to examine the lush greenery surrounding them.

The men rested under a side porch entwined with ivy. Sun and shadow crisscrossed the lattice work. After a spell, LeComte's words rang out. "How do I know you are a man to be trusted? You appear out of nowhere, making an offer to trade a steam engine for my expert rope maker and his son. How do I know you do not plan to employ them at Madame DeSalle's, under her direction?" LeComte puffed from his pipe.

Edward's tenor voice answered, "I assure you as a southern gentleman of New Orleans, the offer I make to you is sound."

Brianna tiptoed within earshot and got a clear view through the lattice.

LeComte picked his teeth with his fingernail. "What makes you so interested in Richard and Moses, when I have other slaves equally skilled?" He blinked at the smoke from the pipe, then out in the direction of the fields.

Edward stretched his legs in front of him. "I need your rope maker and his son for a new building project I wish to start in San Francisco. I would rather employ my own craftsmen than rely on finding men when I arrive. They overcharge."

"So, what would I gain in return?" The flesh waggled under the master's chin. "You would rob me of two of my best slaves. What would you offer in their place?" He stopped to tamp some tobacco into his pipe.

Edward delivered his words with a smooth determination. "I knew you would be of that mind, sir. As a speculator, I am always ready for the next question. I can offer you a brand new steam engine that will crush your cane. We have it in my father's shipyard, delivered this summer from New York. Think of how many slaves that would replace." He leaned back in the chair, a half-grin on his face.

LeComte gave Edward a keen gaze. "I already have a steam mill. How is this better than what I already have?" He twisted a large diamond on his overstuffed pinkie finger.

Edward rested his hand on his chin. "The answer is not that it is better, although I would venture to say that the quality of this engine is of the highest in America. No, what I offer will expand your field of operations."

LeComte eased forward in his chair. "Make yourself plain, Spina, for I have little time to waste." His words flared with impatience.

Edward unfolded a drawing from his waistcoat pocket and handed it to LeComte. He moved his chair closer and pointed at the illustration.

"You see, Monsieur, instead of crushing the same amount as you are able to mill today, this engine will add productivity, increasing your profits by at least half. You will be the envy of every plantation in the South."

LeComte examined the drawing, fingering the wattle of skin under his chin. His voice rang with doubt. "And how, may I ask, would I accomplish that feat?"

Edward's tone was firm. "You could produce sugar faster and on a grand scale. Instead of using slaves in production and milling, you could plant and tend more cane. I saw many of your fields lying fallow on our buggy ride here. Those would be full and thriving with cane should you agree to take the steam engine for your boys."

"Hmmm." LeComte angled his head. He studied the diagram. Pipe smoke lingered like a phantom above his head.

After a moment, Edward said, "I could have your steam engine here by barge at the end of this week."

LeComte's tight expression relaxed into a smile. "In time to mill the cane in my northwest field."

Edward sat back, absorbing LeComte's reaction. He continued, "If you need a bill of lading to ensure my word, I will have my courier place it in your hands no later than tomorrow morning."

LeComte inclined his head, deep in thought. The steady hum of insects filled the silence. Then he spoke. "I must admit, I find your offer enticing." His stout fingers tapped the diagram. His pipe lay on its side on the table. White smoke continued to drift from its chamber.

As soon as she was sure they were going to seal the bargain, Brianna indulged her growing curiosity. What were the workings of the plantation like? This was a good time to slip away. She'd always wondered if the fields stretched away for miles, the cotton-pickers struggling under sacks of cane, as the stories said.

From the corner of her eye, she noticed Edward look up to see her gliding away from them. He checked his pocket watch, then tucked it back into his vest pocket. He called out, "Brianna, do not go far since we aim to depart soon enough."

She clicked open her fan. "I want only to catch a bit of breeze is all, Edward." She followed the wooden railing that led her around to the rear of the balcony. From that point, her view led away from the house.

In the distance, wooden slave shanties sat on risers, built to keep the huts off the damp ground inhabited by snakes, lubber grasshoppers, carpenter ants, and black beetles. The bush katydid's *fft . . . fft* and *zzz . . . zzz . . . zzz* notes stirred in the air around her. Colored children skipped rope among green groves of magnolia. Women young and old washed sheets in open cisterns, mended work clothes, and stirred cast iron pots that steamed over open fires. White men bearing whips rode horseback into the distant fields where speckled human forms moved up and down rows of mature cane. Men shoved giant stalks onto wagons behind them.

A straw-hatted white man on horseback rode through the cane field, wielding a bullwhip. She flinched and drew back. Every now and then, he would let the whip fly with a terrifying crack above his head, and rows of workers would bow and cringe. Though she could not hear his words, she knew the man was Galsworthy. She pressed her fan across her nose and mouth. He must not recognize her.

Her head grew faint, and the terror of that night in the parlor house replayed itself in frightening detail. His hands closed around her throat, his nubby fingers pawing her breasts, he had pushed himself on her, spreading her legs wide with his knees. Unsure whether it was the effect of the mint julep or the heat, she sagged against the white balustrade. Galsworthy must not see her.

Edward rounded the corner of the portico and caught her. "Brianna, are you ill?"

She gasped, "I want to leave now. Please, Edward. I will explain later. We must go."

He took her by the arm and steadied her footsteps. "I came to find you. We are a success." She relaxed into the comfort of his body as they stepped across the now empty balcony. Lace curtains shifted inside the front windows as they passed. Who was watching? The sweet aroma of pipe tobacco still lingered in the air, and LeComte's empty chair continued to rock.

No one walked them down the steps to the shady entrance of the lower porch. No one saw them off to their buggy waiting at the end of the row of live oak. Yet someone watched them drive away.

A green coach drawn by two bays waited to pass them on the narrow road. As they went by, Brianna recognized Mr. Moreau. He perched among some cartons inside the carriage, a roll of measuring tape hanging around his neck. He lifted his top hat as they passed. Why would he be going to the plantation? No doubt he was making a delivery.

Brianna's thoughts returned to Moreau and the hat shop. The curtain. The feet. What had Moreau overheard and what would he tell LeComte when he visited the plantation after her and Edward? Surely LeComte would discuss the gambler and his companion, knowing they had just left. She gazed after the spinning carriage wheels that grew smaller and smaller in the distance. At least in San Francisco, she'd never have to see such a distasteful man.

Forty-Two

GET OFF YOUR HORSE

Not long after Moreau's departure, as the noonday sun descended into deeper shadows, Pierre LeComte cantered down the path into the sugar cane fields on his white stallion, Gabriel. On an ordinary day, he relished acting the role of a king who surveyed his domain. Slaves carried hoes, picks, and shovels back to the main work barn. Soon they would take their late afternoon meal of refuse and stale bread, the custom of this plantation. He passed a rebellious slave who withered in the stocks. The men would go back to cut cane in the cooler weather of the evening when the river breezes rose to cool the sweat from their foreheads.

Moreau's recent words paraded in LeComte's mind: *Galsworthy . . . torture . . . Richard . . . Moses . . . set free.* He couldn't decide which made him the angrier—Spina's lie about his purpose for trading the steam engine for the slaves, or Galsworthy's violent debauchery in the Vieux

Carré. LeComte's face twisted into a frown and he clutched his diamond-tipped walking stick in one hand, his reins in another. Slaves paused at their chores and doffed their hats as he passed, then shuddered. He loved to make them shiver, but they were not his mission today. Maybe tomorrow, but not today.

Galsworthy sat astride his mare Brigitte under a giant live oak, fanning himself with his straw hat. He looked forward to the ride back to the plantation house, his midday's work done. Cook would fix his favorite Creole chicken over dirty rice and beans. Then back he would go to crack the whip until sunset. Tomorrow was Sunday, the Lord's day. His free day to tarry with the fellow overseers at the saloons, then visit the brothels where he would fall asleep in the arms of a nameless, faceless wench named Sally or Sue. The harlots withstood his cruel, unusual games of the flesh, as long as he flashed an occasional gold coin from the Old Mint. Maybe one of them would let him draw blood after a good ride on the mattress. A bit of saliva dribbled from his mouth.

The master galloped toward him in the distance, red dust flying behind him. The overseer passed a dirty rag over his face and mouth and the back of his neck. He spat out a large hunk of chewing tobacco with his words. "Sonuvabitch, whadda he wan' now?"

One look at LeComte's dark scowl gave him the answer. "Nevah liked dat look." He managed a thin smile as LeComte reined up parallel to his horse.

LeComte's face had swelled into a bulbous red oval in the afternoon heat. He batted away a swarm of flies trying to slake their thirst on the sweat lining his face. A slave who was sheltering under the oak jumped up and took Gabriel's reins. LeComte slid down and planted his feet in the red earth.

Galsworthy leaned his wrists on the pommel of his own saddle to quell the trembling in his hands. Brigitte tossed her mane and nickered her disapproval.

After a stony silence, Galsworthy spoke first. "Something you need, Monsieur?" He peered down at his master.

"Got a question, you no-account." LeComte glared up at him, his eyes sparking. "A question relating to the treatment of my two prize chattel. Get down from there, you buzzard."

Galsworthy tensed, open-mouthed. "I don't know 'bout any two slaves. No slaves atall, nohow. Jest the ones needs workin' and made to work." He closed his lips in a jagged line. Meddling in the affairs of slaves and masters was a hanging deed in Louisiana. Any such charge would be ruinous. He imagined the result of an accusation: the sheriff of the parish would arrest him and with little to no representation, he would be found guilty and put to the rope. No more lustful lie-downs with loose maidens, no more long drinks down by the French Market, no more satisfying lashings on bare black flesh. His life would be over.

LeComte raised his voice. "I say man, get off your horse. I think you know what I'm about. For a long time, I've heard tell about your doings in the Quarter. Brothels, groggeries, gambling dens, and such like. Now I did not mention it to you then because I figured men like you need a way to frolic. But what I did not figure at the time was that I had gone sucker. But now I've heard about your latest incident, your trespassing on Edward Spina's interest in Madame DeSalle's parlor house." He stepped toward him. "Your savagery nearly caused the death of a prostitute."

"I would never trick you, Monsieur." Galsworthy's nose ran, and he brushed a shaking hand across his upper lip. Then his eyes narrowed. "Who told you I would?"

"Moreau, the hatter." The master spat the words out like bitter chaw.

"Who, the what? Don't know the fella." Galsworthy clamped his teeth and rolled his fists into a ball.

LeComte's face contorted. "That's not your concern, now is it? But my concern is that our freed slave Emma was in that parlor house at the time of the walloping you gave the young lady at DeSalle's. And the young lady you whipped happened to be the whore of none other than

Edward Spina, gambler speculator, and son of the most powerful shipbuilding family in the Louisiana territory."

"I didn't have none to do with that." Brigitte shook her head, and as Galsworthy tightened the reins, she shifted on her front legs.

"There's plenty that saw you there and know you did it." LeComte's eyes fixed, his jaw braced like a hawk's before killing its prey.

"I ain't never been there, never." He tucked in his lower lip.

The master cocked his head to one side. "Then how's it happen that Edward Spina's whore's nursemaid is the wife of Richard and mother of Moses? My prime bull and his son?"

"Huh?" Galsworthy cocked an eyebrow.

LeComte's lips twisted into an unearthly grin. "After your attack on his whore, Edward Spina heard about Emma and Richard's separation and about their son Moses. To pile on the agony, Emma told her about your unfounded cruelty to them, my prize bulls, and now Spina will take them in trade from me. What do you suppose they plan to do with them, huh?" He fondled the whip handle in his palm.

"Don't know, Monsieur. Maybe they plans to use them as slaves theyselves." Galsworthy winced. Spina and his whore had been at Halldown that day. Twat and tarnation.

LeComte's spit sprayed out with his words. "No, you idiot! They plan to go to court and file freedom papers for them. Just what we need in New Orleans parish . . . more freed slaves. Now, thanks to that gossip-mongering hatter Moreau, I am soon to be the laughing stock of every plantation owner on the Mississippi." A corded vein pulsed on the side of his neck.

The master remained by the side of Galsworthy's mount, and he yanked Galsworthy's right boot from his stirrup.

Galsworthy yowled. "What are you doing?" The master meant business. Galsworthy's leg swung free, and he kicked his foot wildly toward the stirrup. Before he could regain his foothold, the master reached up, grabbed the pommel of the saddle to steady himself, and with his other hand, beat Galsworthy with his whip handle until the overseer fell off of the horse, his left leg still stuck in the stirrup.

Galsworthy's heart thudded. LeComte's murderous face was silhouetted against the sun.

The only thing Galsworthy could do was to cover his head with his arms as a shield.

The planter's next words bristled an executioner's warning. "I'm too much a southern gentleman to give a horse his head to drag you through my plantation. You'd be a dead man in five minutes, going across the cut cane fields. Wouldn't be much left of you with the cane sharp as tacks."

He peeked through the crook of his arm to see LeComte's mouth form into a scowl. He heard the master's steady inhale—exhale, inhale—exhale. The master was getting on in years; maybe he was not going to continue the beating. Galsworthy kept his head down, blood pulsing through his veins.

After the moment's refreshment, the master resumed his tirade. "No, sir. I'm just going to fire you. Get your fuckin' foot out of that fuckin' stirrup, and walk your dead body off my lands as fast as jack dumpling, else I will hang you myself from this oak. I have done it before and I can do it again. And don't let me catch hide nor hair of you anywhere near my lands. I'll take the cannon Father Auguste left me from Andy Jackson's war and blow you to smithereens as a favor to humanity."

The last thing Galsworthy remembered of the incident was his painful headache and the wound to his pride. Not the least was the loss of his job and his reputation. No plantation owner would hire him as an overseer ever again. He ground his teeth. Now someone would pay, and pay dearly, they would.

Forty-Three

AN ABSENCE OF WINDOWPANES

That same afternoon, Brianna, Edward, and Emma returned to Halldown Plantation in a hired coach, entering into the slave quarters by a remote service road. They filed into a slave cottage, each carrying a carpetbag. A thin woman in a slatted chair nursed a child at her breast. Two toddlers played with wooden toys at her feet. Their small group filled up the lean-to, where Edward had told Brianna fifteen people slept each night.

The faded wood shack graced a small porch that offered meager shade from the sun. Shafts of light cut through three small windows; Brianna noticed the absence of windowpanes. Instead, hand-stitched calico curtains wilted against the windowsills. An old, sick woman rested on a cot; her rheumy eyes stared at the ceiling.

"We come as your friends, Mademoiselle," Edward said.

The young woman rose, the child attached to her breast. "I . . . I have not done nothing wrong." Her eyes widened, her voice tired.

Edward said, "Pardon . . . I didn't get your name."

"Mary," she said.

"Ah, Mary, we're here to fetch away Moses and Richard. They are not in any harm; in fact, they are to be taken someplace safe."

The old sick woman leaned upon an elbow. "What's that, Mary?"

"Hush, Rose, go back to sleep," Mary said. She turned back to the group, her eyes wary. "How am I supposed to know you are telling the truth and not fetching them to use up like some piece of trash or t'other?" Her downturned mouth trembled, and the baby in her arms waved its arms.

Emma stepped toward her. "Mary, it's me, Emma. You remember me? I was here for a long time. Mama to Moses, wife of Richard."

Mary's voice filled with wonder. "Lemme get a good look at you, then. She took halting steps toward her old acquaintance.

Emma reached out and grabbed Mary's hand. "See? I'm all cleaned up now. Remember the master freed me?"

Mary paused, her eyes poring over Emma's face. "Last I remember, you was skin and bones, although I know the master was beholden to you after you saved his daughter. Now it comes back to me . . . it surely does."

"I am sorry to break in, but we don't have much time, Mary. Here's our bill of sale for them." Edward opened a paper and showed her, the tip of his index finger on their scrawled names.

"I cannot read." Mary's eyes darted past them toward the door.

Brianna pointed at the paper. "Here is the seal of Halldown Plantation under the master's signature. I'll read it line for line . . . will you believe us then?"

"Maybe I will." She exchanged a glance with Emma.

After Brianna read her the document at a slow pace, Mary's tense face relaxed into a satisfied peace. She laid her baby in a crude wooden cradle and stepped out to the front porch. From there she called to the neighboring cabin. "Elijah, get me Mos' and Richard from the dinner quarters."

"What for?" A young voice answered.

Suspicion hung in the air like Spanish moss. Brianna noticed that distrust at every level infected the body of a plantation. The master did not trust the slave; the slave did not trust the master. Even the master could not trust another master and a slave could not trust another slave. Sickness ruled the body, and every limb manifested signs of the disease. Deceit ran in the veins of everyone on this land, and it took very little to pierce the boil with deadly results—whipping, caning, hanging, raping, torturing. All was legal within the Black Code, the law of the land.

In the still heat of the cabin, while watching the toddlers play listless games, Brianna heard male voices approaching. All but Rose gathered at the door to watch the men trudge toward the cabin. Richard carried a thick strand of rope over his arm, and Moses held empty dinner plates and utensils to wash at the cabin's pump. The group stepped back as Emma ran out into the yard and the three family members embraced each other. Brianna's eyes burned with joy for them. Yet they could not stay long lest the master change his mind or Galsworthy hear of their pending freedom.

"Emma," Edward called. "We must pack up their things and go. No time to waste."

Soon, the group crowded into the cabin, helping the men who shoved tattered items of clothing into their carpetbags.

"We must be off," Emma said. With a kiss to Rose asleep on the cot and a hug for Mary and her children, they made haste to the frontage road where they stuffed into Edward's carriage, and summoned the driver who awaited them, deep into his cigar and a pint of ale under a nearby tree.

Forty-Four

To Teach a Lesson

New Orleans, Louisiana
September 1850

The party of five settled into Edward's carriage and the horses met the road. The creak of the carriage gained a rhythm. Brianna eyed the slaves with compassion. Richard kept his eyes downcast, focused on his dusty hands. Moses sat by the window and regarded the river as they drove alongside it. Emma reached for Richard's hand and held it as they bounced and jolted over the rutted levee road.

A steamboat kept pace with them as they traveled downriver toward New Orleans. Every now and then, its horn would blow, and the breeze carried the sound of the splashing paddlewheel as it worked its way through the water. Brianna touched Edward's hand, which was looped through her arm, and relaxed on her lap. He looked over at her, his smile devastating in its intensity. How exciting. She and Edward were a family in kind, about to set off on a new adventure together. How good it was to have Emma, Richard, and Moses reunited. The first step had been to gain their custody; the next was their manumission in court.

The sound of *pop-pop* broke the serenity. The passengers' hands flailed out to brace themselves, their faces fading into white ashen masks. The horses neighed and rose up, jerked the carriage, then led it down an embankment. Brianna screamed in terror at the disappearing horizon.

The coach plowed into the untilled field off the roadbed, and the rig screeched on its bolts and hinges as the horses lost their heads and aimed into the oblivion of the far woods. She watched the passengers knock about the interior. They shouted and screamed as their heads thumped against the top of the rig. To her horror, belongings tumbled from racks and opened. The impact sprayed clothes and shoes inside and outside the coach.

A crash into a tupelo tree put an end to the horse's flight. The coachman bounced off the driver's seat and hung upside down over the window, blood streaming down his face. Brianna's heart squeezed in anguish; his eyes were frozen in death. With a final jolt of the carriage, the driver planted face down in the muddy field. Brianna rested speechless, her breath trapped. Where was Edward? God, don't let her lose him now. A live oak branch had poked through the carriage window, narrowly missing her. She fumbled against the bark and lichen that scraped her face.

Edward cried out, "Hell!" She saw him pry open the carriage door. Pistol in hand, he jumped down onto the ground. Another gunshot whistled past, striking against the carriage wheel, setting the vehicle down even farther into the mud.

"Edward!" Brianna crumpled in her seat. Was this bitter battle to be the end of them?

"Stay there, get down, stay down." His voice was firm and commanding.

Brianna waved the others down onto the carriage floor. Where were they? She gazed out the window to see their coach crouched far under the tree branch, partly camouflaged. Meanwhile, Richard lowered the carriage curtains that had ripped from their hooks. A whiz of bullets penetrated the body of the rig.

Moses moaned, "Oh, Mama, I've been hit."

Without hesitation, Brianna reached up and yanked down a curtain from the window facing away from the direction of the bullets. She and Emma fashioned a tourniquet, winding the curtain around his arm above the wound on his left forearm. Blood had spurted everywhere—on their clothes and faces. Mrs. Morgan's handkerchief slid easily from Brianna's pocket, and she wiped away the tears streaming down Moses's face. He clamped his lips tight against the pain.

"Ambrose, protect this boy." She patted her gris-gris bag in her skirt pocket and prayed in the refuge of her faith.

Not long after, a horse's hooves pounded nearer and nearer on the levee road above the field. Brianna closed her eyes and Emma whispered the *Our Father*.

Moses's dark eyes flickered and he fainted.

"He is coming for us, Lord Almighty." Richard's jaw muscles tensed.

Brianna peeked around the curtain drawn against the window. She endured a frustrating moment of confusion, then the two men came into view.

Edward had planted his feet and was aiming a pistol up at Galsworthy who sat astride a field horse atop the levee, holding a shotgun up like a spear. Surely Galsworthy had the upper hand. Edward's was a raw act of courage. Even so, he said, "Galsworthy, go away and leave us in peace. You've done enough damage for one day. Don't harm the innocents when it is me you want."

Edward held the pistol in midair and continued to point it at Galsworthy. Then he walked into the clearing between the carriage and the levee.

Oh, no, Edward, don't sacrifice yourself. Brianna trembled involuntarily. She looked from Edward up to the levee.

Galsworthy's mouth screwed into a sneer. There it was: the same sneer from the moment he'd leaned over her in the parlor house, the demon's pustules festering on his face. She put her fingertips to her mouth. *Ambrose, dear Ambrose, please help us now. If Edward is killed, Galsworthy will come for me again, and he will show me no mercy.* Tears spilled down her cheek, and she wiped them away with a furious swipe.

Galsworthy kneed his mare and she reared up. The bastard was trying to scare Edward, but Edward held his ground, unmoving, his pistol pointed at his opponent.

Brianna waited for Galsworthy's next move. Was she confronting a lightless future without Edward?

A shotgun blast pierced the air, followed by Galsworthy's guttural pitch. "This'll teach a lesson to you, Spina. You'se unschooled in my ways. Next time I don't plan to be so kind." Then he wheeled his mount around and dug his heels into her ribs. He vanished through a whirl of red dust on the Halldown road.

After a period of safe silence that seemed eternal, Edward guided Brianna and the party out of the carriage. They slipped through the muddy field and waited on a dock for a passing keelboat to carry them to downstream to New Orleans. Brianna glanced back and saw the carriage on its side. Bullet holes peppered the vehicle. The horses lay in the mud, much as had the dog in the Quarter, their corpses sinking fast into the boggy soil.

Forty-Five

FLEUR-DE-LIS

New Orleans, Louisiana
September 1850

Judge Josiah Cole fought to catch his breath all morning in the suffocating courtroom filled with tobacco smoke. The breeze entered through a crack in an open window, allowing but a whisper of air. In the corner of his eye, the golden *Fleur-de-Lis* on the white background of the Louisiana flag disappeared, then reappeared in the playful gust. All morning, he had listened to manumission cases, most of which he had dismissed for lack of proof or lack of standing. Louisiana politics had shifted, and now judges were urged to grant fewer slaves their freedom. For months, colored men and women in bedraggled condition had stood before him at the bar, their children beside them, faces upturned, full of hope.

He had denied many their freedom. They would cringe at the hammering of his gavel, their faces heartsick as they trudged away down the lengthy courtroom aisle, the door clanging shut behind them. This morning, his nerves were tattered. His mood traveled up and down. His thoughts strayed to the yellowfin tuna he had tried to hook on the line out in the Gulf last week. Some struggle that had been. And it had broken away to be food on another fisherman's dinner plate. He sighed, wishing for lunchtime and his daughter's peach cobbler.

The court clerk announced the next case. A middle-aged colored man and woman stood before him, their black hair peppered with gray. Next to them waited a young man with a bandaged arm, from an obvious gunshot wound, and he guessed him to be their son by his facial features. The nattily dressed Spina held a Panama hat, and a redheaded woman wore summer flounces. Their eyes peered up at him. So optimistic, he thought. He steeled himself for another round of despair.

The bailiff had them swear on the Holy Bible to tell the truth so help them God, which they all did. After that, the clerk accepted their papers, made notes in a ledger, and nodded to the judge, passing the items across the bar to him.

Brianna turned to view the courtroom packed with onlookers and petitioners. This crowd could become a disorderly lot without the decorum of the court. She heard the comforting sound of the judge beating his gavel and shushing a loud group of petitioners in the back gallery. It was hard to breathe in here; humanity pressed together like tics on a hound.

A baby cried, its whine intensifying until the judge stood up and cried, "Madame, Have mercy on our ears! I pray you to depart this courtroom immediately so we may rest in peace." He made the sign of the cross for good measure, and Brianna heard whispers and shuffling behind her as the unruly family left the chamber. As she watched them, her glance rested on a pair of familiar eyes in the audience. Mr. Moreau from the hat shop was staring at her. Her mouth opened in recognition.

He gave her a sharp nod. Whatever was he doing here? She stiffened, her mind filled with worrisome thoughts. He had been at the plantation that day. Was he a spy for LeComte?

Various human body odors ranging from sweat to excrement wafted through the courtroom, and Brianna held her handkerchief to her nose. Even the Fells Point sewers emitted more pleasing scents. Edward stood next to her, although they refrained from holding hands in front of the judge. From time to time, Edward's gaze returned to her, and his nearness made her senses spin. His thick, wavy hair, his full sensual lips, his muscular body—all served to tempt her. The longer they shared moments together, the longer she wanted to linger in his company, savoring the joy that rose inside of her.

At length, Judge Cole spoke. "Mr. Spina, please advance to the bar."

Edward gave his hat to Richard, then stepped forward and stood looking up at the dais. "Yes, Your Honor."

"From your petition, I see you wish to grant manumission upon these parties, er . . ." He paused a moment, pushing his spectacles further up his nose. "Mr. Richard Lewis and Moses Lewis."

Edward spoke in obliging tones. "Yes, Your Honor."

The judge held up a document so it was visible to the crowd. "And this is your receipt for their payment?"

Brianna squinted, recognizing the scrawl of *Pierre LeComte* she had seen LeComte write that day on the plantation.

"Yes, *Votre Honneur*."

The judge stifled a yawn. "And you are a legal citizen of the parish of New Orleans, state of Louisiana?"

"I am, indeed." Edward's tone was crisp and confident.

"Your papers, please?"

Edward showed his papers and they were noted by the court clerk.

"*Tres bien*, very well." The judge reclined in his squeaky chair. "For what reason are you asking manumission for these parties?" He steepled his fingers, then rested his chin on them.

Edward's eyes focused on him. "I wish to employ them as craftsmen for new buildings in San Francisco."

The judge leaned forward, his pot belly pressed against the bench. "Mr. Spina, are you aware that the laws of manumission are changing?"

Edward gave Brianna a sideways glance. Beads of sweat tickled his forehead. "I do not read the laws, Your Honor, but I do abide by them."

The judge's words dropped like cards before him. "That is all well and good, Mr. Spina, but the recent laws now require that freed slaves post a one-thousand-dollar bond to the court. They are also required to leave the state of Louisiana within thirty days."

This was unexpected news. Edward turned and cast a glance at Brianna. His eyebrows rose, telegraphing to her his surprise. "They are?" He faced the judge, awaiting the next hand.

"Yes, and therefore upon taking ownership and then manumitting these slaves, you must provide the court such funds." The judge scratched his sideburns and sighed.

A moment of silence ensued, the movements of ladies' fans stirring little currents of air in the oven-like chamber. Her rising spirits were drowned by a new wave of fears. Was Edward sure he could afford to pay?

Edward spoke. "I can provide the money with an hour's visit to the bank." There. He had a full house.

The judge gave him a probing gaze. "Very well. Since I have little faith in your reputation as a gambler, I also will need to see the tickets that guarantee them passage on the ship to California. Such tickets need to be stamped to depart within thirty days of today's date." A royal flush.

Edward's knuckles were white against the judge's bench. "I have the tickets at home, but I do not know how quickly I may get to the bank, then to home, and then return with them here, Your Honor."

The judge eyed his pocket watch and looked up. "Mr. Spina, do not misunderstand me. My docket is full and my stomach is empty. The court will recess now. If you do not return with the bond and the tickets by noon, I shall declare your purchase and this manumission null and void. I will have a bailiff take the slaves back to their plantation, and we will be done with it. No other judge will take this case again, for love nor money. You had better pull foot for the bank and home, my son."

"Yes, Your Honor." Edward closed his eyes to regain his composure, and took several steps back.

The bailiff stepped forward and led the waiting party over to a bench at the side under his watch.

Judge Cole pounded the gavel. "Court is in lunch recess for one hour," he announced.

Edward disappeared into the smoke, smells, and stale perfume that was New Orleans.

Forty-Six

A Row of Yellow Teeth

After what seemed an eternity, Brianna exchanged glances with Emma and the men beside her in the visitor's gallery. Although Brianna was hopeful that Edward would make the bank in time, she worried that he wouldn't return from home in time. She held her gris-gris bag and prayed to Ambrose for protection.

Judge Cole reassumed the bench, and he rifled through loose-leaf papers and turned pages of books at his desk. The audience had grown smaller in size; Brianna guessed the afternoon's heatwave may have something to do with it.

Edward's footsteps stamped through the central aisle of the courtroom, and he wove through women's hats and men's jackets on his way to the judge's bench. Brianna watched him wave three tickets in the air. He slid them under the judge's nose, and then passed him a paper, which Brianna guessed to be the bank draft for one thousand dollars.

The judge beamed down at Edward, and he lifted his gavel for a pronouncement. Brianna caught a blur of movement from the corner of her eye. It was then that she recognized Moreau again, standing mid-audience in a gray suit and matching boots. What did that officious little man want now? She shuddered to think.

"May I approach the bench, Your Honor?" Moreau cleared his throat.

The judge's face approximated the red of a cooked crawfish. "Identify yourself!"

"Moreau, the hatter, sir."

"And, Moreau? This must be pertinent to Mr. Spina's case, or I shall call you in contempt. My recess snack is sure to be getting cold, and the froth on my beer will disappear before I can drink it." He glowered.

Brianna and Emma shared glances. Brianna's heart thrummed in her head. *Please, God, no more misery.*

Moreau said, "Your Honor, the very nature of these people who have purchased the slaves is called into question here." He turned his head and Brianna caught a crooked smirk crossing his face.

Brianna's stomach clenched. This little man was an ass.

"What?" the judge bellowed. "Please fill my ear with more information, good fellow."

Moreau projected his speech, his tone cocky and superior. "The money that paid for this manumission has been gotten illegally, since both gambling and prostitution are outlawed in the Crescent City."

"Please identify your interest in this matter. How did you come to know the persons in question, and their acquaintance with the slaves?"

"My friend Galsworthy is overseer at Halldown Plantation." Moreau rocked back on his heels.

Emma clutched her hand, and Brianna felt its moisture.

"Is that where the said slaves were held in bondage?" The judge's right eyebrow lifted higher than his left.

"Yes, and it was there they kidnapped the said slaves." Moreau's upper lip curled, revealing a row of uneven yellow teeth.

The judge set his jaw in a straight line. "It does not make sense, my fellow, that they would kidnap the slaves to bring them to court, the seat of justice. In the court's view, they have provided their evidence of purchase and manumission in a reasonable and timely fashion. If I were you, my little man, I would keep my business at the hatter's and nowhere else. Your request is denied."

Moreau had no choice but to say, "Thank you, Your Honor." Brianna suppressed a laugh as he backed away from the bar, turned, and fled the court.

The judge summoned Richard and Moses to him. He proclaimed the freedom of Richard and Moses for all to hear. He gave a final clobbering of the gavel, then declared afternoon recess for the rest of the day.

That night, over her empty champagne glass at DeSalle's, Brianna said, "I have one more bag to pack for tomorrow's embarkation. It is 2200, and the boat departs tomorrow at 0900 hours. Around them, the parlor house was quiet, except for the occasional squeak of bedsprings from the rooms of entertainment.

"We do not have many belongings," Emma said. Her eyes shone luminous and expectant.

Brianna nodded. "I think it is best to travel light since we must travel over land on the Panama Route. Now we must all go to bed, since the ship leaves so early in the morning."

Emma rose along with Richard and Moses, who said their good-nights, and they all disappeared up the stairs to Emma's room.

Edward yawned and said, "I must away to gather my belongings, my love. Tomorrow it is off to see the elephant. Come, see me to the door so we may say our goodbyes."

She loved his kisses, the way he lingered with his mouth on hers, then stayed close, holding her tight to him afterward. She went to the door and watched him mount his horse, tipping his top hat goodnight.

Forty-Seven

HEAVY LIFTING

New Orleans, Louisiana
September 1850

Deep in the night, Brianna awakened to the smell of smoke. She lay entwined in her bedsheets, wondering. Someone must have left a cigar burning downstairs in the parlor, or perhaps in one of the bedrooms. Probably nothing. She fluffed her pillow and rolled over.

A few minutes passed. What was that? Voices shouted and she rose and opened the shutters to see flickering torches illuminate the street outside the parlor house. Eerie black silhouettes traveled across her bedroom wall. Her pulse quickened. What on earth was going on? Then, she heard a window shattering downstairs in the hallway, and the whoosh of flame igniting something. Her heart skittered in her chest. Someone must have thrown a burning torch into the house.

Smoke drifted under her door, and she opened it to see black tendrils crawling up the walls. "Fire!" she cried, running along hallway to the landing, pounding on bedroom doors. "Run for your lives! Fire!" She started to move toward the front of the house, but the hot wooden boards singed her bare feet, so she made her way downstairs to the servant's entrance in the back. The courtesans appeared one by one, their nightcaps askew, their skimpy *negligées* in disarray. They rubbed their eyes, then held each other's hands out the door into the night.

Emma, Richard, and Moses appeared on the threshold in their street clothes, never having gone to bed since they stayed up, excited about the journey to come.

Celeste scurried past Brianna in a dash to the exit, joining the others as they bounded out of the doorway onto the street.

"Where's Madame DeSalle?" Brianna cried out to Celeste. "And our little Andy?"

"I do not know, Mademoiselle." Celeste looked back, her face lined with sweat.

"First, we must get to safety," Brianna yelled.

Celeste reached out her fingers, and Brianna grasped them. Together they leaped across the street, then turned and faced the parlor house. Wheezing, she peered through the smoke, hoping for a dog's bark.

Neighbors poured out of their doors, and the footman Pierre rattled off on a borrowed horse to summon the fire brigade. The air filled with a choking mixture of smoke and ash, and bystanders bent over, coughing. Madame DeSalle was nowhere in the crowd. Tongues of fire licked upward from the tops of windows, black smoke billowing. If Andy were in there, he wouldn't survive. Tears pricked her eyes, and she brushed them away.

Celeste peered through the smoke at the bystanders huddling outside. "No sign of Madame."

"Then I must find her," Brianna said, pushing her gold-red braid up into her nightcap to get it out of her way.

"No, Mademoiselle, you must not go inside . . . it is all burning now!" Celeste said.

Her words made Brianna even more determined. She threaded her way back to the servant's entrance, avoiding cinders that were flying into the street. The heat in the house was fearsome, and she broke into a sweat that coursed down her face.

She raced to the rear first-floor chamber occupied by Madame DeSalle. *Please God, let the door be unlocked.* Otherwise, Brianna would not know what to do. She turned the knob, and the door gave way. Through the smoky haze, she spied Madame lying prone on the bed, unconscious from drink, no doubt. The woman did love her absinthe. Still no sign of Andy, not even a whimper. The smoke packed her lungs and stung her eyes. She grabbed the portly woman around the waist, but the unconscious DeSalle proved heavy lifting.

A pair of hands appeared from out of the smoke and took Madame's arms, tugging her toward the door. Emma's hands. She'd recognize them anywhere. Emma had held the compresses to her forehead during recovery from Galsworthy's attack.

"Emma," Brianna choked. Her relief was short-lived. She looked up to see hot smoke billow across the ceiling, resembling the dark thunderclouds of summer storms.

"Quick, before we go up with the house," Emma said. With great strength, Emma dragged the unconscious woman across the floor and out the door.

Celeste appeared in the haze and assisted Brianna where she could, kicking away the cinders and warning Emma of burning embers. Showers of sparks pelted them, and they had to stop more than once to see their way through.

Back out in the street facing the parlor house, Brianna heard shouts and firemen appeared with hatchets, the whites of their eyes flashing in the darkness. The last thing Brianna remembered was lying on a blanket in the muddy street. Celeste pressed a cup of water to her lips.

She heard Edward say, "I am here now. Emma, you must care for Richard and Moses. Brianna appears to be stunned, but see, she is drinking now from the cup. "

A dog's yelp, and Brianna recognized Andy's unmistakable yowl. Then something began to lick her face, and she looked up into Andy's eyes, brown and round, his eyelashes singed, smoky cinders darkening his coat.

She heard Celeste ask, "Will Brianna be strong enough to make the journey?"

"She will be." Edward's voice rose, his tone changing from relief to determination.

"Listen to me, Celeste. We must all leave New Orleans. You must come with us. You also are no longer safe here. You have been seen about town with Brianna and Emma. If we leave you behind at DeSalle's, Galsworthy is likely to take revenge upon you. Mark my words, it is most dangerous for you."

"Oui, Monsieur. I will come with you. I never said so, but I was dreading your departure. You are the only family I have now." She paused. "Who would do this?"

"Someone who hates the idea of human freedom," Edward said.

Forty-Eight

A Lantern Sputters

New Orleans, Louisiana
September 1850

At 0845 hours, when Captain Leathers stood at the gangway of *The Steamship Alabama*, his mouth dropped open. Brianna imagined it would be quite a shock to see them all boarding in half-burned clothes. He rushed down the gangway. His hands reached out and took Brianna's arms. "Mind your white suit, Captain. I'm bound to dirty your sleeve."

"Pay it no mind, my dear." His lips brushed the back her hand.

She took limping steps alongside Edward and Celeste. Her lungs tightened from last night's smoke, and she labored to breathe. She checked to make sure Andy padded alongside her. After he'd survived the fire, he would not leave her side.

"We have lost our tickets, mate," Edward said, as he plodded up the planks to the main deck.

"What happened to you?" Leathers asked.

"Parlor house riot, followed by a fire. Nearly killed my family, my friends, and my love. We may still be in danger since the culprits got away." His voice grated from smoke inhalation.

"Make haste as you can. The ship is about to cast off. I will advise your pilot, my friend Captain Evers. We must secret you below deck so that you are not seen by too many people on the wharf. Otherwise, there could be trouble for the ship."

Every step wearied Brianna; her feet were lead weights.

Leathers turned as if taken by a sudden fear. "Any idea who did this?"

"Galsworthy and his henchmen. Moses recognized them as they rode away." A persistent wheeze layered Edward's voice.

"I see."

They struggled up the last step of the gangway and onto the deck. What a relief. Brianna put a hand on Edward's arm, and he signaled the group to stop for a moment. The group gathered together, their breathing labored. Andy stood in the middle, his tail wagging.

Celeste's smoke-mottled face turned toward the captain. She spoke with a new courage. "We also need the ship's doctor, since we have suffered burns and cuts from the fire. Brianna's feet are blistered badly." She pulled two framed pictures out of her satchel and passed them to the captain.

"What are these?"

"Paris. They are precious to us, although they may be singed."

His generous eyes loomed large. "I'll see to it that they are well-stored during the voyage." He passed them to the skipper, and turned back to them. "You are lucky to have escaped alive."

Brianna took a quick look at her surroundings. Men and women gathered on the clipper steamship's deck and dangled handkerchiefs to wave at their friends waiting on the dock below. The steam engine chuffed, and flags flew from the three masts as the sidewheels turned.

Brianna followed Edward's outstretched arm; she hobbled across the deck and down the creaking stepladder to their cabins. The freed slaves followed them, but at the bottom of the ladder, a steamship officer guided them away.

She turned to Edward. "Why must they go with him rather than staying here with us?" Brianna asked. "I fear they may be kidnapped . . . or worse." She gritted her teeth as she thought of losing them.

Edward frowned. "I was fortunate to get them on board, Brianna. There was no more room, and I had to pay the captain handsomely for their berths. In fact, only with Captain Leathers' intervention did Captain Evans risk defying the shipping company by taking too many passengers on board." He shrugged his shoulders. "They will dine with us at our table each night, my love."

Brianna exhaled, pressing her hand on her chest to lessen the pain. "At least I know they are in good hands here with us."

Edward's mouth curved upward. "And no one will bother us in San Francisco. Here, come to the porthole. We will say our own *au revoir* to the Crescent City. We now begin a new chapter." He placed a tender arm around her shoulders as they studied the wharf. Brianna's only regret was not going to Ambrose's resting place to say goodbye, but she consoled herself by remembering the words of Madame LaVeau:

As you waken in the morning,
The first light through the window carries his little smile to you.
Let his light carry you through life,
Guiding your footsteps into the moments of eternal unity with your son.

Celeste stood on the threshold of Brianna's tiny cabin. "One can hardly turn around in here." Her eyes shifted to a lantern sputtering on the wall where it rocked with the ship.

"Look out our porthole." Brianna pointed. "At least we can see the last of America as we make our way out to sea. I have loved it here, you know." She regarded Edward who sat next to her on the cot. "From here we can see the Place D'Armes and even the Cabildo. The French Market must be down there, to the right." She petted Andy's head where he snuggled next to her on the bed.

Celeste's voice softened in wonder. "I am surprised to hear you say this, considering you almost lost your life here."

"It is a miracle we all survived last night." She had lost Ambrose—her second life—here. But Edward would never know about that. She promised herself never to tell him. She looked up at him. "I have loved New Orleans ever since we met that day on St. Peter Street. You showed me a beautiful city I would never have known without you."

He squeezed her hand, his eyes misty and wistful.

This brought to mind her last voyage out of Baltimore's Inner Harbor; the flags flying reminded her of the pelican feather she'd held that day. It was lost in the fire, along with so many other mementoes. She sighed. Those things were not important. They needed to burn up, along with her old life in the old land of Louisiana. She prepared for new adventures and freedom in a land she could not even imagine.

They heard the slamming of hatches and the scrape of the gangway as it thundered away from the ship onto the dock. Shouts and sounds of laughter and goodbyes floated down to where they were below deck.

The ship creaked, and Edward looked out the narrow porthole. Brianna studied the panorama. Celeste peeked out from the space above them.

From their view, Briana saw two figures on horseback pull up to the dock. She shook her head, fear crawling into her chest. "Is that Galsworthy and one of his men?" Brianna asked.

"It sure is . . . but wait. Captain Leathers is talking to them. He is pointing toward Lake Pontchartrain," Edward said. "That's my Leathers . . . the expert poker face."

"Look Edward. They are turning around and riding away in that direction," Celeste said. She pointed north.

The ship's whistle blew, bells clanged, and a cheer rose up from the waving crowd. Andy stood on his hind legs and cocked his head toward the porthole.

"No one will bother us." Brianna repeated Edward's earlier words, watching the white, green, and brown shades of New Orleans fade away downriver to join Baltimore in her patchwork of memories.

Part Three

For a Good Man's Love

But, mistress, know yourself. Down on your knees,
And thank heaven, fasting, for a good man's love ...

William Shakespeare, *As You Like It,* 3.5.60–61

Forty-Nine

FIRST BALCONY

San Francisco, California
April 1856

Brianna and Edward swept out of their coach under the marquee at the American Theater. A crowd gathered around a giant poster on an easel. Brianna pushed her way forward through the capes and top hats so they could view it up close. She pointed with her gloved finger. "Look, Edward! Just as the *Daily Song* said, the Ravels are on stage tonight!"

"I had no reason to doubt you, my love. Remember, I've given up a nice afternoon of poker to keep you happy." He squeezed her hand, and she warmed to his touch.

"Edward, indulge me . . . you usually do. *Nicodemus, or, The Unfortunate Fisherman.* I wonder what that story's about? What will the Ravels come up with next?"

"How do they invent such outrageous titles?" Edward advanced toward the ticket booth, and she followed, gazing around at the splendid jewelry women wore—pearl strands, diamond-drop earrings, and emerald hairclips were only some of the gems gracing their dresses, coats, and hats.

She caught up with Edward and pressed against his side. "Stop teasing. The Ravels are famous all over the world; they're masters of pantomime." It was hard to suppress this kind of excitement—she'd waited for months to see these *artistes*, world famous for their spectacular moves.

"All right. I come only to watch your enjoyment. You make me fall in love with you again no matter what you wear . . . and don't wear." Brianna felt Edward's lips brush her cheek. He dropped several coins in the tray and took tickets from the attendant.

A hot flush traveled through her as she stood waiting, remembering his naked body entwined with hers in bed that morning. She held his arm closer, then stood on tiptoe to whisper in his ear. "Well, if the Ravels are not enough for you, we'll also see the famous Martinettis."

Edward gave the tickets to the vested man inside the theater door. "And who are they, may I ask? A group of Italian tightrope walkers? Wouldn't be surprised. I remember such feats in the Genoa of my childhood." He dropped her hand and leaned over to pitch a spent cigar into a tray in the lobby.

Brianna patted his arm. Maybe he'd like them after all. "I've followed their careers in the broadsheets, and they're world-renowned acrobats with high-flying feats. *The Red Gnome* comes right after the opening scene of *Nicodemus.*" Still chilled from the evening's fog, she adjusted her spring scarf around her neck. She reveled in their banter, her mood buoyant and carefree.

"Frightful." Edward wiped his mouth with a handkerchief. "The torture does not end there." He cast her a look, humor playing about his eyes. She felt his arm under hers while they strolled through the lobby.

"No, it does not." Brianna continued his mock-serious tone. "Louisa saw it last night. The Martinettis dress up in fabulous costume to do the fairy spectacular. It made her believe gnomes and fairies were real. The fairies came out of the walls, and the ceilings, and—"

"Good Lord, I know when to fall asleep." Edward lowered his eyelids. "I'll take a good nap when the lights go out."

In spite of herself, she chuckled. "At least try not to snore, my sweet man." Brianna gazed up into his face. "During the last opera, you sounded like one of the elephants on stage."

"If it happens today, ignore me."

"It's too hard. How can I ignore you when you drool on the shoulder of my best gown?" She opened her Chinese fan and waved away the cloud of cigar smoke in front of them. What a crowd today. It was taking forever to get to their seats.

"Then wake me up." He grinned, showing his receipts to an usher.

The man studied their tickets, then stood back. Brianna caught his searching gaze, and her throat closed up. Why was he scrutinizing them? Had he recognized them, remembering their fame as the madam and gambler from the broadsheets?

"Excuse us, Sir and Madam, have we had the pleasure of your attendance before, um, Mr. and Mrs. . . . oh, dear me, I have quite forgotten your names . . . uh?"

Edward held his shoulders back, his head high. "Spina. Mr. Edward Spina and Miss Brianna Baird."

"But, Sir, the tickets say *first balcony*, you see." The usher grew pale, and he began to suck the space under his half-missing front tooth. "What to do, what to do."

A gentleman behind them cleared his throat; Brianna glanced back at the line growing behind them.

"Well, just show us to our seats, my good man," Edward said. "Whatever could be the matter here? Is there something wrong with the tickets? I bought them from that very nice gentleman over there in the booth just now. I say!" He pressed a gold dollar into the usher's palm.

"It's just that . . . hmmm . . . you will be in the first balcony with the upper classes, Mr. Spina, instead of second with . . . well, you know." The usher smirked, fingering the money, a red tinge coloring his cheeks.

Brianna eyed the man, imagining his amusement that such lower class citizens as she and Edward were attempting to bribe him.

"My good man, if our sitting with the higher ranking members of society is the only problem you're worried about, I suggest you forget about it. It doesn't worry us, does it, my dear?" Spina placed another gold piece in the man's hand.

Brianna stepped toward the usher. "We never mind sitting with the upper classes, as long as they leave us alone. Most of the time, the men leer and the women memorize my gowns so they can have their dressmakers attempt a copy. We've never had an incident, and we've been contributing members of the San Francisco society for five years."

The coins clicked together in the usher's palm. "Very well." He dropped the money in his pocket and escorted them to their seats in the second-to-last row.

Once they were seated for a few moments, Brianna scanned the theater, determined to put aside her negative feelings about the usher. "Isn't this magnificent, Edward? That chandelier is surely the largest I've ever seen . . . and I thought the opera house was grand." She pulled her opera glasses from her pocket and peered through them. Memorable days like this made life worth living.

"Yes, Brianna, it's wonderful, I do agree. I've heard that the chandelier at the Paris Opera House is even grander. One of these days, I plan to suffer through the opera there just for you." Edward settled into his velvet green seat. His legs bumped up against the seats in front of him. "How am I supposed to sit through this when I can't even stretch out my legs? Three hours of sitting, what a chore. It's worse than being cramped into a bungo on the Chagres River. Remember that voyage, so long ago?" He sighed, the teasing back in his voice.

"Edward. You are a trouble. But I disagree. Nothing's worse than being in that boat with the water seeping in around the carpetbags, and the worms crawling in the water, not to mention the giant flying beetles, large as my fist." Brianna shivered, lost in the memory. "I'm happy to be here right now in this opera house. Nothing like a pantomime to help us take our minds off Jeannette."

"Emma told me she'd left her room a shambles when she went away from the house yesterday."

"The tart gave me a turn, and I'm happy she left without more destruction." Brianna lapsed into a thoughtful silence, her mind on the house. Had she been too hard on the girl? Jeannette and General Williams had a turbulent relationship, but all in all, the man asked for Jeanette each time he visited the parlor house, so she always let him have her. In turn, Jeannette never complained about Williams. Maybe she should have pried more into the arguments that Jeannette and Williams engaged in constantly, followed by the loud sexual noises in their chamber.

Brianna chewed on the end of her finger. Of course she herself had been lost and mistaken, too, at one time, just like Jeannette. Maybe the poor girl had fallen in love with the man. But drink had been creeping up on him lately, and Emma had heard rumors that Jeannette was fond of the opium dens. With a pang of guilt for sending the girl away, Brianna felt for the gris-gris bag in her skirt pocket and gave it a squeeze.

Brianna surveyed the crowd of diamond and gold-laden women taking their seats in the balconies, and focused her opera glasses on their fashionable gowns cascading to the floor. The sight of their fine silks and laces brought back memories of Miss Osborne's shop, and her never-ending desire to have her own business someday. Instead, fortune being what it was, there was better money to be made by opening a parlor house rather than a seamstress shop.

She thought about their early days in San Francisco. Few women had been here, and miners roamed the streets, longing for the feel of a woman's skin. With Celeste and Emma's help, their first parlor house had opened, followed by another two in no time. A contrast to the raucous bawdyhouses, theirs provided a private, peaceful setting where prominent men could savor the best in fine wine, French cuisines, and stunning courtesans.

She and Edward had founded their most recent house on Waverly Place a mere two years past. It was their finest. Simple on the outside, but ostentatious on the inside. The walls were lined with velvet and satin, the French champagne flowed freely, and she insisted her girls were treated well. No one there had to parade around in a scant negligée. All the girls were of legal age, dressed in gowns she tailored from Parisian designs.

She broke the silence between them. "Edward, when are we going to Paris? We've been talking about it for years." She made a point to bring it up from time to time so he'd never forget its importance to her.

Edward studied her face a moment. "Sometime next year, I think. It's a long journey from California, but we can take the Grand Tour now that we have made our latest winnings. Our racehorses, Double Eagle and Mississippi, have been doing quite well lately. They were a good investment." He peeled off one of Brianna's gloves, and inserted his finger into center of her palm. He drew figure eights there with his fingertip.

The silken tip of his finger stirred her, and she opened her mouth in unexpected pleasure.

"Do you know what I love about you?" he whispered into her ear.

Brianna breathed out a laughing sigh. "Edward, do not embarrass me. We are in society." Maybe she could suppress her rising passion by surveying the women seated in their balcony— she hoped she might recognize a high-class woman.

He continued. "I love your turned up nose, the tiny freckles that pepper your cheeks, and the way copper mixes with blond streaks in your hair."

The houselights lowered.

"Edward." Brianna withdrew her hand from his. "Save that for to-night." She tapped her closed fan against her lips.

Fifty

SAWDUST AND PERFUME

San Francisco, California
April 1856

Stage lanterns flickered; lights and shadows moved in the orchestra pit. The curtain waved now and then as the props crew prepared stage sets and actors took their places. The white-haired maestro thumbed through the music on his podium while the players tuned their instruments. The box seats held many of the most powerful men and their wives in San Francisco—bankers, judges, and politicians.

A sudden movement jarred the back of Brianna's seat. She turned and noticed prominent banker Charles Lewis and his wife Margaret arranging themselves into the seats behind them. Their faces had been in the broadsheets recently. The society pages reported their frequent attendance at galas and soirées.

Such a mix of people in the theater. Brianna gazed around the interior of her balcony and down at both gentry and miners composing the audience in the pit. These citizens craved the escape of the theater, no matter their occupation. Sawdust mixed with French perfume drifted in the air. Men in deerskin jackets nestled next to women in silk gowns, and all savored the spectacle of the stage and theatergoers around them.

The maestro made sharp taps with his baton on the podium, and the musicians played the first musical bars. The house lights dimmed in their sconces; attendants lit oil lamps lining the stage. The audience silenced, and the lyrical overture to *Nicodemus* echoed through the theater. As was their custom, Brianna held Edward's hand in her lap during the performance.

Ravel, the star performer, parted the red velvet curtains, stepped onstage, then swept them closed behind him. The audience gasped, then clapped and cheered. Foot-pounding reverberated on the wooden floors.

The actor struck an imposing figure as the harlequin—he stood six feet tall, his costume composed of glittering diamond patterns of yellow and red, his head topped with an admiral's hat. His eyes glinted against the stage lights, and he lifted his hand to begin the pantomime routine. The only other mesmerizing figure Brianna had seen like him had been a large-boned Emberá Indian playing the flute in full toucan feathers. But that had been on the Chagres River. So long ago now, but memories, like the turgid blue waters of the river, kept spilling over rocks in her mind, carrying with them the turbulence of their Isthmus crossing.

The second scene progressed and the audience quieted, absorbed in the play. Then something moved in the center of the darkened orchestra seats down below. Brianna saw Edward turn his head, distracted by an interchange among a group of people. He stared at several young men, who looked like moving shadows in the pit. By gosh, they were pointing their fingers at her and Edward in the first balcony. Since social luminaries filled the balcony that night, the lads may be fussing over those folks, surely not her or Edward.

With that thought, she gazed back at the stage. The scenery descended and acrobats floated back and forth on swings or swooped down from trap doors above the stage. Red and yellow costumes flamed against the blue and white of the starry canopy on the stage set. Brianna glanced back at the orchestra. Whatever the fuss had been, it appeared to be over. The audience gasped and applauded at the various twists and turns of the flying acrobats as they flipped over the bars and caught one another's legs.

"There! See?" Voices shouted through the music, coming from the same part of the pit as before.

Brianna squinted down at yet another disturbance. Her annoyance grew. She'd ask Edward to talk to the house management at intermission. They'd have to eject the disruptors. Probably drunk. The men's behavior reminded her of their early days in San Francisco, when any gold miner was a drunken gold miner, and at any moment, a street spectacle could be turned into a muddy melee. The former young men's cries began to disrupt their section of the audience, and a murmur traveled through the theater. She tapped Edward's arm. "Is there a fight down there? Some lads creating a ruckus?"

Those same youths were now on tiptoe, surrounded by other spectators who admonished them. Someone called, "Down in front, boys. Scoundrels, take your seats." Despite warnings, one of the young men called, "Look! Spina!"

Edward's former peace disturbed, he jerked his head in the direction of the sound.

Brianna heard the boy's words ricochet off the walls of the opera house as though *Spee-Na* were the first notes of an aria. She bit her lip and sank a bit lower in her seat. Fear rose inside of her, mixed with a helpless indignation.

Around Brianna and Edward, the diamond-laden matrons of high society exchanged low whispers, their gold jewelry sparkling beneath the wall sconces. Brianna turned around; in the row behind her, next to the Lewises, sat the eminent United States Deputy Marshal General William A. Williams and his wife. Williams was in full military dress, and his epaulets twinkled next to the spangled, bell-shaped skirts of his wife, Tessa. Mrs. Williams fixed a glare at the back of Edward's head.

God knew how much Mrs. Williams despised her, as well. The general frequented their parlor house on more than one night a week. The woman leaned over to her distinguished husband and spoke to him behind her feather-tipped fan. She gathered her pelisse about her. Brianna sat, wondering. Was the woman preparing to leave?

Brianna watched Edward take in the scene down in the orchestra, his calm face hardening into a mask of anger. A patient and calculating man, it took a lot to provoke him. His fingers rounded into fists. She could tell he was getting fed up.

Her own hands were clammy and her breath quickened; she was a part of the sideshow. The spectators pointed at her, their eyes wide, enthralled to see the elegant Brianna Baird, famous Madam, sitting in a high-society first balcony, under the very nose of the US marshal of San Francisco. She knew what they were saying: *Such a scandal! How could she dare?*

To make matters worse, she guessed the lads downstairs had begun to place bets on whether or not the general would arrest her, the madam who was forbidden to be in high-society seats. They'd hope for even more melodrama off-stage. Maybe even the arrival of a Black Maria, followed by a jail sentence. Brianna cringed at the horror of her situation.

General Williams' coat rustled; he rose from the seat behind Edward. Out of the corner of her eye, Brianna saw Mrs. Williams' grim expression. The woman stayed put. Edward turned his head, his glance following the general as he exited the first balcony through the side door. Without a doubt, the general would follow the back hallway down to the foyer where he would probably demand to see the manager. As she looked back at his empty seat, she imagined the scene below, where the general would demand his way. On occasion, she and Edward had been rejected by high society. This would not be the first time, nor likely the last.

Fifty-One

A Rumble of Complaint

San Francisco, California
April 1856

Downstairs, General Williams surveyed the foyer filled with theatergoers who were too late to enter the show. He joined men at the bar and threw back a glass of whiskey. He glared at the barman. "I demand to see the management."

Williams' stomach rumbled a complaint. He slapped his white kid gloves against his free hand. The onion soup he had for lunch crawled back up his raw throat, and he burped loudly. The barman disappeared into a side office.

In a few moments, a bald man emerged through the crowd and walked toward the general, then stopped to bow.

The general was pleased to see the manager grovel in the presence of the great one. If he'd had a ring, he would have extended his hand. Instead, he savored the man's low scraping before him.

The man spoke in a wavering tone. "General Williams, I would not be so bold as to—"

Williams snapped, his patience taut as barbed wire. "Be bold enough to get rid of that distasteful blot Spina and his courtesan. You know as well as I do that fallen women have their section in the third tier."

Meanwhile, the general turned and noticed a group of well-heeled latecomers forming an audience around them as he conversed with the manager. Men in red-lined black cloaks and women in bell-shaped sleeves gestured toward them as they glided past in the foyer. San Franciscans loved a spectacle, but the general wanted no part of it.

He looked again at the manager, noting a wet sheen on the man's face. He could usually sweat out a fool in order to get his way, and could command respect with a simple glance. A flash of pride crossed his mind: as a southern gentleman, he had grown up with his own personal slave. It was so entertaining to intimidate men of lower rank; in fact, it made life worth living.

The manager mumbled, "Well, yes, but . . ." He took out a ragged brown handkerchief and wiped his face, as if trying to erase it so he would not be noticed by the pool of observers.

Williams ignored the bystanders. His steady eyes followed the circular movements of the man's hand as he cleaned his cheeks, forehead, ears, and nose. He took a step closer to him. "But what, man?"

The manager blew his nose and dabbed at his eyes. He blabbered, "Well, General, I would ask him to leave, but you see, he did pay handsomely for those first-balcony seats."

Williams clenched his fists, holding them at his sides. "I say, either that sporting fellow goes or I do. I do not want my lovely wife in contact with that sister of misery. And you would be quite wise in the future to bar the Spinas' admission to the American Theater altogether." He rose to his six-foot height. "I shall not hesitate to report this incident to Captain William Tecumseh Sherman who is soon to take command as major general of the California Militia in our fair city."

He heard a ripple of commentary ebb and flow through the bystanders.

The manager took a step backward. "Yes, um, well, dreadfully, uh, most dreadfully—"

Williams persisted. "Your theater is on a path to perdition, my fellow, and you would be wise to consider its influence on your young patrons. Those young men coming from mines and dockyards are innocent, unschooled."

The manager stammered and wound his handkerchief through his fingers.

The general seized his moment. "Do not place their moral lives in jeopardy by allowing such degradation as Brianna Spina to permeate your establishment. Their poor mothers back in Atlanta would be weeping to think what they are exposed to here in what is reputed to be a fine theater." He stood back, satisfied he'd pressed the moral issue. Now he stood on a high cliff looking down at the sinners the manager entertained.

The manager sniffed. "You have a point, there, General, yes, oh, yes, you do, you do." He stepped back into a bowing, backward track toward a door marked OFFICE.

The general trailed him, his long finger pointing at the manager's nose.

Edward turned and contemplated the empty seat behind him. Since the general had been a dutiful patron of the parlor house for the past year, he was familiar with the famous man's imposing attitude. No doubt the man was lodging a complaint about him and Brianna down below to please his wife. Nothing to be concerned about. He yawned. It had happened before, and was sure to happen again.

He had gained respect for his skills at the tables during his five years in the young city. San Franciscans were a mixture of cultures and ethnicities and they accepted—no, tolerated—the risk taker, the outsider. Edward, the gambler, had fit right in. Any man with initiative could place his bets in business and industry. Fortunes rose and fell with the sun each day. One man's triumph became another's folly. The legacy of the gold rush lingered in the rollicking, devil-may-care city, a city that was still prey to the novelty of extraordinary wealth and crushing poverty.

Edward tapped his fingers on the arms of his seat, his mind wandering. New Orleans had been an excellent training ground for his dealings in this perilous town; the evil underbelly of humanity appeared here as well, and Edward recognized it in the people he saw and the cruelty he witnessed. The docks of Genoa, the wharf of New Orleans, and the bay of San Francisco—all of these harvested the lawless from countries all over the world. Human life was expendable; men and women were good as long as they were useful. Port cities received bloodlust and the lust for women's flesh with the incoming cargo. Other men may threaten him, but not the general, whose lascivious needs were satisfied inside their parlor house.

Despite the series of disturbances, the show progressed as scheduled. Their hands laced together, Edward and Brianna followed the onstage antics of the Martinettis' high wire act. Edward quite forgot the earlier disturbance. He turned to admire his lovely companion who sat next to him, her skin luminous in the soft reflected light, her full breasts reminding him of his urge to kiss her again and again.

That was the reason Edward went to the theater when Brianna pestered him to accompany her. Never mind the acts on stage. He cherished his time alone with her in the darkness, where he could admire and appreciate her beauty. She had grown up from the youngster he had won in his triumphant toss of the double eagle. The love they shared matured each day, developing into a ready acceptance of each other's strengths and weaknesses. He continued to ask for her hand in marriage, knowing full well she would always turn him down. Although he never held it against her, he always wondered why.

At intermission, the theater attendants lowered the stage lights. Hallway sconces blazed, and Brianna and Edward stood and stretched their legs. Brianna lifted her opera glasses and looked up at other areas of the theater. In the lens, she spied two young men who fondled harlots up in their designated second balcony. Brianna's stomach tightened.

Her parlor house was oceans away from such uncouth public behavior, yet the general public associated her with the lowest of women. At times like these, she wished she could go to Paris right away to open her seamstress shop. There she'd melt into the anonymous crowds she'd seen in the broadsheets. Celeste had told her of the cafés and charming villages of France. The way artists stood along the Seine, dabbing paint on their easels.

"Champagne, *ma chérie*?" Edward's voice broke into her thoughts. A white-coated waiter strolled through the aisles, champagne fizzing in the glasses on his tray.

Brianna's eyes surveyed the crowd below in the orchestra as patrons milled out to the bar. A group of lads glanced up, and one called out, "Strumpet!" Her face burned hot as melting lead.

Edward moved closer to her, and she felt the strength of his arm around her waist. He whispered, "Pay no mind, my love. They admire your beauty and wish they could be sitting in my place. Mere boys."

"I know." Brianna sat back down and examined the scuffs on the seatback in front of her.

He reclined next to her, and lowered his voice. "No maybes or words of doubt, Brianna. We own property and a business in this town like everyone else in this balcony. We have a right to be here, same as they do."

Her sidelong gaze met his. "You may be right. Those boys are so young. They know nothing of the world. I was an innocent when I first came to New Orleans."

His voice bristled. "They will soon learn the world is an unfriendly place for those who taunt others in a strange town."

Brianna shivered, pulling her fur closely about her shoulders.

The lights dimmed once again, and *The Red Gnome*, the fairy extravaganza, burst on stage, accompanied by notes from a piccolo. The good fairy entered from stage right, then flitted across the stage, her wings catching streams of light as she danced. Smoke machines pumped out dark clouds and from a trap door rose two lovers in an embrace.

This time, the noise in the row behind Brianna was too loud to ignore. The general must have returned to their balcony. Behind them, the swish of skirts and sliding of footsteps preceded a series of excuse me's. What was going on? Horsehair crinolines and bulky coats bumped her head from behind. Was the general summoning his wife to leave?

Brianna gazed back to see Mrs. Williams standing up in the row behind her. The woman was pulling her red velvet cloak about her shoulders. Her face purple with pent-up rage, she spat out words to her companion. "Imagine, Mrs. Lewis. A queen of sin allowed in the first balcony! Wait until the mayor hears about this. I shall speak to him myself. Brianna Spina mixing with genteel society. This is the height of moral decay."

With a flash of gold epaulets and a clanking sidearm, the red-faced general guided his party down the stairs and out of the box. Thank God for small favors. Brianna reached for Edward's hand and held it tight against her heart.

Fifty-Two

THE EMPTY PROMISE

San Francisco, California
April 1856

That evening at home in the parlor house kitchen on Waverly Place, Brianna warmed herself next to Edward at the stove. The marine fog had chilled their carriage on the way home from the theater, and her teeth chattered as she removed her damp coat and hung it on the wooden hook by the door.

After each day's affairs and before retiring to bed, Celeste fixed a delightful spread of sweetmeats and fruit, topped off with a variety of teas she'd purchased with Cook at the Chinese markets. Brianna leaned over the table and popped a confection into her mouth. "These are such good madeleines, Celeste! I daresay I'll have another." Andy pawed her leg, and she gave him a bite.

Edward nibbled on fruit and closed his eyes. "Try some of these grapes. They taste like candy."

After the staff would go to bed, Brianna looked forward to this cherished time with Edward, when they shared their reactions to the day. Sheltered from the cold, foggy night, this little meal was intimate and cozy. As usual, Celeste said goodnight and the swinging door squeaked shut behind her.

Brianna's thoughts traveled to household affairs. Right now, Emma and Richard would be managing the parlor house guests and the doves in the other side of the house. The goings-on were most discreet. In the five years they had lived in San Francisco, they had catered to high-ranked gentlemen from the upper reaches of San Francisco society, and the house was well-ordered, thanks to secret contributions to the San Francisco police who patrolled Waverly Place in return. Although their customer Williams was a US marshal, he was aware of the doings of the local police, and he turned a blind eye. He wouldn't dream of spoiling a good thing. Neither would his superiors, many of whom frequented such houses. And San Francisco's finest was fond of charitable donations, no matter the source.

After supper, champagne and light musical entertainment was followed by dancing, and then the girls and their customers went to their beds and slept through the night.

Edward's brown eyes shone against the candlelight. He held up the teapot and asked, "Another cup of jasmine tea, my dear? I would be delighted to pour." His respectful manners contrasted with the Spenser of long ago who'd served her last or not at all.

"Am I worthy of another cup of tea?" She freed her copper colored braid from her chignon, and it swung across her breast.

Brianna followed Edward's gaze as it traced the braid sweeping down over her shoulder. She felt a gentle tug as his fingertips fondled the fringe. "What do you mean by that? Are you worthy? Do not be ridiculous. You are a southern lady, my intended, and worth more to me than any new-minted gold piece won at the faro tables." On an ordinary night, she'd reach out and lure him with a series of kisses, first light, then deeper. Yet tonight had been far from ordinary—she prickled at the thought of her recent humiliation in the theater.

She held out her teacup and he tipped over the pot, pouring the Jasmine into the cup, the smell of flowers rising up in the steam. "I am most grateful." She bit her bottom lip as dark thoughts pervaded their moment together. "All the same, please be cautious, Edward. You never know who may call upon you next to protect my reputation. General Williams looked angry to see us in first balcony . . . it was his wife's influence. He's never like that when he comes here." She prayed that Edward would listen to her as he usually did.

He dropped a lump of sugar into his cup. "I agree. Even though he seemed angry, most likely on account of Jeannette, Mrs. Williams is stoking the fire. No doubt she's learned that he comes here. News travels like the bay sharks in this town. The very idea that we were sitting in the balcony right in front of her must have been too much to bear. One can hardly blame the poor thing."

"I don't know. He's like a mad dog worrying the end of a stick. That man continues to claim he came out at the little end of the horn with Jeannette. The night she left, he was upset with us because we couldn't give him another girl in her place. The other girls were taken already. I told him we'd have to interview other girls, but he was miffed and stomped out. He could cause us trouble."

"Is that so?" Edward's face darkened as he sipped his tea.

The swinging door between the hall and kitchen squeaked open, followed by Celeste.

Brianna looked up. Had the girl been eavesdropping as usual?

Celeste moved a tray of blueberry muffins from the sideboard to the table. Her voice sounded a soft French chime. "*Pardon*, Monsieur, Madame. I hear through the cooks that Mrs. Williams is a devilish one. She thinks she is superior to God, and she is most cruel to her household every day. If she did not pay them well, she would have no servants at all, *sacré bleu*!"

Brianna leaned forward, her elbows on the table. "Did you hear that, Edward? That woman has a mean streak. We certainly don't know the influence she has on General Williams. Together, they could harm our peaceful business."

"I'm not afraid of that, but I won't allow those hypocrites to cast a blight on you. After all, you are a Goddess compared to Mrs. Williams." She recognized angry flickering at the back of his eyes.

Old fears stirred inside of her. Edward had the same black look that night on the boat from Panama City. The night the thief had tried to rob him while he slept. The ruffian had pulled the moneybag from under his leg where he slept on his hammock. She'd reached across and tapped Edward, who'd cocked his revolver. That same glare had crossed his eyes then, right before he'd shot the thief between the eyes.

Brianna set down her teacup. "My dear Edward, she's married, and I choose not to be. For that, I have a black mark in her book and the book of her high society. You and I both know I will remain in the underworld compared to her place in the first balcony."

"Oh!" Celeste fanned her fingertips over her mouth. "I forgot to tell you, Father Gabriel left his calling card again today." Pulling it out of her pocket, she passed it to Edward, then stood as if awaiting further directions.

"Quite all right, Celeste. Quite all right." Edward gave a catlike stretch.

With that, Celeste tugged off her white apron and hanged it on the kitchen hook.

"Sleep well," Brianna said.

Celeste stepped out and the door squeaked behind her.

"On that matter of marriage, my love." Edward faced Brianna, his hands caressing her shoulders.

"Please, Edward, haven't we said enough about it?"

He cocked his head. "But we are not immoral. Father Gabriel lets us into his church and gives us communion, even though you are not a baptized Catholic." He reached out and took her hand in his.

Brianna's voice was firm. "Father Gabriel hopes that someday, we'll stop living in sin and become one in the holy sacrament of matrimony. That way, we'll no longer be a blot for him, too. He'll feel that he's done his duty in gathering two errant sheep into his flock. I, on the other hand, do not want to take a ceremonial husband. We'd appear to the town as the daughter of joy and her pimp." She slid her hand away and crossed her arms over her chest.

His mouth turned down in a frown. "I want to marry you."

"Edward, I'm not ready, and I don't know if or when I'll ever be." She could see moisture glistening in his dark eyes. "I can promise you true love."

Brianna paused for a moment. True love? Spenser had promised her that and so much more. At least she'd thought so, and then look what had happened. The dark swirling waters closing over Ambrose rose up in her mind.

Loosening her arms, she leaned her head against his chest. "Don't you see? We're different from the rest of the world. Because of our professions, we're outcast, ridiculed in high society. Even though your friends say you're straight as a string, and I know you to be more ethical than any other man, our world has ranked you elsewhere."

He shrugged and rolled up his sleeves. "All the same, Brianna, I have a duty to defend you and what we have built, no matter what others think. These are men's affairs . . . not women's. My profession is legitimate; it is even licensed by the state of California. I have as much courage . . . or more . . . than Williams. He may face guns in his line of work, but I face deadly odds, winner-take-all, every day I leave this house."

"Not women's affairs?" Brianna's voice rose. "And my profession? Does it not take courage?"

Although Edward drew away from her, she gave in to an angry force building inside herself. "Do you think I enjoy matching men with these young girls every night, when deep in my heart, I know the girls' lives are in ruins, each day, each liaison chipping away at their foundations as human beings?"

"But . . . I thought you enjoyed running the business."

"It's been a way to make a living here, Edward, that is all. Enjoyment? Never. Truth to tell, I'm not sure I can go on doing it much longer. Watching Jeannette suffer from her disease made me realize how deadly this business is." Brianna fought against a shiver that seemed to take hold of her.

His brows knit together. "I wasn't aware you felt so deeply about this."

She tapped her foot. "When will we have enough saved so we may move to France where I can open my sewing business? My hands itch to put patterns together again, rather than sewing them for soiled doves, as I do now." She blinked up at the ceiling so he wouldn't see her tears brimming.

Brianna tilted her head and saw a shadow cross his face. Edward looked so hurt. She rather regretted the way she'd responded to his promise of true love. She'd need to think about that. Had she been smothering her belief that he loved her, much as one would smother a mouse with a pillow?

Edward gave a sigh. "I have asked for your patience, my dear, about going to France. Consider the other side of the coin. Thanks to you, our girls provide a needed service to the men of this town, and they are forever grateful. Have you seen the gifts they bring their chosen ones? And the girls are more than loving companions. When the men are lonely or shut away from their preoccupied society wives, the girls serve as confidantes, friends, sounding-boards. After Jeannette left, the tension in the house vanished and the laughter is coming back into the girls. That is . . . most of the time." He ran his fingers through Brianna's hair, and loosened strands fell around her face. Edward's touch relaxed her the way the hot climate in Panama had dulled her energy and filled her with a sleepy bliss.

"All right, I'll practice patience, but I'm serious about France." Brianna looked up into his eyes. "Every day, young women knock at our door seeking work. I won't be satisfied until I find the right new girl for our house."

The back of Edward's fingers stroked her cheek. "Here we have a pleasant society, and I will do all in my power to keep it so until we leave for Paris. Come here, my sweetest blossom, sit on my lap so I may undo that luxurious braid of yours." His look radiated heat and desire. He gathered her into the snug harbor of his arms.

"This has been tempting me all evening." His hands combed open her braid, and he massaged her hair.

Gentle currents of desire awakened within her. Brianna found his passionate challenge impossible to resist.

"Marry me," Edward whispered. His breath came fast against her neck, and he raised her chin. His tongue parted her lips. His kiss was soft, yet deep and urgent. He brought her to her feet, and carried her up the stairs to bed.

Fifty-Three

BEGINNER'S LUCK

San Francisco, California
April 1856

After midnight the following day, Edward tipped brandy from a snifter, considering his next move. The last meager dice roll gave Edward one move plus two. Now Doc Poppy advanced one checker across the backgammon board. An unlit cigar perched on the side of Edward's lip as he sipped, his eyes intent on the green surface. Doc hopped his checkers with glee over the board on a lucky roll of five and six. His bright eyes reminded Edward of a spider monkey in the Panamanian wild.

Usually he could beat Doc hands down, but tonight was a different story, and his two gold pieces depended on it. Not a great deal of money, but a loss all the same. Poppy always played with Edward for practice and always lost. When Poppy won, Edward would fume inside until he outmaneuvered him during the next game.

Edward loved the back room of The Berkeley Saloon, its gamblers tucked into its warmth on these cold San Francisco nights. The fog-steamed windows hid players from drunken observers staggering home on the planked streets. In their secluded dens, serious gamblers could get to work at draw poker, faro, and craps, creeping to bed in the early morning hours, the mist cloaking their identities. They would sleep all day, then return to their tables the following night.

Doc Poppy cleared his throat. "I heard about last night at the American Theater." He motioned for Edward to roll his set of dice, then wound a lanky arm through the slats of his own chair.

"What about it?" Edward asked. What did the town stir in its pot tonight?

"Hear tell General Williams made quite a fool of himself in the foyer. Folks are saying he threatened the theater manager. Do you know he backed the poor man all the way into his office 'til the man slammed the door in his face?"

"Probably on a drunken spree. Not the first time he's been rambunctious." Edward shook his head as he lit a cigar.

Doc Poppy continued, "Heard tell his highfalutin' wife kicked a fuss about you and Brianna sitting in the first balcony . . . matter of fact, he was mad as a March hare."

"Do tell, so was he now?" Edward had seen Williams rage at various drivers and bartenders in the past, so this was not news to him. He also knew Williams had made a scene downstairs at the theater. Since he was used to being the object of gossip, Edward shrugged his shoulders and rolled a double. "Bout time," he said, grinning.

Doc Poppy groaned and said, "You always come from behind, you devil." He scratched his chest, considering his next move.

"Not always, Doc, not always." Edward enjoyed the easy company of Doc Poppy. He did not make men friends easily. A gambler's luck came and went. To trust was to make oneself vulnerable in this chaotic western drama in which a surprising act unfolded every day.

Long used to shifting alliances, Edward stayed away from rowdies and kept his thoughts to himself. The only person he shared most everything with was Brianna, and that because she had captured his heart and soul.

At the end of the game, Edward collected his modest winnings. "Doc, let me buy you a glass of champagne before we head home? It's the least I can do for you since you let me beat you every night."

Doc laughed and patted him on the back. "All right, chap, but this was just your beginner's luck. You wait 'til I warm up tomorrow night. I will be hard to catch. You will have to run fast in the poker game with me and the Hansen Boys from Sacramento." Doc got up and stretched his long arms into an arc above his head.

"Well, your running fast is my slow motion." Edward chuckled, reaching out his hands and gathering up his winnings.

One moment followed another until the men stood side by side at the bar. Red Hayes, the burly bartender, poured them each a flute of French champagne. Edward lit his cigar and puffed. Smoke clouds hovered over the wanton maidens and young miners embracing on the corner chairs.

Through the haze at the end of the bar, Edward spied a most dreaded sight—the figure of General Williams, US Marshal. He had on a gray wool coat; his red scarf lay next to him on the bar. A silver star glistened on his chest. Edward's heart thumped. He hoped to finish his drink and escape to avoid a meeting. Edward had nothing good to say to Williams after what had transpired the previous night.

"Will! How good to see you!" Doc Poppy unfurled his long arm in greeting and sidled down to the far end of the bar.

Edward swallowed hard. He knew what was coming next. The acid from the champagne burned in his chest. Damned hypocrite, Poppy.

"Edward, come over and meet my good friend, General Williams." Doc waved him over.

Edward feared his own reaction more than Williams'. He looked to the door, but the circumstance trapped him. To leave now would draw too much attention to himself. This was worse than eating stewed iguana with the Emberás on the Chagres. Every bite of the stringy meat had made him want to retch.

"William, meet my backgammon rival, Edward Spina," Poppy said, his mouth curving upward in a smile.

Edward tensed. Was Poppy trying to force a meeting with the general?

"Pleasure." Williams extended a hand, but Edward did not shake it. He wanted no part of Poppy's pretense. The general sneered and dropped his outstretched arm.

Yet Edward would not be entirely rude. That was not his way. Instead, he chose to bow, assuming a southern drawl. "Evenin', General." Edward opened his coat to show off his gold watch chain, which he knew would glitter against his red velvet waistcoat. In that way, Williams would know he was not the only southerner familiar with a gentleman's art.

He met the general's gaze. The man peered down at Edward from the bridge of his long nose.

Edward's cardsharp mind read the motives behind the man's disdain. He staked a mental bet that the general's wife had held a tirade last night when they got home. The general didn't need the American Theater when he lived full time with a woman who wore two faces—one a socialite, the other a shrew. The general might not be anxious for an encore. Yet, as Edward looked up at the general's narrowing eyes, Edward came to a realization. *He needs to squash me like the gambling beetle he sees me to be.*

Williams broke under Edward's fixed gaze. "Spina, I need a word with you. Could you excuse us for a moment, Poppy?" With that statement, Williams did not look at Edward, but past him, attempting to cause Edward to look around for someone else the general may be addressing. However, Edward was wary of this old lawman's trick.

Edward heard Doc Poppy mumble to Red Hayes, "Do I see Williams trying to be nice to Spina?"

The bartender shook his head, "Not like the general. Wonder what his mischief is?"

Edward followed Williams through the swinging doors and out onto the boardwalk. The saloon's lights shone out onto the vapory street, full of drunken miners. Young men in pairs and trios stumbled through the muck, some stopping to vomit or urinate at intervals. Horses neighed at their hitching posts, some abandoned by intoxicated riders.

His gaze flickered back into the saloon; his allies had stayed inside. The US marshal could have him clapped in irons on a whim. However, the lawman did not have grounds to arrest him. Instead, the general wanted to provoke him so he could satisfy his personal vendetta. Edward did not have to be his victim. He had a right to civil liberties granted to all citizens of California.

Williams wobbled on the plank sidewalks as soon as they got out the saloon door. Alarm bells rang in Edward's head; his stomach tightened into a sailor's knot. The general had drunk too much. Not a good sign. Although Edward pushed against him, the general's strong arms maneuvered his back against the wall. Then he extended an arm, blocking Edward's way back into the Berkeley. Edward's eyes watered at the pungent whiskey on the man's breath.

Williams slurred his words. "Let me be direct, *s-shir*. You set me up with that pus-ridden whore, Jeannette. You said she was the finest from Paris. I only found out about her condition this week on the *s-shtreets*. Then you brought your whore-woman Baird into the American last night in a deliberate attempt to blacken my name and that of my dear wife. In fact, you called me a whoreson to my face, you scoundrel."

Edward would not stand for this nonsense, especially from a drunk wearing a US marshal's badge. Any customer in a parlor house could get the clap. That was a risk any patron understood. And no one would call his Brianna a whore-woman. "My wife is no whore. She is virginal compared to that slut of yours who was all dolled up like some well-ridden tramp. I never talked to you in the theater, so how could I call you a whoreson?"

Edward's muscles tensed as Williams reached into a deep pocket, and pulled out a tan glove. He felt the rush of air as the glove flashed past his face. He ducked out of the general's reach and fled back through the doors to the safety of Poppy and Hayes.

Edward yelled as he turned, taking long steps back into the saloon. "Have I any friends in here? This man is challenging me to a duel!" His breath issued like shots from a cannon.

Inside, the bar crowd stared, hypnotized. Card players listened, patrons held up drinks, the semi-nude waitress paused. All eyes shifted from side to side, their heads unmoving. Spina's fear vibrated through the bar, and they felt the jolt of Williams' challenge. A facial slap meant the beginning of the end for a poor shot with a pistol. Many gamblers went down that way. Though masters of strategy and chance, a betting man was a poor match against a war veteran. Spina beat Williams in a duel? A hero of the Mexican War, General Williams was by far the better shot.

Williams clattered back into the saloon, his steps etching a zigzag pattern on the sawdust floor. He smiled, a blob of drool escaping his lip, and then announced to the crowd, "I promised to slap this man's face, and I aim to do it now." Any gun-toting drunk was a menace; the crowd shrank into dark corners. Drinkers dropped for cover, and many guests hid under their tables.

Lucy Carlson, the kitchen maid, gasped. "Oh, you mustn't do that." She ducked down into her pots and pans.

Even from his distance, Edward could see the man's scowl as he spoke to Lucy. "I mustn't? Where'd you go, you filthy bastard?" Williams licked his teeth as he looked around. Edward flinched; the general advanced toward him. He looked up in horror to see the man's puffy cheeks now tinged with purple, the mottled bits of white skin the color of sand fleas. And then he knew. All the signals came together at this crossroads—he was facing a madman.

Out of the corner of his eye, Edward saw two lovers cower on the floor under a corner table, their arms entwined.

Silence filled the room, the nooks and crannies of the saloon radiating fear, uncertainty.

The general's bulk filled the passage between Edward and the door.

Edward stilled his chest, a technique he'd learned on the Genoa docks. When a man felt fear, he must not show it.

Doc Poppy's voice made a surgical incision into the tension. "Well, now, gentlemen." His voice assumed a tone of geniality as though they'd been at a garden party. "Do come back as friends and finish our bottle of champagne. I am sure this thing can be worked out with a simple bit of conver—"

"To hell it can," Edward said. He grabbed his greatcoat, put on his top hat, and took deft steps around the general, avoiding the long reach of the man's arms. He strode out into the street, at once grateful for the milky wrap of fog that shrouded him.

After a blurry few moments, Red Hayes and the bar crowd knew Williams had lost the hand he had tried to play. Folding his greatcoat about him like a blanket, the man sashayed out.

Flapping a towel against his leg, Red considered the situation. The small audience inside the Berkeley had seen the best entertainment of the night played out before them. San Francisco loved theater in real life. At dawn, most inhabitants of the young city would now know what had transpired and where. Such events enhanced the reputation of a public house. Any time the bar's name appeared in the broadsheets, it was worth a paid advertisement—unless, of course, someone had shot up the place, which proved costly in the long run.

Red Hayes remarked to Lucy, who stood washing glasses, "I don't know how that business happened. Spina was sober. Williams was the one who was tight . . . and he's the law."

"Quite puzzling," Lucy said. She set a cup on a towel. "That is why so few decent women stay in this town. Some of the lawmen are more violent than the criminals."

Fifty-Four

THAT SWEET RIVER

San Francisco, California
April 1856

Back home at Waverly Place, Edward slipped off his topcoat and muffler. He sat down and Richard helped him edge off his boots. He looked at Richard's downturned head, the top of his dark curly hair mixed with gray. Despite Edward's insistence on removing his own boots, Richard continued to perform the ritual. After a while, Edward had stopped resisting, realizing that Richard was expressing a form of gratitude.

The man's right hand was missing two fingers, and Edward saddened. Such a horrifying scene in Panama City: Richard extending his hand, his face crumpling in agony, jiggers creating bunches of odd hills under the skin of his last two fingers. The hills were crammed with flea eggs that fed off his tissues. The doc had said his case was too far gone, and the parasites were bound to take his whole hand in short order, so they had to amputate the fingers.

Emma's soft voice interrupted Edward's grisly memory, her hands outstretched with his usual brandy snifter and favorite slippers. Andy put his paws up against his leg.

Edward reached out, petted Andy, and took the slippers. "Thank you, Emma." He turned toward Richard. "Mighty cold tonight. Breeze coming in off the wharf swirls the fog around. Gets into a man's bones." He slid his stockinged feet into the softness. With her usual thoughtfulness, Emma had heated them at the fireside. How they spoiled him.

"Monsieur Spina," Richard said, "Here's hot brandy Emma made special for you. Takes the chill off."

"Thank you, Emma." Edward took a sip and his expression relaxed. "Anything I should know about?" He tousled Andy's ears.

"No, we had an uneventful night, and we are at full occupancy. But, of course, you should talk to Mademoiselle about that. Last I checked, she was already asleep." Emma passed a lit candle to Richard, who led their way up the dark stairs to Edward's bedroom. "Good night, Monsieur." She turned the knob for him, and then disappeared with Richard down the hallway, the light from their candle growing dimmer as they strolled away.

Once inside, Spina sat on the edge of the bed where Brianna lay adrift in a sea of dreams, her arm cradling her head against the pillow. A nearly-spent candle had sputtered wax, but there was still enough light to illuminate her. He took a moment to appreciate her beauty—the soft play of her red lips against the white rose of her skin. Her round breasts rose and fell with each breath.

How Brianna distracted him. He would think of her upturned nose and her long, lacy eyelashes in the midst of a poker game, and inevitably lose that hand. Edward would imagine her hand caressing his manhood and forget to place a bet. He never tired of admiring her beauty, and at times, he wondered at the miracle of having her in his life.

She brought him joy unlike any other woman in New Orleans he had known before. Each day, Edward learned more about this complex creature whose life he had lifted from the streets. Yes, he had saved her from degradation, but she had also worked hard to build the life they had dreamed of in San Francisco. Now he could not imagine living one day without her.

Edward fondled one of her golden curls, remembering the young, lost girl he had met on St. Peter Street. She had grown into a Madam. Brianna showed great courage to run a parlor house, to ignore the taunts and smirks of finely dressed San Francisco gentry in the streets. Every day she had to deal with the many problems of her doves who were tender creatures, many not long for this life. Yet every obstacle seemed to make her stronger rather than weaker.

She was suited for the West—the rollicking existence matched her adventurous spirit, and she thrived here. Edward loved the way she ran the parlor house, her way of resisting their enemies, and her help in planning their future.

Brianna twitched her nose, and she opened her eyes to take in her beloved. She sat up straight. "I smell burning."

"It was the candle . . . see?" He held up the candleholder, the wax dripping into a puddle at its side.

Brianna reached out her arms to him, so he blew out the candle and crawled onto the bed next to her, nestling against her cheek on the pink pillow. The tip of one breast poked out of her nightgown, its soft, round shape beckoning in the darkness. His hand cupped that breast, feeling its firmness. Desire rose in him, and he drew her closer, welcoming her soft kisses against his cheeks, lips, and eyes. He rose on one elbow, and lingered over her upturned face, her eyes like deep pools of water. Edward wanted to dive deep into those waters, to lose himself in the sweet river delta between her legs. She opened her legs and he pulled off the covers and lifted her nightgown over her, revealing the ivory skin of her belly, the red-blond swirl of hair between her hips.

He sank his face into her delta, his tongue seeking out the perfumed center of her pink flesh. Brianna moaned, and caressed the top of his head, her fingers making broad circular motions. He spent time tasting the fruit that gave way beneath his tongue, and as her moans strengthened, he thrust his tongue inside her, making a circular sweep that matched her own caresses.

"Come to me, now," he heard her whisper, her voice choked with longing.

"Oh, my love," Edward murmured, and she rolled over, her back facing toward him, and he thrust his spear deep into the river of waters, the ether, the intersection of her and him, the place of *together, never apart.* Each motion into her made the world tremble, the earth shake, the very core of him come near to explosion, like standing on a canyon cliff, like standing in the ocean, deep, deep, deep.

Their cries, their moans, their sighs intermingled, and together they called each other's names, the names all lovers call with the hope and joy of eternal fulfillment. He burst into her, the flame penetrating the water's depth, creating underwater shooting stars arrayed in patterns and pulses unlike any he had seen in the skies at night, skies he had gazed upon from the docks at Genoa, the docks of New Orleans, the docks of San Francisco. He needed to search no more for the essence of his life, the match to light his soul. Brianna was lying next to him, her breast still rising and falling, her eyes twinkling up at him in the candlelight.

Fifty-Five

NOT A WIFE

San Francisco, California
April 1856

That same evening in her tiled hallway, a gaunt, red-eyed Tessa Williams gathered her husband's greatcoat and belongings, damp from the pea-soupy streets. "You've been drinking again." She heard a plunk as she dropped the items on the reception table. "You promised you would stop."

Williams looked down at her with a stale annoyance. "Yes, well I guess I slipped tonight." His voice rang with an insincerity born of working with criminals. After years of pursuits and arrests, the law knew how to wrap cotton around the truth.

"Quite a slip this time, Will, since you can't hardly stand up by yourself." Right now, he filled her with nothing but disgust.

He leaned against her and their maid Gloria as they mounted the stairs to their bedroom.

Tessa wanted more information about his doings tonight. "You didn't run into any trouble after your watch ended, did you?" she asked.

He collapsed on his back across their bed and lay moaning, his chest rising and falling. His jacket was opened to reveal his waistcoat, US marshal's badge, and watch chain dangling from the chest pocket. Tessa motioned to Gloria and they each took a leg and pulled his boots off, one at a time, dropping them on the floorboards with a thud.

"Spina," he muttered. His head lolled back and forth against the bed.

Tessa bent over him. Was he having a bad dream? Maybe some part of him could hear her. The mattress sagged where she settled on the bed. She mopped his spittle with her own handkerchief. "That Spina again. Didn't I tell you to avoid him? He and his fallen woman will insult someone else, and that will be the end of him. Let someone else take care of him . . . not you."

Williams lifted one eyelid. "Bastard." His eyes rolled side to side like marbles under his eyelids. From the corner of her eye, Tessa saw Gloria take a back step and lean against the wall, her face ashen. Poor girl wasn't used to such talk. As a matter of fact, neither was she.

"I will not have that language in my house, Will. And your drunken behavior has got to stop. Wait until my good father in Washington City hears about this. He will come out himself to take me back home, if need be. I cannot see you doing this to yourself." She saw their life as a cracked and splintered window. Where was the grand house, the traveling abroad, the fine gowns he'd promised her?

"Your Honor." He sighed. Drool pooled on his lips, then trickled into his beard.

Tessa curled her lip at the sickening familiarity of his inertia. As she rose from the mattress, he rolled over and sprawled, semi-conscious against the pillows.

"I think I had better sleep down the hall again tonight. Oh, and Gloria, let's not forget the chamber pot and a bowl in case he loses his dinner and other things." She cringed at the vivid memory of the last foul mess he made. She could not remember when they had last shared their marriage bed. Will never reached out to her anymore; their hugs and kisses had ended some time past. The more he drank, the less he seemed to care about her—she felt like an object in the house—a chair, a desk, or a table. But not a wife.

Gloria's timid voice broke into her thoughts. "Mrs. Williams, should I bring the bowl and the same towels we used last week to bathe the general?"

"I think so, even though last week, he missed the bowl and the pot completely." She sighed as she watched the man's bloated belly rise and fall. Why had she ever believed Will's empty promises?

Fifty-Six

IF YOU MUST

San Francisco, California
April 1856

The next morning, Tessa Williams perched on her Queen Anne chair in the parlor, half an ear on the gossip shared by the ladies of the San Francisco Sewing Club, and half an ear cocked for her husband's footsteps. The women chattered about last night's American Theater show while they worked on their needlepoint, darning, and crochet. With impeccable manners, they kept their eyes focused on their materials, their ears perked for the next round of gossip.

Tessa considered. Though social etiquette prevented these women from engaging in life on the streets, they knew all about it secondhand. She heard the general's heavy footsteps shake the floor of the foyer outside. The women stopped their usual chatter; their eyes shifted to the double doors leading to the noise.

Trying to control her erratic heartbeat, Tessa padded to the parlor door, her knitting in her hands. "Don't forget your top hat, General."

She looked back down into the five expectant faces of women who sought fuel to stoke their gossip engine for the next three days. "Excuse me, ladies." She bowed, ignoring their raised eyebrows and sharpened glances.

Tessa closed the double doors behind her. "Will? Where did you get your hat?"

He fingered the brim of his top hat. "Gloria gave it to me." His whisper was hoarse.

She stepped toward him. "Why are you going out so early today, dear?"

Rather than answer her, he looked away. Mrs. Williams blocked the front door so that her husband would face her. Will's face was bloated as a bog.

Tessa said, "Shouldn't you take some biscuit and egg first? Cook is preparing an excellent pheasant for the Sewing Club luncheon, and we have plenty of chocolate mousse for dessert." She could usually tempt him to stay with food.

Today his red, muscle-twitching face told her he had another idea in mind. "No, my dear, let me go. I have business to attend to, and there is no time to waste."

"What kind of business? You do need to eat, Will, especially with your heavy consumption of spirits."

He acted oblivious to the strain in Tessa's voice. "I will eat out with Dr. Poppy."

"Oh, are you meeting Doc? Good. He takes care of your welfare . . . especially, well, you know, when you overdo."

"No need to be concerned." He scowled at her.

"Wait a minute, Will." She glanced at the double doors leading into the parlor, imagining the ladies' heads bobbing up to eavesdrop on their conversation, then down to refocus on their needlework. She motioned him into the side parlor and closed the French doors behind her.

Tessa placed her hands on his forearms. "Please do not do anything unfortunate today."

The general's swollen face peered down at her. His eyes balanced on purple bags. Day-drunk, his pores breathed out whiskey. A sore oozed yellow pus at the corner of his lower lip.

"Stop." He pulled his arms from hers, then lifted her away from the doors as though she were a lamp in the way.

It was as Tessa had suspected: He was up to something this morning. "Will, don't jeopardize what you've worked so hard this many years to accomplish! You have citations on the wall, letters from the president, recognitions from more senators and dignitaries than I can count. You have a general's uniform hanging in the wardrobe. Don't let this one slight at the American Theater bother you and ruin it all. Do not squander our future, all in praise of demon alcohol." She crossed her arms, her heart throbbing in her chest.

What she recognized as hatred flickered in Will's bloodshot eyes. "I cannot let it go. Spina must be punished." He stepped over to the gun rack, and lifted off a Colt 1848 holster pistol.

Tessa stared at the gun, then clasped her hands in prayer. "Remember David's Psalm 34, 'The Lord is nigh unto them that are of a broken heart; and saveth such as be of a contrite spirit.' Be contrite, Will. Forgive."

He rumbled, "Ah ha! But remember, I stand for justice." His purpled mouth twisted like a mourning ribbon.

"But do you have to do justice when you are angry and troubled? Why not wait until you are calm, with all your faculties. Rash decisions carry deadly consequences."

Will peered down at her from beneath rugged brows. "Woman, have you known me to be rash when vengeance must be done?"

The word *vengeance* gnawed away at her trust. Tessa reached up and gripped his shoulder with the palm of her right hand. "Yes, I have known you to be rash. Outsiders may not see you as a hothead, but I have known you as one in this house."

"Madame, I assure you, I will simply pursue the law. That is all I intend to do today. Stand aside, for I plan to leave our house." He brushed past her and headed again for the front door.

A wave of anxiety swept over her. "I have but one question, Will. Do you love me? For if you do, leave your pistol with me. Then promise me you will come home sober and free from harm." Tessa neared him, her hands outstretched.

Will slammed the gun into her hands and she stepped backward from the force. "If I must." He glared, his voice harsh.

He clanged open the French doors, and stepped out.

Tessa followed him outside and stood watching from the front stoop. He wove his way down the hill toward the center of town. Praise heaven her father would never know about this.

Gloria's soft voice whispered behind her, "May I put that pistol in the armory, Mrs. Williams?"

"Yes, Gloria, you may." Relieved to be rid of the gun, Tessa placed it into the maid's open hands and returned to the Sewing Club.

Fifty-Seven

BAD DANCE PARTNERS

San Francisco, California
April 1856

Early that same afternoon, Doc Poppy kept an eye on Williams, who sat high on his barstool at the Bank Exchange on Market Street. The general regaled his companions with tales of past glories on and off the battlefield. He had a following of friends who could hold as much or more pisco punch as he and continue to do business the same day.

Over the years, Doc Poppy had witnessed enough scenes to know Williams and liquor were bad dance partners. The longer Williams danced, the slower he moved, until demon drink laid him on the floor or on a backroom cot to snore it off. Doc and his friends knew the man's weakness, yet in his early cups, the general made a lively storyteller who entertained them for hours.

Overhearing their remarks, Doc could tell the crowd sensed tension in the general this afternoon. A bitter edge framed the man's words. He seemed unable to abandon last night's confrontation with Spina, an event already fading into the annals of local memory.

When Williams began to slur his words, Doc rose and broke up the group. He recognized the telltale signs of a Williams binge in the general's unfocused expression. Once started, this man drank to the finish line. Doc shooed several out the door of the Exchange, yet many friends stayed on, curious to view Williams' next act.

Doc refused Williams' offer of a drink, but he was determined to stay by his side. He settled into a chair in their midst and listened to the end of his battlefield tale. Sensing the general's rising anger, he put his arm under his elbow and guided him out of the Bank Exchange toward home.

On their way out the door, Doc observed several men shaking their heads. One man remarked, "Spina had better watch out." Some said Spina had it coming; others held nothing against the gambling man. The peace loving Spina was nowhere in sight, yet all expected to hear news of a duel within hours. They placed bets on the general, but only one bet on the gambler.

Doc's mission was to get Williams home to the Missus, where she would keep him out of trouble. They had made it a half block away from the Exchange when the general slumped against him out in the wind-whipped street. "*Nevah* fear, Doc, I'm on my way home to the wife, my *prishon* warden," Williams said. A thin trail of yellow bile etched its way down his chin.

Poppy strengthened his hold on the man's arm. "I need a gentleman's promise," he said.

Williams slurred. "For *Gah's* sake, my good man, *whaddo* you take me for . . . a liar?"

"At times, yes, Williams, 'specially when you want something," Poppy said. "A promise will suffice. Then I will feel confident that you are not going to demand a duel." Doc leaned against the general to prop him up, but Williams shook him off.

"*Yesh*, I said, I *a-am* on my way *h-home*," he blubbered. A bricklayer's cart moved past, nearly knocking him over.

Poppy shook his head, helpless to change his friend's direction. "Well, then, until tomorrow."

"Farewell, Doc," Williams blinked a few times, holding his arms out to break his fall against the wall of a haberdashery.

Poppy persisted. "Sure you don't want me to summon a carriage to take you home to the Missus?"

Williams waved at him, and Poppy observed him as he zigzagged away in the opposite direction. Although somewhat concerned, Doc took Williams' objection in stride. He'd learned from seeing many of his patients turn into corpses that it was wise not to intervene in the affairs of angry men. That was the violent way of things in their city beside the bay. Underdogs did not last long. Such was the evening madness in a city grown too big too fast, its plank streets webbing in all directions away from the wharf toward the distant hills.

Down Montgomery Street, General Williams stopped to examine an oversized onion in a vegetable stall, then he turned back to make sure Poppy had disappeared toward the wharf. Good riddance. He had put on a drunk act to get rid of the good doctor. Anger simmered within him. Sonuvabitch. Not too much longer now and Spina would learn his lesson.

To be sure, Williams' burning stomach testified to the many belts of whiskey he had taken that afternoon, but all his pain would go away with one simple twist of the knife on his belt. He rubbed his chin as he contemplated. Rather than kill Spina on impact, first he would maim him, just as he himself had been infected by that tart at the parlor house. With any luck, Spina's wound would ooze and the man would die in agony. Were Spina to die earlier, so much the better. Self-defense—easy to justify in court. Any jury would believe the general. The reward of taking Spina's slime off the streets could not be weighed in gold shavings.

The Berkeley Saloon stood deserted that afternoon, and Williams' footsteps echoed through the empty barroom. He scanned the establishment; the sound of familiar voices in the kitchen brought back the previous night's events. Intent on finding Spina, Williams made for the back parlor. He surveyed the empty scene of last night's backgammon game. Strange. The empty room made him edgy. Sweat pearled on his upper lip. "Hayes? Hayes!" He called out in hopes of rousing the lazy, no-good bartender.

"What can I get you this afternoon, General?" A deep voice sounded from the kitchen, then a hand parted the red-checked kitchen curtain behind the bar. Hayes waddled out, a greasy apron wrinkled over his stomach.

"The *ushual*." the general said. He picked away some crust that gathered at the corners of his eyes. "And full chisel. I don't *wanna* wait."

Hayes slid over a double shot in a glass-etched tumbler. "Anything to eat with your whisky?" he asked.

The general put his hand around the glass. Maybe Hayes could be useful. "Yeah, as a matter *uh* fact, I could chew on a little information." He gulped down two fingers of whiskey and wiped his lips on his sleeve.

Hayes' hand quivered as he wiped it on his apron.

The general fingered his empty glass. He'd put the bartender a bit off guard. "*Sheen* Doc Poppy?"

Hayes grunted as he slapped a towel over his shoulder. "'Bout an hour ago. Said he had an amputation to do, then planned to come back here for dinner. The Mrs. is cooking up a venison stew tonight. Always pulls in the crowd, then they stay to drink and gamble. Want to try some, General? Mighty tasty. Steady you a bit."

"*Nah* tonight," he said. Despite the haze of liquor, the general saw the curtain move behind the bar. The kitchen staff was eavesdropping. The new telegraph had nothing on lightning-fast mouth-to-mouth communication in this town.

Hayes spoke. "Want me to send Doc Poppy to you? Where will you be tonight, General?"

Williams laid on the drunk accent. "*Nah* necessary. I seek Edward *Shhhpina*." He blinked, pretending to bring the two Hayeses into focus as one.

Hayes avoided his eyes and worked a rag into a spot on the bar. "This here chaw is the devil to get out. Fellows miss the spittoon on occasion."

The general planted both his elbows on the bar. He extended his right arm and clamped a hand over Hayes' moving rag.

The bartender looked up, his eyes wide as chestnuts.

Williams lifted Hayes' hand away from the rag and plunked it on the bar top. "By the way, I heard from the magistrate your taxes have not been paid on this place for a year." His now-sober voice carried both the wrath of the deranged and the clank of a jailer's keys.

The bartender pulled his hand from the general's grasp and squinted. "Uh . . . Spina? He was here not a half hour ago. He and Aspinall had words with Mrs. Hayes about her doings for tonight's big poker game with the Hansen Boys. Spina wanted her to add plenty of taters and peas to her stewpot. Adamant about those peas." His voice grew softer. "Also asked for sherry in the stew . . . said it gave it a refined taste. The man is always talking about New Orleans cooking."

Hayes wiped the rag down the counter, sidling away from the general. "Those southerners always have a different idea about food, don't they, General? After all, you would know, being from the South and all. I, myself, well I come from Maine . . . different flavors."

The general glanced back at the empty glass and gold coin he had left on the bar. The swinging doors of the saloon squeaked on his way out.

Fifty-Eight

MOONCAKES AND TEA

San Francisco, California
April 1856

Late that same morning, Brianna batted away a pesky seagull from her straw bonnet. She lifted her skirts to avoid the many mud puddles and dung piles on *Tangren Jie*, or Chinese Street. Women's chatter poured out of high windows; crashing cymbals burst out of temple doors. The parlor house stood midblock. Its second-floor windows were open, giving Brianna hope that Mei Li, the famous madam, was home today. Mei Li had come to the Bay City in 1851, and since then, had built up a famous parlor house through her own grit and determination.

Brianna knocked on the door and scanned up and down the narrow street. Laundry hung on lines strung between the buildings, and multicolored lanterns floated on wires above her head. Since there was no immediate answer, she peeked through a grilled window on the same floor. A girl sat on a wooden chair in the corner. It was hard to see inside since the window was dirty, but Brianna was intrigued, so she squinted hard. At first, the girl seemed to be a statue, but something about her seemed real. Mei Li expected perfection and complete obedience from the Chinese girls who came from her own province of Canton. She beat them when they did not obey, or cast them into the streets. Was this girl being punished for something she'd done?

Brianna remembered that all the judges knew the Chinese madam. Mei Li made frequent appearances in court, arguing on behalf of her Cantonese girls and her property rights. So far, Brianna had happily avoided court appearances; she'd kept the policemen well-supplied with flowers and perfume for their wives, with an occasional sampling of honey from her girls.

A moment afterward, a young boy with a long queue draped over his shoulder opened the door a crack. In response to her request to see Mei Li, he muttered in Cantonese and pointed down the street to the fish market.

Along Brianna's route, carts and construction workers threw up dust clouds where new buildings were going up. Men and boys pushed wheelbarrows and hammered nails into boards. Masons slathered gray mortar onto red bricks, the clay dust flying. Brianna held Mrs. Morgan's handkerchief against her mouth. Her thoughts returned to Mei Li, her confidante. Each of them worked to keep the police and politicians happy in the Bay City. The police came to their brothels to remove the occasional unruly customer in exchange for a handsome sum. The politicians came to enjoy a bit of unstructured female companionship in exchange for anonymity. Mouths were closed; everyone was happy.

Brianna stepped into a tea shop and pointed to a drawer containing her favorite tea, jasmine. A Chinese gentleman with a long white beard filled an envelope with the tea, and she dropped a coin into his hand, noting his long, manicured finger nails. She stepped out of the shop and continued strolling through the crowds of men in purple, black, and tan tang jackets, long pants, and soft-soled shoes. Above her head swung salmon-colored lanterns mixed with red flags that were embellished with gold Chinese lettering. Around her, the chatter of Cantonese and English filled the air, making its own discordant music.

She smelled Johnny's Fish Market before she ever saw it, the odors of crab, halibut, and jacksmelt mixing with ginger and lemon. She bowed her head as customary to the two men having their usual smoke outside the shop, drawing from their long pipes and lounging in their mandarin jackets against the doorframe. Brianna spotted Mei Li in a red silk wrap, studying fresh oysters behind the counter. The sign in Cantonese and English read FRESH OYSTERS JUST IN FROM TOMALES BAY. Mei Li poked a single chopstick at the vendor's face. Her Cantonese dialect fed music into the stream of voices. Her friend was haggling over the lowest price for that seafood.

Brianna joined her friend at the display counter. Mei Li met her gaze. When she smiled, her penciled eyebrows rode high. She wore her jet-black hair pulled back in a tight bun at the nape of her neck and a white chrysanthemum behind her ear. Standing on tiptoe in her lotus shoes, she asked, "Are they fresh, Johnny?"

He nodded, answering in rapid-fire Cantonese; Brianna guessed his meaning, based on his gestures. "Just in this morning."

Brianna waited for Mei Li's questions, which generally came after Johnny's offer. Once again, she interpreted the signals as Mei Li pointed her chopstick at the oysters and then at Johnny's face. Mei Li's voice challenged him. "You sure? The shell looks very dry . . . it should be wet if it's fresh. Let me feel them, please."

As Johnny reached into his basket to pull out an oyster for her to sample, the tiny woman greeted Brianna in English with a deep bow. "Good morning, Miss Baird, how are you?" She had a faint British accent, having been taught English by missionaries in her native Hong Kong.

Brianna bowed in return and gazed into her friend's nut brown eyes. "I am fine, Mrs. Li, and I am looking for fresh oysters, too. My men crave them with their champagne each evening. They love them along with the fresh salmon Richard has been smoking in the southern style."

"Ah yes," Mei Li tested the oyster with her bare fingers; she took her chopstick and pried open the shell to check the contents. Satisfied, she said in English this time, "These are medium fresh, so I want a lower price than the sign. They came in yesterday, correct, Johnny?"

Brianna interrupted. "But, the sign says *fresh within the hour.*"

"Yes. They try to sell all the old ones. I never make a mistake." She winked at Brianna.

Johnny bobbed, his bald head sweating as he gathered her usual order. From observations Brianna had made of these two over the years, she knew that Mei Li was one of Johnny's most discriminating customers, and that he respected her. Mrs. Li surged higher on her platform shoes, switching to Cantonese. "Only this time, I want a double order. Two packages."

Brianna loved watching their interactions, veiled behind the mysterious Cantonese intonations. Mei and Johnny shared a private joke, and Brianna stood patient while they giggled like schoolchildren. Within a few minutes, Johnny pushed two brown paper packages across the counter. Mei dropped a pile of coins into the vendor's hand and turned to leave the market.

While reaching up to take the package, Brianna sensed the hard tip of Mei Li's chopstick on her arm. She looked down into Mei's face. The Chinese madam said, "Wait. Johnny will send his delivery boy to our houses. That's why I gave him so many coins today."

Brianna said, "Thank you, Mrs. Li . . . most kind of you."

A small boy with a bouncing black queue ran up to them, bowed, then grabbed the packages from their hands. He bent low and swiftly ran out of the exit.

"Johnny says you're a very nice customer." Mei Li tucked a strand of black hair behind her ear.

"Good of you to say." In turn, Brianna dropped her coins into her companion's outstretched hand, and they skirted dung piles and mud puddles across the street to their customary teahouse.

Inside, over freshly baked mooncakes and a pot of green tea, they talked of their business interests and daily affairs in their parlor houses. Brianna felt at home here with Mei Li; they shared common interests, and over time they had developed a bond of trust that transcended culture and custom. Mei Li's girls came from Hong Kong. Most spoke Cantonese, no English. She maintained a firm hand on her business, and on the men who frequented her house. She had taught her younger friend much about managing others.

Brianna lifted her teacup and sipped the hot, green tea, letting it warm her throat. "I had to turn Jeannette out some time ago." She heard a measure of anxiety in her own voice.

Mei Li's thinly penciled eyebrows rose. "Why? The usual?"

To their way of thinking, *the usual* referred to the clap, or venereal disease, which was grounds for a parlor girl's immediate dismissal.

Brianna felt a surge of nausea. "She had putrid lesions on her cheek and around her lips. She was fond of the opium dens—too fond. A nasty business she created on her own hook." Somehow, saying it aloud brought back the image of the girl's oozing sores.

Mei Li's eyebrows pinched together. "I wonder where she will go." Her red dress glimmered in the smoky light. "Surely not to one of the local politicians. No one would take her in if she is in such a condition."

Brianna frowned. "I don't know. I keep the girls exclusively for one man each night. I saw how fast the girls got sick in New Orleans brothels when they lay with several men each night. After a time, they looked bedraggled and started acting funny in the head."

"Was Jeannette sick when she came to your house?" Mei Li asked. Her smooth forehead wrinkled. Her eyes narrowed and she pulled out her chopstick from a long sleeve. Brianna watched her stir the tea leaves in the bottom of her cup.

"She may have been sick before she got to us." Brianna nibbled the edge of her cake. "She could have taken sick in Paris and hidden her condition."

Mei Li stiffened in her chair. "This talk makes me feel unclean. We must keep our girls clean or there is much suffering."

Those words sobered Brianna. She thought about the sad but inevitable part of their brothel business. Once a girl complained of a swelling or if a pustule erupted on her face, that girl lost her position. Some girls fell into disgrace through overuse of opium or liquor. On rare occasions, Brianna and Mei took pity on some girls, even helping them pack their bags and paying their passage home to the nearest relative. Most often, however, diseased girls left with no home to return to, only to show up later in a pile of corpses heaped on a wagon to be buried—or burned if diseased—at the cemetery on Russian Hill.

On those occasions when a neighborhood policeman traced a dead girl back to her brothel, Mei Li would contact the secret society, who would ship their bodies back to Canton province for a proper burial with their ancestors. Brianna would send her girls' corpses to the pauper's graveyard where the body would molder forever in an unmarked trench.

Brianna could not forget the details of Jeannette's ragged face. "The poor dove is now on the streets. Most likely, she will find a desperate young sailor who wants to share her bed."

Mei Li's eyes widened. "Jeannette's fate brings bad luck to Waverly Street."

A chilly bay breeze whirled scraps of paper in the street, and Brianna pulled her cape closer around her neck. "We need a streak of good luck to take away this bad loss," Mei Li said. Cymbals crashed from a balcony above as a band practiced. Although Brianna heard the crashing every day, she still felt a start at the sound, like distant thunder.

Mei Li guided her friend by her arm. She pointed to a three-story structure, decorated with ornate balconies and Chinese lanterns. "Let us go upstairs to Tien Hau Temple. We'll ask for good fortunes today, to fill our empty teapot."

"If we must." Brianna shrugged. "Do you remember the last time you translated for me? Mr. Wu told me I would break out in rashes, one after the other. That never happened."

"You never break out. You avoid eating frog legs." Mei Li's eyes gleamed.

"You don't miss a thing," Brianna sensed her mood lighten at the prospect of seeing into the future.

Brianna followed Mei up the narrow staircase. At the top, Mr. Wu met them, his hands outstretched, his long arms emerging from the baggy sleeves of his jacket. She matched his deep bow, then lingered with him a moment, her eyes adjusting to the dim lighting and the tranquil atmosphere.

As they stood in front of the altar housing the Goddess Mazu, Brianna bowed three times, imitating Mei Li. On a first visit long ago, she'd learned that Tien Hau was the first Buddhist temple built in Chinatown. Today, the air was filled with sharp incense from burning sticks, and the *shu zhu* beads clacked as worshippers chanted their mantras. Gold statuary, flowers, and fruit adorned the red- and black-lacquered altar. Crimson and yellow lanterns suspended from the ceiling.

When it was her turn to kneel on the riser before the altar, she thought of a question for the Goddess. She must find out if Edward's love was as true as he promised.

On past temple visits, Mr. Wu had taught her that each inquiry had to follow an ancient pattern. Sometimes the answers did not come out plainly, and she would have to ask Mei Li to interpret them.

This time she asked the Goddess, "Will I receive true love in *Gum Saan*, San Francisco?" Following the age-old tradition, she shook the canister of divination sticks, and watched one tumble to the ground. Brianna grabbed a stick from the floor, and handed it to Mei Li.

She watched at a side table while Mei Li consulted with Mr. Wu. She held her breath. What if she did not receive true love? Wu ran a long fingernail across the number on her stick, then thumbed through various books. Turning, he addressed them in Cantonese, which Mei Li translated.

"Someone seeks revenge for an imaginary wrong. Receive true love . . . yes."

Fifty-Nine

LET'S MAKE A TOAST

San Francisco, California
April 1856

In the back kitchen behind the bar at the Berkeley, Red Hayes stirred boiling stew in the large, cast iron pot, trying not burn it. He propped open the alley door. The late afternoon breeze carried with it the steady beat of horses' hooves and the low moan of a distant horn on the bay.

Paxie, the stray cat, yowled from the side street. Hayes cut off some venison fat from meat on the carving board and cast it to her. From around the corner appeared a group of tiny kittens who gathered around Paxie, waiting for a morsel to fall their way. Hayes was a fool for small critters; he filled a bowl with fresh cream and laid it on the stoop, lingering to watch the kittens lap up their treat.

As he turned to stir the stew again over the stove, Hayes heard the unmistakable, booming voice of the tipsy General Williams passing by on Clay Street. "Pray he does not return." Hayes made a vigorous sign of the cross. "I don't want any trouble from that rascal . . . bad for business."

After footsteps reverberated on wooden planks outside, the saloon door's hinges squealed a warning. Hayes crossed himself a second time. "What now?" He lingered over the stew, bubbling in reply. He grunted, lifting the heavy pot off the burner, then wiped his hands on his apron. Spina's voice echoed in from the bar. "Thaddeus? Any drink in the house?"

"This ought to be good," Hayes murmured to the crucifix over the sink. Stretching his face into a smile, he opened the curtain to greet the party of three gentlemen, their dusty hats lying on the bar.

"Thirsty again, General?" Hayes set out his best cut-glass tumblers, one for each man.

The general held his head high, his jaw square. "Never turn down a drink." He wiped the back of his hand across his lips, and stood apart from the two men.

Spina tilted his head. "Henry Aspinall, meet our favorite barman, Thaddeus 'Red' Hayes."

"Pleased." Aspinall lay his top hat on the bar.

Hayes depicted an ease he didn't necessarily feel. "Pleasured, I'm sure." He swept his hand toward the collection of whiskeys glittering against the mirror behind him. "The usual?" He set a basket of sourdough bread out on the bar, and waited for a reply.

The general left his place at the end of the bar and elbowed between Spina and Aspinall. "No, this evening I want French champagne. Let us make a toast!"

Today, as on many days, Hayes marveled at the general's ability to hold his liquor until he made a steep descent into oblivion. A couple of weeks ago, Williams had lain face-down under a table in the corner, stinking of fecal matter as he did right now, and no one could rouse him. Hayes popped the cork, and poured the fizzing liquid into the general's glass. Wouldn't be long 'til this fellow would star in his own funeral procession down to the Mission. He'd seen his kind of drinking death before.

"By all means, a cheer," Spina said. The bubbles clung to the gambler's mustache as he sipped from his flute.

"What are we toasting, my friends? Let me in on the secret?" Aspinall's innocent tone carried no understanding of the previous conflict.

Hayes filled all the glasses and then stepped away to wipe the oaken bar. From there, he studied the men.

"I think we should toast our first meeting of the day," said Williams. He held up his glass.

"An excellent idea." Spina's eyes slitted, wary.

The three men clinked their flutes in unison.

Aspinall asked, "And where was your last meeting, may I ask? Were you two together in military service?"

"In a manner of speaking," said Williams.

"Yes, you might say that we were in a skirmish," Spina said. He sipped from his flute.

Hayes cringed, picturing Williams' threatening gestures from the night before.

"Ah, I see." Aspinall lifted a piece of sourdough bread from the basket on the bar and chewed on a piece.

"An incident of thievery at the American Theater," Williams said. His face flamed like a lit match.

"What was stolen?" Aspinall asked. "Spina, you know I love a mystery." Aspinall turned and faced the general. "Pray tell, General, was it a theft of gold? Or was it your wife's diamonds?"

"Nothing as serious as all that," Spina said, over his own shoulder to Aspinall.

"No?" The general's eyes darted from Aspinall's face to Spina's, where they froze. "Nothing serious, but indeed a theft all the same."

Hayes saw Spina's jaw muscle tighten, leading to a sudden decline in the merriment. An unearthly silence ensued. He stepped back toward the group. "Another glass before I step away, gentlemen?" He worried about the half-cooked stew. Maybe if he stopped pouring, they would take their conflict elsewhere. Their kind of trouble was bad for business.

"None for me," said Spina. His hand covered his flute, bubbles popping through the spaces between his fingers.

Hayes watched Spina fix a glance on Williams. The bartender cracked his knuckles on one hand, then the other, waiting for Williams' response. The general's eyes were crisscrossed with red lines, his shirt cuffs gray with ground-in dirt, and a strange yellow crust speckled the skin around his mouth. Even by San Francisco standards, where baths were costly and few, this man was unwashed.

Hayes tilted his head, assessing the situation. Yes, he decided—if the general wanted more, he could go elsewhere. This would be the general's last pour from this house tonight.

The general broke the silence. "Yes for me." He gave Spina an unrelenting glare. Then he did the unthinkable. General Williams grabbed the entire bottle from the counter, gulped down the rest of the champagne, and pushed the empty container away from him down the bar.

Hayes stood back from his side of the bar, his hands flat on the wood surface. Lord of Mercy, what else did this creature have in mind?

"Another bottle to go *arround*," Williams ordered. His speech slowed like a wagon with a bent axel.

Hayes was ready for him, his voice measured. "No, no, sorry to say, General, we're out of champagne tonight. More bottles of Reims in tomorrow." He prayed for help from above.

"What the hell?" Williams said, a frown creasing his face "I like not to be denied my *pull-leshure*." He passed the back of his hand across his dripping lips and shook off some drops of saliva that had gathered on the back of his hand.

Spina and Aspinall exchanged nervous glances.

Hayes suspected the men knew what he knew: the alcohol was taking effect on the general's mind. Too far gone to reason. "Another shipment's coming in off the wharf tomorrow. Lots of celebrating recently . . . a new Mariposa claim has been yielding lots of ore. Been pouring it like water." He wiped a towel around the base of the last bottle, and hid it below the bar.

Hayes steeled himself for the next reply. Based on the man's frequent visits, he knew caution.

"What's a fellow supposed to drink, then?" Williams' mouth curled into a vicious smirk.

Spina looked toward the door.

Williams tapped his index finger on the bar. "Can't drink the water, you know, for fear of the ague. What's a *thhirsty* man supposed to do in this town? Drink his own piss?"

Hayes shook his head. Williams whined a lot like those kittens in the alley this afternoon. No wonder people hated the general. Those who called themselves his friends hung about him out of fear. Hayes saw the tense Spina grip his hat. He guessed Spina was sensing an unlucky hand. In the meantime, Aspinall's coins pinged on the bar.

Spina said, "Thanks, Thaddeus, but I must take your leave, for a faro game awaits me at the Blue Wing." Cold dislike had erased his usual congenial expression.

"Mr. Spina, you are always welcome." Hayes set their empty flutes on the kitchen tray. He heard the smacking sound of the general's hand patting Spina's back.

"Mind if I accompany you to the Blue Wing?" General Williams' voice grated.

Spina did not utter a word.

As they sauntered out, Aspinall turned and tipped his hat to Hayes.

Hayes' skin grew cold as he watched the group fade into the street. Evening fog rolled in, chilling the city after a warm, sunny day. Yet there might still be trouble from the general tonight. If Edward came back for a game with the Hansen Boys, might Williams return?

Here's another prayer, Lord. Hayes signed another cross just for good measure to make sure the Man Above saw it. "Please keep Spina safe . . .

he's a good man. No telling what Williams is up to. He shivered as Paxie did when a strange dog lurked in the alley.

Back in the kitchen, Hayes shut the alley door against the breeze and heaved the pot back on the burner. He tossed another log on the embers in the wood stove. The stew would soon be ready for the dinner crowd.

Sixty

THE DOWNWARD SLICE

San Francisco, California
April 1856

Edward's face prickled cold under the misty fog that night. He hurried toward Waverly Place, glad he had made a quick break away from Williams, avoiding his offer of another drink at the Blue Wing. He was past due at home; his stomach rumbled. Tonight was Richard's night to cook gumbo, and he had promised Brianna he would be home early to enjoy it with her before his poker game with the Hansen Boys. He imagined his favorite oysters laced with garlic, and doubled his pace toward home.

Between evening affairs and day duties, Edward and Brianna often collapsed into bed, finding the other fast asleep. Tonight would be different. They would have time to hold and caress each other before he had to go out again. Edward gazed at a crab seller on the corner, seeing Brianna's vision in the steam from his pot. Her red-gold hair had formed a halo about her head this morning as she shrugged him into his cape and sent him off with a luscious embrace.

Edward's bliss-filled vision flitted away as he ran to cross in front of a slow-moving stagecoach. Once past, he bent down to brush loose dust off his trousers. All of a sudden, he was taken aback. Why did he persist in asking for her hand, knowing she would turn him down? Was he a simpleton? He stopped to feel a fresh apple at a fruit stand. No, he muttered to himself. He asked her because he could not live one day without her; because she was the heart and soul he never had; because her breath was his breath.

He dropped a coin into the till and bit into the golden fruit. Life would end should Brianna ever leave him, and he never wanted to push her too far. She always looked so forlorn when he mentioned marriage, and he only held out hope that with time, she would want to marry him, and indeed, it would be her notion, not his.

A hussy's laughter broke out of a brightly lit saloon, soon followed by a group of young miners who jostled Edward. Diners crossed the music-filled, fog-shrouded streets. The women were gaily bonneted and caped, and the men were in top hats and high boots, polished for the evening's outing.

Edward threw his apple core into the street, and watched two rats emerge from the darkness to fight for it. In stride, he pulled his gold pocket watch out of his velvet waistcoat, and checked the time. He considered the busy streets. Past six. He would find a quicker way to get through this crowd. He picked his way around couples meandering by shop windows, and said his excuse me's to the war widows in black lace. The fog moved in, swirling around corners, and he pulled his cape more closely about him.

As he rounded the vaporous corner of Clay and Leidesdorff Streets, Edward ran smack into the outstretched arm of General William A. Williams.

The general slurred, "*Shhpina*, I have lost my appetite for dinner tonight. You have been no end to damnable trouble."

Edward swerved out of the way to avoid Williams' long reach, but the general caught his forearm. The pain of the lunatic's grip was matched only by the gambler's outrage at the trap into which he'd fallen.

Williams' mug lay in half shadow in front of Edward. He was backlit by the oil lamps inside a tavern. Edward's arm went numb under Williams' iron fist. The maniac made a half-turn, and he could see the general's face glowing a bloated, hellish crimson.

Edward peered at the general's drunken bulk. He appeared about to explode out of his skin, a gruesome thought. Edward recoiled and covered his nose with his cape. What an infernal beast. He tried to shake Williams off, so he stepped off the curb. "I thought our matter was settled, Sir."

Yet the general persisted, dropping Edward's arm, then clutching him around the shoulders. Together, in silence, they staggered down the south side of the street toward DuPont.

Nothing in New Orleans had prepared him for this encounter. Not even one of the thieves he'd fought off on the Isthmus Crossing compared to this brute. Talk about Williams' ungodly strength. There seemed to be no reasoning with him, so Edward abandoned that idea and hoped to escape through a quick maneuver.

Williams' red eyes protruded from his sockets. "No matter is settled, Edward, until I see you in a coffin."

Rather than use the violence of which he was capable, Edward decided to rely on strategy, taking steps forward to slow the general's pace if he continued to drag him. Williams had all the power, and Edward had none. To make it worse, his opponent had the force of the law behind him. Anything Edward did to defend himself against the general would be suspect. He focused on the road ahead, trusting that the general would be so drunk, he would either collapse or give up.

What was that? Something metal clanked in the street. Edward exhaled puffs of air against Williams's arm in the cool night. His pulse quickened. Now he was sure that the general had unsheathed his knife.

He watched the scabbard bounce into the road. Where was the knife? In Williams' hand? Though the general had the weapon, Edward had his wits. He tore away from the general's grip. A downward slice of steel whipped the air next to Edward's ear. His gun—there! He slid his own loaded derringer named Betsy out of his coat pocket, and in terror, he thrust the general aside.

The general howled, throwing Edward back against the wall, and twining his hands around Edward's neck.

Edward's struggled to breathe, but the general's massive fingers expanded around his neck, and his vision began to go dark. One chance before the assailant made a downward thrust. Go, Betsy! He pulled the trigger. The pistol discharged into the general's body, the kick knocking Edward sideways against the building. The general's limp weight pinned Edward in a ghastly embrace; Edward looked into the general's wide, bloodshot eyes, and stepping a foot to the side, he let the corpse slide to the ground.

Edward rose up on rubbery legs. The horizon tilted up and down. A steamy spread of blood covered the general's chest. Edward froze, grasping his gun, conscious of a yelling crowd appearing like grains of rice pouring out of a gunnysack. Edward was grabbed, mauled, and mishandled by several faceless men, and from that moment on, all bets were off.

Sixty-One

SNUG AGAINST HER BREAST

San Francisco, California
April 1856

Midway down Leidesdorff, a certain lady of the night, Jeannette LeBrun, crept onto the porch stoop of a shuttered hat shop. She gathered her tattered belongings around her, preparing for an evening repast. Out of her bag, she brought a meat bone fished from a refuse pile earlier in the afternoon, and a raw potato. Lean pickings today, but it would have to do.

She fondled General Williams' gold coins in her pocket. He'd thrown them to her after their rough sexual encounter in the alleyway earlier in the day. Though she was no longer at the parlor house, he would seek her out and have her against piers, lean-tos, and lampposts. *Pah.* He didn't seem to fear getting the clap from her. As long as he paid handsomely, she would overlook his pawing and thrusting.

Of a sudden, she got up and peered down the street in the direction of a noise. An opportunity? Two male voices pierced the air, and she pondered. The voices resembled those of Williams and Spina. Were they arguing? Her spirits rose. In the Bay City, an argument could lead to a gunshot. With any luck, a corpse would lie in the street, and with any more luck, she'd get to the body before the crowds picked it clean.

Jeannette's heart doubled a beat: would she find some money in the victim's pockets? Adding to today's gold coins, she might have enough for a stagecoach to Sacramento where folks said it was warmer. She'd have to hurry. Her threadbare shoes met the dusty road—faster now, faster—toward Leidesdorff and Clay. Right—it was those two men.

She swooped onto the porch of The Miner's Hotel where she had a clear view of the scene. Then a gunshot rang out, an unmistakable pop that made her wince. The taller man—yes, it was definitely Williams—collapsed onto the shorter man, Spina, her former employer. What was going on? Spina lowered Williams onto the ground, then stood staring down at him. Jeannette glanced in the other direction to see men approaching—a grocer, his apron flying; a bartender, a towel over his shoulder; then a businessman, his top hat careening off to the side of his head. As she rejoined the street, they followed behind her at a distance, their heels thudding as they met the ground.

Jeannette got there first, breathless. Spina had stepped away from Williams, a faraway look in his eyes. He stood as silent as the corpse at his feet. Something had taken possession of him, but she had no chance to figure that out. Williams' bulk lay splayed out on the street, his head cradled in a pile of horse dung.

She heard shouts behind her now—no time to check his pockets. Damn the man, along with herself. But what was that? In the street, less than three feet from Williams, lay—yes, now she was sure—a knife. After money, the next best thing. A knife meant protection. She grabbed it up, tucked it into her chemise, and resumed a casual pace back through the oncoming crowds to her perch on the stoop.

By now the masses were rushing past, and sprinkled among them were policemen on horseback. Some men grabbed Spina and the policeman jumped off his horse and shackled him. They dragged him further down the street. Probably to jail.

Before anyone noticed, Jeannette crept back down Leidesdorff to her porch stoop. She curled up, pulled her rags about her, and patted the cold, sharp blade of the knife inside her chemise. Lucky for her, she'd been first on the scene. Lucky for her, the weapon lay snug against her breast . . . until the day she may have to use it.

Sixty-Two

IN MEN'S HANDS

San Francisco, California
April 1856

Brianna's day was restless, haunted by her visit to Tien Hau temple. Mr. Wu's fortune played a chant in her head: *Someone seeks revenge for an imaginary wrong.* She tried to sweep dust from the parlor, but the worries returned. Who was that someone? What wrong had been imaginary? While she worked with Celeste to bake a cake, her fears persisted. Then, when she tried to pay bills at the kitchen table, her accounts would not balance, so she bit her pencil in frustration.

That evening, the household set about their usual tasks. Emma rested her hand on the broom handle; Richard held the soup ladle up to his lips over the gumbo boiling on the stove, and Celeste darned stockings. Brianna looked up. She could hear Cantonese utterances growing louder from the back door. Accustomed to entering without knocking, Mei Li burst into the kitchen at Waverly Place, and leaned against the wall to catch her breath.

Brianna kicked back her chair and crossed the kitchen. "What is it, Madame Li?"

Richard took her cloak. Mei was quite a sight, her hair askew and a bruise on her elbow where she had fallen getting up the stairs to see them. The madam's appearance was forever perfect, so even one hair out of its red lacquer clip meant something was terribly wrong.

"Oh, it is not I who need the help, Madame Spina, it is you," Mei Li blurted out. She sank into the nearest chair.

Richard helped her out of her Lotus shoes, and Emma put the kettle on to brew her favorite green tea. Celeste said, "*Mon Dieu,*" and brought a towel, which Richard wrapped around Mei's feet. Brianna took a seat next to her, set a hand on her shoulder, and then paused while her friend caught her breath.

Brianna said, "Please tell us what is wrong . . . we haven't seen Edward in hours. He was supposed to come back for supper, and to see me." Her stomach churned. Each minute's passing brought more uncertainty.

Mei put a hand to her chest. "Edward is in jail, accused of killing general Williams. I am so sorry." She coughed to clear the idea from her head, then took a sip of the tea Richard set before her.

Brianna's mind denied the reality of Mei's words. "Oh . . . no . . . that cannot be. They must have another man . . . mistaken identity."

The others all nodded their heads in agreement with Brianna.

Emma's calm voice broke the silence. "In all these years, I have never seen him lose his temper."

"It is true! Monsieur Spina . . . very, very kind." Celeste pushed her darning needle into the sock.

"I agree," Richard said, then placed a bowl of steaming gumbo before Madame Li. She slid a pair of gold-tipped chopsticks out of her sleeve and speared a prawn.

Brianna watched Mei chew the seafood. "Do go on."

Mei Li swallowed, then spoke in a wavering voice. "The whole street is talking about it. My girls were babbling, and I heard it from one of them. I went downstairs to Officer Porter who said the vigilante mobs are gathering and they will be ringing the bell at the Monumental Engine Company—Big Six—to call the men to arms. The Vigilantes are a force to fear, and if they are after Edward, I am afraid for his life."

She stirred her soup as she continued. "When the Vigilantes hold a trial, they do not even call the proper witnesses. I lost many friends in '51, many of them innocent. You have no idea what they can do to a man. The men were half dead before they met the noose." Mei's charcoaled eye makeup blurred, dark rivulets bled through the rouged circles on her cheeks.

Brianna listened to Mei Li, now believing the worst about Edward. Here at last, she and Edward had achieved their dream only to have it shattered by some stupid, jealous socialite. "It was Williams' wife. She put him up to it," Brianna said. She remembered the boys' fingers as they pointed up at her two nights ago. *Strumpet.* All because of Mrs. Williams. Hatred mixed with humiliation filled her thoughts. Why did she feel so helpless? How could she confront such rage, especially if the Vigilantes decided to put Edward on trial?

Emma moved to Brianna's side, and Brianna sensed her comforting presence.

Mei Li said, "People say you made Edward kill him. Oh, forgive me, I was so afraid I forgot this . . . someone passed me this for you in the street. Here, take it." She pulled a tattered envelope out of her mysterious sleeve and passed it to her friend.

Brianna's composure was so delicate; she was afraid of the letter. What if it gave her even more bitter news? Brianna set the letter on the table, and said, "His wife wanted me dead. I know she did. She wouldn't get over us being at the American Theater that night. Instead of taking it out on her husband for coming here to our parlor house, she's seeking vengeance against me. So, she knew how to kill me by murdering my Edward!" Brianna sobbed into Emma's apron. "Why hadn't the general come after me first?" She rose up, her tears gleaming as they trickled down her cheeks. "I would be quite willing to die if Edward could live."

A hush filled the kitchen, the only sound the *plop-plop* of the gumbo forgotten on the stove.

"No, no." Emma soothed Brianna while patting the yellow ribbons in her curls. "Your death is not the solution." She made the sign of the cross. "Instead, you must think first. It is no different here than when they lynch my people in the South. In fact, many of these Vigilante people are Southerners. They like their noose high and their whisky strong. Part of their evening's entertainment. These people never change, but you are different. You have a brain."

"But what good is intelligence, Emma, when a town turns against you?" The roaring crackle of timbers from the fire in New Orleans jammed into her thoughts.

"It is worth quite a lot, Mademoiselle," Emma said, her large hands on Brianna's shoulders. "You also have something . . . someone . . . worth fighting for, whereas all those brute Vigilantes want is excitement, a Roman spectacle at the circus."

Andy stood on his hind legs, barking at a noise outside the kitchen window.

Celeste drew back the curtained window and observed the scene. "Look! The throngs are thick and moving fast . . . I do not see any ladies. Where are they all going?"

Richard joined her at the window. "I'm not sure, but those men are carrying rifles."

Brianna said, "Of course there aren't any women. It would not be safe for women out there at night. Even *our* type of women." Andy jumped in to her lap, and Brianna pressed her face into the soft fur at the top of his head.

Mei Li's voice hardened. "My girls said Sam Brannan made a speech in favor of the lynch law over at the Occidental Hotel. He complained that law and order has broken down in our Yerba Buena as it did in '51, and that it is time to put the law back in men's hands." This time she speared a carrot with her chopstick. "Always in *men's* hands."

"That is what I mean," Emma said, and her eyes shifted from Mei Li to Brianna. "You must use your woman's wiles so that men do not know you have power when indeed you do."

Overwhelmed by this sudden turn of events, Brianna failed to grasp all that Emma and Mei Li were saying. She remembered the second part of Mr. Wu's fortune: *Receive true love . . . yes.* She put her hand in her pocket and wrapped her fingers around the gris-gris bag. She reached out and fingered the unopened envelope, letting her hands feel the nubby vellum. She'd open it alone when no one would see her sobs.

Emma and Brianna worked together in an upstairs bedroom in the gathering evening.

Emma held up a garment. "But why do you want to wear my dirty housedress and apron, Miss Brianna?"

Brianna shrugged into the smock. Too tight up top, too loose below the waist. "See, Emma, it just fits. I thought you and I were roughly the same shape. Unfortunately, I don't have the lovely hips you have; too much up here." Brianna cupped her breasts, giving a disappointed sigh. She looked down to see Andy gazing up at her.

Emma angled her head as she observed Brianna. "Most ladies would say the opposite, Miss Brianna. The most desirable figures in *Godey's* fashion books all show women endowed above the waist, not below. The perfect X is what is necessary to fill out the latest gowns, I'm told, at least by our parlor girls."

"Ah, you've been watching when Giacomo comes to fit the girls with my new designs every month."

"Well, yes." A smile crossed Emma's lips, and her eyes had a faraway look.

"I see." Brianna looked over her shoulder as Emma finished tying the apron in back. "The next time Giacomo comes, remind me you need a new frock for the summer season. I will include you in the fitting."

Brianna paused, considering how to complete her disguise. "Oh, I know. Emma, please hand me the smudge pot from my dressing table. There . . . would you smear some on both my cheeks . . . make it look like mud. Your *Godey's Lady's Book* would be horrified. That is how I wish to appear."

Brianna turned around and faced Emma. "You are a combination of mother and sister to me. I am forever grateful to you for all you have meant to me and Edward," she said.

Emma's eyes wrinkled as her own mother's used to do. "Where to at this late hour? The streets are full of men, armed and dangerous."

"Yes, I know. But this is something I must do right now." Brianna struggled into Emma's greatcoat and pulled her slouchy hat deep over her face. "Just tell me. If you saw me on a dark street, would you recognize me, Emma?"

"No, I would not know you." Emma gave a deep sigh. "Please be careful. Richard, Moses, and I are truly grateful for our lives together. Without you, we would have gone into eternity forever apart. With your help, Moses learned to read and write with the tutor. Without you, he never would have gotten the job at the dry goods store. The owner, Mr. Hobbs, allows that he sets store by the hard work Moses does for him."

"We are a family of sorts, are we not?" Brianna wiped a misty eye with the corner of her sleeve. She straightened herself. "Now, I must be off. Hand me the envelope and I'll put it in my pocket. Excellent."

Andy jumped up in the chair, watching. He angled his head first one way, then the other.

Sixty-Three

WINE GONE SOUR

San Francisco, California
April 1856

Winds from Montgomery Street and the Wharf whooshed around street corners. Chilled, Brianna drew her cloak about her. The streets blazed with small crowds carrying torches. She could hear them talking about the murder of General Williams. At the end of a dark alley between two wooden crates, Brianna set eyes on a woman. The darkened form in a chemise was covered with an oily bed cloth; she pressed what appeared to be chicken scraps and lettuce into her mouth. "*Merde*," she swore in French, spitting out a pebble hidden inside a loaf of bread. Recoiling from Brianna, she sheltered her food as a bear would hug her cub. "Go away!" She sprayed food bits into the air.

"Jeannette, is that you?" Brianna's voice echoed along the brick alleyway. A rat skittered out of its hiding place, and Brianna rose on tiptoe as it sped past her skirts. Her heart thrummed in her ears.

Jeannette did not move; instead, she intensified her grip on her belongings.

Brianna would have to gain her trust. She held out the tattered letter Jeannette had sent her. "See? Your letter. Speak to me."

"Who are you?" Jeannette pulled her long legs in closer and shrank back.

"I am Brianna Baird, your former madam. I must talk to you. May I come closer?"

The woman shrugged. "Not too close." Her red-rimmed eyes looked glassy, and as she turned her head, a cadaverous sheen manifested on her waxen cheeks. An open sore oozed on her lip.

Brianna recognized Jeanette's bitter battle: disease and starvation would weaken her day by day until she shriveled away. She remembered her own struggles in New Orleans, and so humbled, she knelt down in front of Jeannette. Her voice was soft and gentle. "You say in the letter that you have the knife . . . Williams' knife."

"That I do," Jeannette said. She peered through sunken eyes. "Have you told anyone else at the house? Madame Li?"

"No, Jeannette, I have not. No one else knows but me."

"How do I know that you have not told some twisted lie and the police aren't right behind you? Eh? What reassurance do I have?" A bruise swelled on Jeanette's cheek.

"Reassurance?" Brianna felt an anger rising within her she had not felt before. "Jeannette, listen to me! You have the only evidence that can possibly save Monsieur Spina from the rope. Without it, the Vigilantes will dispense with the trial, take him from the Battery Street Jail, and hang him at any minute. You alone have the knife that proves my husband shot General Williams in self-defense."

"Yes, I do, and it is worth much." Her round eyes shrank to dots in the ashen face.

"I am willing to do anything, pay anything, to have that knife."

"You will never have this knife, Mademoiselle Baird." Jeannette hissed. "We need to talk about the past . . . my past, and the reason you turned me out into the street like a dog. Do you know I was raped my first night on the street, out in the middle of Portsmouth Square by a gang of toughs? Australians. Called the Sydney Ducks. Do you know a policeman looked on and laughed? I am still bleeding. The only revenge I have is that they are suffering the clap by now, and that they have carried their curse back to their home country where they can spread it even further. *Mon Dieu*!" Jeannette spat, then wept aloud and rocked from side to side.

Brianna heard her own sharp gasp. What a dreadful tale. "I am sorry," Brianna said. She crouched down closer, speechless at the pitiable sight. A question burned inside her. "How did you get . . . um . . . sick? Surely not at our house. Your customers wore the French letters we gave you, didn't they?"

"Yes, yes, of course they did. I made them put them on, right in front of me . . . except for one time. It turns out that one time was all it took." Jeannette looked out into mid-space. "I got the disease from the Irish ship captain from New York who visited last summer. God save me, I did not see his sores until the morning, and then I knew I was in danger.

"Danger?"

"A few days after, I had a painful sore down there, getting worse and worse. To top it off, I felt sick and dizzy."

"You never thought of coming to me?"

"I feared you would cast me out then and there. So, I went to see one of my friends, a girl at Madame Li's. I told her about my pains. She took me to a Chinese *herboriste*. He gave me some kind of green paste to use, but the sores kept coming."

Brianna imagined the scene: the girl opening her legs, inserting the green paste on the end of a stick, her sores raw and pussy. Nausea rose in her gut, followed by sympathy for Jeannette's plight. "Whenever did you start taking the drugs?"

"I first began the opium to take away the symptoms. One of Madame Li's had used it, and she invited me to a secret den where the Chinese go to smoke. It helped to dull the pain for a spell. But the sores began to spread down there, and one night, I bled all over Judge Kimball."

"I'm surprised he didn't mention it to me."

Jeannette's voice was acrid as wine gone sour. "You don't understand, do you? There's a code among girls and a code among Johns. The rules forbid sharing certain things with the Madam, things that cause trouble. But then Judge Kimball told your other customer, the mayor, about my illness, and my secret was out."

The ground was hard under Brianna's knees, pebbles grinding into the skin beneath her skirts. "What happened the night of the fight?"

The woman's lip curled in a sneer. "I was taking shelter on the streets, and I saw two men fighting down the block. Their voices sounded familiar. When I drew near, I recognized Mr. Spina struggling against someone. The general was trying to stab Mr. Spina with a knife. Mr. Spina drew a gun and shot the general. The knife bounced away and I picked it up before the crowd got there. I have no love for either one of you, Miss Baird. I plan to keep the knife. That way, Spina cannot argue self-defense. It is a good way to pay Spina back for all he, and you, did to me."

"So, you have the knife, but there is something I can't figure out. Jeannette, why didn't you tell me or Celeste right away that you were sick instead of going to the opium sellers? We could have taken care to send you back to France to your *famille*. I sent you away because you had the clap and were using opium. Had I known about your disease before it spread, I would have acted differently."

"My God. I would never go back to France. I have no *famille*. They put me out onto the streets of Rouen when I was ten. All that is over now. The Chinese herbalist says I am dying; it will only be a matter of time. The nuns will not take me in. I tried. They said I am the devil's girl and am bound for hell. Nothing can be done." Soot mixed with tears on her face.

"So, Jeannette, why bother to send me the letter?" Brianna crept closer.

Jeanette looked at her, surprise mixed with indignation. "Madame Spina, you say I should have told you right away that I was sick. But you don't realize how badly you treated me. In fact, you ignored me throughout my stay with you. As long as I obeyed the house rules and entertained the men, you hardly spoke to me. That is, until you saw signs of my illness.

Then you were very cruel to send me away without letting me tell you my side of the story. You came in that morning, threw my clothes in a bag, and then cast me out into the street like a mongrel. I knew I was wrong. I only wanted you to hear me out. I knew I had little time left, and that soon enough you would know about my condition."

Jeanette paused, her face a wreath of shame.

Brianna knew that disgrace.

Jeannette continued. "Examine your heart, Miss Baird. Haven't you ever been lost, alone? Hurting? Afraid? Perhaps so alone you thought death would be a tender gift?" Jeannette sobbed into her rags.

Brianna heard Jeannette's questions, but her mind wandered into a labyrinth. She saw Father casting her down the stairs and aiming plates at her. She felt again the pain of that day and the numb desolation of gathering her belongings, knowing she had no home, and possibly would never have a home again. And as Brianna gazed at Jeannette, she saw herself, and she knew she had played the role of her own father in ignoring, then casting out this lost girl.

Fear had driven her to get rid of Jeannette, yet she now knew that fear had driven her father to rid himself of the humiliation and despair he could not face. Instead, by forgiving his daughter, Father could have paved a path from his own dungeon into the light. Now, somehow, Brianna had been given a second chance to forgive this girl whom she had sent away to die, and that was a sign she must surely act upon.

"Here," Brianna said, placing ten gold coins in Jeannette's hand. The girl's cracked fingers made a fist around the money.

"I was wrong, Jeannette, to treat you the way I did. You were hurt and in despair, and I discarded you, forgetting how lost I once was, and could be again, should luck turn against me. Come back to my house.

Emma will run a hot bath for you. Take back your old bedroom and live out your days in peace. I will not have you spend one more night in pain and misery. Please, please come."

Jeannette pulled back, her face gray and forlorn. "No, Madame, I will never come back to you. I may only have a few more days left to live. I wish to spend them with any serenity left in my heart. With my knife. Now, go and leave me alone." She shrouded her head with her lice-infested blanket, rolled herself into a tight ball, and turned as hard as stone.

Sixty-Four

THE SWEET STENCH OF DEATH

San Francisco, California
April 1856

At ten o'clock the next Monday morning, Brianna looked over at Emma, both of them well-disguised as young miners. They sat in spectator chairs in the city marshal's office in the Jenny Lind City Hall, awaiting the results of the general's inquest. They surveyed the rowdy crowd flowing in, prepared for the hearing.

Emma leaned toward Brianna. "I am glad we are in this getup, Mademoiselle. Look at all the angry men's faces, I cringe to think what is in their minds."

"Revenge is in their thoughts, sure as I breathe."

"It was that way in Louisiana, too. Why are people so quick to judge?"

"I wish I knew . . . I fear so for our Edward." Brianna regarded her deliberately grubby hands, and her thoughts floated into the next room where a few minutes ago, she and Emma had filed passed Williams' body lying in state on a table for the crowd. The corpse still lay there, bloated and green, coins on the man's eyes, in full dress uniform, a white cloth tied above his head to hold the jaw closed.

The sweet stench of death continued to permeate Brianna's senses. *Ick*. She pressed a red miner's scarf to her nose in hopes of quelling the nausea. Although she'd seen plenty of dead bodies lying on street corners in New Orleans, she could only glance in horror, then look away. What had existed in hearsay now took shape as reality: Williams was stone dead and Edward accused of his murder.

Edward sat at a table, his back to her. If only she could see his face, but he looked straight ahead. What he must be feeling and thinking right now, Brianna could only guess.

The verdict was expected any minute. "Did you see the size of the mob at the jailhouse?" Brianna asked. She peered over at Emma and brushed away the drifts of hair that poked out from her floppy straw hat.

Between nervous glances around the room, Emma spoke in a whisper. "More amazing was the number of Vigilante troops. Did you see? Must have been fifty armed men."

"Madame Li said they were an ordered bunch, like an army. They scare the bejesus out of me."

Emma flinched. "Don't swear, Mademoiselle, God will hear you . . . even now."

Brianna pointed her tin cup, carried as part of her disguise, toward a stately looking woman in a black feathered hat perched in the front row. "That's Mrs. Williams sitting over there."

Emma whispered, "She's handsome enough."

"Enough for what, Emma?"

"To hold her husband's interest, Mademoiselle."

"Looks deceive, dear Emma. Sometimes people's insides don't match their outsides."

"Makes me grateful for my Richard." Emma exhaled softly.

"Yes. He is a good man. Look there, Emma. There's evidence laid out on the table." Emma whispered, "His gun?"

"Edward's derringer, named Betsy." Brianna swallowed a sob escaping her throat. The import of what had happened began to sink in.

The judge's voice penetrated the smoky haze. "Has the coroner's jury come to a verdict?"

"Yes, Your Honor, we have."

"Would the foreman please read the jury's findings?"

A hush filled the room. Brianna's mouth went dry as a tickling weed.

A tall, lanky juror held a paper in his hand and pushed his spectacles farther up his nose. "William A. Williams came to his death by a pistol shot fired from the hands of one Edward Spina the night of Saturday, April 19th, between the hours of six and seven o'clock, at the corner of Clay and Leidesdorff streets in the city of San Francisco, in front of a store occupied by Fox and O'Connor."

Brianna's hand clutched Emma's arm, then removed it, mindful of her disguise.

"Williams was deprived of his life by the said Spina; and from the facts produced, the jury believes the said act was premeditated."

"Oh, no." Brianna covered her mouth to stifle a cry of wild pain.

A loud *huzzah* resounded from the gallery. A shout rang out. Feet pounded the wood floors.

A husky male voice called out, "'Bout time we get some law and order in this town."

The judge rose at the bench and pounded his gavel. "Order!" When he had regained silence in his court, he sat down again. "Will the defendant rise?"

Edward and a scrawny young attorney, provided by the bar, got to their feet. The judge said, "Since the jury has spoken, I order the prisoner returned to the jail to await trial on the charge of capital murder."

Another set of cheers rose from the floorboards to the rafters of the courtroom. The bailiffs crossed the room and took Edward in hand. His ball and chain slid and dragged behind him on the floor, his hands bound behind him with heavy chains and locks.

As they filed out among the celebratory crowd of men, Brianna heard Mr. Hawkes say to his companion, "Brianna Spina's fault. She put him up to it." The owner of The Fishtrap Café nodded in response. "She should swing right next to him, as an example to all the women who might consider such a thing. I'm tired of all the ballot-box stuffing going on. Law and order has gone to rack and ruin in our city. I'm going over to join the Vigilantes."

"Me, too," said Mr. Hawkes.

Through her newfound grief, Brianna whispered a prayer: *God, keep Edward from the rope.*

Sixty-Five

THE MIDST OF CHAOS

San Francisco, California
April 1856

An hour had passed since Brianna had left Emma at the parlor house. Brianna knew she must act quickly, for she had few friends in this town at the moment. She considered their situation. If the goal of the Vigilante movement was to displace the government in power, none of them were safe. After changing back into her day dress and cloak, Brianna followed the backdoor alley to Mei Li's parlor house.

A Chinese musical group was practicing on an upstairs floor, and the sound of their familiar crashing cymbals filled the street. She noticed the windows were tightly shuttered on the brick house. A houseboy peeked through the iron bars of the heavy door, then ushered Brianna in with much bowing and ceremony.

She heard Mei Li's high-pitched voice lecturing the cook in the kitchen, in half-Cantonese, half-English. "Not enough chicken in the broth . . . what . . . did you steal from me? Last night's wonton soup was horrible!"

Brianna cringed, expecting the crash of a thrown pot at any moment. Standing behind the houseboy as he opened the kitchen door, Brianna saw her friend poke her chopstick into the poor cook's back, and he yowled.

Brianna crossed into the kitchen, the smell of fried vegetables surrounding her. "Mei, I have so much to tell you."

Mei Li turned and smiled. "Oh! My good friend! Madame Spina!" She banished the butler, snapped opened her fan, and shot a menacing glare over her shoulder at the cook. She took Brianna's arm. "Come, sit. No one will bother us in here."

She led Brianna out of the kitchen, and they descended onto large satin cushions that filled the floor in Mei's drawing room, where bright sunbeams illuminated the red walls. A small golden statue of a rotund Buddha, one hand raised, illuminated a niche in the corner.

Brianna removed her gloves. "I went to the inquest." She looked down at her hands, still smudged from this morning's disguise. "I am most troubled."

"I heard the verdict from my friends at court. I have many friends in the court system; it's the best way to help my girls. Unfortunately, I asked for their help, but they all had other cases, too busy to help you and Edward. Corruption is everywhere in this town."

Brianna felt Mei pat her arm and a shock ran through her. She said, "Edward is in great danger." She'd known this, but to say it to another gave it truth.

Her friend's voice lowered. "I know. My friends tried to give money to the judge. Impossible, they said. No one was saved." She gave her head one firm shake, her gold hairpiece dangling against her black chignon. "The city government will hang Mr. Edward for fear the town will riot. Then the Vigilantes will have him. Edward is a pawn in their hands. His life is a tool for one group getting power, that is all. I saw many such things as a girl in Hong Kong."

"I know you speak the truth, but my mind is a muddle." Brianna searched Mei Li's face, hoping for illumination.

Mei Li tilted her head. "I have one question. Why would he shoot Williams?"

Brianna fixed her eyes on the oil lamp next to her. "Let me think, Mei Li. It's all been so sudden." She paused to gather her thoughts. "All right. Here's what I know. Edward shot Williams in self-defense. The only piece of evidence on Edward's behalf is the knife. Jeannette saw the fight from a distance, and grabbed the knife from the ground afterward. Now she won't give it up. My fear is that even if she did surrender it, no one would believe her, even if she presented it to the magistrate. She's a lowly prostitute with no voice. I'm desperate . . . at my wit's end. I can't imagine what to do."

"I must think." Mei Li's eyes closed, and she leaned back in her black lacquer chair. She stroked her chin with her closed fan. "In the midst of chaos, there is also opportunity. So says our famous Chinese warrior, Sun Tzu."

"Yes, you have told me other things he has said," Brianna said, wiping her eyes. A silent moment passed, enveloping them both.

Then Mei said, "I think I know of an opportunity. I helped a famous man once with a murder case involving a Chinese prostitute. I translated and got evidence for him. He is a criminal lawyer, Colonel F.T. Billings. He does not think like other men; he is independent.

Brianna's eyes widened. "Where can I find him?" She moved to the edge of her chair.

Mei put out her hand. "Be wise, Madame Spina, rather than hasty. Plan your words well before you go to see him. Make your case to him. Convince him of all the ways your husband is a good man. He will need to be persuaded why he must take such a lost cause."

"How can I best prepare and convince him?"

"Same as our Chinese women—with your wits and pocketbook. I will send a messenger to him to ask to see you. In the meantime, take this." Mei Li reached over and pulled a Chinese charm out of a red brocade box.

Brianna felt her friend's warm hands press the object into her hand. She looked down at the small, white-jade Buddha on a red string that was nestled in her palm.

"Carry this with you, *mèimei*, younger sister. It will bring you good luck, for right now, you are a woman warrior going into battle."

Brianna nestled it next to the gris-gris in her bag. Double protection in the land of crisscross.

Sixty-Six

ANSWERS TO MY PRAYERS

San Francisco, California
April 1856

On the following morning, the aroma of French perfume and freshly baked croissants filled the air around Brianna and Emma as they waited in the antechamber of F.T. Billings, the venerable defense attorney. Male voices murmured on the other side of the wall. Matthew Primm, the secretary, opened the door with a flourish.

The balding Primm ushered in Brianna and Emma, making room for their broad skirts. He announced, "The Mrs. Brianna Spina party, Mr. Billings. The lawyer pointed to the telltale croissant crumbs on Matthew Primm's lips and he chuckled. Her bit of baked bribery had worked—she'd gotten in to see the great man earlier than expected.

Brianna took a deep breath as the distinguished attorney and his loyal friend Governor Foote stood up from their comfortable chairs, where they enjoyed a drop of brandy before the lunch hour. Brianna lifted the black veil over her hat, and she and Emma settled into the chairs facing his massive desk.

Emma rested the basket of croissants on Mr. Billings' desk and then sat back. Brianna noticed the lack of dust on the many law books upright on the bookshelves behind him.

Under the most modest circumstances, Mr. Billings would make a most imposing impression. His gray, curly hair framed his long face and bushy sideburns. His eyes were clear and blue, his gaze serene.

After an exchange of greetings, the attorney strode to an open side window and shut it. "That pounding is constant! When will they ever be done building and rebuilding this town? Now, what may I do for you, Miss Baird?" His dark brows knit with curiosity as he scanned the basket of croissants on his desk.

Governor Foote said, "Ladies, if you would like, I will take my leave. Many clients prefer a confidential meeting with Mr. Billings."

Brianna raised her eyebrows. "Oh, no, Governor, please stay. I have nothing to hide here, as my maid Emma knows. I am so grateful to both of you for hearing my case." She brushed a lock of hair out of her eyes, and Mr. Billings smiled.

"You are not at all what your repu—" He stopped, wordless, unusual for a lawyer of great stature in this town. He cleared his throat instead.

"You mean I do not look like a madam." Brianna managed a smile. "I take that as a compliment, Mr. Billings. I trade merely in the oldest of professions, and thanks to the grace of the Almighty, Mr. Spina treats me as his wife." She fondled the gris-gris bag in her pocket.

"You have lived here in Yerba Buena awhile?" Governor Foote sipped his brandy. His white hair hung about his collar in long waves.

"For the past few years, my husband and I have built up our parlor house concern from scratch, and we have made many friends in the trade. He has been successful at cards, having learned at the tables in New Orleans as just a young boy. He also plays the horses, and now we have two prizewinning studs, named Mississippi and Double Eagle. We have a faithful group at Waverly Place, and our house is an orderly one. Our gentlemen are regular, and we do not accept transients, only permanent residents of San Francisco . . . of certain means, of course." Brianna held her head up high.

The lawyer's tone was somber. "I know you are here about your husband, Miss Baird. Please tell me of your concerns." He opened a desk drawer, extracted a sheet of vellum, then dipped his pen in an inkwell.

Brianna's head began to spin, and as if knowing this, Emma reached across from her chair, and put her hand on Brianna's.

Emma whispered, "Go on, Mademoiselle."

Brianna took a breath. "Have you read the coroner's inquest report?"

"Yes, I have," Billings said, glancing at Governor Foote, who raised his eyebrows in return.

She continued. "In that instance, I will spare you the facts of the case. I need you to save my husband's life, Mr. Billings. It is a very simple matter, you see. He did not murder General Williams. In fact, he shot his derringer in self-defense. The general was insane, sir; he could not tolerate his tumbler of Monongahela. The whole town knows that when he drank too much, he lost his temper."

Governor Foote broke in. "What Miss Baird says is true. Williams' capacity for liquor and anger was legendary."

Brianna closed her eyes, feeling a rising glimmer of hope that they might understand her.

Billings scratched his pen across the page. He lifted his head, studying her face. "Do go on, Miss Baird."

"Edward has never had a run-in with the law in his life, Mr. Billings. He possesses a calm personality, and he's capable of reading the humor of others very well. He has told me of his many near-violent incidences, especially in this town where trouble walks the street every day." A tear trickled down her cheek, and she reached into her pocket for the embroidered handkerchief Mrs. Morgan had given her back in Baltimore.

Brianna blew her nose loudly. "One of our former girls, named Jeannette, had a tryst over a period of time with the general at our parlor house. After that, the general complained of the clap. It is true that Jeanette had the pustules, and she still has them. I know since I tracked her down after the shooting and found her in an alleyway. The poor thing claims she rushed to the murder scene with the crowd and saw a knife on the pavement near his dead body. After that, she picked it up and hid it on her person, planning to keep it for her own protection. The poor soul would not surrender it to me. But I know she would give it to one such as yourself."

Billings tapped the paper lightly with his fingers. "Do go on."

A knot formed in Brianna's stomach. "My husband will be framed by the Vigilantes without your help. In their zeal for law and order in San Francisco, they're bent on destroying it. They'll use my husband as an example, but he is an innocent man. Only you have the power, influence, and respect in this town to defend him. Please consider taking his case. I know you will save him from the noose. Find Jeannette. Defend Edward. Without you, he is sure to hang, sir." She held the handkerchief to both eyes for a moment to stop their stinging.

Governor Foote broke in. "But Miss Baird, Mr. Billings rarely takes a lost cause. He is eminent and does not have to accept just any case now. Plus, consider the expense, good lady. He charges more than any defense attorney in this town."

She threw up her hands. "Name your price, Mr. Billings. I'll meet any price you name. Mr. Spina and I have much in the way of savings."

Billings paused, pen down. He steepled his hands under his chin. The grandfather clock chimed the hour, then resumed its methodical ticking.

Brianna's heart thundered as a few moments passed. What would she do if he refused to take her case?

His bushy eyebrows joined as one. "Miss Baird, since your case will require hiring a team of lawyers, I put your fee at thirty thousand dollars, no more, no less. You must understand, this case is very risky for me.

With the town boiling with Vigilantes, there is no predicting the verdict. Why, my very practice of law in this town could be compromised."

Foote cleared his throat. "He is saying that you may lose not on the matter of law or principle, but because the Vigilante committee could take the case away from the courts. That is what happened in 1851."

Brianna heard Emma's sharp intake of breath, but she held her head steady, her gaze firm. She glanced first at Foote, who clutched his burned-out cigar between two fingers, then cast her full attention on Billings' face.

Billings angled his head as he regarded Brianna. "The governor is right, Miss Baird. In '51, the Vigilantes held a makeshift trial court, and the accused were hanged almost immediately. To my mind, the crowd is in a similar hot mood today. Many of those same men brag that they still have their original uniforms and bayonets. Any money you spend today on your case may be wasted."

Brianna clenched her fists. "I know what happened in '51. The Vigilantes hanged guilty men that time. My husband is being singled out, just because of his profession. Nothing more, nothing less. Against my banker's advice, I have a Wells Fargo draft for two thousand dollars, much of my savings. The rest is in gold coins. I have half of your fee with me today, sir. The rest you shall have delivered by nightfall." Emma placed an envelope on Billings' desk. Then she loosened her purse strings, overturned the pouch, and all eyes followed the glittering cascade of gold coins that fell across his desk.

Both men rose, their eyes widening. Foote guided the rolling coins along the edge so they would not fall to the floor.

Then Billings called Mr. Primm, who burst through the door. All knew he had been eavesdropping. "Matthew, get me a container for this coinage, please, right away." Mr. Primm hurried back in with a leather pouch, into which Billings scooped the money. "Now Primm, be so kind as to put it in the safe." The man disappeared out the door with the bag.

They all sat back down, but Brianna stayed on the edge of her chair. "What are the next steps, Mr. Billings? We have so little time to prepare.

Edward is to be arraigned during the session of the Fourth District Court in two weeks."

Billings leaned forward. "Yes, indeed, there is little time. Yet, it can be done and will be done. Your case is worthy, and I will summon my team immediately. It is of high importance to locate Jeannette and the knife."

Brianna placed her hand over her heart. "Mr. Billings, I am forever grateful. I know this is a difficult, maybe even hopeless case, but I cannot lose my husband. I love him so. Please do all you can to save his life."

Foote guided her out of her chair and laced his arm in hers. "Young lady, you and your entire household are in great danger. Please take the utmost precautions in the streets. The town is crazed, and bullets have been fired in the air in the midst of public meetings. Do not go out of your house without an escort."

"I would add, do not go out unless you are armed, Miss Baird." Billings frowned.

"Yes, I know." Brianna pulled a revolver out of her reticule and placed it on the desk. "I know how to shoot well, as do all of my girls. I will defend my house."

The two men nodded at each other.

She returned the gun to her bag. "Gentlemen, I will expect a messenger at my house on Waverly Place with the next steps we must pursue." She dropped her gris-gris bag into the safety of her pocket. Without listening for a reply, Brianna pulled the veil back down onto her face, and Emma took her arm and walked her to the door. She turned and surveyed the bookshelf behind the broad desk. Her voice rose as she said, "Mr. Billings, inside all those legal books behind you, there lies the answers to my prayers."

"Would that were true, Miss Baird. Would that were true." He gave her a faraway glance as he closed the door behind her.

From the window, Billings and Foote observed Miss Baird step into her carriage, accompanied by her maid. The black window shade had been fastened down on the carriage, concealing their identities.

Foote leaned back and tapped his brandy glass. "She is quite a spark."

Billings gave a slight smile. "That may be part of the trouble."

Sixty-Seven

UNTIL PROVEN GUILTY

San Francisco, California
April 1856

The next day's early morning sunshine poured through an open window from the sky above Waverly Place. It seemed like yesterday that Brianna had looked out at the Fell Inn from Miss Osborne's. What was the commotion in the street today? Brianna's house never received visitors before breakfast, yet she saw food carts rattle up in front of the house, their ponies snorting in the mist. Then larger carriages and traps halted, exhaling men, women, and children. Hawkers appeared, selling toys and candy in the narrow street. Brianna stepped back and groaned loudly. Their audience had arrived.

Emma hovered nearby. She stepped in front of Brianna and closed the window. "Pay them no mind, Brianna. There are always those that make a festival out of ill-fortune. Doesn't seem to matter where we are . . . bad folks are bad to the core." She plumped pillows on the Spinas' bed, and pulled up the orange counterpane.

Brianna sat down at her writing desk. Andy nudged her leg, and she gathered him into her lap. She welcomed the quiet moment to compose a letter to Edward. She'd ask Richard to take it to the jail that morning. The words came easily, flowing from her steel pen.

My dearest Edward,

I miss you so much, my darling. We are all concerned about your well-being, and Richard has packed some meats and vegetables, along with Emma's croissants for you. There are threats to my life now, and I dare not come to the jail for fear I may be taken off the street.

Are they treating you well, or are they being awful to you? I cannot imagine my love spending one night in that horrible place, especially for the crime of self-defense. You are innocent until proven guilty, but they are treating you otherwise.

I do not want to tell you anything that could be seen by prying eyes, since spies are everywhere, according to our good friends who are watching the Vigilantes grow in power.

I managed to convince F.T. Billings to be your defense counsel, and he assured me he would bring together several lawyers to act on your behalf. He is most qualified and esteemed.

I wish I could be there with you right now in order to make your days more comfortable and your nights more hopeful. I know that with the Almighty's help, we will prevail, since there is justice in the world. Do not lose hope, for our household is behind you, praying for you, and loving you forever.

Yours until the end of time,
Brianna

Lost in the world of her letter, Brianna imagined Edward's tattered form sitting on a dirty makeshift bed in the middle of a cell rife with vermin. The cells had bars on the windows, not glass, and even in spring, the nights were damp and chilled, the bay wind biting the unprotected prisoner. She caressed Andy's ears, picturing her Edward eating from a tin plate. What would be on it? Maybe a crust of bread or a rotten chicken leg. They treated prisoners no better than dogs, and those accused of killing a general, better yet a US marshal, would receive treatment reserved for the lowest of animals. She worried most about Edward's intolerance for dirt and his love of good dress and polite manners. He'd built up a life for himself filled with beautiful things and elegant people. Jail wasn't a suitable place for him.

"Emma," she called.

"Yes, Miss Baird," Emma stepped in, her arms laden with sheets and towels.

"I need to see Richard. Is he in the house?"

"Yes, I believe he returned from the stables. What do you need from him, may I ask?"

Her words tumbled out. "I'll start crying again if I have to say it twice, so please find him, and then I'll tell the both of you what I need. Please hurry."

After a few moments, Richard's hunched form darkened the bedroom, and he held his hat in his hands. "Emma said you needed me right away. I am here to do anything for you." His face radiated a gentle eagerness.

Brianna's jaw clenched. "Richard, this errand will take grit and cunning. Within the items for Edward is hidden a message I am sending. If the jailer finds it before Edward, this could jeopardize Edward's entire case. Not only I, but also you could be arrested for delivering secret information to a prisoner. Are you willing to do it?"

Richard's bent back straightened a bit. "I will do anything if it helps Mr. Spina. You both got me and my Emma away from New Orleans. You saved our lives. What can I do?"

Brianna planted her feet as she faced him. "First, I need you to pack a carpetbag with Mr. Edward's blue silk pajamas, his slippers, and his bathrobe. Then, put in a newly pressed shirt, pants, his not-so-favorite vest . . . this is jail, after all . . . and his cravat and coat. A change of socks and undergarments also. You know of those matters, not I, since you dressed him every day. One last question. Do they allow shaving implements into the jail?"

Richard's forehead wrinkled. "No Ma'am, a razor could hurt someone."

"Yes, of course, I am not thinking straight." Brianna closed the envelope and held it up to a candle to light the sealing wax.

Richard asked, "Do you want me to deliver that message to Mr. Spina along with the carpetbag?"

"Yes. Now, when you get to the jail, ask for Sheriff Jamison, a personal friend of mine, and let him know you have these items to give to Mr. Spina. Let the sheriff know he is, of course, free to inspect the items for weapons, but guarantee that he will not find anything objectionable inside. That way, he will trust you. He knows me well and is thankful for my donations to the sheriffs and fire brigade of this town. He is sure to comply." Brianna pressed her lips together.

"Yes, Ma'am."

"Oh, and Richard, do take along a dozen of Emma's freshly baked croissants from this morning's batch. They're filled with apricot preserves. He will like that." She gazed into his eyes.

"Yes, Ma'am." Richard headed toward Mr. Spina's dressing room to pack the bags.

Sixty-Eight

THE WOODEN BOX

San Francisco, California
April 1856

That afternoon's sunlight streamed through the dining-room windows. Brianna and Emma were conferring about which china to set out for the evening's fancy parlor house dinner. Andy's bark rang through the house. It was his panic howl, not the friendly yelp reserved for neighbors. A heavy doorknocker sounded against the outside door. Brianna observed the play of tension wrinkling Emma's features, mirroring her own fears.

"Who that could be?" Brianna asked. Her heart skittered in her chest.

Celeste took long steps out of the kitchen and brushed past them toward the door. "Shh, Andy." She bent down and picked up Andy, who wriggled in her arms.

Brianna was mystified and more than a little concerned. If the Vigilantes decided to force their way in, there would be nowhere to hide.

She heard Celeste's soft murmur at the door. "Oui, Monsieur. We're closed for business now."

A forceful male voice said, "I need to see Miss Baird. A matter of utmost urgency." The door closed and heavy boots pounded on the hallway's wooden floor.

Emma and Brianna exchanged glances of recognition. That tenor voice belonged to Governor Foote.

Brianna looked toward Emma. "Please go see the governor into the drawing room. I'll be there shortly. Whatever could he want?"

"Maybe he has more news of the case." Emma patted Brianna's arm and headed out to the hallway.

As Brianna neatened the stray locks of her bun and set her lace collar into place, she imagined Edward in jail, his head in his hands. She had to continue her quest to save his life. This was not just for her now: for the first time, she must repay all the favors he had given her since that fateful day of the coin toss in New Orleans. She hardened her resolve and followed in Emma's footsteps.

The governor's top hat rested in his hands, and he stood at the edge of a chair.

Brianna forced a smooth smile of confidence as she strode over and extended her hand, then dipped in a quick curtsy.

He nodded and folded his legs into the stiff armchair, his lips in a thin straight line. He set the box next to him on the floor.

Brianna's eyes flickered over the box. "Governor, to what does my humble house owe the honor?" She waved a trembling hand toward Emma. "Please bring some of Celeste's pressed coffee and don't forget some extra cookies for the governor."

Emma curtsied and disappeared into the hallway.

Brianna said, "Do please make yourself comfortable." She paused to catch her breath.

The governor gave her a curt nod. “In fact, I have little time.”

A subtle warning layered his tone. “Very well, sir.” Brianna chewed her bottom lip as she sank into her chair, patting down the layers of her billowing skirts.

Foote lifted the pleat of his topcoat as he sat so as not to wrinkle the back of it. He placed his hat on the side table, moving aside a china bowl filled with chocolates. He peered at the wall. “I see you’ve got a lovely painting of Paris. Have you visited?”

Brianna took his choice of subject as a trick to disarm her. With reluctance, her eyes followed his gaze to the painting. “No, my secretary, Celeste, was born there, and she has a natural gift for artwork. She sketched that from memory and worked on painting it for many months last year. I had it framed at a shop on Clay Street. Isn’t it grand?” She tensed as she struggled to contain her uncertainties. What could be in the box?

“Yes, indeed,” he said. “Sadly, I’m not here to talk about paintings, Miss Baird.” He looked at her much as one regards a lost puppy wandering in the highroad.

Brianna's hands formed a knot in her lap to stop their quivering. “Have you brought me news of Edward’s case?”

The governor nodded. “I’ve come directly from Billings’ office with a message and a delivery. Don’t fault me, for I’m merely conveying the word.” He rubbed the back of his neck as though it ached.

Brianna’s voice cut into the calmness. “Your news, Governor?” She shut her eyes, fearing the worst. She wanted to trust him, but that box disturbed her.

China cups clinked on a silver tray, followed by Emma’s soft voice asking, “Would the governor prefer cream? Sugar?”

Brianna felt Emma put a warm cup into her hands, and she opened her eyes again, gathering her senses. She swallowed hard to stifle the fears that marched through her like Vigilantes on parade, their top hats and bayonet-tipped rifles surrounding Edward. The swirl of cream and sugar brought her momentarily to that long-ago day in New Orleans, the flashing parrot feathers, Madame DeSalle.

Brianna looked at the governor, and noticed that his face was a gloomy shade of gray. He dangled a spoon in his *café au lait.* "Mr. Billings arranged for a private detective to find the whereabouts of your Miss Jeannette, the possible witness and bearer of the knife."

Was there a ray of hope? Maybe Jeannette was convinced to help Edward.

Brianna said, "I'm pleased to hear of this. She's living on our city streets, so she should be easy to find."

The governor sipped his café, his voice comforting, yet unsettling. "That's part of my message today, unfortunate as it is."

Brianna leaned forward, her fingers clenching her cup. "Go ahead. I don't shrink from the truth. I have no choice."

"The police have searched every alley and byway of our fair city, but as yet, there's been no sign of her. Many young women have shown up in the morgue, but she has not been seen there, either. Sometimes they are thrown into the bay and end up being eaten by the sharks."

After a moment of stunned silence, Brianna choked out her words. "Oh, no, it can't be. I spoke to her a day or two ago. She was gaunt, frail, yes, but . . ." The image of a waterlogged body flashed through her mind. She'd seen them in Baltimore as a young girl, and remembered their mottled, white torsos; missing head, arms, and legs.

Foote's eyes glistened with compassion. "The detective told the venerable Mr. Billings that they are continuing to search for her, but if they cannot find her, the defense will have a weak case without the knife."

Brianna's eyes searched his. "Did the detectives see any sign of the knife? She had to have it. She could have dropped it in an alley, or anywhere for that matter." She had a sudden, disturbing thought. "Oh no, what if she'd cast it into the bay in an ultimate act of revenge?"

He shook his head. "No knife in the streets or alleys, according to the detectives. They did check Washerwoman's Lagoon. No sign of it. If she's thrown the knife into the bay, it will be impossible to find." The governor's voice was distant, and she felt him bobbing away from her like a buoy loosed from its anchor.

A white, floating pillow, trailing blood, crossed her imagination. Could Jeannette now be in the waters of the bay, food for sea life? "Oh, I see. How horrible."

Resting her cup on the side table, she got up, and crossed the room. She traced her fingers over a pressed-flower painting on the wall. "Poor Jeannette," she said.

An empty silence surrounded them.

The governor cleared his throat.

Brianna's weary hand fell heavily from the painting onto her apron skirt. She turned around and faced him. "There's more?"

"After this news, Mr. Billings reviewed your situation," he said.

"Good, I know he's making some sound decisions, and . . ." Her voice was shakier than she wanted it to be.

"He's declined to take your case."

A moan left her lips. "Why ever not? Can't he see how desperate we are?"

"He thinks it will be an uphill battle without a witness or evidence. He can't spend the time necessary to prepare a case he can't ever win." The governor shook his head, his compassion vanishing into the dark spaces of the room.

Brianna's face flamed. "So, I hear two reasons why Mr. Billings is refusing to take my case. First, he's afraid of his political future and that of his law firm. Second, he has no time for it. Right?" A gnawing emptiness reminded her of the nights Father had left her family all alone in Baltimore.

The skin bunched around his eyes. "Yes, when you put it that way, Miss Baird, that's true."

Somehow, Brianna managed to sit down and lean toward the governor. "Well, I do believe he's afraid for his future, and perhaps his own life, if he takes the case. I don't believe he doesn't have time. He promised he would assemble a team of lawyers to help him, and he has the power and influence in California to do that. He could also summon other lawyers in the United States if he chose to." She glared at him as though he were in the witness box at a trial.

Foote's lips resumed their thin, straight line. He rose, regarding her with the sharp, black eyes of a politician. "Miss Baird, those are matters I know nothing about. I've given you the message . . . now for the delivery." He clicked open the wooden box and lifted out a sack.

Brianna's eyes widened. "The money! How could he return it?" Brianna steadied her voice against incoming waves of anger. "Governor, I've got no quarrel with you. As you stated, you're merely the messenger. I've got a message for you to take back to Mr. Billings, however. He's an officer of the court; I insist that he take my husband's case."

The governor regarded Brianna in silence; his hand gripped the brim of his hat. Did she see painful recognition in his eyes?

She stepped out of the chair, then leaned against the back of it to gather strength. Her skirts billowed about her in soft waves. "Tell him to come to my house at the hour of ten tomorrow morning for further discussion. He agreed to mount a capital defense, and now he wants to withdraw?"

The governor's lips parted and he raised an eyebrow. Yet no words were said.

Brianna brushed her closed fist across her lips. "Don't misunderstand me, Governor, I won't accept his refusal. And, in good faith, I won't take back the payment I made. Please return it to him. Edward's life is at stake. I can do no less for him."

Foote peered down at her, still clutching the bag. "But, Miss Baird . . ."

Brianna lifted up the empty box and took a step closer to him. "Any further discussion will take place here at my house tomorrow morning, not a moment sooner, nor later. That is my will and the will of poor Mr. Spina, God protect him."

Foote kept a civil tone. “Very well, as you wish.”

Brianna gently tugged the bag from his arms, placed the bag inside the box, then passed it back. In silence, he put the cover on the box, and latched it.

Cleansing tears broke free and streamed down Brianna’s face. She could no longer hold in the pent-up anguish. Without bidding the governor good day, she rushed from the room and knocked over the side table with her full skirts.

Andy yelped and fled into the hallway.

Ignoring the crash of china cups, Brianna ran up the stairs, threw herself on her bed, and spoke furious prayers into her gris-gris bag.

A silent, downcast Emma let the governor out the front entrance. As the heavy door swung shut behind him, he observed the box in his arms. “Well, I’ll be. That’s quite a woman. Wait until old Billings hears about this.” Then he headed toward his favorite barstool at the Bank Exchange, his mind on a glass of tawny port.

Sixty-Nine

LITTLE NOOSES

San Francisco, California
April 1856

The next day, Brianna couldn't help herself. The ebb and flow of voices in the crowd outside drew her to the window. She parted the heavy damask curtain and lifted it to one side, holding it with her fingers. Down in the street, afternoon picnickers feasted on pickles, roast chicken, and fruit pies from impromptu food stands set up for the occasion. Someone pointed up at her, and in her mind, she saw the theater boys' fingers raised up with the word *strumpet* on their lips. She dropped the curtain and watched it sway for a moment.

Remembering the governor's remark, Brianna aimed her gaze again at Celeste's drawing of Paris. "Take me away, Lord, anywhere but here. Why must I go through this horror?" Her fingers caressed the smoke-licked frame. Dreams of Paris drifted away into the ether, along with her future, which looked increasingly dim.

Three o'clock. Colonel Billings was late. Brianna sat and waited, threading her fingers through her thick amber hair and examining the curls in her hand. At last, the heavy door knocker pounded and she heard the sound of Richard greeting the visitors at the door. She patted her dress, ran her tongue across her lips, and opened wide the drawing room double doors.

An unsmiling Billings strode over the threshold, his gold watch chain catching the light.

Brianna forced a greeting. "Good morning, Colonel. Please sit down. Plenty of room on the sofa." Her own voice sounded false and brittle.

The colonel did not make eye contact with her. Why didn't he return her glance? The bitter taste of bile rose in her throat. What was worse, the governor pulled out the leather coin satchel from under his greatcoat and set it on the floor. Had he given up on Edward, too?

Emma reached out and took the colonel's hat and cane.

Brianna sidestepped the bag of gold. She gave her most cheerful greeting to the older man. "Governor Foote, good morning. You gentlemen are looking well today." It soothed her to play the polite hostess, even in crisis. Father's whippings during her Baltimore childhood had taught her a measure of self-control. A hiccup caught in her throat. The whalebone stays of her corset held her upright and they dug into her flesh. They would steady her in times of need. Whenever she had let her emotions go, she got into trouble, and then would always have to make amends as time passed. "Blessed are the meek," she whispered under her breath.

"What was that?" The governor cupped his ear. "You know, my hearing has never been the same after the battles and cannon fire I've witnessed. Kills the hearing and the nerves, you see."

Brianna managed a shrug. "Nothing. I am so glad you are here with us, governor." His crinkled eyes bored into hers. Her heart skipped beats. Her emotions compelled her to explode, uncontrolled, like wild horses bursting out of a corral. Yet she held herself with calm.

Billings perched on the edge of the sofa. She observed the great man who had testified before the supreme court of the land. His large eyebrows clumped together, his face tense as dried cowhide. His eyes were slitted wide enough for anyone to spot the whites in a long, filmy line. Any minute, his tongue would flick out like a lizard's. He glanced sideways at the governor and kept a deathlike silence.

"Colonel Billings," Brianna began. Billings looked away, but she persisted. "Colonel, I know you consider me maligned, poor, weak, and wicked. Yet I am not. I come from minister's stock in Baltimore, and my mother and father brought me up in the ways of the Lord. I trusted the wrong boy and was banished to New Orleans. There, when I faced starvation, I met the gentle Edward Spina, who helped me find shelter and protected me from the vile life to which I was destined. Only through God's grace do I exist here before you and the governor."

Brianna watched Billings fix a stare at the decorative trim on a corner of the ceiling as though memorizing its design. She stepped over and looked down at him, blocking his view. She swallowed, a hiccup bubbling up. "Colonel Billings, you must hear me." She inhaled quickly. "The night of the fight, I know Edward would not stand for any insults to my name. General Williams called me the lowest of women. Even with Edward's calmness, Williams provoked him for days to pay him back for embarrassing his wife that night in the American Theater."

Billings said, "We know of Williams' drunkenness and violent behavior." His voice contained a dismissive tone.

Her eyes drilled his face. "Yes, Colonel, all of San Francisco is aware of his cruel streak. He has intimidated many proprietors. He threatened and humiliated people. That is how he worked his ways. Most folks laughed it off because he was tipsy on duty most days."

"Even General Tecumseh Sherman found him troublesome," Foote added, then scratched his chin.

She continued. "It is a hard matter when a lawman is a drunk and a rowdy, Colonel. Especially in a Vigilante town, where any minute, the law is grabbed by those who think they are above it."

Billings sat in a frozen pose, his face like the Buddha in Tien Hau Temple.

What was the use? Billings' mind was on other things, not her. Another, more significant case than hers. How useless and small she must appear to him.

Brianna strode to the opposite window and held open the lace curtain covering the alcove. Thrill seekers milled about outside, and when they saw her at the open window, a low roar went up from the crowd, parents pointing her out to their families.

Children held up little nooses as toys, some even with makeshift dolls hanging by their necks. "Brianna Spina! Hang her, too!" Grimacing, she let the curtain fall. Darkness settled back into the room.

So alone, so lost. These men could walk out the door any minute. They were her only hope. *Please Lord, give them the strength to do what was right.*

The gentlemen sat silent as the street laughter filtered through the heavy drapery. Billings sank back into the sofa cushion, his features as blank as a death mask. Foote stirred the embers in the fireplace.

Brianna's lengthy skirts tugged at her waist as she knelt on the rug before Billings, raising her eyes to him.

"Please help me, dear Colonel Billings. I am all he has. If I don't help him, no one else will. It is my duty. The town is too frightened to intervene. They will arrest anyone who advocates for him, all except for you. You hold such importance that they would not dare. The Vigilante ranks are growing daily; the troops muster now at Fort Gunnybags on Sacramento Street. All the businessmen of this town are joining. Any person of influence has now signed up."

Billings cut his eyes toward the window. "Listen to that crowd outside. Mob violence runs this town. Rocks were thrown through my office window yesterday, and I have received anonymous messages threatening death if I pursue your case."

"I am sorry. Yet I am begging you for Edward's life, now, Colonel Billings. He is unjustly accused, and without your help, he will die an innocent man. He did not murder General Williams. Ask Emma, Richard, Celeste, and any of my girls. Interview the business people we know, our banker, any of our personal friends. Doctor Poppy. People at the gambling houses and bars he frequented."

Billings lowered his brows. "One of the messages threatened to kill my mother who lives with me. She's old and frail and cannot withstand fear. I cannot go before a judge under these conditions and risk my relatives." His voice contained the sharp edge of fear.

Still on her knees, Brianna folded her hands as if in prayer. She continued. "Trust in the Lord, for he is good. Believe in his protection and mercy. There are times during which we must risk everything to protect the innocent. One day, you will be able to teach other juries the value of integrity."

Billings shook his head, his eyes stony.

She went on. "As for your mother's safety, send her away where she is safe outside California. The Vigilantes' call is not as loud as they think. With your power and connections, you would find safe harbor for your relatives until the trial is over and the threat subsides."

Billings rested his chin on his knuckles. "It is not only that matter, but also the future of my reputation. To have lost in the cause to save a gambler's life? It does not reflect upon my purity of heart, and fellow members of the bar may believe I have lots my wits to defend such a lowly member of society."

Brianna's fists clenched. "Forget Edward's title or status . . . forget his connection to me, a so-called whore, a gambler's maiden, who communes with the lowest of the low in God's eyes. Only you, Colonel Billings, only you can save us . . . him . . . from dangling at the end of the rope they are testing right now at Fort Gunnybags. I will not see my beloved strangling at the end of that cord. And God in his mercy knows he would die an innocent man."

Again, a stony silence reigned, but Brianna saw a slight twitch in Billings' eyes as he gazed up at her. He had heard her now; she was sure of it.

She continued. "How much lower into the dirt must I go, Colonel? I am a Magdalene, after all. A woman loved by Christ, forgiven for all her sins. Those outside will not be the first to cast a stone at a wanton woman . . . it has already been done centuries past."

Billings stiffened, silent once more.

Somewhere deep inside of Brianna, her rage boiled. She must contain it. The force of it quickened inside her spirit: a rolling river full of dreams of Paris, her father's thrown cups, her mother's bowed head on the table, the coin toss, the *beignets*, on and on like a torrent, a flood, cleansing, pushing, ending with her little Ambrose.

"You will take our case." Her voice rose strong and firm, impassioned but in control. "By heaven and God's mercy, you will take our case. You will not deny the soul beating inside the body of our dear Edward. If you do not take it on for me, do it for all who know and love him. Do it for them."

Foote wiped a corner of his eye, and Billings' shoulders relaxed somewhat.

Brianna paused and drew a breath. "You will use all of your tremendous talent and love for humanity to teach this world about justice. You will risk losing your friends and ruining your reputation to defend this innocent. Yes, Colonel Billings, you will defend Edward Spina or you will die regretting it."

She reached over to him. Her arms curled around his neck, her head nestled onto his chest.

He leaned back, arms outstretched, his eyebrows arched in surprise. "Oh my dear woman." Billings' voice broke. He reached out his hand, and patted her head as he would the daughter he'd never had.

She squeezed her eyes shut. She could no longer speak. She had done all she could. The rest was up to the Divine.

She heard his voice vibrate through his chest. "I am not much for sentimentality," he said. "Yet your speech has schooled me not to fear, but instead to forge ahead in his defense." With gentle hands, Billings lifted Brianna up and set her back where she'd rested on the floor.

"And what about your mother? How might you keep her safe?" Foote frowned over at Billings.

The lawyer paused a moment. "I will send her to my sister Patrice in Boston. They will be safe in the fortress of Beacon Hill society."

Brianna felt as though a weight had been lifted. "Do I dare believe it? What does he mean, Governor?" she asked, her eyes on Billings, who sat transfixed.

The governor spoke as though they were best friends. "It means he will take your case, dear woman."

Relief poured out of Brianna. Her voluminous skirts pooled in circles around her slim body on the rug. She ran her hands over the satin garment that fanned about her, its lace and velvet intertwined.

"Are you quite all right, Miss Baird?" Billings asked.

"Oh, yes, I am fine. Light and airy. I am floating." She focused up on their beards and cravats, then closed her eyes to see green ferns dancing in the sunlight. There was hope after all.

She prayed aloud, "God, can we postpone our date with Paris? I need to marry Edward."

The gentlemen helped Emma lift Brianna onto the fainting couch. Emma's gentle hands put a pillow under her head and tucked a quilt around her. Andy leaped up next to her and she felt his rough tongue lick her cheek.

With her hand on Andy's head, she asked, "What's that sound, Emma?" She reached out and grasped Emma's outstretched hand.

"The clinking of coins in the satchel they carry. Richard is showing the men out to their coach, Mademoiselle."

"Have we done it, Emma?"

"Yes, *you* have."

Seventy

TIME TO LEAD THE CHARGE

San Francisco, California
April 1856

Moments after, during the carriage ride through DuPont, Kearny, and other muddy streets, the horses gained speed, then halted every so often for a stray dog who crossed the road or a sodden miner fallen in the mud. As Billings considered the passing scenes, he ignored Foote's idle chatter. Instead, he remembered the emerald spark in Brianna's eyes, framed by feathered eyelashes. She had spoken with such decency, such love for her man. It had taken him back to his childhood in Virginia. What had been her name? Ah, yes, Helena, the schoolmaster had called her. But to him, she was Helen, like Helen of Troy. The face that launched a thousand ships.

He had never married, but instead had given himself up to the law. Justice had been his bride after the Mexican war. Others came home to their sweethearts; he embraced the bar. Instead of pursuing women in laces, he admired dusty tomes. Instead of playing with his own apple-cheeked infants, he researched with law clerks. He prided himself on tucking his emotions away.

Yet, Brianna had touched him as no woman had since Helena. Her pleas for mercy and justice reminded him of their Shakespearean playacting in the Fredericksberg orchards. What was the drama? *Merchant of Venice.* He softened. A vision of Helena's auburn hair, porcelain skin, and soft voice floated in front of him. She recited Portia's speech. He mouthed the words along with the apparition. How did it go? Oh yes…

The quality of mercy is not strain'd,
It droppeth as the gentle rain from heaven
Upon the place beneath: it is twice blest;
It blesseth him that gives and him that takes . . .

It was his time, his duty. Time to provide mercy, and bless the downtrodden, the weary and the hopeless. He would go into battle for his Helen, and for Brianna, the wondrous creature who had asked for his help. To hell with the dust and tedium of his lawbooks. It was time to lead the charge.

Seventy-One

PURIFICATION

San Francisco, California
April 1856

A week droned by. Edward sat in the courtroom, twisting his freshly laundered handkerchief into a knot. Billings sat next to him, conferring with his fellow lawyers. To pass the time, Edward counted the marks on the dingy courtroom walls. He examined his own manacled hands and dirty fingernails. Disgusting. Blood caked and dried on his wrists; his ankles ached from their iron shackles.

Edward looked down at his clothing. This velvet waistcoat had been a poor choice—Richard should have known the room would be balmy. What was the need for fancy garments and highly fashionable boots when a man was to be hanged? Each breath was now a gift. How many more did he have? His mouth was dry as a withered magnolia leaf, and sweat lay in itchy tracks down his spine.

Restless, Edward raised his eyes again and scanned the courtroom. The judge presided on an oak bench, behind which was a large United

States flag with thirty-one stars hung on the wall next to a portrait of George Washington. The jury box was filled with men he had seen about town: a pioneer, a banker, a storeowner, a nut peddler, a painter, a carpenter. All eyed him with suspicion. How many of them were friends of the famous general he had shot? He tensed, for at that moment, the gallery behind him boomed with jeers and insults, the public in no mood for mercy. The guard posted at the door held back the crowd gathered in the anteroom, and he knew a line snaked all the way out to the front of the courthouse.

The judge's gavel pounded on the wooden dais, calling the session to order. The festive atmosphere faded and the majestic serenity of justice prevailed.

Prosecutor Thomas Harrison rose and faced the jury. "The facts of the case are these." He passed a detailed street map of San Francisco City to the jury foreman, who then advanced it to the eleven men in the jury box. Harrison's forceful, steady voice rang through the courtroom. "On the evening of April 19th, General Williams and Edward Spina walked arm in arm down Clay to Leidesdorff Street in conversation.

"At a certain point, an argument ensued. General Williams carried no weapons and Spina, a derringer pistol. They turned onto Leidesdorff near the entrance of The Miner's Hotel, at which point Spina pushed Williams against the wall, holding the derringer to his chest. They wrestled for possession of the gun. The defense alleges the victim carried a knife and held it above Spina's chest. To date the defense has not presented any evidence that Williams was carrying a knife in his sheath." Edward turned his ear to catch the murmur of disapproval rising and falling through the observers behind him.

He noticed Harrison hook one thumb in his waistcoat pocket. "Gentlemen, you are charged with a great responsibility. Mr. Spina, the prisoner, is accused of the capital crime of murder for which the punishment is hanging. You are required to determine whether or not the prisoner committed the murder of the victim General Williams."

The prosecutor laid out his case with matter-of-fact indifference, and Edward wondered if the man ever considered the value of the human life that hung in the balance; in this case, *his* life.

Edward listened, each word of Harrison's a dull thud in his ears. "The prosecution will prove that Spina planned and committed cold-blooded murder. He acted to avenge the humiliation that he suffered when the general challenged him to a duel by slapping him across the face, a contest that Spina was too cowardly to accept. We will also prove that the general did not have a knife." The prosecutor sniffed and hunched down at the prosecution's table.

Edward heard the swish of Billings' coat as he rose and marched to the jury box. "The prisoner asks not for mercy, but for the assurance of a fair and just opinion from you gentlemen. The defense will show that General Williams was in deadly pursuit of Spina to avenge the insult he suffered from two nights prior at the American Theater. Williams had a history of drunken, hot-headed behavior."

The jury's eyes followed the attorney as he paced in front of them. "The next night at the Berkeley Saloon, Williams slapped Spina's face, attempting to incite him to a duel. The day after, he searched the town looking for Spina. When he found Spina next to the entrance of the Miner's Hotel, he pulled a knife with the intent to kill Mr. Spina. The accused struggled against Williams, and he shot him in self-defense. The gentlemen of the jury will see that the facts that we present will require a verdict of acquittal."

After a short recess, the prosecution summoned Captain Elijah Brennan to the witness stand. The seasoned navy man held an air of authority, his bearing highlighted by a bristling red beard and sunburned face.

Edward squinted at the man. He could not recall ever seeing him before.

Mr. Harrison began the questioning. "Captain Brennan, please tell the jury what you saw on the night in question on Leidesdorff Street."

Pointing to Spina, Brennan said, "I saw that man over there push, then shove the taller, burlier man with him."

Spina flinched, the end of Brennan's finger reminding him of the general's dagger tip.

"Were the two men having an argument?"

Brennan nodded. "I could not hear what they were saying, but their faces were red and one looked drunk."

Harrison asked, "Which one was drunk?"

Brennan answered, "The defendant over there." The finger rose again and stabbed in Spina's direction. Edward steeled himself.

Harrison asked, his hand caressing the witness stand, "What makes you think he might have been drunk?"

Brennan said, "He hung on to the side of the building during the argument to steady himself."

Harrison continued. "What happened next?"

Brennan said, "Next, I saw the shorter man pull a small gun that looked like a derringer from under his coat, and then grab the taller man by his lapel."

Following standard court procedure, Harrison stopped. "Do you see the shorter man in this courtroom today?"

"Yes, he is right over there." He pointed at Spina.

"What did he do with the gun?" Harrison asked.

"He put it to the taller man's chest and then I heard two gunshots fired."

"Continue, please."

"The shorter man pulled away, started down the street, and the tall man fell to the ground."

Harrison stepped away, then faced the witness. "You said in your written statement that you were the first person to reach the victim lying on the ground. Is that correct?"

"Yes, I did."

"Was he breathing?"

"No, sir. His eyes were rolled back in his head and he did not breathe. Blood seeped out onto his coat, from a chest wound, I figure."

Edward had no recollection of any of this, so he took in each detail and painted the scene on his imaginary canvas. He filled in the color of red as they described the blood, and the yellow-sparked flash of Betsy discharging her bullet into the general.

Seventy-Two

WE SPEAK OF FEAR

San Francisco, California
May 1856

During eight more days of testimony, the prosecution produced nine witnesses; only one mentioned hearing a knife sheath drop on the ground. And no one among them testified to seeing Williams wield the knife. Late on the ninth day, the defense summoned Andrew Peterson to the witness stand. Edward sat up, recognizing the man. Nicknamed "The Quaker," Peterson's hands trembled from time to time, perhaps the result of some childhood illness. His frequent tremors caused many in the crowd to snicker, which assisted the prosecution.

F.T. Billings rose and addressed Peterson. "How do you know Mr. Spina?"

Peterson shook but his voice was steady. "We would frequent the tables together in games of faro and backgammon. I've beaten him a time or two." He smiled, his tongue visible through a gap where two front teeth should have been.

Billings stepped forward. "How do you know General Williams?"

Peterson spoke again. "I know him as a drunken bully and a cheat at cards."

Harrison burst from his seat. "Objection! Irrelevant, Your Honor."

Judge Eckles frowned. "Overruled."

Billings asked, "On Saturday night, did you see the argument between Williams and Spina on Leidesdorff Street?"

"Yes, I did." A slight tremor passed through Peterson's shoulders.

Billings waved his hand toward the jury box. "Could you please describe to the men of the jury what you saw?"

Peterson's voice echoed in the high-ceilinged courtroom. "I saw two men walking along Leidesdorff Street, their voices raised, their fists clenched."

"Did you hear what they said?"

Peterson continued. "I heard Williams threaten Spina. He said, 'You have it coming, you sonovabitch, after what you did to my wife.'"

Billings' face appeared calm. "What did Mr. Spina say in response?"

"'Leave me the hell alone. I want no quarrel.'"

"Can you describe what next you saw?"

Peterson said, "I saw General Williams draw a sheath from under his coat with his left hand. He then pulled a knife out of the sheath with his right hand and held it over Mr. Spina."

Again, Edward envisioned the tip of the knife. He considered. Had Betsy not done her job that night, maybe the general would be sitting here in his place. Or maybe not, since the city would be reluctant to prosecute such a large and powerful figure, a hero of the Mexican War.

"How did the defendant react?" Billings looked back and Spina met his gaze.

"He grabbed Williams with his left hand and shot him with his right. The crowd closed in and I could not see anything else."

Billings asked, "How large was the knife?"

Peterson said, "It was a heavy knife of considerable length."

Each evening after a day at the courthouse, Brianna would huddle around the kitchen table with Emma, Richard, and Celeste, discussing the day's events. The night of Peterson's testimony, a sharp knock resounded at the back door. Brianna's pulse quickened: another riotous crowd outside?

A muffled voice muttered, "Jamison. It's urgent."

Richard crossed toward the stoop and turned the doorknob. Jamison stepped over the threshold, followed by a top-hatted Billings, his black cloak swinging about his shoulders.

"Greetings all," Jamison said. Then turning to Billings, he murmured, "I'll be outside waiting in the paddy wagon."

Billings said, "This won't take long, Sheriff."

As if on cue, Emma, Richard, and Celeste left the kitchen.

Billings paced across the kitchen and sat next to Brianna at the table.

She felt the press of his gloved hand on hers. "You've come to see me. Why?"

"The trial is not going well for us."

"I don't understand . . . Peterson's testimony should be proof enough that there was a knife at the scene."

"In an ordinary time, Madame, that might be so. But we live in extraordinary times, do we not? The Vigilantes are stirring and the populace is demanding a restoration of law and order in this town. Without the actual knife, our case is weakened. The populace will claim that a notorious madam of means has bought off the witness."

"But that's a lie."

"No matter . . . people believe what they want to believe. And the broadsheets are railing against Edward, crying out for his execution."

"I don't understand how an entire town can turn against one man."

"There's nothing to understand . . . they are ruled by fear."

"Fear."

"Yes, they think finding Edward innocent will open the door to further crime and corruption. The broadsheets fan the flames of public opinion, and the extremists will take over the city. We speak of fear? That is mine."

Seventy-Three

WHAT KIND OF GOD

San Francisco, California
May 1856

The following day, Brianna entered town dressed in a blond-wigged disguise, her head covered by a hooded cloak. A cold wind whipped into the bay from the Pacific Ocean, the kind of day when a breeze could lift up a small child. On a tip from a pipe-smoking sailor, Brianna found Jeannette holed up in a dinghy tied to a pier at the foot of Montgomery Street. She lay in freezing silence under a piece of canvas splattered with seagull droppings.

Brianna pulled up her skirts, dangled her legs over the pier, and sat down. She called through the wind, "Jeannette LeBrun, is that you?" A breeze whipped her petticoats, and she bound the skirts under her knees to keep her legs covered.

A pair of bloodshot eyes peered out from under the top of the filthy covering.

"Who wants to know?"

"It's me, Brianna." Her own teeth were chattering—why hadn't she brought a blanket with her?

"Baird? Go away, I don't want to talk to you." Jeannette's voice was low and bitter.

Brianna searched her face. "Jeanette, please, you must listen. Edward's situation has gotten so much worse. The papers call for his hanging now, and every day the trial drags on, the jurors grow ready to convict him and send him to the noose."

"He brought it on himself." Jeannette drew the canvas down to her neck. Her twisted smile revealed a set of brown and broken teeth. The tide surged, and her dinghy rose up and down, straining its moorings.

Brianna breathed in, holding back her rising anger. "No, Jeannette, Williams brought it on him. You know Edward shot him in self-defense, and you have the evidence that can save his life."

Jeannette rolled her eyes. "I've told you before, I'm not interested. Haven't you heard I'm dying? A ship's doctor from the clipper ship *Osborne* saw me here and he felt my pulse and checked my signs. He says I have not much longer, that I'm hot with fever and my heartbeat is weak."

A stevedore pushed a handcart onto the pier, its metal wheels grinding into the wooden slats.

Brianna waited for the noise to pass, then she patted the edge of the canvas cover. "Jeannette, please listen to me. Do you care about your soul? Do you wish to go to heaven?"

"Heaven! What chance is there that I may go to heaven? God turned his back on me when my mother rented me out to men at the age of five. What kind of God would let that happen to a little girl?"

The power of Jeannette's resentment resonated deep within Brianna. How often had she herself thought the same about her father? She paused for a moment, studying the speckled brown hills surrounding the azure bay. Then she leaned as far over the pier as she could so Jeannette could see her clearly. "There is no end to the possibility of heaven . . . even at the last minute, the worst criminals are saved if they repent and do a merciful act for another. I, too, had lived under desperate circumstances, long ago, far away. Instead of speaking to a woman on a pier, I had to soothe my dead infant in preparation for his water burial."

Brianna saw Jeannette's eyes widen and fix on her face, so she continued. "It was only after enduring many trials that I realized that my own foolish stubbornness had led me nowhere. Then I had the chance with Edward to save the lives of two slaves who lived under a cruel and heartless villain. I gave myself to their salvation in order to release myself from bondage . . . a spiritual prison in which I had found myself."

Jeannette nodded in silence.

"Please, Jeannette, consider what you could do to save yourself and your soul. If you but go to court and tell the judge you have the knife and show it to him, you will save Edward's life. He will die if you don't."

With that, Jeannette turned her head and appeared to listen, one ear cocked toward Brianna. "Tell me how," she said.

Seventy-Four

SPORTING BUSINESS

San Francisco, California
May 1856

As four more days of testimony passed, Edward wearied from the constant flow of yammering speeches. Was the court's motive for dragging along a string of witnesses to wear out the jurors so they would rule in the prosecution's favor, simply to be done with the case?

Edward observed the jury fidgeting in their chairs, their eyes traveling to the courthouse clock. What were they thinking about? Their boats needed caulking, roofs needed repairing, and stores needed restocking. The pool of gallery spectators grew smaller each day the trial dragged on, and Edward knew the citizens relied on the broadsheets to provide the missing details.

Billings rose and addressed the judge. "Your Honor, the defense calls Jeannette LeBrun to the witness stand.

Harrison sprang up, his voice bristling. "Your Honor, the prosecution was not informed of this witness."

A chorus of murmurs sounded from the courtroom.

The judge pounded the gavel to quell the noisy spectators. "In my chambers, counselors."

Although Edward knew Billings would call Jeannette as a witness today, his fingers tightened, his knuckles as white as Andy's dog bones. Billings had only told him she'd been located. Nothing more. Questions paraded through his consciousness: Where had Billings found her? How much had he paid her to testify? Had she agreed to appear in order to wreak revenge on him and Brianna? Would Jeannette twist another kind of knife into his gut, a slash forever separating him from his beloved?

The judge led the parade out of chambers into the courtroom, and the attorneys resumed their posts.

Edward turned to see the courtroom door open wide. A wan ghost of a woman took halting steps with the bailiff toward the witness stand. Jeannette stared out of hollowed eyes, and her breath came in low, rasping sounds.

After the swearing-in, the bailiff held Jeanette's arm as she hobbled into the witness box. She then began to cough—a deep, sputum-filled heave, and the bailiff passed her a handkerchief.

The crowd's murmurs transformed into audible cries of *whore!* until the judge pounded his gavel. Edward looked around him, ignoring the black looks cast his way from various observers. Somewhat relieved by the chaos, he focused on the front of the room with interest. At least the bystanders had targeted someone else for a change.

Harrison was the first to confront the witness. The prosecutor advanced to Jeannette on the witness stand. "Here at the trial's end, you decided to come forth with the evidence?" His tone blended sarcasm with disdain.

"Yes, I did." Her voice was faint, barely audible.

Harrison's voice grew louder. "Were you coerced by any person or persons to testify?"

"No, I was not."

"Were you paid by any person or persons to testify?"

She shook her head. "No one paid me. I heard about the trial, and that it was going badly for Mr. Spina."

Harrison said, "So, on a whim, you changed your mind?"

"No, I am dying. A ship's doctor told me I may not last the month. Consumption has torn my lungs. I wish to purify myself of all hatred and make peace with God and my enemies."

Harrison asked, "Even peace with Mr. Spina?" He shot a disgusted glance at the jury.

"Only I am responsible for my sins. I do not wish to be the cause of Mr. Spina's punishment when he shot the general in self-defense."

When his turn came for questioning, Billings set a steady hand on the witness box. "Miss LeBrun, tell us how you are acquainted with the deceased, one General Williams."

"The general had done sporting business with me."

"Where was this?"

"At the parlor house run by Edward Spina and his wife, Brianna."

"So you and the victim were acquainted. For how long had you done business?"

"Almost a year."

Billings asked. "Now, on the night in question, did you encounter either of the two men, Spina or Williams?"

"Yes, but even before that, the very drunk general took me into an alley and forced himself on my person, then he threw some dollar coins at me as he left."

The crowd roared its disapproval, and the judge pounded his gavel as he cried, "Order!"

Prosecutor Harrison rose, his face red. "Objection. Not relevant, Your Honor."

Billings pivoted, and faced the judge. "Your Honor, it is relevant since we gain a picture of the general's unsavory character."

The judge frowned. "Very well. Overruled." Then he turned to Jeannette. "Miss LeBrun, kindly stay on your account of the murder scene. That is all."

Jeannette dabbed her forehead. "Yes, Your Honor."

Billings resumed. "Tell us what you saw transpire between the two men."

Jeannette said, "I saw General Williams, his back to the entrance of the Miner's Hotel on Leidesdorff. In his hand was a large dagger. I heard a clatter when the sheath hit the ground and bounced away."

Billings asked, "Did you see Mr. Spina with General Williams?"

She nodded. "Yes. I saw him pull a derringer pistol from his pocket, grab the dagger from the general's hand, and then hold the pistol against his chest."

Billings looked at the jury. "Did you see Spina fire the gun?"

Jeannette shook her head. "No, but I heard a gunshot."

"Did you see the general afterward?"

"Yes. He fell onto Mr. Spina, who then lowered the general onto the ground. Then, after I got there, a crowd came and rushed away with Mr. Spina down Montgomery."

Billings stroked his chin. "Then what did you do?"

"I saw the knife lying nearby in the dirt. I picked it up and held it under my shawl."

Billings continued. "Did you know you were concealing important evidence by removing it from the scene of the crime?"

Jeannette had a coughing spell, and the bailiff furnished her a glass of what appeared to be brandy from the judge's chambers. After a sip, she continued. "I did not care, Mr. Billings."

With that, her head lolled forward onto her chest. Two bailiffs rushed forward and escorted her out of the courtroom.

Seventy-Five

LIGHT WITHIN THE SHADOWS

San Francisco, California
May 1856

The next day's dawn signaled the last day of the trial. *Thank God for that,* Edward thought. His mind was full of trial images. Each time the crowd had scoffed and mocked the testimony, Edward had sat smaller than small. Each time they had mentioned Brianna's name, a shock wave had rippled through the gallery's women and children, as though encountering a leper in their midst. Each time Edward had been called to the stand, they had stood and taunted, calling him a whore-monger, a pimp.

At one point, the judge nearly lost control of the room. In unison, the gallery had cried, "Hang him, hang him!" They acted like fans cheering a rowing team on his beloved Mississippi. Each piece of new evidence had led to hooting and ridicule.

Edward's only hope was for Brianna's love. He imagined his red haired angel, her long tresses spread out on the pillow as he caressed her sweet face and mingled his kisses with her own. Such a deep need united them, both physically and spiritually. They had been together now through so many episodes; they were close and comfortable.

No woman ever understood him like Brianna. Who else loved him so well? And he still lost his head over her, for he could never get enough of her. Her skin carried a natural perfume so sweet he could catch a whiff on his body many hours after their lovemaking. This drove him mad with desire.

And she was good for him. Without her, he would have lived the gambler's nocturnal existence. Win or lose; take the house; lose it again; place your bets, gentlemen. Another round? Alone again, sleeping all day, then out into the solitary poker club, the saloon, the establishment. An occasional visit to a house of ill repute, finding a poor vixen to listen to his troubles. Brianna had shown him the light within the shadows, another existence that he never dreamed possible. An existence of order and logic and kindness.

Did Edward dare to hope for their future? His chances of living were slim to none. Yet, he still dreamed of freedom. How would their life together be different now that all this had happened? Could he thank her enough for getting the best attorney in the state to represent him? Brianna spoke for him when all around town, men wanted to quash his voice and send him to the gallows yesterday, today, and tomorrow for killing a lawman.

Back to the present. All witnesses had been called; now it was time for Billings to make his closing statements to the jury. Some words and not others sank in as the great man spoke to the jury. He was telling the citizenry that although she was a lowly madam, Brianna was of noble character since she had spent a fortune supporting Edward's defense: "Brianna fell from grace early in her life, and she is counted among the queens of sin who will never be heard in the rooms of polite society."

Hearing her name, Edward sat up, fully expecting to hear more defamatory cries from the gallery, but instead, the room silenced.

Billings continued. "The defendant is known to be gentle, kind, and forgiving. He was known to lend money to his fellow gamblers, even after a winning round. He was followed by General Williams, who wished a duel to gain satisfaction after his appearance at the theater. If any of you had been confronted by such a drunken, vengeful man, much taller than you, you may be called upon to seek relief in self-defense.

Edward remembered his Italian Catholic priest in Genoa, up on the altar reading the New Testament. Billings captivated the spectators as much as had that priest.

The defense attorney's voice thundered. "Edward Spina and Brianna have maintained a common-law bond since 1850. They have founded a business together, and police reports state that there is little disturbance at the parlor house."

Edward wet his cracked lips, happy to think of their mutual attachment. Not just for one day, but for eternity. That much he knew. Edward had pulled an ace from the deck when he had drawn Brianna from the streets of New Orleans. A dull ache throbbed in his gut when he thought of his many marriage proposals and her many elaborate refusals. She simply could not marry and he had long ago accepted that.

Billings' voice rang out. "Their bonds continue until one of them dies, thus they are so attached."

Edward looked up at his attorney. There was no relief in life without Brianna, and Edward saw them together in a sailboat at anchor, their love a secret only until now. Billings painted their lives on a canvas before the world, a world that knew only profanity and excitement. This was simply a circus to San Francisco. After today's verdict and his certain death, Edward knew the populous would move on to follow the next bloody conflict.

He heard Billings again. "Rare indeed is a man who would defend the honor of the one he loves before a knife." Spina scanned the gallery, and within the sea of faces, he spied a young, golden haired woman who gazed at him. She must not be more than eighteen. Just about Brianna's age in New Orleans. She heard the story. Did she understand? Could she fathom such a deep love that a woman would sell her dear belongings to raise the money for her lover's defense, to protect him from the injustice before him? She looked so sweet and harmless. May she stay that way in life, rather than turning into these shrews who believed themselves above the God who made us all.

Billings railed against the testimony that claimed that Spina had planned the shooting death of Williams. "There is not one thing the prosecution has said that is in accordance with truth and justice; there is not one version the other side has given that is based on testimony and facts." The man was powerful with words. Many listeners dabbed their eyes with their handkerchiefs.

Billings went on, pacing before the jury box. "And, as you consider the merit and weight of the prisoner's judgment, consider the testimony of Jeannette, the dying wretch who took the knife, at first with the intention of revenge, but then realizing that only the Divine can mete out justice, came forward with the evidence to clear his name. Let her be the example of one who makes amends, to inspire your just and fair rendering of judgment in the eyes of the Almighty, who will judge us all."

Edward heard the courtroom resound with weeping and sniffling. The jury filed out of their box and a whirl of bodies advanced upon him. The strong arms of Sheriff Jamison and his deputy laced through his. He looked down to see the leather peeling on his boots, the result of cuts made by the iron shackles around his ankles. Back to jail, then the agony of awaiting the verdict.

"Let us go, Edward." He looked up into the shaggy eyebrows of his old friend, the sheriff. "Time for chow." He pictured the gruel puddled in a bowl on the table in his cell. His ravenous stomach growled.

Seventy-Six

THEY CARRY TORCHES

San Francisco, California
May 1856

Brianna pulled a shawl about her. On most days, her kitchen bustled with Celeste's food preparations. Today, the room stood gloomy and silent despite its occupants. Andy whimpered as if sensing the worst, and he lay down on his cushion, his brown eyes large and worried.

Emma had become very quiet as the day progressed.

"How many hours has it been since the jury started deliberating?" Celeste asked.

Brianna took the plate of cold sand dabs from Celeste's outstretched hands. "By my count, forty-one," she said. "Too many to wait." She put the plate on the table, then massaged her neck with her right hand.

"When is Richard supposed to come back?" Celeste asked Emma, who handed her the salt and pepper.

"Any time now. I told him not to be late for dinner. He does love his fried trout from the gold streams." She stared over at his empty place at the table, the hot steam rising from the fish on the plate.

Brianna stared at the white flakes on her fork, then put it down. She had no appetite.

Andy perked his ears and wagged his tail.

Richard's voice rang out from the front hallway, and the front door thudded shut, shaking the frame building. "A hung jury!" He burst into the dining room, and a comical grin played upon his face.

"Great news, Richard," cried Emma, as she jumped up and hugged her husband.

Brianna rose, gasping. Could this be true?

Richard took a step back, his eyes darting around the room.

Brianna was curious about the change in his face. "What now?" She shifted to keep her balance.

"There's something else," Richard said. Brianna's chest tightened like a vise.

Richard's mouth thinned with unhappiness. This was not their usual, forthright Richard.

"Tell us, Richard. Please sit down. Don't hold anything back," Brianna said.

He was strangely silent.

Brianna noticed the only sound in the room was water dripping from a wet rag into a pan in the sink.

Celeste eased a plate in front of him. "The usual to drink?" she asked.

"Bourbon tonight. I need strength," Richard replied.

Celeste poured a drink from a large bottle, then set the tumbler before Richard on the table. He downed a straight shot, then continued. "It was as thus—the jury came back, asking to be relieved because they could not agree after all this time. They begged mercy of the court to go back to their families and businesses, and the court granted their request."

"Hmmm, sounds suspicious to me." Emma's quavering voice set the tone.

Brianna contemplated Emma's word *suspicious*. Of all people, Emma would recognize questionable verdicts after having lived in New Orleans where justice did not exist for the rank and file. Brianna breathed out. When will this misery be over?

Richard pulled out a scrap of paper from his pocket. "Moses wrote this down for me since I do not know how."

Brianna took it from him. "My, this scrawl is hard to read, but here it is. First ballot: six voted for murder, five for manslaughter, one voted for acquittal. Then, the vote was six and six: murder or manslaughter. When it got to the third ballot, seven went for murder, and five for manslaughter. By the fourth ballot, eight went for murder, and four went for manslaughter." Brianna's voice lowered to a whisper, and she fell into a silent web of thoughts.

Brianna stared into mid-space. Had the jury continued deliberating, the verdict would have been twelve for murder. Each ballot cast led Edward closer to the scaffold. The squeaky chair wobbled under her, and she laid the paper on the table. How much despair was it possible for a human to feel?

"Yes, Mademoiselle, it was a hung jury." Richard's eyes glistened.

"Poor, poor Monsieur Edward," said Celeste, stirring her tea.

Richard's voice pierced the gloom. "There is something more you should know."

Brianna twisted her hands together. "What would that be? You've already told me enough to break my heart."

Doom wrapped around his words. "There's been another murder . . . this time, Peter McCutcheon, the editor of *The Daily Song*, has been shot in the street. They've caught the culprit, but I couldn't get the fellow's name. Now there are more Vigilante mobs in the streets. I fear not only for Edward now, but for all of us. The law is losing control of the city."

Those words spurred Brianna to action. She turned to Celeste. "Celeste, please go upstairs and tell the girls to gather their things. The house will remain closed for an indefinite period of time. Tell them to go to a safe house, preferably out of the city."

"Oui," said Celeste. "I have a friend in Sacramento named Patrice. They can stay with her until we send for them again." She turned and disappeared through the kitchen door.

Brianna said, "Emma, please get their stage fare ready and summon the coach with the dark curtains so no one recognizes them."

Richard returned from the drawing-room window. "The earlier crowd has been joined by an even larger mob in front of the house. They all carry torches tonight, Mademoiselle. We need to get our girls out by the back door and through the alley. I will make sure they take the coach elsewhere. We must hurry."

Brianna's voice sharpened. "Snuff out the candles and turn off the oil lamps inside the house."

A knock sounded at the back door. Andy sniffed the air around the transom, rather than barking this time. He must recognize the scent. It was a friend.

She crossed the room and opened the door a crack.

Sheriff Jamison stood there, hat in hand. His white moustache and goatee formed a triangle around his mouth. Without so much as a greeting, he said, "Miss Baird, I have posted four guards, two in the front and two at your back door. The Vigilante mobs are growing and they are meeting at Portsmouth Square. I see you are putting out the lamps now. Good idea. You should all grab your weapons and find a place to hide within the house. Where is the best location?"

Brianna's throat grew tight. "We will go to the attic, but Sheriff, do you really think they will hurt us?"

"No telling, Miss Baird. Best be cautious. Mob violence is unpredictable. I lived through 1851, and these times are just as frightening. What weapons do you have in your house?"

"Four shotguns and three revolvers, to my knowledge."

"Good. I will get your girls out of here under cover, but you and your servants should take shelter in your attic." His wrinkled face puckered with concern. "I would offer to take all of you, but if the mobs got wind of Brianna in the coach, they might attack us in force. They've even mobbed the police and the jails, so our meager protection would be useless against them."

At the sound of footsteps, Brianna turned to see her girls appear in the doorway, their flowered nightgowns peeking through gaps in their capes. They carried satchels with skirts and blouses sticking out the edges.

Jamison cleared his throat. "Where should we send your girls?"

Celeste passed a hastily written note to him.

He opened out the letter and Brianna watched his eyes scan the scrawl. He folded it up and tucked it into his coat pocket. "Sacramento, eh? Very well. We'll see they get out of the city safely."

Brianna faced Emma. "Please put all the food you can into one of the market crates. Richard, can you fill the milk cans with water from the pump in the alleyway? We'll carry all of it into the attic with our weapons."

Sheriff Jamison said, "My officers will signal when you should leave the house or when it is all clear. How can they communicate when you are in the attic?"

"Does anyone have a whistle strong enough to be heard above the mobs?" Brianna grasped his arm.

"Yes, Miss Baird. You will hear three short blasts when the mob has dispersed. But for now, clear your house and get upstairs to safety."

Seventy-Seven

THAT INFERNAL RACKET

San Francisco, California
May 1856

Edward, the prisoner, shuffled the deck, and Al, the guard, cut the cards, each reaching through the iron bars separating them. The two men had developed an easy companionship. Edward reflected that stranger things had probably happened in the annals of jail relationships, and it wasn't odd that the prisoner and freed man took a liking to each other. In a sense, both of them were prisoners: one to the four walls; the other to the boredom of the job.

Since his imprisonment, Edward knew little of life outside the stockades except for the information he gleaned during his rides to and from the courthouse in Sheriff Jamison's paddy wagon. He gladly received Richard's daily visits with the newspaper, and he read about his own case. The longer the delay, the worse his chances were of survival.

Each day, he heard stirrings outside the jail and he read the condemning words of Peter McCutcheon, the editor of *The Daily Song*. The journalist pointed to Edward's hung jury two days ago as an act of corruption in a town facing criminal lawlessness. McCutcheon railed in his editorials against gamblers and prostitutes. Each day's news was full of tension: robberies, murders, and rapes filled the pages.

A former Vigilante himself, McCutcheon's incendiary words were a siren call for law and order in a city gone morally astray. As a result, the populace was now stirring for vengeance, and the broadsheets said Vigilantes had put out the call for enrollments. If they reinstated their militia, they would threaten to take over the system of law and order in San Francisco. Folks said that back in '51, their vengeance was swift and brutal.

Edward's thoughts shifted to his present circumstance. Which was worse? The urine stench permeating the cell or the gnawing rats scrambling on him at night? Thank God for Brianna's visits one hour a week. If not for her and his Italian translation of The Bible, he would go mad.

Edward grew restless from the endless waiting until his new trial. Billings had visited the previous day with news of the legal process, and had left him with little hope. A trial would be set for early summer. He pictured the bitter, sour faces of the men on his next jury, licking their lips with thoughts of retribution.

Please, God. Let it be right away.

Edward turned back toward the game at hand. "You've got me again, Al . . . I'm running scared." He joked as his partner cut the cards.

"You should be nervous, Mr. Spina, for I had a run of luck yesterday." Al dealt the deck.

"Yep, I shouldn't have taught you to play so well, *amico*."

"You don't even have to teach me, Mr. Spina, because you show me each time you win. I just follow your lead." A missing-tooth grin brightened Al's face.

"Aces high or low?" Edward asked.

"High, of course. Want a sip of my hot coffee, Edward? I can pass it through the bars to you." Al's good will rippled through his chubby frame.

"No, thanks, when I'm playing, I only crave whisky." Edward licked his lips.

Al snickered. "You know I ain't about to provide that in here. Want me to lose my job? Have to put food on the table for my missus and the four tots. Brought 'em all the way from Kansas in '52. Thought the wagon train was hell; even here in gold country it's been a darned hard life."

"Where did the name Al come from?" Edward shuffled the deck, holding the cards out.

The guard cut the deck. "It's Aloysius, if you must know. My mother was more Catholic than the church. I think it was in honor of some saint or other." He steepled his fingers.

Edward dealt the cards. "Would be hard to shorten a name like that."

"Sure enough, it's been a cross to bear." Al peered at his hand.

Edward nodded as he drew an ace. "High card," he announced. The rumblings of wagons approaching, horses neighing, and men shouting broke his attention.

Al's grin vanished, and a scowl took its place. "Damn! Can't a person play a decent hand around here without that infernal racket?"

Edward flicked a card with the end of his finger and looked up. "You're right, my friend. Outside this place, the crowd noises have calmed down plenty lately."

A bash sounded outside the hallway.

"What's going on out there?" Al called.

Another crash and the door to the cell block flung open and spurs jangled on the wood as men burst in, pushing a prisoner ahead of them. Spina's mouth went bone dry. The prisoner was none other than the notorious politician, James L. Carew. For years his pictures had been plastered all over the broadsheets. He was nothing other than a living scandal and a fraud.

Al leaped to his feet, kicking his card stool out of the way. Edward stuffed the lucky deck under his pillow and reclined on his cot. He couldn't help but stare at the commotion as Sheriff Jamison worked to open the lock of the next cell, and then grunted as he heaved the prisoner inside.

"Fuck you all!" Carew pronounced. "I haven't done a bit what you all say!" He continued to shout profanities until his voice grew hoarse, and a loud bang echoed as he threw himself against the bars separating his cell from Spina's.

"Murder, James L. Carew! That's what you've done!" Jamison stood red-faced, his goatee bristling white against his dark-blue sheriff's uniform.

Hatred wallpapered Carew's features. "Peter McCutcheon deserved what he got." His chest heaved. "Fucker slandered my name all over his paper, all over this town. Now everyone believes I'm a crook."

Al stepped up, his three chins waggling. "Well, Carew, hear tell you've been in Sing before. Wouldn't be nothin' to think you was a crook. You *are* a crook."

Carew frowned, then he spat out his words. "Jamison, I say too bad McCutcheon didn't have a knife or gun on him. Then I could claim self-defense like your bastard Spina sitting over there, taking his ease and comfort. You watch. I'll swing and he'll walk away. And he's as guilty as I am, only he's a sleazy, low-life card player; Italian cock-sucking whore-monger."

Spina's eyes shifted side to side. He burned, a low coal-fire starting in his stomach pits, then traveling up to his jugular. Carew's murder of Peter McCutcheon would provoke more than the usual violence in the city. And that would be his death sentence.

Now, as in '51, Vigilante soldiers traveled in from all areas of the state. Former San Francisco vigilante troop members had waited in the shadows, and with one blink, they were out in the light of day, bayonets fixed, at attention, marching, parading, intimidating. They'd take the town from the government, from the governor, from the sheriff, and they'd do what they darned well pleased with it.

And it wouldn't matter if Edward was innocent or guilty; their justice and their laws ruled with fear. A solid, steely vengeance that had no mercy, a bloodlust that would turn back upon the Vigilantes, so no one was safe. Hysteria run riot. Gone were the days when an elegant, mild-mannered card player walked the streets of San Francisco with a madam on his arm. Winds of change were blowing in from the bay, and this town would never be the same. He watched the scene unfold between Carew and Jamison in the next cell.

"You've got quite a reputation, young man, as a fighter and a ballot-box stuffer in this town," Jamison said, his green eyes flashing.

"Should have killed McCutcheon long before that night." Carew bit a hangnail on a dirty finger.

"Maybe so, but you wouldn't have gotten off. McCutcheon had eleven bullets in him when Doc Poppy saw him. Said one of them just missed his heart."

"Bagley counted twenty shots fired that night . . . not all of them from me," Carew smirked, his eyes wide and rangy.

Jamison scolded, "What about all of your self-appointed high positions? You're inspector of elections in the Sixth Ward? How many ballots rigged? You're a liar and a fake, Carew."

The prisoner slapped his knee. "And a proud member of the Volunteer Fire Department, Engine Number 10."

Spina had heard enough. By murdering McCutcheon, Carew had destroyed any chances either man had of freedom. By murdering McCutcheon, Carew had thumbed his nose at the voice of law and order, the darling of those enraged by what they saw as the lack of civil order.

Edward looked down in time to see a cockroach climb over his dusty boot. He stared at the beetle as it descended onto the ground, its slick, black body resembling a hearse. Would his own coffin be made from a ship's timbers? And what about his funeral procession? He imagined it winding down planked streets to the Mission. He envisioned a priest at the graveyard, his finger outstretched toward Edward's resting place, the trees waving in the sea breeze of the graveyard. Was that his Brianna, weeping over his open tomb?

As Spina began to see the impact of McCutcheon's murder on his next trial, the heat rose into his muscles, and he strategized his next move. He'd punish Carew, whose vengeance caused his own impending death and the subsequent loss of his Brianna.

As a seagull's cry met the waning sunlight, a purple cast blanketed Spina's cell. The spring days were getting longer, so it must be close to 8:30 at night. He crept across his cell to check Carew's form. The man lay half on his bunk, half on the floor, in deep sleep.

Spina shook his head. "The devil incarnate," he whispered, "can fall asleep anywhere." He held his nose, his eyes watering from the stink of the man. "Too busy to bathe, I guess. Must have relieved himself without using the outhouse."

A strange quietude reigned outside. No yelling of crowds, no children's cries as they played games within the encircling mobs. Al had eased his watch on Spina since the attention was now on the murderous Carew. Where was Al? He expected to see him at his usual post outside Carew's cell. He bent his head, angling his view down the hallway. In the light of a half-burned candle, there sat the guard, his roly-poly chest rising and falling, while in deep dreams, he embraced the tabletop.

Spina sighed. "Good, Al won't hear this." Genovese justice was swift and silent. Spina's childhood had taught him what to do.

He fingered a spoon he had stolen from the gruel bowl that evening. He looked at his carpetbag on the floor. Some time back, Brianna had brought him a long cravat, in case he wished to dress as well in the jail as in the gambling hells. He stuffed it into his pocket, hidden under his linen overshirt. "Psst!" he whispered.

Carew's form twitched in place but did not stir.

Edward raised his voice a notch. "I say, Carew." Carew rolled off his cot, toppling onto the dirt floor. He lay there, semi-conscious.

Spina persisted. "Carew, come here! Want to talk to you. My man, wake up! Wake up now!"

Carew blinked and growled, sitting up like a bear disturbed from hibernation. He rubbed his dusty head. "What do you want, whoreson? I don't plan to commune with your sort. You're grease. One of those filthy Italians. You belong with the maggots, Spina." He held his nose.

"Hmmm, indeed. I agree. We Italians are a filthy lot, aren't we?" Spina hissed.

"Yeah." Carew rubbed his dirt-pitted fists in his eyes.

"But we're a lot better than you micks, I suspect." Spina knew an Irishman's pressure point, and he aimed right for it.

Bingo, the man was on his feet like a pirate, putting up his fists, "Cussing lick-finger!"

Spina danced behind the cell bars separating them. "Come and get it, you mule-hipped knothead!"

Carew's cheeks puffed, as did his chest.

Spina continued his taunts. "You know what they say about you Irish? Can't keep your pants on. That is why you have so many children running around town. Potato eaters, slime, vermin. Now that's a true mick! Come on over here and let's conversate. Shh . . . be quiet or the guards will hear, quiet now, you ugly mick, come on over, you slimeball . . . I want to show you the garrote."

Like a bear baited by a dog, Carew lumbered up to the cell bars. He stuck his paw-like fists through first one opening, then another, as Spina continued to gibe him.

"Come here, let me show you an old, medieval Italian fight move."

"I ain't skeerd, show me what you got," Carew said.

In a move he had learned as a teenager on the docks of New Orleans, Spina grabbed Carew's left arm and pulled it around inside his cell. As Carew flailed, Spina tore the cravat from his pocket and threaded it through the bars and around his neck, drawing it taut.

As Carew turned, Spina stabilized the neckerchief with a spoon, making a tight knot. He pinned Carew's head so that it faced back into the man's cell, pulling Carew's other arm behind him. Pulling the cravat down, Edward made a double knot so that his prey could not move. One tug on the band, and Spina could strangle him. He paused, one jerk short of execution.

Right now, no need to kill him. Edward had done a simple act of torture to repay this idiot for taking his own life from him, thus destroying Brianna's future.

Carew's breath came in rasps; he struggled against the bars, his hands flailing wildly.

"Carew," Spina spat. "You've put the noose around both our necks with your stupidity. I could have been a free man but for your ass for a brain. But what I am doing will make your hanging more painful. That's my motive. And believe me, you will hang. Whether next to me, before or after, is no matter. Now you'll suffer greater death pains with the noose around your neck than ever before. Oh, and by the way, you've bedded more whores in your life than I ever have in mine, and I'm sure you have cocksores to prove it."

Spina pulled the garrote tighter and tighter, rubbing it from side to side until a line of blood burst from Carew's neck onto the cravat, and a red trickle appeared on his shirt. Carew choked; his hands flew to his neck. Spina's hands held firm. Carew went limp, passed out against the cell bars.

"As I said, I do not mean to kill you, you *figlio di putana*, son of a whore. Only to make your neck so raw and painful, the Vigilante noose will chafe and bite you, your pain sublime. And God himself will laugh that the biggest devil in hell will get his due."

Spina tossed the spoon in the hallway, and hid the cravat in his valise. He surveyed his night's work. "Good," he said. "Sweet dreams."

The next morning, as a sleepy Al served breakfast to Carew, Spina watched the guard stare at the bloody marks and bruises on Carew's neck. He remarked, "Looks like you tried to hang yourself there, mate."

Carew glanced over at Spina through the bars. He bit into his hard tack. "What are you talking about, ugly mug?"

Spina lowered his gaze, then cracked his knuckles loudly.

Al left well enough alone.

Spina guessed Al's conclusion. The world would be better served if the gambler did the job before the Vigilantes got to Carew. Less trouble for everyone.

Seventy-Eight

DESIRING SO IN NAME

San Francisco, California
May 1856

After five days in the attic, Sheriff Jamison signaled the all-clear. Brianna and Emma could not decide whether to be relieved or even more frightened. Sheriff Jamison advised them that local Vigilantes had taken over governance of the city, so a temporary semblance of law and order reigned again in the Bay. Crowds no longer rallied in front of the parlor house; the usual merchants and peddlers traded their wares on Waverly. She anticipated the worst when the Sheriff told her the Vigilantes had transferred Edward to their Sacramento Street warehouse, nicknamed Fort Gunnybags. The previous day, the Committee had held a new secret trial.

The next two days, Richard carried an exchange of messages between Brianna and Billings. Brianna agreed to meet Billings and Foote on the outskirts of the city. Any recognition would be dangerous, so she had Richard saddle up their gentle mare, Julianne, and dressed as a young man, she headed into the hills to their meeting point on the Mission Plank Road. Emma had insisted Brianna carry a pistol in a holster and smudge her face in way that suggested she had a short-cut beard. She tied her hair in a topknot, then covered it with a floppy, low-slung hat.

Brianna rode up to the gentlemen standing by their horses, the three o'clock sun casting lazy shadows over the hillsides on 9th Street. An occasional house or two speckled the knolls around them, and they heard the occasional bleating of a goat or the moo of a cow. The roads were wet from a recent rain shower, and after the men helped Brianna off her horse, her boots sank into the sandy mud. She dropped Julianne's reins and the horse meandered off to a side pasture to nibble some weeds.

Brianna's heart thumped in her chest. "Please, gentlemen, no formalities. I wish to know the verdict." Her eye caught the breezes rustling the mounds of grass flowing across the green hills.

Billings spoke, his voice soft, as if to soothe the tension she felt. "Miss Baird, it is as you have feared. The committee met in secret and declared him guilty. Most of the witnesses from the original trial have long since left the city out of fear."

Foote stepped forward. "I assisted wherever I could, Miss Baird, but I am afraid he was guilty to them before the proceedings ever began."

To her own surprise, she did not flinch. "How is Edward?"

Billings fingered his riding whip. "He received the verdict calmly, and thanked the committee for considering his case."

Foote coughed, and Julianne the horse snuffled in the weed patch.

Brianna's fingers trembled. "I have been told that Vigilante justice is rapid. When is the execution?" Nausea rose in her belly along with despair.

Foote's shoulders drooped. "Tomorrow when the Vigilante bell signals the funeral procession of Peter McCutcheon. Mr. Spina and Carew are to hang at the same time."

A numbness settled in Brianna's arms and legs. Billings stepped forward and pressed a paper into her hand. "From Mr. Spina," he said.

Billings and Foote exchanged nods. "We will give you some privacy as you read the letter, Madame," Billings said. They stepped away with their horses, and she trudged through the mud over to Julianne. She unfolded the letter and leaned against the mare's side.

My dearest Brianna,

Tomorrow they will come for my life, and I must do their bidding. It is of no use to proclaim my innocence, since I have been tried and convicted in the court of public hatred. It is useless to ask for pity or forgiveness, since they appear to have none in their hearts.

Father Gabriel is with me now, and he assures me I will go to God since he knows I shot in self-defense. He, along with you, knows my heart and my conscience is clear. My dearest, I have a last request before I go to my Heavenly Father. I ask this now with all the earnestness of a dying man. Please marry me. There is still time. Father Gabriel has told me he can marry us before the execution. Although after tomorrow, we will not be together as one, our marriage will signal the union of our hearts forever. I know you did not marry me for reasons of distrust, based on your past trials. Yet if you consider, I have served as your faithful husband now for six years, and had I been granted life, I would have continued to be yours until we both were parted through death. We have so little time left. Please consider uniting our blessed hearts together as one.

Your husband in heart, desiring so in name,
Edward

Brianna spun and faced the mare's side, crushing the letter to her chest as she held onto the saddle. She'd been more than stupid to resist his offers of marriage all these many years. She'd been blind to his goodness, to his patience, to the kindness he showed by humbly waiting for her. Rather than following his wishes, she had denied Ambrose the father he would have deserved, even though it would have been in name only.

Not only had she forsaken Ambrose, but she'd also punished herself. She had held Edward at arm's length rather than accepting him fully into her heart where he truly belonged. Hadn't he proved his faithfulness over and over again, both in New Orleans and San Francisco? There'd never been a time when she doubted his love. She saw now that she had taken advantage of his trust and loyalty, rather than returning the trust she owed him.

Brianna beat a fist against her chest. How had she been so blind? Even now, despite her many rejections, he wanted her, heart and soul, on his deathbed. How could she deny such purity of heart?

She picked her way back through the sludge to Billings and Foote. "Gentlemen, I have a simple message for you to carry back to Mr. Spina." The world brightened as she regarded the men.

Billings regarded her. "Do you wish to write it? If so, I have carried on my horse some paper and a pencil."

"No, that won't be necessary." Brianna said.

Foote asked, "And your message?"

Her voice was steady. "The message is simply this one word: *yes*."

On her ride back home, the green grasses, the smells of the earth, the bleats of the sheep, even the puffy clouds sailing over the hills, carried new life to her senses.

Seventy-Nine

PARALLEL ROPES

San Francisco, California
May 1856

The next day, Brianna clung to Billings' arm while they wended their way through the carefree throng on Sacramento Street. Emma had dressed Brianna in a long, black wig, mantilla, and white and red Spanish-style skirt to avoid recognition. Although Brianna still faced some risk of danger if she were recognized, Billings encouraged her to accompany him, and she felt safe in his company.

On a typical day, Frank Mazzetta would be tending to his special lamb roasting on a spit in front of his small market. A line would form around the block when Frank cooked. His spicy garlic and grease concoction made one's mouth water for days in anticipation. Brianna's parlor house patrons enjoyed his leg of lamb along with the French champagne and caviar.

Brianna always stopped to exchange pleasantries, giving Frank a written order for that evening's soirée. Frank would eye the list as he poked the embers, garlic steam rising in gusts around them. Today, however, Frank's store stood dark, the shades drawn. The lamb spit stood abandoned outside, white grease hardened in the tray.

Instead, today she spied Frank and his children occupying a plot of ground on the muddy flat of the square facing the Vigilante Headquarters that they had named Fort Gunnybags. Brianna guessed the family angled for a good view of the executions while they ate lunch. As she took Billings' arm and turned to mount the steps, she opened her fan to conceal her face. Over the top of it, she glimpsed young Jimmy shoot a marble with characteristic cruelty at his sister, Carmela. Her cries, mingled with Frank's shouts, told Brianna the marble had hit the target, those cries piercing the murmurs of the crowd. Her jaw clenched. They were waiting for her Edward, the star of today's show.

Upstairs in the Vigilante Headquarters, Edward's eyes fastened on the manacles around his ankles, the powdery stench of dust and urine coating his throat. He reclined on a storeroom cot on the second floor of the warehouse, where he studied the many boxes and crates stacked up in the corners. His head pounded with an eternal headache; his legs cramped, stiff from lack of movement.

The nameless Vigilante guard slipped in the usual tray of brown glop with a fork attached, along with a watery brown broth slopping within a gray tin cup. Edward, each day more surprised at how much better the rations were tasting, noticed his muscles shrinking on his arms and legs. He picked up the bowl, noticing how much heavier it had become in one week. After he set it back down, he lifted the crucifix Brianna had brought from the parlor house, then held it to his lips.

Before he could reach for his rations, the rising thrum of activities down in the square drifted in through the open window—horses trotted, Vigilantes shouted commands, and hammers pounded nails against the scaffold. Every sound mixed with the next to form a ribbon of fear winding through him. A fiddler tuned his instrument, his discordant melody threading through the murmur of the gathering crowd. Keys grated in locks; boots' heels pounded in the corridor.

Edward gazed up as Brianna swept into the room on the arm of attorney Billings. "Brianna," he said. She was spring to him, the embodiment of all things soft and loving.

Father Gabriel padded behind them, his white-rope belt flashing against his brown Franciscan robes.

Brianna pulled her black mantilla off her shoulders, revealing her white cape and full red and white skirt, fringed with black Spanish lace. She unpeeled her black wig, and auburn tresses circled her ears in the latest style.

This getup tickled Edward, and despite his sad situation, he burst into laughter. "You were let in? I'm surprised. You look like Lola Montez in that getup." He rubbed his dry and itchy eyes, then rose and extended a wobbly hand. "Mr. Billings, Father Gabriel, I am in your debt."

He felt the touch of Brianna's white-gloved hand on his arm.

"Edward, I came as soon as Mr. Billings called. Moses pulled the hack out of the stables and we raced here as fast as we could." Brianna pulled back, removing her glove.

Edward felt her soft, pink hand close around his. Did she know he was already retreating into his inner core? Did she know he was protecting himself from the horror-filled scenes of his own death at the end of the noose? He searched her face for relief.

Brianna turned to Father Gabriel and stood eyeball-to-eyeball with the tipsy reverend.

Her voice was solemn. "Two things. First, Father, I insist on having time alone with Mr. Spina so that we can prepare for the sacraments." Brianna held her mantilla up to her nose. Even from Edward's seated position, he could smell the priest's alcoholic vapors.

"*Si, Signorina*, but we don't have much time." Father Gabriel nodded, his Italian brown eyes floating under heavy lids. "I need to stay in their good graces." He looked toward the guard outside the cell. "There is the matter of a stolen chalice and candle holders they are helping me recover."

Father prodded. "You have fifteen minutes, Miss Baird, and then we must conduct the marriage rites. The Vigilantes have set the time, and we must stay within the limits. If we don't, there is the danger they will throw us out . . . that is, all except Edward." Pearls of sweat appeared on his forehead.

Brianna waved away his remark. "I insist on Mr. Spina's being dressed to be married in his best suit." She pointed to a multi-colored carpetbag that Billings had required she bring inside with her.

Father Gabriel frowned. "But there is no time for that."

"Yes there is, and you know it." Brianna's eyes blazed, her pupils large and dark. Father Gabriel stepped back on unsteady feet, a sheepish look on his face.

Edward grinned. That was his Brianna—on fire. He had watched her use the same authority while running her parlor house.

Father murmured, "As you wish, Miss Baird." Her words had penetrated his layers of alcoholic fog.

Billings bowed, tipped his hat, then backed out of the cell. Edward saw Billings turn his back to them, but the lawyer sat down on a chair within calling distance. Father Gabriel followed suit, then perched next to Billings on a rickety stool.

After Father Gabriel left the room, Brianna noticed a black nit crossing Edward's scalp, evidence of his neglect in filthy jails for the last three months. A straggly beard aged him beyond his thirty-six years. Underneath the beard, his cheekbones rode high on his face, and emaciation grayed his once-handsome features. Crust from an untreated cut festered yellow on his ear, and she seethed. How dare they? The manacles carved purple marks on his wrists. She had no intention of allowing the Vigilantes to prevail over them. Edward Spina would not be married, then buried in this condition. He was famous for his impeccable taste and cleanliness.

In better times, she would have gone into combat with the Committee of Vigilance, decrying the brutality and injustice of Edward's condition. In better times, she would have ranted and raved to Billings, pleading with him to use his best legal maneuvers to free Edward. But in these times, she felt helpless, for she knew her lover had lost not only his freedom, but now also his life. All because the Vigilantes would not treat her case with justice. And with that loss, she had no more energy left, except to give Edward as much love as she could within the space of two hours.

"Edward." She sat and faced him on his cot. "Colonel Billings will take you and dress you in your best suit."

"Yes, Brianna." He nodded, and she sensed obedience in his voice. So unlike the Edward of old who had guided her through the chaotic streets of New Orleans.

In a moment, Billings appeared, his face kind and apologetic. A sob sprang from Brianna's throat when Billings helped Edward up from the cot and guided him from the room. Each step forward brought them closer to the end. Brianna's handkerchief failed to absorb the tears running down her face, and she looked down to see her white linen bodice stained with them. She dabbed at the moisture with her black mantilla. Trying to distract herself, she sat on a crate of dishes and made X's and O's with the heel of her black-pointed shoe in the sawdust on the floor. She coiled her fingers through the black ringlets of the wig on her lap. *Stay strong for Edward; stay strong for yourself.* She closed her eyes against the pain that laced around her more tightly each moment.

Hooting and hollering filtered in through the open windows as the crowds grew outside. Brianna bit her lip. How like the Romans gathering at the coliseum, waiting to see lions tear apart the gladiators. The shouts of the carpenters mingled with their pounding and adjusting of boards on the scaffold. A mysterious force drew Brianna out of the cell and over to the windows facing Sacramento Street.

A wave of dizziness pushed her to the window's side wall where she stretched out her hands for support. A pair of parallel ropes dropped, then dangled in front of her outside the tall, open window. She leaned out the window and saw the workmen up on the roof and over on the scaffold. The massive cables jerked up and down as the crew adjusted the length from the pulleys attached to the roof above. The heavy lines unraveled as they fell, then swung wildly until men snapped them down onto the platform below. The workmen on the boards caught the rope ends, their gloved hands forming them into the nooses for Edward and Carew. What would poor Edward feel when that rope tightened around his neck?

Brianna gazed past the scaffolding and down at the square. Her eyes caught the gray tips of bayonets that were fixed atop the raised rifles of the Committee of Vigilance. The soldiers marched in company, their shiny high hats and bow ties prominent in the daylight. The militia lined up in strict formation in front of the warehouse entrance to prevent anyone from entering the building. Between her and the militia were six to seven one-foot-high gunnysacks, filled with bulk. Among them, the committee had situated cannons for double protection. The crowd filled the perimeter of the square in front of the warehouse and spilled out onto the side streets. Here and there, young men in caps hawked sweets and beer to the thirsty, sun-drenched crowd.

Brianna's rising sense of outrage took her by surprise. *An ordinary day for them to make some money.* She shook her head, disgusted. Would she have the strength to endure this day? She wove her way back to the cell and sat back down on the cot.

Eighty

SO GOOD TO ME

San Francisco, California
May 1856

After a few moments, Father Gabriel's heavy shoes thudded back into the room, and behind him Edward shuffled, dragging a ball and chain. The formal attire he wore did nothing to disguise the faded daguerreotype of her Edward, her lover, her friend. Yet he could still make her blush. What was it about him that she found irresistible? Despite their age difference, he'd always treated her as an equal, like a lady. He was steady, and she trusted him.

Billings located a dusty blanket and hung up a makeshift curtain to shelter the couple from the soldiers and workmen passing by.

In semi-darkness, they sat together on the sagging cot to share their last words. Brianna combed his hair and mustache, something she used to do every night before bed. She loved his thick, black hair, sweeping over his collar in rolling curls.

Father Gabriel disappeared around the corner, brushing away a drunken tear. "Mrs. Emma wants a word with me," he said.

Billings shadowed him out the door while pointing to his open pocket watch.

Once alone, Brianna put her arm around Edward's broad shoulders, hugging him close to her breast. "You look so good to me." She took his face in her hands, and kissed his nose, mouth, eyes, cheeks—long, studied kisses, as though painting designs with her lips. "Good enough to eat." She imagined her lips lighting embers long since burned out.

She felt the soft tips of his fingers as they brushed the hair from her forehead. "Brianna, I am in fear." He rested back on the cot and took her in his arms, and his fingers searched through the layers of lace for her inviting body, a perfect fit for his own. How well she remembered this. Their past was a canvas painted with scenes like this—hours thus enraptured, skin on skin.

Brianna's lips nuzzled his ear. "I failed you."

Edward stroked her hair. "You did the best you could."

She propped herself up on an elbow and he gazed up at her. "I didn't spend enough money on your defense. I should have made a court appearance. Acted more hysterical. Raised more eyebrows."

Edward's eyes were round and luminous in his sunken face. He caressed her cheek with the back of his hand. "From all I hear, you raised enough hell for the both of us."

"Hell?" She shook her head. "Not nearly enough."

"Oh, hush, that's all over now." He pulled her back down and patted her head as he used to do when she was but a young girl in New Orleans.

"What can I do now without you? How can I go on?" She fought off the internal knotting of her throat.

Edward cradled her more closely on his chest. "Brianna, promise me something."

"Anything, my love, anything." Brianna held her lips against his cheek. She wanted to remember this forever.

His voice mingled grief with desire. "That we are buried together at the Mission."

"I can arrange that. It is sacred ground. I do not know how right now, but I can do that." She stroked his cheek with the back of her hand.

His whisper grew hoarse. "I asked Father Gabriel. He is making arrangements so we can be buried side by side."

She pulled back. "But I'm not Catholic . . . I'm also surprised he's performing our ceremony, rather than a judge. Isn't that against Catholic law?"

Edward gave her a sideways glance. "The bishop has a big appetite for charitable contributions."

"So you paid him off?"

"With Billings' help." His eyes crinkled upward.

"I see." Brianna tucked her body even closer to his. "Any other requests, my love?"

"Second, and most important, I want you go on striving without me. Keep the parlor houses, and live your life knowing that I am always there with you, no matter what." He swallowed.

"That's a large demand for me, Edward." She wept, tears burning her eyelids.

He raised his chin. "I know, my girl. You have strength and confidence. You're not going to be called Mrs. Spina for nothing."

Wordless, she held him tight, as close as she had held Ambrose before releasing him into the Mississippi.

He sighed. "You're be mine for all eternity, you know. It took my dying wish to get you to marry me. After all those years of trying to convince you."

After a pause during which Brianna struggled against a sob, she said,

"I was always afraid of being a wife instead of a woman. I never saw myself as respectable, even though I wanted dignity."

Edward turned his head toward her. "I recognize that. And yet I hold you on the highest of pedestals. You rank higher than any of richest high-society women on Nob Hill." He ran his fingers through her hair, and she buried her face against his shoulder.

A lone tear snuck from a corner of her eye. "I . . . I couldn't trust any man, not after—"

"I know . . . not after losing Ambrose." Edward's voice spoke of the tender understanding gained from watching Brianna battle painful thoughts for years.

Brianna stiffened like Miss Rose's mannequin. "How do you know about Ambrose? I never told a soul."

His fingers trailed down her cheek. "Emma told me everything. One day, last year, I found your gris-gris bag on the floor of our bedroom, and I knew it meant something to you . . . something about you . . . and I had to know. So I pestered the poor woman until she told me your secret."

Brianna sobbed and pulled Edward to her chest. "Edward, I . . . don't know what to say. I lost my baby, now I am to lose you, too?"

He pulled away, gazing up at her. "I feel as though Ambrose was my child, too, and when I held the gris-gris, I could feel his love for you." Edward's eyes looked faraway, his voice as tender as soft May rains.

The guard cleared his throat outside the chamber. Brianna felt Edward's muscles tense under her. She nuzzled his cheek. "I have but one more question, Edward."

"Yes. Anything." His arms encircled her body as though protecting her from all harm.

"Did you shoot Williams in self-defense? I must know. No matter the answer, I will be on your side. Your truth will give me strength and hope to go on without you."

Edward's eyes traveled from her face up to the ceiling. "I truly believe so. I have mulled it over thousands of times since it happened. I dream about it, even when I am awake. In the scene, I see his hand move to his jacket pocket, and I know he is going to draw his knife. He pulls out the knife and takes a slice, barely missing me."

Brianna let out a huge breath. "That is all I need, Edward. Forever." The cot creaked under them and they clenched each other, castaways adrift on a stormy sea. And Brianna knew those few moments of safe haven were the most honest they had ever shared.

Eighty-One

THE WILTING ROSE

San Francisco, California
May 1856

A half an hour ticked away. Brianna wondered as she watched Father Gabriel wobble on his feet. If he fell over, he might land on top of her or Edward. The plump priest reeked of whiskey, his bulbous red nose and vein-laced cheeks punctuating the mottled face. Would he make it through the ceremony before the Vigilante bell sounded on the roof, signaling the beginning of the end?

She held Mrs. Morgan's handkerchief up to her nose to quell the priest's vapors. How did the priest manage to stay upright without losing his balance? According to Emma, Father Gabriel had spent the previous night at Darby's, celebrating the guilty verdict of the same man to whom he would administer Last Confession, Holy Matrimony, and the last rites within minutes of each other.

Yet even within the chaos of pounding and banging, and the shouts of the mob outside, Brianna surrendered to a lightness, a type of bliss that far exceeded this marriage, this ring, this day. A line from her Baltimore hymnal played in her head. *This is the day the Lord has made. Let us rejoice and be glad in it.* After all, she was giving Edward what he so long desired and what she'd so long denied him—her promise to love him forever.

What odd times these were. Men were enemies and friends, saints and sinners, all at the same time. A flask bulged out of the priest's hip pocket. Brianna frowned at his stained and crooked Roman collar. His pudgy neck protruded, giving him a rakish appearance. So like her own father. What was the link between loving God and loving the bottle? Oh well, it mattered little. In giving herself to Edward, a great freedom lifted her up.

Shafts of light from the tall, parallel windows highlighted them. Edward's shackles rattled and grooved the wooden floor. She blinked at dusty sunbeams; was she dreaming? This scene blurred like New Orleans lace. Crates, barrels, and boxes surrounded them, and Father Gabriel rested his breviary on a barrel. The priest stifled a burp, and he perched the wedding ring on his own pinky finger to hold it in place.

Edward's wan smile penetrated Brianna's clouds of uncertainty. Brianna looked at her life as if it belonged to someone else. Here she was, one of the most accomplished madams of San Francisco, her parlor house a favorite haunt of the rich and powerful men of her times. Yet, in marrying Edward, she was as shy as she had been as a wee child in Baltimore, who used to hide behind her mother's skirts when callers came for tea. Brianna saw that moment at Miss Osborne's shop when she had spied her first madam from the window. How she had changed since those early days. How she had collected experiences. How she had loved.

How handsome Edward was today, despite their deadly circumstances. A drop of sweat lingered on his forehead. Was he as scared as she? His eyes had sunken, and lines had deepened around them. The poor man had retreated behind a veil of pain.

How often had Brianna overlooked the many little gifts he'd given her? Boxes of chocolates to make her laugh, buggy rides out to Ocean

Beach to point out the whales? When he had reached out to hold her, how often had she been too busy with the girls to pay attention to him? She clenched her teeth, filled with regret.

Annie had once said that death makes life worth living. Brianna now looked at Edward in a new way, now that she would lose him. Never had Edward seemed so desirable, kind, or noble than in this moment. If only Annie were here today to give her hope and strength.

They posed before the priest, Brianna in a black mantilla cascading over her white jacket, and Edward next to her in his black morning coat and red cravat. She looked down at the trembling red rose in her fingers, a rose Richard had plucked for her from the back garden of Waverly Place. Where was Emma? Good—right beside her, calm and serene. At Edward's side, Richard straightened himself with a dignified posture.

Father Gabriel cleared his throat and made the sign of the cross. "*In nomine Patris et Filii et Spiritus Sancti.*"

"Amen," Brianna heard them all say.

The priest passed the ring to Richard and then flipped through the well-worn pages of his leather-bound breviary. He placed the red-ribbon bookmark against the inner spine of the prayer book. Brianna glanced at two Vigilante guards at the door, who glared at them. Her breath quickened. On a whim, they could put a halt to the wedding.

"Edward Spina, wilt thou take Brianna Baird, here present, for thy lawful wife, according to the rite of our holy Mother the Church?"

Edward said, "I will."

Brianna caught his misty-eyed gaze.

"Brianna Baird, wilt thou take Edward Spina, here present, for thy lawful husband, according the rite of our holy Mother the Church?"

"I will."

"Will you now join your right hands?"

Edward's gentle fingers relaxed on top of Brianna's hand, and she was startled at the longing she found within his eyes. She wanted to stay there forever in that space, the sunbeams supporting them.

"I, Edward Spina, take thee, Brianna Baird, for my lawful wife, to have and to hold, from this day forward, for better, for worse, for richer, for poorer, in sickness and in health, until death do us part."

Brianna paused, swallowing the last remnants of fear in marrying, knowing that she could trust this man with all her being.

"Do go on, Brianna," the priest encouraged.

"I, Brianna Baird, take thee, Edward Spina, for my lawful husband, to have and to hold, from this day forward, for better, for worse, for richer, for poorer, in sickness and in health, until death do us part."

Father Gabriel intoned in Latin, "I join you together in marriage, in the name of the Father, and of the Son, and of the Holy Ghost. Amen."

Richard picked up and held out a small silver bowl filled with holy water, and the priest dipped his fingers into it, then sprinkled droplets onto Brianna and Edward.

Brianna welcomed the cool spray, as cleansing and pure as their blessed vows.

Father Gabriel shifted his gaze toward Richard. "The ring, please?"

Richard pulled it from his pocket. He then passed it to the priest, but it tumbled from the priest's shaky hand. Brianna watched it roll between Edward's shackled legs, then underneath the storage crates.

Hysteria mixed with desperation rose in Brianna's throat. Richard scrambled to find the ring where it landed between two boxes. He stood up, holding it out to the priest, who took it from him.

Out of the corner of Brianna's eye, she saw Emma's eyes follow Richard, then close for a moment. Her calm demeanor gave Brianna peace and soothed her jittery nerves. Father Gabriel passed the ring to Edward.

The Vigilante guard cleared his throat in a warning. Not much time left. Edward slid the ring onto her trembling finger, guiding it over her knuckle and into place. She inhaled sharply— the ring breathed out light from a cluster of small rubies forming a small rise, its gold filigree cupping a large diamond, its facets absorbing, then reflecting the rainbow of colors surrounding them.

Brianna had little time to admire it, for next she heard guards clomping toward them, chains clanking, from the outer hallway. They were coming to take Edward. *Please no, not yet,* she prayed. Their high hats, bearded faces, and blue jackets darkened the hallway and cast shadows into the room.

The priest raised his hand to stop the men. "Time for holy communion." Father Gabriel's brows lifted and he made the sign of the cross.

The guards stopped in the doorway and upon hearing the priest's words, they frowned, leaning against their rifles.

Brianna suppressed her sobs.

Richard whispered, "You must be strong . . . for your new husband." A fatal resignation settled on his features.

Edward reached across and held Brianna's hands. Father Gabriel gave him the sacrament of holy communion, placing the white wafer on his tongue.

Brianna did not step forward to receive the host, since she was not a baptized Catholic.

Then, the priest stepped back, and Brianna imitated the movements of Edward's hands as he made the sign of the cross before both of them. "I then pronounce—"

Without waiting for the final declaration, Edward drew Brianna to him and nuzzled her ear. He pulled away, his eyes flickering over her face. "Be brave, Brianna. Live as I have taught you to live. Stay strong. Independent." He set her back, hands on her shoulders.

Would she ever be able to be as brave as he was right now? She gazed into his eyes, dark liquid pools reflecting the sunlight from the tall windows.

Edward leaned toward the priest. "I am ready now, Father, for the last rites. He swiveled slowly, the ball and chain rumbling. "I will wait for you to join me, Brianna."

The Vigilante bell on the roof pierced the air, and they startled. All eleven-hundred pounds of the bell chimed, and Brianna, among the rest of those in Fort Gunnybags, went deaf in those minutes. The Boston bell's peals summoned onlookers within a ten-mile radius.

Amid the clamor, Father Gabriel shot out the words, "I then pronounce you man and wife."

Captured in Edward's arms, Brianna opened herself to his kisses, knowing this would be their last embrace. Her body entwined within his shelter, their bodies two braided strands of kelp resembling those washed up at Ocean Beach. She heard the calm, soothing words of Marie LaVeau:

Let his light carry you through life,
Guiding your footsteps into the moments of eternal unity with your son.

For a moment, all movement stopped. The clanking in the distance grew louder, accompanied by the dull thrum of boots on wood. The militia were coming. Billings and Father Gabriel pulled Edward away from Brianna. When Edward's grip loosened, then faded, she lost a part of herself, her friend, confidante, and lover. What would she do without him?

A Vigilante militiaman stepped in without fanfare, his sword swinging at his hip, took Edward's arm, and led him stumbling away in the direction of his cell, the drag of his ball and chain sounding a *dot-dot-dash* like the Morse code she'd once heard at the station house on Telegraph Hill.

Brianna's mantilla floated to the floor. She leaned against Billings' chest, sensing his cradling arms enclosing her as though she were the child he'd never had. She felt Emma's hands set the mantilla back up on her head and shoulders. Brianna pulled the veil close about her face. It was as though half of her life were being taken away, as though her body were about to be cut in half, like the magician's girl in the box.

But this was no magic. This was real.

She squeezed away the tears, aware for a moment: the rescued black mantilla drifting over her white cape resembled the habit of an Ursuline nun. Again, she could hear the gentle intonations of the Voodoo Queen.

Be open to love.
Other loves.
Your man's love.
So Be It.

Father Gabriel shadowed Edward and the guards back to his cell for the private sacraments of penance and extreme unction, the rite for the dying. Brianna tried to keep hold of her fragile self-control. Every time his ball and chain raked across the floor, she rode waves of apprehension. Yet she would give him strength. "I hear you're an expert gambler, Mr. Spina," Brianna said.

She trailed behind Father Gabriel toward the cell, and then, while leaning against the doorframe, she watched him sink down on the cot. He reached over and gathered the chain's links and the ball so they no longer chafed against his leg.

His sunken eyes focused on the ceiling. "And the odds are best in heaven, I'm told."

She gazed through the bars of the cell and looked up at the ceiling along with him. "Win a feathery cloud for us to live on."

He turned to her and forced a grin. "Think God will lend us a privacy curtain . . . now and then?"

"Yes, my love, you know He will." Brianna throat was so tight, she had trouble getting out the words.

"Farewell, my love," he sobbed.

She clung to the cell bars. "Godspeed, my Edward." Her voice mingled with his one last time. She continued, "They want a show? We'll give them a better show than the American Theater. Be brave. I'll join you soon in heaven. They have magnificent parlor houses up there, I'm told."

Emma stepped over, her kind presence filling the blank space where Edward had stood.

Brianna reached out and grasped Emma's arm. "What will Father Gabriel do with Edward?" she asked.

Emma's dark, upturned eyes gleamed, reminding Brianna of Marie LaVeau as she spoke. "Edward will tell Father Gabriel his sins and ask for forgiveness. Then Father will anoint him with holy oil so that he will go to his death purified and whole in the eyes of God."

Edward gazed back at Brianna from his cot inside the cell. A smile crossed his lips. "That's my girl; our new home is at the Mission."

Eighty-Two

THE FAINT SMILE

San Francisco, California
May 1856

Father shooed away the guards, who allowed only Doc Poppy inside as a witness to the sacrament. A makeshift blanket was hung across the cell door to create the illusion of privacy. Emma's strong arms encircled Brianna's shoulders, and she led Brianna to a seat down the hallway. They rested together in a weary silence.

Brianna's thoughts led her into a dark tunnel. This was a slow death, but nothing compared to what Edward would endure.

Emma's soft hands held hers. With each passing moment, a strange peacefulness settled over Brianna. For the first time in her life, she knew she'd carry on and do the right thing, since Edward's life and his bravery had made their mark so strongly upon her. She wanted it to be over so she could take his broken body away from the scene of shouting and rumbling outside. She guessed more than a thousand people were waiting in the square outside, the profane atmosphere robbing the air of justice.

After a few moments, Father Gabriel dashed out of the cell, his white surplice flying and the violet stole flashing around his neck. Doc Poppy followed on his heels, calling, "Guards, guards!"

Brianna pushed herself up to stand, her shaky arms clutching the back of the chair. "Doc Poppy! Whatever's the matter? Has something happened to Edward?"

Doc turned back and looked down at her as though unseeing. "Please stay here, my dear."

Brianna saw Emma reach out, and she felt the grasp of her hand.

Brianna studied Emma's even expression, calm as the Mississippi at low tide. "What is going on?" Brianna asked. She knew she had to control her emotions, but every part of her wanted to go to Edward.

Emma spoke in a stern tone. "Madame, you must remain calm, lest you also be arrested. Remember where you are and who you are."

"Very well, Emma, but only for now." Brianna sounded resigned, but she burned inside. She stepped away from Emma, then sank back into the chair and bent down, her elbows resting on her knees.

A string of ants crossed in front of her, hauling a dead fly. Why couldn't the ants pick up her sorrows, too, and take them away?

Brianna watched several Vigilante guards descend upon the cell, the leather visors of their high hats reflecting rays of light from the windows. Their mutton chops and ill-fitting uniforms spoke of men trying to relive their glory days from the Mexican War a decade before. What were they trying to prove now in the name of justice?

Father Gabriel came out and knelt before Brianna, his white surplice a stark contrast against the brown Franciscan robes beneath. He tipped his head, his dry lips slightly apart.

"Father, do speak or I'll fall apart. What's happened to Edward? I know something is wrong. What is it?"

"My dear, it appears the Lord has intervened and carried him to heaven before the noose could have its way with him." He looked up at the rafters as though the almighty God appeared there.

"Do say more . . . I don't understand. I have to see him."

She felt Emma's firm hands encircle her forearm.

Father Gabriel showed a sudden sobriety. "Not yet. Doc Poppy is examining him with a stethoscope on both his chest and back. The Vigilante guards are acting as witnesses."

Brianna's heart raced. "I must go to him. I must—"

Emma's soft voice filled the space between them. "I think you must stay where you are, Madame, and let the doctor do his work. If he is revived, they'll take him to the scaffold, and you will be pushed aside. There's danger for you unless you abide by the doctor's wishes."

The priest drew up two chairs and mumbled the *Our Father*. Brianna sat across from him in numb silence, witnessing the prayer. He took her hand and held it in his. The smell of alcohol had faded from his breath, and he no longer appeared tipsy. Within the priest's grasp, she sought comfort in praying for the eternal peace Edward may have now or in the future. The worst part was not knowing. Was he alive, dead, or about to hang, dropped by a noose so suddenly that he would asphyxiate, his struggle to breathe audible to those watching from inside the Vigilante Headquarters?

Within a few moments, church bells clanged, joined by the Vigilante bell on the roof. Compelled by some force beyond her, Brianna rose to her feet.

Father Gabriel said, "You don't have to go to see, Brianna."

She pressed his hands away. "I must," she said.

Emma's steady presence lent her strength.

"Do not leave me," Brianna said to Emma.

Emma said, "I am here by your side."

Brianna and Emma rose and made their way to the warehouse window. Brianna swept a drifting cobweb away and looked out through the twelve-foot-high windows onto the square. Through the open window she could hear the crowd roar as the guards hoisted the struggling Carew out onto the twin scaffolds. The wiry Irishman clawed and fought his guards, and with each thrust and parry, the audience cheered, holding their penny candies and pink-cheeked children high in the air. Brianna followed the proceedings with a morbid fascination.

She had a clear view from the window. Below, lining the entrance to the Fort, Vigilante sentinels froze at attention, their bayonets perpendicular to their high hats. Father had taken Brianna's family to the courthouse square in Baltimore to witness executions when she was a young girl. He'd meant it to be a lesson to them. Hanging men usually cried out and then jerked violently at the edge of the rope. The crowd below waited expectantly, for the convulsions were the best part of the show.

The hangman stepped through the open window onto the platform, his black muslin gown and black cap bearing witness to the finality of the act he was about to perform. Was that the sound of teeth clicking together? Brianna shuddered. The hangman had two odd habits, that of clicking his false teeth together and of wringing his hands. She was mesmerized. Standing taller than six feet, he symbolized the Destroyer from the book of Revelations, his purpose to inspire fear and loathing in the general population.

The crowd silenced. Carew went limp in the guards' arms. From the warehouse window, Brianna surveyed upturned faces and open mouths. Even the twitchiest children quieted under the executioner's spell.

Another movement caught Brianna's attention—a guard passed a white kerchief through the window, which the hangman grabbed, then used to blindfold Carew. With a click of his teeth, the hangman looped the noose over the prisoner's head, then cinched it around his neck. Carew recoiled. Brianna saw the rope bite into his flesh. Had it hurt him?

Feeling nauseated, she grasped the window casement for support. Edward would be next to feel the hangman's pinch.

The executioner issued a loud grunt, his teeth clattering as he spoke. "Do you wish to give your final words to the people?"

The crowd bellowed, "Wake up, Carew! Hell's awaiting!"

In response, Carew raved for a good ten minutes. The mobs lost temporary interest; parents and children lined up for syllabubs at refreshment stands. Few in the crowd seemed to listen to what he said. Men and boys threw balls to each other; women suckled their infants. The executioner examined his fingernails, first on one hand, then the other.

At the next sounding of the Vigilante bell, Brianna heard a collective hush from the crowd below. Brianna spotted Peter McCutcheon's funeral cortege, replete with black curtained carriage, black-plumed stallions, and Vigilante battalions both leading and following the hearse. They rounded the corner of Montgomery and Washington Streets, the place where Carew had shot McCutcheon dead.

As arranged, the scaffold dropped with a whoosh, Carew's body fell, then halted at the end of the noose. He writhed, then dangled in midair, framed high against the brick walls of Fort Gunnybags. The mobs below danced and cheered, this time their bare fists raised high. The rope groaned against wooden beams, bearing the weight of Carew's body as it swung from side to side. The hangman stood erect on the scaffold, his arms akimbo. What was he thinking as he eyed the crowd? Who among them would be next?

Afterward, a strange, empty silence ensued. A Vigilante soldier poked his head out a window and summoned the executioner back inside the building. He then pulled down the window, locked it, and drew the black curtain, signaling the end of the day's spectacle.

From her window, Brianna spied the subdued crowd filing home. Sun-bonneted women carried picnic baskets, and small boys and girls followed. She noticed that there were small effigies of hanging men and executioners dangling from their wrists. All appeared satisfied that real justice had been done by the Vigilantes—for now.

Brianna put a hand on Emma's shoulder. "Wait a moment . . . what about Edward?" She blinked through tears brimming in her eyes.

Emma whispered, "Perhaps there's been a change of plans. Best not to say anything that might upset the Vigilantes."

Brianna heard the sound of heavy boots on wooden boards, followed by a breathless Doc Poppy bending down over her, his expression grim. "We must take you home, Brianna. Right away before they change their minds and decide to arrest you."

One thought crossed Brianna's mind: God help the next criminal who crossed the Committee.

Eighty-Three

GOLD FILIGREE

San Francisco, California
May 1856

In the twilight of that day, Brianna sat alone on her fainting couch. Outside, the fog now shrouded the streets and darkened the parlor. Andy lay snoring against the side of her hip. As with all executions, she knew fierce debate ensued in the saloons and gambling houses of San Francisco. The Victorian city was enchanted with death, she mused. In the semi-darkness, her fingers caressed the newspaper she'd been reading. *The Daily Song* reported that half the city thought Spina's death before hanging beat out Carew's dancing at the end of the rope.

She shook her head. San Francisco city had missed the best and final act. Her poor Edward had never regained consciousness, and Doc Poppy had pronounced him dead. After slipping out through the back door of Fort Gunnybags, Brianna had met Nathaniel Gray, the undertaker, who took her husband's body back to his mortuary on Sacramento Street and prepared him for burial. Brianna sent Richard to give him Edward's finest linen suit and ordered his favorite silk crimson cravat to be placed around his collar.

Brianna picked up a matchstick from the box on the table, struck it against the sandpaper, and lit a candle. The candle sputtered, and she watched its wax dripping down the side into the brass holder. Now Brianna could hear Emma moving around in the adjacent kitchen. Along with preparing for tomorrow's funeral for Edward, Emma and Richard were arranging their subsequent departure from San Francisco.

Even though Brianna was relieved the worst was over, she couldn't control the disquieting images that kept popping into her mind. Had Edward's handsome face already begun sinking into the dark mask of death? At rest lay her teacher, friend, lover, and now, her beloved husband for eternity. Rather than wallow in sadness, she was determined to give him serenity at last. She fingered her ring and smelled her red rose. He had died a hero in glorious battle. Relief lightened the darkness. She would bury him deep and safe from prying eyes.

Andy whimpered, his round chocolate colored eyes studying her. She tousled the fur on the crown of his head. "It's true, Andy. San Francisco can't hurt our Edward anymore." Something flickered on her hand. How could she forget her new memory? Her eyes lingered on the wedding ring, the gold filigree radiant in the candlelight.

In the breezy morning of the following day, Brianna stood in a black veil, holding a white rose. Next to her was Father Gabriel, who sprinkled holy water over the coffin in the churchyard of Mission Dolores. Feeling the prick of the thorny stem, she gazed into the white petals fanning out from a tight central bud. White for purity of heart. Billings had planted a red rosebush next to the gravesite under a redwood sapling. Father Gabriel had reserved the spot next to it for her own grave, for she wished to be buried next to the man who had taught her the meaning of love. The priest paid no mind that she was not Catholic, nor that she was a daughter of the night. Was this gesture out of respect to Edward? Her answer came in the form of the prayer he chose to say over Edward's coffin.

Lord,

Make me an instrument of your peace.

Where there is injury, pardon.

Brianna listened to the wind whipping across the hills surrounding them. *Injury . . . pardon.* The small redwood trees planted nearby gave out a whisper of joy. *Injury . . . pardon.* Resignation replaced her former despair. Now all she wanted was safety for Edward, and peace. Oh please, God—give him peace.

Men's shouts caught Brianna's attention. Across from them, in the Irish section of the graveyard, a pair of laboring men were digging the site of Carew's new resting place. She noticed the Irish burial grounds were across from the Italians where Edward would now reside for eternity. The sound of a light thump brought her back to Edward's burial. Now Father Gabriel's hands were raised and he was releasing sand and dirt onto the coffin lid.

Brianna pictured Edward lying inside, his long, feathered eyelashes swept shut in the darkness. He had rescued her from a life of prostitution, taught her to be a proper lady in New Orleans, and led her to San Francisco, where she had found herself a madam who owned her own business. In that role she had become a woman. And now, even without Edward, she would continue toward a higher cause to help Celeste find her lost mother in Paris. "You'll never be alone, Edward, even when I am in Paris." She kissed the coffin lid. "You will always have my heart."

Eighty-Four

FAMILIAR SAILS

San Francisco, California
May 1856

A mere two days after the burial, Brianna looked up at the familiar sails unfurling against the mast. A series of small signal flags were flapping against the wind. She held her cloak tight about her in the California sea air, and a mixed feeling of regret and excitement took hold of her. She would miss the Bay City and all its quirky pleasures. After all, this had been her and Edward's home for years.

Brianna heard Celeste's footsteps as she came up from the lower decks, and they joined each other to observe the brown hills of Monterey, now becoming a small, windswept point behind them. The brown California coastline grew fainter, replaced by the blue-gray ocean dotted with white-capped waves.

Celeste's voice carried on the wind. "I am happy to return to France, but yet I worry that life there will be the same as when I left . . . harsh, with much fighting and starvation. It has been several years since I have seen Maman, and when I find her, I will not let her go." A tear glinted in the corner of one eye, and she brushed it off.

Brianna reached over and patted her hand. "I want her to come live with us in Paris when we find her." She felt a blast of cold air strike her ear, and she shivered, drawing her hood close about her head. "You know, I will miss Mei Li. Thank God she agreed to take the parlor house and manage it for me. If she hadn't agreed, I don't know what I would have done."

Celeste looped an arm under Brianna's. "Now is not the time for us to worry about that. Please let us go below decks. Madame Emma has prepared a surprise for you."

Brianna let out a deep breath. "I've had all the surprises I need for one season." She gathered her up skirts, and together with Celeste, walked to the steps leading down to the lower deck.

At Emma's cabin, Brianna stopped and knocked. She felt Celeste press her shoulder against her own.

"One moment, Madame." From within, Emma's voice sounded nervous.

Brianna turned and grinned at Celeste. "How does she always know it's me?"

Celeste laughed. "I think it is her Haitian voodoo that makes her see all things."

The door creaked open, and just then, the ship encountered a wave, and they lurched forward and back. Brianna lost her balance and stumbled forward into the cabin, landing against Richard, who caught her in his arms.

While straightening herself, Brianna noticed the form of a body under the blanket on the cabin cot. "Who is that?"

Emma stepped forward. "We were preparing more of a surprise for you, but now that you're here . . ."

Richard pulled off the blanket, revealing Edward's huddled form. Curled up in death, he resembled drawings of an unborn child she'd seen at Mrs. Morgan's.

"What have you done?" Brianna eyed them with suspicion, anger and fear rising inside of her like a tide building against the shore.

Richard resettled the blanket over Edward's shoulders. "We saved him with Haitian voodoo potions that make fake sleep. Remember the wedding? We ground up the powder and dipped the host the priest carried in it. We didn't know if it would be enough to work, but it did stop his heart temporarily."

"Where did you get this drug?" Brianna pressed a hand to her lips. What had they done to poor Edward?

Emma stepped forward. "I carried all my potions with me from New Orleans. I learned the formulas from Madame LaVeau."

"How did you unbury him?" A wild tear found its way down Brianna's cheek before she could swipe it away.

"That was simple," Richard said. "Celeste distracted the night guard at the Mission while Father Gabriel and I dug up the coffin, just in time. We had only a half hour or it would have been too late, and he would have suffocated."

"And you never told me?"

Emma said, "We couldn't tell anyone for fear we would be found out. We traveled by carriage to Monterey and brought him onto the ship under the cover of night. He was barely breathing at the time, but his pulse is getting stronger now. There is a still a risk, Madame."

Brianna knotted her hands together. "Of what? Lord help us, we get him back, just to have him be gone again?" How much more agony did she have to endure?

Emma continued. "In Haiti, the *bokors*, or priests, use these potions to make zombies out of their enemies. Most often, the person who receives potion is never himself afterward."

"In what way?" Brianna's pulse throbbed in her ears.

"Loss of memory, trouble thinking, paralysis."

"Oh, no. Could that mean . . .?" Brianna imagined Edward's future: bedridden, a gray, vegetable-like creature, slowly fading away in a back bedroom of some dank lodging house in Paris. What if his mind was gone but his body whole? What if she rued the day he had not been hanged instead?

Richard's voice emerged through the fog of her anxiety. His leathered palm patted her fisted hand. "We will have to wait and see, Madame. With the fresh sea air and Captain Leathers' fine food on board our ship, the chances of his recovery are good. He's suffered a great test. Even without the potion, he will be a changed man."

Emma said, "He may be different, but thank God he's still alive."

"Yes," Brianna sighed. She must be grateful. She settled at the edge of Edward's bed, and outlined his profile with her fingers: Roman nose, mustache, full lips, then thick, black curls framing his head. This was her Edward, sure enough. And despite the passage of time, no matter what, he was now and always would be her dear husband.

Brianna withdrew the gris-gris bag from her pocket. A faint shuffle of footsteps. Good. They had known she needed quiet. Emma, Richard, and Celeste closed the cabin door, leaving her alone with Edward.

Pressing the small sack into Edward's fingers, Brianna said, "I will be yours until you no longer feel the emptiness consume you. When you are strong and powerful within yourself. When the loneliness does not take and shred you like a snakeskin. When you feel whole and at peace with God. Above all else, I will be yours when you are patient with others, with yourself, and with love. You are still young. You do not know what lies ahead, just as you never knew what lurked behind when you were a child."

Was she mistaken, or did she see a faint smile cross her husband's lips?

Brianna took Edward's limp body and held him to her chest, chanting softly to him in a slow rhythm, a gentle flow that continued to nurture him, drawing him deep into her soul.

Epilogue

Paris, France
October 1861

The years flew by. San Francisco's retired Sheriff Jamison and his eight-year-old grandson Andrew dodged the oncoming foot traffic on Rue de Rivoli, Paris, a stop on their European grand tour. A middle-aged couple passed, the woman striking in her blue bonnet and flaming red hair. Holding her arm and wielding a cane was a gray-haired gentleman, dressed in a top hat and the latest French *manteau.*

Jamison stopped and tapped his grandson's shoulder, staring at the man and woman.

The man leaned on his cane and dragged one leg behind the other. From time to time, the woman would murmur in his ear as they wove through the crowd.

Jamison's gaze followed the couple's path across the street. He shook his head. "I swear I've seen those people before."

"Where, Grandpa?" Andrew asked.

Jamison scratched his cheek. "Somewhere long ago, but I can't quite place them."

As they waited to cross the street, Jamison noticed the man in the *manteau* plant a kiss on the red-haired woman's lips. Curious. So familiar, yet surely it couldn't be them, not *here.*

Andrew's voice broke into his thoughts. "You promised me hot chocolate, Grandpa." The boy pointed to a café a few paces away.

"Of course, my lad." Jamison grinned, then led his grandson into the shop. He paused, gazing up at the bell above the door, listening to its chime.

To this day, New Orleans ship captains report this unusual sighting: every now and then, on a clear May night, a flame-haired woman wrapped in silver starlight hovers over the pier. She kisses a small gris-gris bag, then casts it deep into the waters of the Mississippi.

So Be It.

Afterword

My story of Brianna Baird and Edward Spina is based loosely on the historical persons of Belle and Charles Cora whom I fictionalized in order to amplify several topics: the position of women, antebellum slavery, New Orleans Voodoo, and the role of the Chinese in the development of America's cultural fabric. Of course, the actual history ends with Charles' hanging by the Vigilantes, and both he and Belle are buried, side by side, in the Mission Dolores graveyard in San Francisco. Their story may be found in the *City of the Golden Fifties* by Pauline Jacobson (1941).

Although I used many references to create this book, here are a few for those who want to find out more about some of the topics mentioned.

On Baltimore and its surrounds: I visited the Fells Point Historic District and the historic Admiral Fell Inn, which is a Historic Hotels of America member, a program of the National Trust for Historic Preservation. The Horse You Came In On Saloon, formerly called a tavern, is associated with the life and tragic death of Edgar Allan Poe, who died in Baltimore. The Inner Harbor continues to glisten in the sunlight, a living testimonial to the seafaring heritage of Baltimore and Fells Point. I referred to *Walking Baltimore* by Evan Balkan (2013); On the history of Fells Point, I relied on *The Fells Point Story* by Norman Rukert (1976).

On prostitution in America: *Daughters of Joy, Sisters of Misery* by Anne M. Butler (1987); *Upstairs Girls: Prostitution in the American West* by Michael Rutter (2005); *Their Sisters' Keepers* by Marilyn Wood Hill (1993); *Confidence Men and Painted Women: A Study of Middle-Class Culture in America, 1830-1870* by Karen Halttunen (1982); *Brothels, Depravity, and Abandoned Women: Illegal Sex in Antebellum New Orleans by* Judith Kelleher Schafer *(2009); The Madams of San Francisco* by Curt Gentry (1964).

On slavery and manumission in antebellum America: *The Rattling Chains: Slave Unrest and Revolt in the Antebellum South* by Nicholas Halasz (1966); *Twelve Years a Slave* by Solomon Northrup, first published in 1853, 2014 edition; *Ar'n't I A Woman? Female Slaves in the Plantation South* by Deborah Gray White, 1999 edition; *Beyond Bondage: Free Women of Color in the Americas*, David Barry Gaspar and Darlene Clark Hine, editors, (2004); *Soul by Soul: Life Inside the Antebellum Slave Market* by Walter Johnson (1999).

On 1850s fashion: *Victorian and Edwardian Fashions from "La Mode Illustree"* by Joanne Olian, editor (19980; *Historic Dress in America: 1607-1870* by Elisabeth McClellan (1904); *Victorian and Edwardian Fashion: A Photographic Survey*, Alison Gernsheim 1981. Here I wish to thank my fellow author, Cheryl Stapp, for her excellent tutorial on the many layers of clothing a woman wore in the 1850s.

On New Orleans: I visited the Vieux Carre' and its rich historical sites. I took a paddle wheeler on the Mississippi, an alligator cruise on the bayou, and paid a visit to Laura and Oak Alley Plantations. I referenced the following: *Walking Tours of Old New Orleans* by Stanley Clisby Arthur (2012); *The French Quarter* by Herbert Asbury (1936, 2003).

For Voodoo: *The Serpent and The Rainbow* by Wade Davis (1997); *A New Orleans Voudou Priestess: The Legend and Reality of Marie Laveau* by Carolyn Morrow Long (2007);

On San Francisco: Having been a former resident of San Francisco, and having worked near Chinatown and Market Street, I had long wished to write a novel about the Victorian era. I revisited the Mission

Dolores, Chinatown, Waverly Place, and Portsmouth Square. Sadly, many buildings have changed since the 1908 earthquake, yet one can still trace the routes of earlier days. Indeed, a visit to Chinatown today differs in tone but not the spirit of 1850s.

For historic 1850s San Francisco: I relied on *The Fantastic City* by Amelia Ransome Neville (1932); *The Annals of San Francisco* by Soule, Gihon and Nisbet, (1855, 1999); *San Francisco 1846-1856: From Hamlet to City* by Roger W. Lotchin (1997); *The Barbary Coast*, Herbert Asbury (1947);

For the Chinese in San Francisco: I am thankful for the guidance of the Chinese Historical Society who provided me with advice and resources, among which is *A History of the Chinese in California, A Syllabus*, Chinn and Choy, editors, (1984). I read *Chinese San Francisco: 1850-1943 – A Trans-Pacific Community* by Yong Chen (2000); *The Chinese Looking Glass* by Dennis Bloodworth, (1967).

Acknowledgments

It takes a town to raise a novel. The builder must first lay the foundation, so I thank the many people of Fells Point, Baltimore; New Orleans, Louisiana; and San Francisco, California. Through their gracious hospitality and assistance during my historical research travels, they helped to lend verisimilitude to the many locations mentioned in the book.

This novel's walls, doors, and windows were created with the assistance of the members of my writing groups. Early inspiration came from Zoe Keithley, my writing mentor. Shoring up various manuscript versions were Robert Pacholik, John Clewett, Kathy Boyd Fellure, Pam S. Dunn, Kitty Haspel, Carolyn Bakken, Sarah Armstrong-Garner, Paula Zaby, Daniel Babka, Rick Davis, Dennis Mahoney, Kathleen Torian Taylor, Cheryl Stapp, Lorna Norisse, and Margaret Duarte. In addition, Mark Weideranders, Antoinette May, and Erika Mailman provided much encouragement along the path to publication.

My editor, Christopher Rose, sweated along with me as we pounded nails into many drafts and cut away excess timber. His meticulous attention to detail and unflagging support helped me bring this project to life.

Many thanks to all of you.

About the Author

Novelist and historian Gini Grossenbacher is one of California's respected and sought-after creative writing coaches and educators. She is a prominent literacy activist and developed an award-winning and innovative curriculum for the teaching of literature and the language arts in school districts and private academies across Northern California. Gini is a sought-after speaker and literary critic who has appeared in print and broadcast media on the subject of great authors and the joys of historical fiction.

Gini is a liberal arts graduate of Lewis & Clark College, one of the oldest institutions of higher education in the American West, has done postgraduate work in European history and Italian literature in ancient Perugia, and has a master's degree in educational governance from one of the nation's most important and prolific postgraduate campuses for school and university leadership.

Gini is also a lifelong forensic historian with a special hands-on interest in the recovery of women's narratives too often neglected in the stories nations and great cities tell about their origins. She has done in-place literary and historical research across five continents and wandered back alleys and elegant high streets from Bangkok and Kyoto to Singapore, from Mexico City and Martinique to Caracas, from London and Paris to Rome and the medieval hills and historic towns where Francis and Clare of Assisi reinvented European monasticism.

Madam of My Heart is Gini's debut novel, the first in *The American Madams* series. To learn more or request Gini as a speaker, go to *www.ginigrossenbacher.com*.

50808311R00291

Made in the USA
San Bernardino, CA
04 July 2017